HEARTS *Awakening*

Hearts Awakening

Delia Parr

BETHANY HOUSE PUBLISHERS

Minneapolis, Minnesota

Hearts Awakening

Cover design by John Hamilton Design

Published by Bethany House Publishers
11400 Hampshire Avenue South
Bloomington, Minnesota 55438

Bethany House Publishers is a division of
Baker Publishing Group, Grand Rapids, Michigan.

Printed in the United States of America

Library of Congress Cataloging-in-Publication Data

Parr, Delia.
Hearts Awakening / Delia Parr.
p. cm.
ISBN 978-0-7642-0670-2 (pbk.)
1. Widows—Fiction. 2. Housekeepers—Fiction. 3. Pennsylvania—History—18th century—Fiction. I. Title.
PS3566.A7527H435 20010
813'.54—dc22

2009040893

Dedicated to my turtle-lover sister,

Carol Beth,

my story editor, beach buddy, friend,
and inspiration, as well as a loving wife
and mother and caring hospice nurse who helps
so many as they prepare to go home.
You are, dear sister,
one of His finest gifts to so many
people who are blessed to be
able to love you back.

One

AUGUST 1840
HARRISBURG, PENNSYLVANIA

While other women her age were busy preparing a hearty breakfast for their families in snug, warm homes that crowded the city or dotted the outlying farms, Elvira Kilmer was hurrying down an unfamiliar roadway, hugging the woods along the eastern shoreline of Dillon's Island to meet a total stranger.

The air was heavy with the sweet scent of apples that grew in the orchards filling the interior of the island. But it was not enough to ease the heavy resentment that beat in Ellie's heart, and her thin, well-mended cape did little more to ward off the uncommon nip in the air than her tattered faith could warm the chill in her spirit.

Yawning, she caught a brief glimpse of the Susquehanna River through a break in the trees that lined either side of the roadway and wondered what it would be like to simply drift away to a place where she was the only one who had control over her life.

Ellie snorted, tugged her cape tighter, and trudged forward. She had just taken a couple of sidesteps to avoid a deep ridge in the roadway when a raccoon darted out of the woods right in front of her. Startled, she swirled about, tripped over her own skirts, and toppled into the brush, snagging her cape on a low branch in the process.

Thankfully, she found the wherewithal to grab on to a small sapling to keep from pitching forward and landing flat on her face. Swaying a bit, she gasped for air and wondered if her heart would burst before it stopped pounding in her ears.

When she finally caught her breath, she glanced down and saw that she had landed smack in the middle of a patch of blackberries. Relief that the thorns on the brambles had not pierced through her cape and skirts was short-lived, however, once she got back to her feet to see what damage she had done to her garments.

Her gloves, which had kept her hands from being scraped, were sticky with tree sap, and the mends she had made just the other day had torn open again, which meant the gloves were now destined for the trash pit. To make matters worse, there was a wide tear in her cape, just above the hem, and she groaned out loud. She could mend that tear easily enough, but the blackberry stains on her cape and her gray skirts would be almost impossible to remove.

Ellie yanked off her gloves and stuffed them into her pocket before easing back to the roadway. "I needed to ruin my cape *and* my work gown *and* my gloves? Now? When I'm due at Mr. Smith's? I look like a . . . a ragamuffin!"

Chest heaving, she swiped at her tears and stomped both

of her work boots free of dirt before resuming her journey. "I thought you were going to help me, Lord. I've trusted in you all my life, yet no matter how hard I've prayed or how hard I've tried to live by your Word, I always end up with . . . with nothing but disappointment," she cried, giving voice to the despair that seemed to have found a permanent home in her spirit.

Apparently frightened by her cry, a trio of small birds burst out of a nearby tree and soared up toward the clouds. She paused to watch them, flying side by side, until they disappeared from view. And, despite the frustration and uncertainty that welled within, she prayed she might one day fully embrace His promise to protect all of His creations, even a trembling follower as she had become.

Ellie continued on her way and spied the rear of the small farmhouse at the southern end of the island, where a single wisp of smoke curled up from a chimney on the near side of the building. She approached the house with the hope that Jackson Smith would be so grateful she had arrived he would not be put off by her unkempt appearance and send her right back to the city—where she would no doubt receive another less-than-gracious welcome.

When she reached the kitchen door at the back of the house, she swallowed hard and paused to straighten the folds on her cape to try to hide the blackberry stains, but there were so many she soon gave up. After smoothing her hair one last time, she took a deep breath for courage and knocked on the kitchen door. And then again. She was about to knock a third time but dropped her hand when she finally heard the sound of heavy footsteps approaching the door.

Her mouth went dry, but she kept her back straight and her shoulders square as she planted a smile on her face.

When the door finally swung open, she took a step back and stared up at the very attractive man standing there. To her surprise, he appeared to be only in his late twenties—a good three or four years her junior—but as she suspected, he wore the weathered tan of a man who carved his way through life by working outdoors in the orchards that covered the tiny island. His summer-bleached brown hair was cropped short, and the dark blue eyes staring back at her beneath heavy brows were fierce with pride and determination. The heavy crease across his brow, however, testified to his weariness, if not the sorrow of losing his wife scarcely six months ago.

"Mr. Smith? I'm Elvira Kilmer. I believe you were told to expect me this morning," she said in a clear, steady voice, though her heart pounded against the wall of her chest. Either he would allow her inside or he would send her straight back to the city, where she would no doubt end up homeless and penniless by the time the sun set.

Again.

Two

Relief, rather than contempt, flashed through Jackson Smith's gaze, and he stepped back to allow her to enter. "Please come in."

Nearly weak with relief herself, Ellie swallowed hard and gratefully entered the dimly lit kitchen, which turned out to be little more than a workroom. The light of early morning barely managed to filter through the two grimy kitchen windows closed tight against the fresh air outside. She could not even see the woods that separated the house from the vast acres of orchards on the island.

The warmth in the room, however, felt good after walking in the chill of early morning for over two hours, but she would not have complained if the room had been ice-cold. Now that she had been invited into the house, she was determined to convince him to let her stay. When her footsteps crunched over dirt and grime that littered the wide-plank floor, she knew without even looking down that it needed a good sweeping, if not a solid scrubbing.

Jackson cringed as his boots crunched over the floor, too. "As you must have noticed already, we've managed to track in a good amount of dirt. I hope Reverend Shore and your cousin Mark told you how incredibly grateful I am that you've volunteered to help out here with the housekeeping and such. I'm afraid the house needs a good scrubbing," he added meekly.

"That's easy enough to do," Ellie said as she glanced around the kitchen.

"May I take your cape?"

She swallowed hard again, slipped out of her cape, and handed it to him, all too aware of the badly stained skirts on her gown, which were now in full view. When his hand brushed hers for the briefest of moments, she felt a warm blush steal across her cheeks, then grow even warmer when he studied her stained garments.

Embarrassed by her appearance, she offered him a weak smile. When her thoughts focused on how handsome he was instead of how desperately she needed to assure him of her housekeeping skills, she quickly explained her mishap in hopes of convincing him she was not usually so unkempt.

"I'm not hurt," she insisted as she concluded her tale. "My cape and gown actually took the brunt of my fall. I didn't have time to return to the city to change, and I really must apologize for arriving here looking so unkempt, but—"

"I'm far more worried that you might have been hurt than I am about the state of your apparel," he quipped before turning and hanging her cape on a wooden peg by the door. "Are you certain you feel up to working here today?" he asked as he approached her again. "Perhaps I should speak to your cousin about postponing your start here and—"

"No, please. I'm fine," she insisted, fearful that her cousin would use this as the very excuse he needed to get rid of her for good.

He shook his head. "I'm afraid there could be any number of critters scurrying about on the island at this hour. They're quite harmless, but I'd rather not take the risk that you might be frightened and fall again. I'll speak to Michael Grant. Instead of letting you walk here alone from the landing after ferrying you across the river, he can walk with you."

"That won't be necessary. I'll just keep an eye out for critters, now that I know they're out and about," she insisted before opening the door to a subject that was much more important to her. "I'm afraid I haven't any references to give you, but—"

"References?" He shook his head and smiled. "I admit that I don't know your cousin all that well, but anyone Reverend Shore recommends doesn't need any references. His assurances that you're a competent housekeeper are enough for me, although I daresay the good reverend would be far more pleased if I brought my sons to Sunday services on a regular basis than he'd be with my expression of faith in his judgment."

Ellie swallowed hard, reluctant, if not unwilling, to tell him that she had yet to meet Reverend Shore. Or that she had not seen her cousin in more than ten years until yesterday. Considering all that, she felt she was in no position to give him her opinion about his church attendance.

"I'm certain I can get your house back to rights," she offered, anxious to prove her mettle and twice as anxious not to give him any cause to complain to her cousin about having to provide her with an escort.

Turning away, she glanced around the room. To her dismay, neglect was everywhere. The hodge-podge of jugs, cookware, tableware, and supplies on the shelves lining the outer wall on either side of the cookstove were either dusty with misuse or splattered with remnants of recent meals. The modern Step Top cooking stove itself was shrouded with grease and gunk. Lingering cooking smells, intensified by the heat in the kitchen, left no room for the heady scent of apples that had lined her way here.

The worktable in the center of the small room, as well as the drying table next to the indoor water pump, was littered with dirty dishes. Indeed, the only clear space in the entire room was on one of the window seats.

Disappointed not to have an old-fashioned hearth to use to prepare meals, Ellie sucked in her breath. Why women would give up cooking on an open hearth for an iron contraption that demanded constant cleaning and attention made no sense to her at all. Granted, she could easily scrub the cookstove clean, but actually using it to prepare meals for the next two weeks would be altogether a greater challenge for her—a challenge she had no choice but to meet.

Convinced her open-hearth cooking skills were probably as outdated as she was on the marriage market, she took a tenuous step closer to the cookstove to get a better look at the controls.

"I never did get around to setting the cookstove out on the side porch for the summer," he offered a bit sheepishly.

"Then the unusually cool weather today is a blessing," she managed, overwhelmed by the prospect of using this cookstove, as well as the work this kitchen demanded. If the rest of the house fared as poorly, she had no doubt she would need far more than the two weeks she promised to work here to set it to rights. Ellie wondered what her cousin would have to say about that.

Curious to see more of the house, she glanced through the doorway into the great room, where she saw his two motherless little boys sitting patiently at the dining table, only steps away, waiting for someone to make their breakfast. Just beyond them, a maze of wooden blocks they must have been playing with just before she arrived littered the floor between the fireplace in the center of the room and the front window.

The two boys were dressed identically in dark blue linen overalls and beige flannel shirts, just like their father's. The younger boy's clothing hung on his small frame, and she suspected he was wearing some of his brother's hand-offs well before he should have given up his baby clothes. Their faces had been scrubbed clean, but their hair needed a good brushing, and she imagined there was more than a speck of dirt under their fingernails.

But it was the needy look on those two precious little faces that reached straight into her heart and tugged hard enough to prick her conscience. Hard enough to remind her that she was a woman of compassion. And definitely hard enough to suggest to her that God must have sent her here not for one, but two very good reasons, who were staring right back at her.

Jackson walked around her to enter the great room and stand protectively behind his sons. "This is Daniel. He's five," he said, squeezing the older boy's shoulder first. "And this is Ethan."

Ellie laid the cloth down on the worktable and joined the man and his sons in the great room.

"Boys, Spinster Kilmer came to help us for a few weeks. I'll expect you to do as she tells you while she's here," he added sternly.

"You can call me Miss Ellie," she offered, noting the look of distrust in both the boys' gazes.

Daniel straightened his shoulders. With fawn brown hair and dark blue eyes, he looked at her with the same fierce gaze as his father and pointed to his younger brother. "Ethan's only three. He likes griddle cakes for breakfast. A lot. Can you cook griddle cakes? We're hungry."

Ethan's eyes widened with expectation, but he did not say a word. Apparently, he was much shyer than his older brother. He had his brother's coloring, but he had a slimmer build and a slick of hair on the back of his head that stuck up like a sapling that had taken root in a bed of low grass.

"Don't be so impatient, Daniel. The poor woman just got here. She has not even seen the rest of the house," his father cautioned.

"I can do that later. Right now I'm feeling hungry, too," Ellie insisted, particularly since she had not eaten anything before setting out today. Grateful that the cookstove had already been heated up, she smiled. "How about I make a good stack of griddle cakes for all of us? I'll need some help, though, since I'm not accustomed to your kitchen," she said.

Daniel scrambled off his chair, helped his younger brother down, and held his hand to keep him next to him. "I can reach the jug of maple syrup," he explained, holding tight to his brother's hand, although Ethan did not seem anxious to help.

"See if you can find the crock of butter, too," she suggested.

"Ethan can get that," Daniel offered but looked up at his father. After getting a nod of approval, he led his brother into the kitchen.

Despite her misgivings about making breakfast using that

cookstove, Ellie kept her smile on her face and followed the boys into the kitchen, with Jackson close behind her. She spied a tired, dingy apron hanging from a peg on the wall next to the side door and quickly put it on.

"I should think it's been very difficult to fend for yourself and the boys, especially at mealtime," she said as she moved behind the table and started to clear a place to work.

Standing just inside the doorway, the man reached out and put a hand on each of his son's shoulders as they attempted to race past him to take the maple syrup and crock of butter to the table. "Slow down or you'll drop those," he warned before releasing them and looking back at her again. "You met Michael Grant when he ferried you over here. His wife, Alice, and their daughter have been kind enough to help out here and there when they could. They've made extra at mealtimes some days and sent it over, but it's been . . . difficult otherwise, since my last housekeeper left some weeks ago."

She moistened a rag at the pump, wiped off the cleared space on the table, and swallowed the lump in her throat. The man was young, healthy, and attractive to boot. The only reason she could fathom that he had not remarried, instead of relying on hired help, had to be that he was still grieving for the woman he had loved and lost scarcely six months ago. "Is there a bake oven outside?" she asked hopefully.

He shrugged. "That hasn't been used for years. The entrance to the root cellar is outside, though, and there's fresh milk in the jug over there on the shelves, along with a basket of eggs. Daniel can show you where everything else is you might need today, but Ethan . . ."

He paused and lowered his voice. "Ethan hasn't really spoken since his mother passed."

Surprised that her cousin had not bothered to tell her about little Ethan's difficulties, Ellie nodded. "I'm sure Daniel will let me know if his brother needs anything."

"He will indeed. I really do need to head out to the orchards, where Michael and the men he hired for the day are waiting for me by now. Unless . . . unless you think you might need my help getting started here," he added, shifting his gaze nervously from her to his sons.

"What about breakfast for yourself?"

He shook his head. "Unless I want to lose the best of this early crop of Maiden Blush apples, I've got to get them off the trees, boxed up, and shipped east. Otherwise, I'll be hard pressed to hold on to my customers there when the later apples are ready to harvest. I wouldn't object if you sent Daniel out with something for me in a bit, though. He knows where I'll be. Otherwise, I'll be back for dinner around one," he added before turning to his sons. "Be good, boys."

Walking past her, he grabbed a straw hat off the peg by the back door and slipped outside, leaving Ellie alone with one mess of a kitchen, a newfangled cookstove she barely knew how to use, and two very hungry little boys charging back to help her.

Three

Later that afternoon, Ellie was counting the minutes until Jackson Smith returned home for supper, even though she feared he might tell her not to come back again when he did.

Standing at the water pump, she rinsed out the cleaning rag again, bent down, and washed the last of the mud from the floor she had just scrubbed clean for the third time that day.

While she did, two very remorseful, very silent, boys sat side by side on one of the wide window seats. They were not the main reason she needed to escape, although taking care of Daniel and Ethan had consumed more energy than she had anticipated. Her dismal failures in the kitchen today, which chipped away at her pride as a good cook, were solely responsible for her dour thoughts.

Even though she had opened up both windows and propped

open the side door until it got too cold in the room and she had to close them, her failures today stretched limp and heavy across the entire kitchen, like bedsheets hung up to dry on a windless day. The acrid smell of burnt griddle cakes from breakfast, along with the bread she had baked and burned and the pungent odor of undercooked, greasy sausage from dinner, still permeated the room.

In fact, there remained two sad loaves of bread, visible testimony to her inability to control the heat in the oven in the top tier of the cookstove while she attempted to manage the heat and cook on the middle tier. Bending down, she swiped at a bit of mud on the floor she had missed, thoroughly disgusted with herself. She had a good sense of what Cousin Mark would say and do if he knew how badly she was faring today, and her frown deepened.

That confounded cookstove! If she were to prove herself a capable housekeeper—and in turn receive a reference from Jackson Smith—it centered around mastering that contraption. And unless she did exactly that, and rather quickly, she doubted he would want her to finish out the two weeks he had been promised. Without a reference, she would never be able to secure a permanent position for herself, which would give her the dignity of finally making her own way in this world, instead of relying on her cousin's charity, such as it was.

Determined to earn that reference, she rinsed out her cleaning rag one last time and laid it flat to dry. Before tackling her next important task, she glanced over at the two boys sitting on the far side of the room. There was more than enough room for both boys to sit together on the overly wide window seat, a feature she had noted on the other windows on the first floor.

Ethan was still watching out the window for his father,

which he had done most of the day. Daniel, however, was sitting straight and tall, staring at her, his open distrust of her still simmering in the depths of his dark blue eyes, which were remarkably like his father's. Handling Daniel had proven to be a greater challenge than dealing with Ethan's inability to speak, but their latest bout of mischief tested the very limits of her patience.

"There," she said, patting the cloth. "The kitchen floor is good and clean again, and I expect both of you to help me keep it that way. Let's take one more look at those shoes of yours while we wait for the floor to dry a bit more," she said sternly.

Daniel's bravado crumbled as she tiptoed over to them. "I got all the mud off me and Ethan. I didn't mean to get any on you. It was an accident," he insisted in a trembling voice.

Regretting her harsh tone, Ellie stopped in front of him, looked down at her gown, and sighed. Winning this child's trust would take love and patience, not cold words. "There's a reason why I wear this dark work gown. It doesn't show the dirt or the mud, although it does show blackberry stains rather well," she added with a smile.

She shook her gown and apron to show him no trace of the mud remained without telling him that even if he had gotten mud on the soiled apron she had borrowed, it would have been hard to spot it among the stains that were too ingrained in the fabric to ever soak away.

"Do you . . . do you want me to get you one of Pappy's belts now?"

She drew back her head and furrowed her brow. "One of his belts?"

He nodded. "So you can strap me like Mrs. Hill did when we were bad. But please don't strap Ethan," he said and scrunched a little closer to his brother before lowering his voice. "He's too little."

Blinking back her disbelief that anyone would strap these two boys for such a minor incident, if ever, Ellie drew in a long breath and knelt down in front of the five-year-old. "Who's Mrs. Hill?" she asked, wondering if this was the housekeeper Jackson Smith had mentioned had left just a few weeks ago.

Daniel scrunched up his face. "She was a keeperhouse, but Pappy made her leave 'cause she was bad to me and Ethan."

"You mean a housekeeper," she corrected gently.

He nodded. "Pappy told her he was the only one who could strap us, even though he never does. Then he told her she had to pack up and go, and she couldn't never, ever come back," he added, puffing out his chest.

Ellie let out a long breath, even as her admiration for the man grew. "Well, good for your father," she replied. "But don't worry. I have no intention of strapping either one of you, and I've reminded you more than once already that I'm only going to be here for two weeks."

Smiling, she patted the soles of their shoes. "Besides, it's partly my fault that you two wound up marching through that big mud puddle on the side of the house."

When Daniel's eyes opened wide, she chuckled. "I should have known not to ask you two boys to sit on the side porch while I scrubbed the kitchen floor."

Daniel eyed her suspiciously. "Why not?"

"Because I know there isn't a mud puddle in this whole world that wouldn't invite little boys to trudge through it. If I'd kept you inside to play with your blocks in the first place, you wouldn't have gotten into trouble now, would you?"

When a grin lit his face for the very first time that day, she narrowed her gaze. "I still expect you and your brother to be more obedient, like your father told you to be," she admonished gently. "Now, if you and Ethan would like to apologize, I think I can promise we can put the whole episode to rest."

He narrowed his gaze. "You won't tell Pappy?"

"If your father asks me about what happened, I'll have to tell him. Otherwise, I don't see why I should mention it, do you?"

His head bobbed from side to side. "I'm sorry I didn't stay on the porch," he blurted and tugged on Ethan's shirt. "You're sorry, too, aren't you, Ethan?"

Ethan turned his head around, nodded once, then returned his attention to the window.

Daniel slipped off the window seat and stood next to her. "You made a big, big pot of soup. We'll have lots and lots to eat, so you don't have to come back tomorrow," he suggested.

"You'll need more than a pot of leftover soup to eat tomorrow, and I haven't finished cleaning the house yet, either," she ventured, although she would not blame Jackson if he agreed with Daniel that they could make do with soup instead of more burnt meals. Fortunately, the man had a sweet tooth, which made her perfectly baked apple turnovers today the only saving grace to the entire dinner she had served.

Since the other odors were still overpowering the smell of the soup she had set to cook earlier, she made her way over to the cookstove to check on it. As usual, Ethan seemed oblivious to her very presence in the room, but Daniel was right on her heels when she took one look into the pot of soup and froze.

No steam.

No bubbles around the edges, either.

With her heart racing, she took the spoon and poked at one of the potatoes and then another. "Rock hard." Gingerly, she tapped the side of the pot with her fingertips. "Scarcely warm. Mercy! There's not enough heat," she grumbled. Ellie opened the side plate on the oven and shook her head. The firewood inside was nothing but embers. "No wood."

Daniel poked his head beside hers to look inside the stove. "My mama never forgot to add the wood."

Ellie frowned. "Perhaps not, but I promised you soup for supper, and soup you shall have," she declared and headed off to the side porch to get more wood.

Daniel raced ahead of her and helped her carry some hickory wood back to the stove. Even though she rebuilt the fire quickly, she had little hope the soup would be done in time for supper.

"You already broked some promises today. You shouldn't make a promise if you're not gonna keep it," Daniel said glumly.

She stilled and glanced down at him. "I broke a promise? When?"

His gaze narrowed. "You said you'd make a good stack of griddle cakes, but you burned them and they tasted bad. You said you were sorry and you wouldn't burn nothin' again, and then you burned the bread."

Instinctively, Ellie stiffened her back. "I didn't burn the griddle cakes or the bread on purpose. I just had a little trouble with the oven and this . . . this cookstove," she explained, surprised at how sensitive she was to the child's criticism.

"My mama didn't burn nothin' like you do. She was a good cook," he muttered.

Ellie stirred the soup, hoping it would heat faster if she did. "I'm sure your mother was a very good cook, but I didn't burn the apple turnovers today. And I didn't completely ruin the bread. Now that I've cut off the burnt crust on the two loaves that are left, I promise the bread will taste better with supper tonight, and that's one promise I know I can keep."

"Is that the only one?" Daniel whispered, his dark eyes troubled.

"No, that's not the only one," she replied, thinking she knew what was really bothering him. "We've already discussed that you and Ethan were wrong to slip outside and get yourselves all muddied up while I was scrubbing the floor in the kitchen today. Since you've both apologized, I don't intend to break my promise not to mention it to your father," she reminded him.

"Lots of people don't keep their promises," Daniel insisted, apparently unimpressed by her reassurances.

She cocked a brow. "Like who?"

"My mother promised she wouldn't be gone long," he whispered, then returned to the window to sit with his brother.

Before Ellie could find her voice to reply to his poignant words, Daniel let out a whoop. "Pappy's coming!" he cried, tugging Ethan down. Together they scurried out the back door to meet their father.

Ellie smiled as she watched the boys tear out of the house with such enthusiasm. As a child she had looked forward to having her own father return at the end of the day, too, and listening later as her parents shared an accounting of their day with each other.

Growing up, she never suspected she would never know the joy of married life or having children of her own, which made her memories all the more bittersweet. Shaking her head, she turned her attention back to the soup, which was just beginning to simmer now. The layers of responsibility she had lovingly accepted had all but erased her childhood dreams of marriage and children, and she could not afford to add to the resentments that already tested her very faith in God by resurrecting those dreams now.

While she stirred the soup and waited for the boys and their father to return to the house, she looked over to a side window, caught a glimpse of her reflection, and sighed. Her features were as unremarkable as her dark brown eyes and hair, which she simply parted in the middle and pulled back in a single braid. The freckles that skipped across the top of her cheeks had gotten darker during the summer months, which was her own fault. Contrary to custom, she did not favor wearing a hat or bonnet and often dropped the hood on her cape so she could feel the warmth of the sun on her head.

Leaning closer to get a better look, she noted the crinkles at the corner of her eyes and just a hint of wrinkles forming across her brow and frowned again. She carried every one of her thirty-one years on her face, and after working hard all day cooking and cleaning and taking care of those two boys, she could feel every one of them, too. And she had a good two-hour walk back to her cousin's home ahead of her.

Startled back to reality when Jackson opened the back door and stepped inside, holding a son by either hand, she began stirring the soup again. She hoped the steam that had just started bubbling off the soup would explain the warm blush on her cheeks and braced herself for Jackson's disappointment when he learned his supper was not waiting for him.

Daniel tried to tug his father toward the cookstove. "Come see, Pappy! We're having soup for supper. Miss Ellie didn't burn it 'cause she forgot to put enough wood in the cookstove, but I helped her carry in more wood. Wanna see?"

Jackson frowned and let go of his boys long enough to stick his hat on the peg by the door. "Is that fresh bread I see on the table, too?"

"Nope. It's the same burned bread," Daniel offered. "Miss Ellie cut off all the black parts."

Ellie managed half a smile, in spite of the boy's apparent glee at pointing out her deficiencies. "I'm afraid I'm still trying to master this cookstove of yours. The soup isn't quite ready yet, so you'll have to wait a bit longer than you might like for supper tonight."

Frowning again, he ruffled the hair on his sons' heads. "I suppose we can wait a spell for supper, if we must, but there's no sense wasting time. You two boys come with me and help me put some apples I picked today into the root cellar. Maybe Miss Ellie will have time to make a couple of apple pies for us tomorrow," he added hopefully.

Even though she had managed to make perfectly baked apple turnovers earlier, she could only pray that the pies would be a success and not just more disasters like the bread had been. "I'll try."

When he glanced around the kitchen, where she even had the windows sparkling clean, his frown finally eased into a smile. "You managed to clean all this today? With the boys underfoot?"

"We never really left the kitchen for long," she replied, taking no small measure of satisfaction in the surprise that laced his words. "Ethan even took a bit of a nap here with us, so I'm afraid I didn't get to do much more than sweep out the rest of the first floor. I was hoping to tackle the great room and the parlor tomorrow," she ventured, hoping he would be pleased enough with her cleaning efforts to overlook her failures at the stove and allow her to return another day.

"That would be fine. More than fine. Thank you."

Relief washed over her. "You're very welcome. I noticed earlier today that the room on the first floor next to the staircase is locked. If you'd like me to clean that room, too, I'll need the key. And I need a key for the door at the bottom of the staircase, as well, although I doubt I'll get as far as cleaning the upstairs tomorrow."

"There's no need to clean the room downstairs. We haven't used it at all since the housekeeper left. Just remind me to leave the key to the staircase when you get here tomorrow," he countered.

Relieved that he actually wanted her to return, yet anxious to start her long trek back to the city, she untied her apron. "I should start back now. I'd rather not travel much after dusk."

He cocked a brow. "What about your supper?"

"I really can't wait for the soup to finish cooking. I'll have something to eat at home," she insisted, even though she had little more than a tin of crackers set aside for herself to eat in her room. "Did you make arrangements for Mr. Grant to meet me at the landing again to ferry me back across the river?"

"He'll be waiting for you."

Taking a deep breath, she hung up her apron, donned her cape, and tied it closed. "I'll see you all in the morning," she offered and slipped past them and out the door just as the sun started sinking close to the horizon.

Determined to have a better day in the kitchen tomorrow, she made her way through the backyard to the narrow roadway that led to the landing at the north end of the island, alert for any sign of critters. When her stomach started to growl, she detoured through a narrow copse of trees into one of the orchards and snatched up a pair of apples that had fallen to the ground. She stuffed one into her cape pocket and ate the other along the way.

With visions of perfectly baked apple pies sitting on Jackson

Smith's dinner table tomorrow dancing through her head, she said a quick prayer that God might offer her a bit more help as she struggled with that cookstove, if only to earn a reference from Jackson Smith two weeks from now.

Unless Cousin Mark had other plans for her—plans that involved yet more penance.

Four

Jackson Smith did not like the decision he had finally made during the night but reckoned he could live with it, just as he had learned to live with the fact that God had rarely, if ever, answered any of his prayers over the past twenty-eight years.

Three days after Spinster Ellie Kilmer had shown up on his doorstep, he raced for home, arriving just after the break of dawn and well before the rain that threatened to make this a miserably wet day. Without any hope that another alternative would present itself, he knew he had to act now. Today. Or lose the only prospect he had to insure that his two boys would have someone to care for them during the day.

After storing his coat on the peg just inside the kitchen door, he checked the cookstove to make sure there was still enough wood in the fire to last until it was time to make breakfast and dashed straight to the parlor. Spinster Kilmer should arrive any minute now, and he stoked the fire in the fireplace back to life, determined to convince her that the offer he was about to give her was simply too lucrative, if not attractive, to turn down.

Once the fire was blazing, he stood up, drew in a long breath, and turned his back to the fire to glance around the parlor. She had just cleaned the room yesterday, and he could find no fault with her housekeeping talents. Still, he let out a sigh. Her obvious lack of skill in the kitchen had not given him much to look forward to at mealtimes, but he hoped the woman would soon learn how to put a meal on the table that was neither burned nor undercooked. In the meantime, he would simply have to survive on her desserts, which were her one claim to success in the kitchen.

Most importantly, however, now that the fall harvest was at its peak, he needed someone to care for his boys—someone he could trust and rely on, day in and day out, so he could devote his energies from dawn to dusk to his orchards.

Unfortunately, since she had only been coming here for the past two days, he still knew very little about her, other than the fact that she was utterly dependent upon her cousin for a place to live, which is what Reverend Shore had told him. Since she had just arrived in Harrisburg and had spent all of her days working in his household, he doubted she had learned much about Jackson, either, which suited his plan quite well.

From firsthand experience, however, he knew that this woman was not adverse to hard work. In fact, he could not think of any other woman who would have walked back and forth from the city to here for the past two days without complaint, let alone any recompense for her efforts. She also had not backed down from her commitment to continue coming here, even though the boys—especially Daniel—had not made it easy for her.

A soft rap at the kitchen door sent him charging straight back to the kitchen. Pausing to stop and square his shoulders, he then crossed the room, kicked something lying on the floor, and saw that it was one of the boys' blocks skidding across the planking. Grumbling under his breath, he retrieved the block, slipped it into his pocket, and scanned the room to make sure he had not missed another one before he opened the door.

Wearing her badly stained, but mended, cape, Spinster Kilmer stood waiting, tall and fit but with extremely common features and a full-freckled face. She was, in all truth, the plainest woman Jackson had ever seen, without a single redeeming feature, save for her dark, expressive eyes, but even they were just a tad too small for her face. In sum, there was little to admire about her looks, a fact that reinforced his plans for her future.

"Good morning," he said, stepping back to allow her inside.

She passed him by, removed her cape, and hung it up next to his coat before covering her stained gown with a freshly laundered apron. "Indeed, it is a good morning, considering I managed to get here ahead of the rain," she said. "Either I'm dreaming or someone's already started a fire in the cookstove."

He cleared his throat. "With rain coming, I need to get out to the orchards earlier than usual, so I decided to start the fire for you. I started one in the parlor, as well. Since you've had a long walk to get here again today, perhaps you'd like to sit down and warm up a bit before cooking breakfast," he offered as he closed the door.

She frowned as she tied her apron into place. "I really

shouldn't dawdle, especially since you want an early start today. Besides, I imagine the boys will be up soon, and I need to make some griddle cakes, preferably ones that aren't burned."

He swallowed hard and decided to plunge ahead. "The boys aren't here."

She furrowed her brow. "They're not here? Where are they?"

Realizing that either his tone of voice had been too harsh or he had given her the impression he did not want his boys here with her today, he smiled. "They're with the Grants because I wanted to speak to you for few moments. Without any interruptions," he added.

"I see," she said quietly.

Her eyes flashed with disappointment, if not a slight bit of fear, before he led her directly to the parlor, where he nodded toward the settee. When she took a seat there, she folded her hands on her lap.

He pulled over the single chair in the room and sat down in front of her. Oddly, even though the settee was lower than his chair, she sat tall enough that they were at eye level with each other. He could see the desperation that now simmered in her gaze, as if she anticipated he was going to relieve her of her duties here, when in fact, he had quite the opposite intention.

Before he could decide how to begin, however, she stiffened her back and lifted her chin just enough to give him a glimpse of her mettle. "Although I've apologized for the meals I made for all of you again yesterday, I'd like to do so again. I'm afraid I'm much more accustomed to cooking over an open hearth. Your cookstove has presented more of a challenge than I'd hoped it would these past two days, but I'm quite certain that I'll be able to—"

"The boys and I have survived quite well, indeed far better than if I'd attempted to cook for us," he insisted, hoping to ease her concerns.

She did not hide her surprise. "You're being more than kind, but if you're planning to offer me a permanent position here as your housekeeper, I'm afraid I must decline."

"Why is that?" he asked as he leaned back in his chair. Although he was convinced now that his first idea, to offer her a position here as a housekeeper, would have been a mistake, he was curious to know her reasons for not being interested.

She drew in a long breath. "Even if I wanted to consider the opportunity, I'm afraid my cousin has already made other arrangements for me."

"What kind of arrangements?" he asked, anxious to know if those arrangements might very well conflict with his own plans for her.

She glanced down at her hands and paused for several long moments, as if collecting her thoughts or her wits or both. When she finally looked up, her eyes were simmering with emotion, but he could not tell if she was deeply embarrassed by what she was about to say or if she simply found it uncomfortable sharing it with someone she scarcely knew. "As you know, my cousin and his wife each operate their own shops at the Emporium. I'll be taking care of all of the housekeeping duties for Cousin Mark's wife, Olivia, so she can spend more time with her customers."

"I see," he murmured, pleased that she had confirmed what Reverend Shore had told him: Spinster Kilmer had no home of her own and was only living with her cousin because necessity demanded it.

"With winter soon coming, she already has quite a few orders to fill for capes and winter wear, and there'll no doubt be more," she explained. "Apparently, her work is impeccable, and her shop is quite popular."

"My late wife, Rebecca, thought so. If I recall correctly, Olivia made her favorite cape. It was a soft blue, almost the exact color of her eyes."

Ellie paled, obviously distraught that she had stirred up memories of his late wife. "I'm sorry. I . . . I didn't know that she . . . I mean I didn't mean to remind you . . . or to bring up—"

"You didn't," he insisted and shifted in his seat, wondering exactly how much this woman knew about Rebecca and the scandal attached to her death—a scandal that now tainted his own name. "I'll need to fetch the boys back home soon, but there are some matters I really do need to discuss with you before I do."

He sat up straight and tensed his back, all too aware that his future and his boys' future depended on how convincing he could be. "As you must know by now, I do indeed need household help of a more permanent nature. To be perfectly honest, I wasn't going to ask you to consider a position here as my housekeeper at all."

Her eyes widened. "You weren't?"

"No," he admitted. "Living out here on Dillon's Island makes it troublesome, if not too time-consuming, for you to travel between here and Harrisburg on a permanent basis. I truly appreciate your willingness to do so these past few days without any form of payment from me for your time and efforts."

To his surprise, she actually blushed, but the pale pink that mottled her cheeks did little to make her even slightly attractive.

"I also realize that any housekeeper I might hire would need to live here," he added, "which would—"

"Which would make it impossible for me to consider, because it wouldn't be at all proper," she said and smiled as if she really meant it.

"No, it certainly wouldn't," he admitted and dismissed any concern that this utterly plain woman would tempt him or any other man. "I didn't have to worry about that problem with Widow Mason, the first housekeeper I hired. She was well past fifty, I believe. Widow Hill was a bit older, but neither of them lasted for more than a few months," he said, unable to stifle his disgust with both of the women. "You and I, on the other hand, are quite a bit closer in age. Neither one of us should invite the gossip that would ignite if you started living here as my housekeeper."

Her cheeks flamed a deeper pink, reminding him of the blush on the yellow apples he had been harvesting. "I'd be more than happy to make inquiries on your behalf in the city, or speak to Reverend Shore for you," she suggested.

"To be perfectly honest, I wasn't going to ask for your help in finding a housekeeper, because I don't want to subject the boys to a constant stream of different women in our home. I thought . . . well, I thought perhaps we might get married instead," he blurted and stared at her, waiting to see her reaction and praying all the while she would not bolt from the room and run all the way back to the city, even if she had to swim across the river to get there.

Fortunately, she remained seated, but her eyes opened wide. She batted her lashes, hard, like the wings on a bird caught in a snare. Her mouth dropped open for a moment before she closed it to moisten her lips. "M-married? Did you say we should get married?" she asked, shaking her head as if she could not believe her own ears.

He drew in a long breath and nodded. "Yes, I did."

"You can't be serious!"

"I'm perfectly serious," he insisted and stiffened his back again so he sat as erectly as she did.

"You actually want me to marry you."

"Yes, I do."

"But you scarcely know me," she argued.

"I know enough," he countered defensively.

"After I spent but a few days working here in the house with your sons while you were out in the orchards working? Unless I'm mistaken, this is the first real conversation we've actually had that didn't involve what the boys had done during the day or what work needed doing."

"That may be true, but—"

"But you still expect me to seriously consider marrying you."

He shifted in his seat. "Well, I wouldn't say I expected you to agree as much as I was hoping—"

"That's ridiculous," she said and waved off the very idea with one of her hands. "You're an incredibly hardworking man, you provide well for your family, and you're handsome to boot. There must be a dozen women in Harrisburg who'd be more than willing to marry you," she quipped.

He grunted. "Then you'd be wrong."

"I don't think so," she insisted. "Why? Why wouldn't they want to marry you?"

He swallowed hard, reluctant to discuss the deep pain of Rebecca's betrayal or the scandal that had escalated with her untimely death. "My marriage to Rebecca wasn't a particularly happy one, and there was more than a bit of gossip about us, both before and after she died," he offered weakly, refusing to label the gossip as scandal for fear of completely turning this woman against his proposal.

Ellie waved her hand in the air. Again. "I care as much about gossip as I do for salted fish, which is to say I avoid it as much as possible." She paused. "Was there any truth to this so-called gossip?"

He stiffened. "A fair bit. Yes. A good bit of it, I should rightly say," he admitted, waiting for her to reject him now, just like several young women had already done when he approached the idea of courting them, although those women were obviously far more aware of his situation than Ellie was.

She nodded slowly, but he noticed a slight twitch to her lips. "Were you . . . were you always true and faithful to Rebecca?"

Her question caught him off guard, and he flinched. "Of course I was, but I don't see why—"

"Then you should dismiss the gossip as nothing more than malicious prattle, along with any woman foolish enough to let gossip control her decisions about whom she decides to marry or how she decides to live her life." She huffed. "Surely there must be one woman of substance who would be willing to marry you."

"I haven't found her in Harrisburg or anywhere else within fifty miles," he argued. "But even if I could, I'd rather not have my life complicated by marrying any of them. I'd rather marry you."

She narrowed her gaze. " 'Complicated'? Exactly how would marrying any woman, other than me, make your life 'complicated'?"

She huffed again, but he sensed his advantage and held on to it. "Because I'm not looking for a wife to share my bed. Just my name," he blurted. "If truth be told, I've no desire to marry again at all, but I need someone who can help me take care of my sons and keep a clean house and make a good home for them without worrying about how long she'll stay. I need someone of good character they can respect. Someone they can learn to trust."

"But—"

"I want to marry someone like you because . . . because it also occurs to me that you have little more to look forward to in the coming years than living with your cousin and his wife or finding a position in someone else's household and spending the rest of your days as a spinster. I can offer you so much more," he explained and leaned forward just a bit to judge her reaction to his rather provocative, if not insensitive, words.

In reply, she simply stared at him, although the pained expression in her eyes and the deep blush on her cheeks made it clear that she was uncomfortable with his rather stark assessment of her life.

When her gaze darkened with hurt, he softened his voice. "I'm not trying to be unkind. All I really want you to see is that it would serve your interests, as well as mine, if we were to marry. If you think so, too, as I hope you will, we could travel directly to the city and get married this morning. By late afternoon, you could be back here, with your own home to run and two boys to mother as your own. You wouldn't have to depend on your cousin for a place to live or for anything else, ever again," he said gently.

Pausing for a moment, he held her gaze. "I'm not a rich man in my own right, by any means, but I can and will provide well for you as your husband, and I . . . I would hope we could find contentment and . . . and a pleasant companionship with one another as we raise Daniel and Ethan. Together."

Her eyes welled with tears that she visibly struggled to keep at bay. When she did speak, her voice was barely above a whisper. "I trust I may speak to you as frankly as you've spoken to me."

He caught his breath for a moment. "Of course."

She moistened her lips, blinked back her tears, and tilted up her chin. "I believe I may have misspoken earlier. You weren't wrong at all. In fact, you were probably quite right to assume there wouldn't be any other woman who might consider a proposal like yours, because no self-respecting woman ever would. But in all truth, yours isn't a proposal of marriage at all. It's a business proposition. And while I find your proposition interesting, albeit highly unconventional, I'm afraid I must decline," she said and rose from her seat. "Under the circumstances, I think it best if I leave now and trust you can find someone else to tend to your housekeeping needs."

Frowning, he got to his feet. "You're saying no?"

"I'm afraid I must," she whispered.

"Just like that? Without any further discussion or consideration of my proposal?"

"Exactly like that," she said, stepping around him.

He followed her as she crossed the room.

"Would you at least stay to discuss the idea further?"

She stopped, forcing him to do the same, but she did not turn around right away. When she did, her features were pale and her hands were trembling. In the depths of her dark eyes, he saw just a glimmer of hurt she had buried as deeply as his own before a flash of defiance eclipsed it.

"How old are you, Mr. Smith? Precisely."

"Twenty-eight. As of last May."

"Well, as you can no doubt see for yourself, I'm a fair bit older," she countered. "I'm thirty-one years old, and as you were quick to point out so ungallantly, I'm also a spinster. Not by choice, but by circumstances I have no inclination to explain to you. But please know this," she said firmly. "I may be a bit long in the tooth and unduly plain, even by generous standards. I also may not have more than a single coin or two to my name or a room within my cousin's household to call my own, but I'm not desperate enough to accept a proposal of marriage that would make me nothing more than a . . . a solution to your problems. Now if you'll excuse me, I'll take my leave," she whispered and promptly walked out of the room.

Stung by her reproach as much as her refusal, he followed her back to the kitchen, where she ignored him while she removed her apron and donned her cape. "I didn't want to . . . I didn't mean to insult you," he said weakly.

She marched to the back door, paused, and turned around to face him again. "No, I don't imagine you meant to do that at all, but you did," she replied, opened the door, and slipped outside.

He charged after her. "At least let me escort you back to the landing," he suggested, hoping he might be able to change her mind along the way.

She waved off his offer without breaking stride. "Thank you, but I'll find my way by myself," she insisted, but never looked back. Not once.

He braced to a halt and watched her head straight into the woods behind the house, but he knew by the way she walked, with her back rigid and her head held high, that it was useless to follow her to try to change her mind.

It was not the first time he had failed to convince a woman to accept his marriage proposal, but he certainly hoped it would be the last.

His only consolation was that this time, the woman who had spurned him did not take his heart with her when she walked away.

Five

Ellie refused to let her bottom lip even quiver or to allow a single tear to fall as she marched away from the farmhouse.

Once she reached the privacy of the thick woods separating the property from the orchards, however, she unlatched the lock on her well-practiced resolve to keep her feelings to herself and opened the floodgates, releasing emotions she had kept hidden from the rest of the world for a very, very long time.

Leaning flat against a massive swamp maple tree, she rested her forehead against the solid trunk and pressed her open palms to the rough bark. She gulped in shaky breaths of cool air as hot tears flowed down her cheeks, but it was the sense of total abandonment that lay heaviest on her heart.

The notion that Jackson Smith had proposed marriage was shocking, but his offer of a marriage in name only shook the very foundation of her faith. Faith that God loved her and understood how very deeply she had always wanted a husband and a family of her own. Faith that God would end the uncertainties in her life now, and most important, faith that God would never, ever abandon her.

She lowered her gaze, and salty tears that flowed freely now warmed her flaming cheeks. Jackson Smith's unexpected proposal, which played on her plain looks and reduced circumstances, simply added more fuel to the flames of resentment she had tried so hard to extinguish these past few months.

He knew that no other woman would ever consider such a proposal. He had even admitted as much, which made his proposal to her all the more hurtful.

She tasted her tears and swiped at her lips, but the yearning for a family and home of her own resurfaced—a yearning she had set aside willingly for years. As an only child, she had stayed home to care for her elderly parents, finding herself free to marry after their deaths when she was twenty-eight, an antique on the marriage market by anyone's standards.

Her status as an aging spinster had inspired only pity from acquaintances and strangers alike. Even her only two living relatives had little interest in making her a part of their families, seeing her only as a burden to bear.

Bands of anguish, braided with thick strands of rejection and abandonment, tightened around her chest, and she drew in measured breaths of air that was laced with the subtle scent of the nearby orchards. Like the apple trees that were twisted and bent, heavy with fruit ready to be harvested, her spirit bowed low and pressed against the tattered remnants of the faith that had always centered her life.

Desperate for understanding, she folded her hands in prayer. "This man's proposal couldn't be your will or the answer to my prayers," she whispered before wrapping her arms about her waist and bowing her head. Breathing ever so slowly, she continued to silently pray, emptying every vestige of the hurt and embarrassment and disappointment that laced her spirit, until she set aside her burden.

Anxious to be on her way, she looked around. Just beyond the dirt roadway that led to the landing at the other end of the island, she saw a small, shaded clearing a bit deeper in the woods. Inexplicably drawn there, she discovered what appeared to be a small family cemetery. Within a shallow rim of river stones, five thick stone markers lay flat, like pillows, on a bed of dense clover and weeds that nearly obscured them.

She tiptoed closer. Reverently, she bent down and cleared away the overgrowth so she could read the etchings on each of the stones. When she finished, she realized they told the simple tale of the family who had owned and lived on Dillon's Island for some time.

Obviously, the death of Jackson Smith's young wife was not the only tragedy to befall them. According to the headstone in the center, James Gladson, the boys' grandfather, had died only four years ago at the age of eighty-three, but he had been predeceased by not one, but three wives. She scanned the headstones closest to him. The inscription, "Beloved Wife," below the names of his first two wives was different from his third wife, Emily, whose inscription read "Beloved Wife and Mother."

All three women had passed away before celebrating their thirty-fifth birthdays, but apparently Emily had been the only one of his wives to bear a child. Sadly, Emily had died before their daughter, Rebecca, had celebrated her second birthday.

Family tragedy continued with Rebecca's death six months ago at the age of twenty-five. She was buried next to her parents, leaving room for Jackson to lay beside her again, as well as space for their sons and their families one day.

Unbidden questions about the gossip surrounding Rebecca and Jackson's marriage rose and begged for answers, but Ellie nudged them aside out of respect for Rebecca, who was not here to defend herself or offer any explanations.

Moved nearly to tears again, Ellie sat down to rest on the ground next to Rebecca's tombstone, and she could not help but compare her life to the other women buried here.

None of these four women had had all their dreams fulfilled in this world. All had died far too young, and two had died childless. Neither Rebecca nor her mother had even lived long enough to see their children grow to adulthood.

And Ellie dared to complain about her life? Or refused to consider that God had led her here to this island for His purpose?

Confronted with this family's many tragedies, she leaned back on her haunches and clasped her hands together. "Forgive me, Father," she whispered, acknowledging a litany of sins with those three simple, but heart-spoken, words.

When Daniel and Ethan came to her mind, she glanced at Rebecca's tombstone and gave Jackson Smith's proposal more serious thought. Granted, if she accepted his proposal, he would never be her husband in the truest sense of the word, perhaps because he was still grieving for the wife he had loved and lost and simply could not open his heart to love again. But Ellie knew he would respect her and provide well for her, because he seemed to be a man of his word and he truly, truly loved his sons.

She reached over to trace Rebecca's name and sniffled back more tears. If she agreed to the conditions he demanded for their marriage, she would never know the joy of carrying a child in her womb or the pain of burying that child, but she would have both the joy and privilege, if not the challenge, of raising Daniel and Ethan to adulthood.

Ellie would also have a husband, of sorts, of her own. A home to call her own. She would have a respected place in this world. And she would never, ever again have to bow to the authority of her cousins.

Reminded of the reality of her situation within her cousin's household, she swallowed hard. If she returned to the city now, she would be met by a flood of questions from her cousin. Yet given the circumstances of her departure, she suspected even he would support her decision to leave without completing her two weeks, as promised.

But what about Daniel and Ethan? What arrangements would Jackson be able to make for them now that she had left so abruptly? Could she really walk away without any thoughts for their well-being?

Disappointed that she had let her own pride blind her to the needs of those two innocent boys, she paused to reconsider Jackson's proposal more rationally.

When she did, she realized that marrying him would bring great gifts into her life. Gifts she had the free will to accept or deny. Gifts that called her to rely on her faith and her belief that His plan for her life was now unfolding, according to His will, and with blessings, abundant with His grace.

Humbled, if not determined to be the woman of faith she yearned to be, she rose to her feet and brushed the dirt from her skirts. Armed with renewed faith and a sense of purpose that had been missing in her life for too long, she set her mind on protecting her interests, as well as the boys. But before she accepted Jackson's proposal, she needed to know exactly what his offer entailed, particularly since he could easily set her aside one day, seeing as their marriage would never be consummated.

Jackson had admitted he only wanted a wife to help raise his boys, but had he considered what role she would play in any or all of their lives once the boys reached their majority? Would he expect her to leave then, as penniless and homeless as she was now? Or would he allow her to stay and live out the days she had left in his home?

She paused, grateful for the gift of good common sense, as well as an eye for detail, before walking directly back to the house with her back straight and her head held high. She needed answers to those questions—answers that would determine whether she would agree to marry him or not.

Unfortunately, even though she rushed her steps, Jackson Smith was long gone by the time she returned to the house. Disappointed, but not discouraged, she eventually found him working alone in the orchards on the western side of the island, a solitary figure nearly obscured by a crop of pale yellow apples flushed with just a hint of pink.

She lifted her skirts and traipsed down one of the narrow grassy expanses between long rows of apple trees, their limbs bowed close to the earth under the weight of a very healthy harvest. She had to sidestep her way past trees where drop baskets sat filled with apples that had fallen to the ground before anyone could harvest them.

Concerned she might startle the man enough to cause him to fall off his ladder at the crown of a nearby tree, she called out to him when she was a good four trees away. "Mr. Smith?"

In response, he moved a branch out of the way, looked at her, and gentled the branch back in place. "If you need someone to help take you back across the river, you'll likely find Michael Grant back at his house. It's on the north shore. Obviously, he hasn't made it here yet."

"I wasn't looking for Mr. Grant. I . . . I was looking for

you," she ventured and stopped a few feet away from the bottom of the ladder he was standing on.

He looked over his shoulder at her, frowned, and climbed down slowly, protecting the apples he had stored in the canvas pouch secured around his neck and lying against his chest. When he had both feet on solid ground, he turned to face her. "I thought you wanted to leave."

She moistened her lips. "I thought I did, too. I still might."

His gaze softened. "I never intended to insult you with my proposal. I made a mistake. My problems are my own, not yours, and I'll simply have to find another way to solve them." He turned and started back up the ladder.

"Perhaps you don't need to worry about that," she blurted.

He paused and reversed his steps. When he was back down again and facing her, his gaze narrowed with disbelief. "You've reconsidered?"

"Somewhat," she admitted. "I realized I left without giving you the opportunity to explain exactly how this business proposal of yours might work."

He cleared his throat and looked self-conscious for the first time since she had come to this island. "As I said earlier, I'm not a rich man in my own right. In all truth, I haven't a penny to my name."

Her eyes widened. "But this island, the orchards—"

"All held in trust for Daniel and Ethan and subject to the terms of my father-in-law's will," he explained as he removed the white cotton gloves he wore while harvesting. "My father-in-law was a very wealthy man, wealthy enough to indulge his lifelong passion for orcharding, which would provide little more than a middling existence for them all, at best. When he named me executor of his will, as well as the boys' trust, he made sure I'd have the authority to allocate whatever funds

I deemed necessary for their well-being and security, as well as my own, particularly since he assumed . . . that is, he had no reason to believe Rebecca would die so young," he said, shifting nervously from one foot to the other.

"I see," she murmured, surprised to see how uncomfortable he was discussing his situation when he had been so at ease discussing her plight earlier.

"I was going to suggest that I would provide for you quite comfortably, at least until the boys reached their majority. Then you'd be free to stay or to leave, as you or I might prefer."

She swallowed hard. "I might agree to stay only until Ethan reaches legal age, but I'd expect a settlement of some kind when I left, if that's what I decided to do."

"Or if I decided that was best," he said and cocked a brow. "Did you have a figure in mind?"

Surprised he would even consider her demand, she smiled. "No, but I expect you'd be fair when you suggested one."

He moistened his lips. "Two hundred dollars a year, held in trust, until Ethan's eighteenth birthday. Until then, you'd be free to use the accounts I'll set up in the city, within reason, of course."

She shook her head. "That's far too generous. One hundred dollars a year would be sufficient."

"We'll compromise. One hundred fifty a year."

"Agreed." She drew in a long breath. "I'd also need to know that if you died before the boys are of legal age, I'd receive my funds immediately."

He snorted. "You'd take the money and leave the boys, even though they were still young?"

"Of course not, but I'd want access to the funds, since you'd no longer be here to pay the accounts in the city," she insisted. "But I'd also have to have some sort of legal guarantee, in writing, that I'd be allowed to remain here on the island to raise the boys. In return, I'd agree not to . . . not to remarry."

His eyes widened with surprise, if not respect. "Agreed, provided I retain the right to appoint a trustee to act as guardian, if need be."

She nodded, gathered up all of her courage, and pressed on. "Beyond that, I have some additional concerns that would need to be addressed before I could agree to your offer."

"Such as?"

"Such as . . . such as confidentiality," she managed, unable to stop a warm blush from spreading across her cheeks. "Remaining husband and wife in name only is a reality that neither one of us should ever share with anyone, with the exception of the lawyer who would draw up the papers."

"Not even your cousin?" Jackson questioned.

"Especially not my cousin," she insisted, fearful that he would try to make her change her mind about marrying Jackson, although she hoped he might be too relieved to be set free of any responsibility for her to care one way or the other. "Even though no one else would know of our arrangement, I wouldn't be able to tolerate the scandal of a . . . a philandering husband, either, and I must, that is, I'm afraid I'll have to insist on your total fidelity."

His gaze hardened. "While my lawyer can easily draw up papers to reflect what we've discussed in financial terms, I'd also expect you to sign an oath that you'll remain an obedient, dutiful, and faithful wife. If you failed to keep that oath, in any way, I'd move to have the marriage annulled immediately, and any and all financial arrangements will be null and void," he said sternly.

Stung, Ellie resisted the urge to confess that she had already paid quite dearly for being true to her strong moral feelings on the issue of fidelity in marriage.

"In return, you can expect me to act as an honorable husband," he added, as if trying to soften his demands. "Is there anything else?"

She drew in a deep breath, decided not to press the matter of having him sign a similar oath, and slowly let out her breath. One of the advantages of living here on this island was the virtual isolation they would enjoy, far from wagging tongues and the gossipmongers, who liked nothing more than to speculate about matters that did not concern them.

Still, she had one concern and one only that might force her to reject this man's proposal unless he agreed to meet her demand. "The day I arrived at your home, you told me that you haven't attended services regularly since your wife died. If we were to marry, I'd expect you to take the boys and me to Sunday services every week."

He let out a deep breath, as if relieved she had not asked for something more. "Weather permitting, that shouldn't be a problem."

She smiled. "Then I agree and I . . . I accept your proposal."

"You accept?"

"Yes. Yes, I do."

"Good. Then if you have no objection, once I store these apples away, we can pick up the boys and be on our way."

When he smiled and held out his hand, she accepted his handshake, but Ellie wondered what it might have been like had he proposed marriage out of affection for her and kissed her instead.

A dangerous thought indeed for a woman who had just agreed to marry a man who clearly did not love her and only wanted her to be his wife because he needed her to help raise his sons.

And nothing more.

Six

The marriage ceremony itself bore little resemblance to the one Ellie had kept stored in the hope chest of her dreams.

She was flushed from dashing straight from the island to the lawyer's office and then to the parsonage with two reluctant little boys in tow, rather than from the excitement of finally becoming a married woman. She was also still wearing her dark brown work gown with only a single pale pink rose the minister's wife had pinned to the collar to add a hint of beauty.

Instead of close family members, she was surrounded by strangers, including Reverend and Mrs. Shore, whom she had never met in person before today. An older couple, some twenty years her senior, they did not have a gray hair to share between them, and their love for one another lit each of their smiles. Likewise, Ellie had never met Mr. Clemmons, their new boarder, who had also agreed to serve as a witness. But he was a kindly looking man, with as gaunt a figure as she had ever seen.

More important, she scarcely knew the man dressed in work overalls and a flannel shirt who had exchanged vows with her only a heartbeat ago.

Daniel wore a sullen pout, but it was little Ethan's teary silence as he clung to his older brother and stood very still in front of his father that tugged at her heartstrings. Jackson mumbled an apology to her, as well as to the minister, who was anxious to conclude the ceremony so he could finish his dinner.

"I'm sorry. I didn't give a thought to needing a ring," Jackson murmured as his cheeks flushed just a bit pink under the deep tan he wore.

The stately minister peered over his spectacles. "You can always get one later. A ring isn't absolutely necessary for—"

"Nonsense. Of course it is. Every woman wants a ring to wear, even if it's a temporary one," Mrs. Shore insisted and reached into her pocket. When she pulled out her hand and opened it to Jackson, Ellie saw four intricately carved wood rings of various sizes lying in the woman's palm.

"One of the congregants, Mr. Burke, is quite skilled as a whittler, and he's been kind enough to make sure we have a supply of rings on hand, just for occasions like this. I'm certain one will fit your new wife well enough until you can purchase a proper ring," she suggested, giving Ellie a reassuring look.

When Jackson selected one of two rings that looked large enough to fit Ellie's finger, the minister's wife leaned close to Ellie. "I wouldn't wear that ring when you're doing housework.

The wood isn't as durable as silver or gold, but at least you'll have a ring as a memento of this very blessed day."

Ellie smiled back. "Yes, I will. Thank you."

Reverend Shore cleared his throat. "If we can continue . . ."

Jackson held out the ring he had selected for Ellie to see. When she nodded, he addressed the minister. "We're ready now."

"Then as I was saying, place the ring on your wife's finger and join hands."

Ellie's hand trembled as Jackson slid the ring onto her finger. Jackson's hand was cold, if not damp, the only indication he was as nervous as she was.

"The ring is but a symbol of God's endless love and fidelity," the minister intoned. "Journey together from this moment forward, as man and wife, in harmony with His commandments, and He will bless you, guide you, and sustain you through the trials of this life until you are reunited with Him in glory in the next. Amen."

"Amen," Ellie whispered, clinging to those promises instead of thoughts of her cousin's reaction when he discovered she had gotten married without his permission or his blessing.

Jackson's voice cracked when he voiced his "amen," but he held on to her hand and did not let go.

Mrs. Shore dabbed at her eyes with her lace-trimmed handkerchief. "Kiss your bride, Mr. Jackson," she prompted as Mr. Clemmons made a quick retreat back to the dinner table.

Jackson finally let go of Ellie's hand and pressed a chaste kiss to her forehead. "Thank you," he whispered so only she could hear him.

She heard more than his gratitude. She heard relief, a sore

replacement for the expression of love she dreamed she might hear one day from the man she had just married.

"What about you, boys? Daniel? Ethan? Wouldn't you like to kiss your new mother, too?" Mrs. Shore prompted.

"Ethan's hungry, and we wanna go home," Daniel insisted, stopping short of refusing the woman's request while keeping a tight hold on his younger brother's hand.

Jackson let go of Ellie's hand to place his hand on Daniel's shoulder. "We really should go."

"We have another stop to make, and there's a basket of food in the wagon. We were planning to eat on the way back to the island." Ellie tried to keep her voice from reflecting her disappointment, even though she understood the boys' reluctance to show her affection of any kind.

Mrs. Shore smiled gently. "They'll come around. Surely it wouldn't hurt to give them a little snack. I do believe Reverend Shore would like to finish his dinner." She looked down at the boys. "Why don't you two come with me? While I warm up the rest of the reverend's dinner, I have a bit of sugar to sprinkle on a good hunk of buttered bread for you," she offered and turned to her husband. "While I take the boys with me, you can sign the marriage certificate for the newlyweds. Mr. Clemmons and I signed it earlier, as always," she said, escorting both boys to the kitchen with no complaint from either one of them.

Without comment, the minister disappeared into his study.

Left alone with her husband for the first time, Ellie self-consciously twisted the ring on her finger. "What made you choose this ring? Not that it matters. They were all very lovely."

He shrugged. "It was the only one carved from apple wood. I thought that might do best, at least until I can get a more proper ring for you."

She closed her hand tight. "I don't need another ring. I like this one," she replied.

And she truly meant it.

With the shadow of the parsonage of the First United Church of Harrisburg behind her, Ellie sat on the far side of the front seat of the buckboard, anxious about making this one last stop before heading back to the island. Jackson sat in the driver's seat, with Daniel and Ethan sitting safely between them, preoccupied with the sweet treat Mrs. Shore had given them.

The day had warmed up considerably, and bright sunshine warmed the top of her head and bounced off the glass windows on the covered bridge that spanned the river. Below, she could see the rush of the Susquehanna River and marveled at the number of shoppers hustling along the street that hugged the river's path.

Her heart was racing as she anticipated returning to her cousin's home to tell him the news of her marriage—news that would elicit a host of reactions, not the least of which was bound to be unadulterated shock.

Wagon traffic, as well as horse traffic, was heavy, which was not unusual for midday, and she was relieved when Jackson finally turned down Mulberry Lane and parked the wagon around the corner from the Emporium and the shops her cousin and his wife operated.

After Jackson helped her down from her seat, the two boys quickly followed. Using a handkerchief she kept stored in her cape pocket, she wiped the sugary crumbs from their faces and hands. "There. That's better," she said, smiling.

Daniel shrugged and looked up at his father. "Pappy, do we hafta go inside? Ethan's still hungry and wants to go home."

Jackson hefted Ethan into his arms. "We won't be long."

"Just long enough for me to get my things and tell my cousin and his wife that I'll be living on the island with all of you," Ellie offered and held out her hand to her oldest stepson.

Instead, Daniel took his father's hand, and Jackson offered her a look that suggested it might be a good while before she earned the boy's trust.

Determined to wait this child out with sheer patience and love, Ellie started up the lane. By the time they turned at the corner and she saw the unique double-door entrance to the Emporium just a few yards ahead, her heart was pounding. Instinctively, she braced to a halt.

"Nervous?" her husband asked gently.

She moistened her lips, brushed at her skirts, and nodded. "I'm not quite sure how Mark or Olivia will take to our getting married," she admitted, giving voice to her own fears for the first time.

"It's my place to tell them," he argued.

"They're my relatives. I should tell them," Ellie countered. Because it would be inappropriate for her to enter her cousin's tailor shop, which Mark had been quick to point out to her when she made that mistake upon her arrival, she led her new family into the display room in the front of Olivia's shop, where half a dozen winter capes had been artfully arranged to tempt the most discriminating shopper. On the far wall, a sideboard held books of pictures of the latest styles, along with samples of fabric, and several upholstered chairs offered ladies the opportunity to relax in comfort while they made their selections.

Before the bell over the door had stopped tinkling, Olivia

emerged from behind a curtain that separated a pair of small fitting rooms from the main shop. At forty-seven, she was sixteen years older than Ellie, a good six inches shorter, and quite round at the hips, but she was still blessed with classic features and lustrous blond hair that made Ellie feel exceedingly plain just being in the same room with her.

"You're back today. Already?" Olivia noted with disappointment as she stepped aside to let a customer pass by her.

Ellie did not know the woman who followed on Olivia's heels, but the very last thing she wanted to do in front of anyone else was to share the news of her marriage to Jackson Smith with Olivia, especially when the woman was clearly irritated by her arrival.

Olivia smiled at her customer and nodded toward Jackson. "You know Mr. Smith, of course, but this is my husband's cousin, Elvira Kilmer, whom I was telling you about," she said without introducing Ellie, in turn, to the well-to-do woman, who was dressed in a rose-colored brushed linen gown that was far more elegant than Ellie would ever need to wear.

The woman smiled graciously at Ellie. "It's wonderful to hear you've come to Harrisburg to live, especially since your cousin here has told me how kind you've been to volunteer to help Jackson with housekeeping and such. Spinsterhood does have its advantages now and again, I suppose," she murmured before turning all of her attention to the man at Ellie's side without giving Ellie a chance to respond. "How are you and these dear boys of yours really faring, Jackson?"

"We're doing well, Christina. Thank you," he replied, without offering the news that he had just remarried.

"I had a letter from Dorothea the other day," she said and shook her head. "The poor dear is suffering so from the heat in Philadelphia. I wrote to advise her to return home for a visit, since we're enjoying such a cool spell, but I doubt my sister will come. Her husband is very busy with his legal practice, and she's far too devoted to him to leave the city without him."

Ellie would have dismissed the familiarity between this woman and her new husband as nothing more than a conversation between old friends, until she saw his gaze harden and his back stiffen. "I wish her well, of course," he offered tersely and shifted Ethan from one arm to the other.

Olivia, quite tactfully, ended the awkward silence that enveloped the room by addressing her customer. "If you stop back on Monday, I'll have your cape finished by then," she promised.

"I will, and I'll send Dorothea your best when I write back to her," the woman replied before taking her leave.

"I didn't expect you back until much later," Olivia noted, ignoring Jackson and the boys.

Ellie cleared the lump in her throat. "Actually, I didn't come back to stay. I just stopped by to talk to Cousin Mark."

Olivia furrowed her brow and crossed her arms. "Now? It's well past noon, and he has several important customers with him. Whatever it is, you'll have to tell me, then I suggest you be on your way. By the time you get back to the island, there'll be little time to get much work done before you have to head back here again."

Jackson took a step closer to Ellie and placed his hand at her back in unspoken, but welcome, support.

The tingles that skipped up and down her spine were quite unsettling, and Ellie stepped ever so slightly away from him. "I . . . I won't be coming back, Olivia. Mr. Smith offered me the opportunity—"

"Well, it isn't proper for you to stay there as his housekeeper," her cousin's wife insisted as her cheeks began to pink.

"I would hope Mr. Smith would recognize that it would be entirely improper, especially since the scandal—"

"It's entirely proper for me to stay on the island with Mr. Smith and his sons now, because Reverend Shore just married us," Ellie blurted.

Olivia paled and looked from Ellie to Jackson and back to Ellie again. "Married? The two of you? Married?"

"Less than half an hour ago," Ellie said and held out her left hand so the woman could see her ring. "I know it's sudden, and it may take some getting used to, but it's what we both wanted," she continued, dropping her hand back to her side before the fact that the ring was made of wood registered with her cousin's wife. "I was hoping you'd be happy for me, and I want Cousin Mark to be happy, too."

Olivia batted her lashes and shook her head. "Married? You're really married? To . . . to him?"

When Ellie nodded, Olivia stared up at Jackson. "You actually had the gall to marry my husband's cousin?" she squeaked, as if choosing Ellie for his wife was not only absurd, but unthinkable.

"I have the marriage certificate right here, if you'd care to see it," he offered.

"That won't be necessary, will it, Olivia?" Ellie said. "While I get my things, please tell Cousin Mark that Jackson and I would like to speak to him." She turned to her husband. "I won't be long," she promised and smiled at the boys before she disappeared behind the curtain to get to her room at the back of the shop.

To Ellie's frustration, Olivia followed right on her heels. "How could you do such a thing?" Olivia hissed when they reached the small room and Ellie started to pack her few possessions into her travel bag.

"How could I what?"

"How could you marry that man? You scarcely know him, and I daresay you have no idea of the scandal surrounding the last woman he married—scandal you now have added to Mark's good name, since he has the bad fortune to be related to you, and to my name, as well! How am I supposed to explain your marriage to my customers?" she charged. With her breast heaving, she pointed her finger at Ellie as if she were a naughty child. "I told Mark you'd bring nothing but heartache to our home, just like you did to Philip's!"

Stung, Ellie dismissed any concern for her cousin Mark or his brother, Philip, and got down on all fours to search under the cot for one of her slippers. "You don't have to explain anything," she insisted, unwilling to entertain any gossip about the man she had just married. "I really don't know why you're so upset. I should think you and Cousin Mark would be as happy to be rid of any responsibility for me as Cousin Philip had been. Besides, if you were both that worried about having any connection to Jackson Smith, you shouldn't have arranged for me to spend two weeks working as the man's housekeeper," she snapped, then snagged the slipper and tucked it into her bag as she got back to her feet.

As if on cue, Cousin Mark stormed into the room, despite the impropriety of his being there. Judging by the anger flashing in his eyes and the red flush on his fleshy cheeks, Ellie assumed Jackson must have gone into the tailor shop and told him their news. "Working as Smith's housekeeper was meant to be punishment for what you did to Philip, something others could easily have interpreted as nothing more than your being charitable to two motherless children. But to *marry* that man? It's unfathomable! It's unacceptable! And I won't allow it," he bellowed.

Ellie drew in a long breath but refused to be baited into an argument. She glanced around the small room to make sure she had not forgotten anything and snapped her travel bag closed, which only seemed to infuriate him further.

"I was depending on you to help Olivia so she could spend more time in the shop," he snapped.

Ellie tried not to let her cousins' angry words detract from her purpose here or dissuade her from believing she had made a wise decision. Turning about, she met Cousin Mark's gaze and held it. "I'm sure your wife will be fine on her own. Jackson and the boys need me more, and I . . . I need more. He's offered me something that neither you nor Philip were willing to do. He's gladly offered me a home. A real home."

Cousin Mark put his arm around his wife's shoulders. "At the very least, you should have consulted me first before you married him. Once you know the real truth about the man—"

"I'm a thirty-one-year-old spinster. Or I was until today. I shouldn't need to ask anyone's permission, but if I can't have your blessing and well-wishes, then I would simply ask that you accept my decision and refrain from spreading any gossip about my husband."

"At least she'll be living outside of the city on an island and not the man's Sunday house, even though it's on the far side of the city," Mark offered to his stricken wife.

"But people won't be able to forget they're married. He comes to the city for Market Day on Wednesdays, and we'll no doubt see them on Sunday when they come for services, which means the entire congregation will see them together."

He grunted. "Smith hasn't been to services much since his wife died."

Olivia sniffled. "They'll be there. *She'll* make certain of it," she whined, as if Ellie were not standing right there.

Cousin Mark stared at Ellie for several long moments before he let out a long sigh. "It's not too late to change your mind. I'll speak to Reverend Shore myself. Since the marriage hasn't been consummated yet—"

"Please step out of my way," Ellie said firmly, wondering what either one of them would say if they discovered that her marriage was destined to remain unconsummated forever.

Her cousin hissed under his breath. "If you leave now, you leave for good. Don't come running back here when you learn the truth about that man or discover that you won't be welcome in decent homes any more than that husband of yours is."

"I won't. Now if you'll excuse me, I need to leave. The boys are hungry. I promised we'd stop for a picnic on the way home, and Mr. Smith . . . my husband wants to work for a few hours in the orchards before it grows dark."

Cousin Mark and his wife stepped aside. "Fine. Stay married to him. Our reputations as godly people are strong enough to weather the storm of gossip your marriage will ignite," he said and snickered as she passed by them. "Now that I think of it, I couldn't have fashioned a better punishment for you than to have you discover the bitter truth of why Smith actually married you."

She paused and turned to face him. "What truth would that be, Cousin?"

"That he married you because you're so miserably plain and unattractive, he knew no other man would ever want you."

Olivia nodded in agreement. "Which means, of course, he'll never have to worry that you'll betray him like Rebecca did."

Seven

For the second time in his life, Jackson Smith returned to Dillon's Island with a bride he did not love.

And for the second time on his wedding day, he yearned for the woman who had stolen his heart and still kept it, long after she had rejected him for another, instead of the woman who now carried his name.

He waved farewell to Michael Grant, who had helped to ferry them back across the river, and drove the buckboard from the landing at the northern tip of the island toward home. The wagon wheels crunched over the narrow dirt path through the woods lining the eastern shore of the hundred-acre island, carrying him farther away from the sights and sounds and smells of the city and the still-painful memories his marriage today had brought back to the surface.

He drew in a long breath, inhaling the woodsy scent laced with a subtle apple fragrance that reassured him all would soon be right with the life he had created for himself here. Like the apple trees his father-in-law had planted and nurtured for over forty years, Jackson had planted himself here eight years ago and established his roots.

Here he had found the stable home he had been searching for, and here his sons would grow to manhood with strong roots and a solid family to guide them. He shook his head and let out a long sigh. After losing his heart to a woman who had spurned him, he had thought he would be able to create that safe haven here with Rebecca, but he had misjudged her, too. He only hoped he had not repeated those mistakes by misjudging the woman he had just married.

The canopy of trees overhead blocked the sun, and the air was cooler than it had been back in the city. He glanced down at his two sleeping sons, curled up together like a pair of newborn puppies on the well below the seat, looked up at the new Mrs. Jackson Smith, and smiled. She appeared to be dozing, too, apparently quite recovered from the rather cold reception she had received from her cousin and his wife when she told them of her marriage.

Unfortunately, she would face criticism just as severe from many others as news of their marriage spread throughout the city, and he could only hope that she was as immune to gossip as she had claimed to be. He gave the horses free rein to follow the path they knew so well, but he tightened his hold on the narrow strips of leather themselves in case something spooked the animals and he needed to control them.

Given the opportunity to observe Ellie unnoticed, he could not help comparing the two women he had married, however unfair that might be. Life, however, was not always fair, a lesson he had learned when he had been orphaned not long after his eighth birthday.

He looked at Ellie again. Where Rebecca had been a petite, vivacious, but volatile blonde with mischievous blue eyes, Ellie was a solidly built, no-nonsense woman who was nearly as tall as he was.

She also seemed to be a stable, settled, easy-to-please woman, although he still wondered if all she owned had really fit into that small travel bag of hers. He had needed three trunks when he had packed up Rebecca's things and stored them away in the attic.

Rebecca's personality was bolder, too. During the seven years of their marriage, Rebecca's impetuous temperament had not softened with age or motherhood. But he had few regrets. He had married Rebecca out of obligation to her father, and he would do it again, given the circumstances of his life.

After hiring Jackson, James Gladson, Rebecca's father, had treated him as the son he had never had. Marrying the man's daughter and giving him grandsons to carry on the family line seemed little enough to do to repay him, especially when Jackson had no interest in ever marrying anyone other than Dorothea—the first and only woman he had ever loved . . . and then lost to another man.

"Dorothea," he whispered and tightened his hold on the reins. Just whispering her name fanned the embers of passion and desire that had once consumed him, indeed blinded him, to any thoughts other than claiming the raven-haired beauty as his own. Yet still they remained, despite the fact that she was now married to another.

Startled out of his reverie when the buckboard hit an unexpected rut in the road and bounced hard, he instinctively reached out one arm to keep his boys steady. He took a quick glance down at them and chuckled. They had not even woken up; in fact, Daniel's arm was still locked protectively around his younger brother.

The jolt did, on the other hand, rouse his new wife, who grabbed the seat with one hand to keep her balance and simultaneously swung her arm out over the boys. When her hand inadvertently touched his, he grasped it until the wagon settled. "We're steady now," he assured her and freed her hand.

Blushing, she looked around as if trying to get a sense of where she was. "I-I'm sorry. I must have dozed off."

He chuckled. "Riding in a buckboard can rock most people to sleep, especially when the roadway isn't very flat. We're not that far from home now."

Her eyes widened and her blushed deepened. She dropped her gaze to look down at the boys again, as if to make sure they were all right after she had neglected watching over them. "I've been dozing that long?"

He chuckled again. "Don't look so upset. You haven't committed a crime. As you can see, the boys are fine. Just plain tuckered out," he offered, rather pleased that her first concern was for the boys. Rebecca would have pitched herself into a fit of hysterics as soon as the jolt woke her up, right after she lambasted him for driving so poorly.

"Poor babes. It's been a difficult day for them," she crooned as she brushed a lock of hair off Ethan's pale cheek and tugged Daniel's hat back into place.

"It's been a momentous day for all of us," he countered. Despite her nurturing sweetness, which simply appeared to be part of her nature, he had no illusions about the woman he had married. He had been fooled once too often to completely trust any woman, especially a woman he had known only for a few days, but he had no worry that this very plain woman could inspire even a wisp of desire that might distract him.

Nevertheless, he planned to hold a tight rein of authority over her in the coming days. Living an isolated life on the island would make that fairly easy to do without raising the hackles of independence he sensed just beneath the surface of her acquiescent demeanor.

He glanced down at his sons and swallowed hard. He also had no illusions about the adjustment both of them would have to make now that they had a stepmother. He had every intention of stepping back and simply watching how his new wife met the challenge of winning the boys' trust and affection, but he was fully prepared to intervene on their behalf and usurp her authority, if necessary, to protect them.

Despite Rebecca's inconsistent interest in her sons, which ranged from doting to indifferent, depending on her mood, both Daniel and Ethan had adored their mother. Indeed, they still did, and they would not take to Ellie easily.

He turned to Ellie and told her so. "Unfortunately, the boys can't fully grasp the reality that their mother is . . . that she's dead and that she won't ever be coming home again," he explained.

"Daniel's made that very clear, and I can only assume Ethan feels the same way," she replied and paused for a moment. "I'm not trying to pry for curiosity's sake, but if I'm going to help Ethan, especially, I wonder if you would answer a question for me."

He stiffened. He should have expected she would have questions about the circumstances surrounding Rebecca's death, but he had yet to come to terms with them himself. By all rights, he should have been totally honest with Ellie before she had agreed to marry him, but if she insisted on knowing now, he would simply have to tell her the entire ugly truth and hope she would not regret her decision to marry him. "I suppose that would depend on the question."

"Did Ethan stop talking as soon as he learned his mother had died, or did he always have difficulty speaking?"

Relieved that her question was not about the circumstances surrounding Rebecca's death, he swallowed hard. "No, he spoke fairly well, when Daniel gave him the chance, but within the first week after his mother passed, he just stopped talking. Dr. Willows assures me there's nothing physically wrong with Ethan, but the longer it takes for him to start speaking again . . ."

"He'll speak when he's ready, or when he feels he needs to talk. I won't rush the matter," she reassured him.

Jackson checked the road ahead, saw that it was clear, and looked down at his sons again before mentioning something that needed to be settled before they woke up. "I'm not certain how either one of them will take to calling you . . . that is, it might be too soon to expect them to call you Mama. It might be easier if they continued to call you Miss Ellie for now," he suggested and urged the horses forward when they attempted to stop for a snack at a stand of young saplings.

"I've waited many, many years for a child to call me Mama. A few more weeks or months wouldn't matter, but perhaps you could answer another question for me, since the boys are still asleep and we have a few more minutes before we reach home."

He tightened his jaw. "If it's about Rebecca—"

"No," she said, a bit too quickly, and her blush reappeared. "I grew up on a small farm outside of Philadelphia, but your farmstead is quite unlike anything I've seen before," she noted and shifted in her seat.

"Obviously, there's not much different about the house itself, although it's far bigger than what I've been accustomed to. I've been to the root cellar behind the house, and I suppose it isn't all that uncommon to have to use an outdoor entrance, but other than the abandoned bake oven, a sadly neglected herb garden, and a small smokehouse, I didn't see any other outbuildings. No barn or . . . or chicken house. No animals, for that matter," she said, as if truly confused.

"That's because I need to spend all of my time with the orchards. Those were my father-in-law's passion, I'm afraid. Now they're mine, and someday, I hope, that's where Daniel and Ethan will devote most of their energies."

She furrowed her brow. "Then you must depend on the Grants for most of what you need, since you obviously can't purchase and store everything you'd have to buy at market in the city."

He pulled on the reins to halt the horses. "You really don't know much about me or my life on this island, do you?" he asked, letting the horses nibble a spell.

She shook her head. "No, I'm afraid I don't," she murmured.

He set the brake, climbed down, walked around the back of the wagon, and helped her down from her seat after making sure the boys were still sleeping. "It's probably easier to explain if I draw you a map. That way you'll be able to see it and be better prepared, just in case the boys decide to wander off on an adventure, which they've been known to do from time to time."

Taking a stick he found lying along the side of the road, he stood next to her and brushed at the dirt in front of them with the side of his boot to make a blank slate. He outlined the shape of the island with the end of the stick and put an X on the southern tip of the island. "My home . . . our home is here, as you must have guessed, just inside a stand of woods that borders the river's edge. The Grants live here," he said, making a larger X at the opposite end of the island. "The homestead there is the original homestead my father-in-law built when he settled here with his first wife."

"That would have been Abigail, I believe, right?" she asked.

When he narrowed his gaze, she moistened her lips. "I found the family cemetery this morning when I was trying to find my way to the landing."

He nodded. "The cemetery is here," he said, planting another X near the western shore, close to their home, before he drew three lines running from north to south. "These are the dirt roadways connecting our home to the Grant homestead, with the orchards in-between. There's a different variety of apple planted in each section, but I can explain why later, assuming you're interested. The island isn't very wide, and I suspect you'll be able to find your way around it fairly quickly."

"Is it all that safe, or should I worry about ending up face-to-face with another raccoon or a wild critter of some sort?"

"It's safe enough," he insisted, reluctant to frighten her yet with stories of the one or two predators he had seen on the island since he had first moved here. "My father-in-law actually lived at the original homestead with his first and second wives, although he never had any children with them. He didn't build the second house until after he married his third wife, Emily, and learned a good year or so later that he was finally going to be a father. Rebecca was born when he was sixty-two. His wife, I believe, was only twenty-nine. Unfortunately, she died a few years later."

"How sad for them all," Ellie whispered.

Reminded of how his life seemed to mimic his father-in-law's at times, he drew in a long breath, anxious to finish the map as well as his explanation. "As I was saying, my father-in-law was passionate about his orchards, but he was even more devoted to being a father, and he had enough money to indulge himself on both accounts. He hired Michael Grant to come live on the island with his family and run the farm and paid him handsomely, in addition to allowing him to keep whatever profits he might make from the farm."

"That seems quite generous," she noted.

"It was, which might explain why the Grants have stayed here for nearly twenty-five years or so. But in return, they provided my father-in-law and his family with whatever they needed, and I saw no reason to change the arrangement after my father-in-law's death. Michael still keeps our smokehouse filled and the root cellar stocked, and his wife, Alice, along with their daughter, sees that we have all the milk, butter, and eggs we need."

"Then I was right. This is a most unusual place."

"I trust you'll have no problem adjusting."

She actually grinned. "To less work? No, not at all. I'll make good use of the extra time I'll have by spending it with the boys. After I give the entire house a thorough cleaning," she added. "Would you have any objections if I tried weeding and replanting the herb garden? There are a few herbs I might be able to harvest before the first frost, assuming I have the time to—"

"It's your garden. The island is your home now, too. You can do whatever you like here, as long as Daniel and Ethan remain your first priority. But remember: You can't ever leave this island alone, or take the boys with you, under any circumstances. Any," he insisted.

Judging by how quickly she dropped her gaze, he had probably spoken too harshly to her, but experience had been more than harsh to him, too.

"Pappy?"

He looked up and saw Daniel standing next to Ethan in the front of the buckboard. "It's about time you two woke up," he said, helping Ellie back into the wagon. "There's still enough left of the day for me to work in the orchards for a few hours before it gets dark. I could surely use your help filling up those drop baskets, Daniel," he said as he climbed back into his seat.

Ethan pouted, but Daniel edged closer to him. "I'll help, and I think Ethan wants to help, too, but maybe you should take Miss Ellie back home to the city first. That way she can get home before it gets too dark to cross the river."

Jackson met Ellie's troubled gaze and shook his head. "Miss Ellie won't be going home to the city. Miss Ellie and I were married today, remember? Her home is with us now. She's my wife," he said gently.

"Mama's not gonna like that," Daniel warned, holding tight to his brother's hand. "She's gonna be real, real mad at you when she gets back."

Eight

Ellie decided to wait until Jackson and Daniel were well on their way to the orchards and out of sight before attempting to lure Ethan away from the kitchen window.

While she unpacked the basket containing the remnants of their picnic on their way home, she also sorted through her other tasks for the afternoon: Keep Ethan occupied. Unpack her travel bag. Start supper. Find a sewing basket. Discover a way to help the boys' broken hearts to heal. And find a way to silence the echo of her cousins' harsh parting words.

She removed several cooked eggs from the basket and stored them on the middle shelf next to the crock of butter, caught a glimpse of her wooden wedding ring, and tried not to think about Cousin Mark's hurtful claim that Jackson had married her because she was so unattractive. Not because it was not true. She'd known all of her life that she was plainer than most women, despite her parents' insistence otherwise. Jackson himself had practically admitted as much when he had made his unusual proposal.

She turned, walked back to the basket, removed the scraps of leftover bread, and set them into a bowl. She had made leftovers like these into a sweet pudding for dessert many, many times, but she had no hope of transforming Olivia's snide remark that Jackson's first wife, Rebecca, had been unfaithful. Her comment was mean and malicious, and while it made Cousin Mark's words more hurtful, it also set Ellie to thinking.

While Jackson had admitted that his first marriage had been troubled and that there had been gossip about it, he had vehemently claimed he had been faithful to his wife. At the time, Ellie had never considered that his wife had been guilty of the ultimate betrayal within their marriage.

If it were true, then the fact that he wanted an extremely plain wife like Ellie made even more sense. By marrying her, he would not be troubled by the possibility that she would betray him, since no other man would want her. But it also meant that he was not troubled by the possibility he could ever be tempted to become more than her husband in name only, either.

What would Jackson think if she told him why she had been put out of Cousin Philip's home in Philadelphia? But more important, why hadn't Jackson been honest with her and told her the nature of the gossip that obviously still surrounded his marriage to Rebecca? Didn't he think she had a right to know? Or didn't he care about her feelings at all?

Hoping work would silence thoughts far too troubling to resolve at the moment, Ellie scrunched down next to Ethan to meet him at eye level. "I could surely use some help unpacking my travel bag, but I'm not certain if I can find my way to my new room. Will you help me?" she asked and offered him her hand.

Ethan hesitated at first, his gaze wary. When he took her hand, she let out a sigh of relief and held on tight as he scrambled down from his seat.

Without saying a word, he led her through the kitchen and past the door at the bottom of the enclosed staircase that led up to the bedrooms on the second floor. He stopped at the very next open doorway, taking two steps inside before stopping abruptly.

Standing alongside him, she gave the room she would call her own a good look. She smiled, despite the dust and musty odor in the room, which had been closed off for a good number of weeks. The room itself might have been considered modest in size by most people, but it was larger than any bedroom she had ever had as a child or as an adult. Ever.

The dark blue quilt on the large double bed, the oversized trunk at the foot, on which Jackson had set her travel bag, and the heavy chest of drawers had probably suited the boys' grandfather when this had been his bedroom. But the delicate lady's desk set in the corner between two large windows that splashed the room with light most definitely appealed to her, almost as much as the small stove that would keep the room warm in winter.

Ellie made an exaggerated effort to sniff the air and crinkled her nose. "It's smelly in here. Maybe we should open those windows first."

With a quick nod, Ethan let go of her hand, raced to the nearest window ledge, and climbed up before she was halfway there. "You're awfully quick," she murmured and planted herself directly behind him so he would not topple off and get hurt.

Unfortunately, despite both their efforts, the window simply would not budge. "Let's try this," she suggested and tapped around the bottom frame with the side of her fist to loosen the sash. She waited until Ethan repeated what she had done before she set her feet and tried to lift the sash again.

"Up it goes," she gritted and got rewarded for her efforts with a gush of fresh air and just the hint of a smile from her stepson.

Once they had opened the second window, he actually offered her a full smile that stole her heart. "You're a good, strong boy. Thank you for helping me." She smoothed his stubborn cowlick, which refused to surrender and lie down.

As fast as lightning, he ran across the room and knelt on top of the trunk next to her travel bag, stirring up dust in the process.

She chuckled her way over to him and wondered how she would find the energy to keep up with him every day. "You're very fast, too. Let's see how quick I can be at emptying out that travel bag of mine," she suggested and opened it up.

When he poked his face straight into the bag, she chuckled again. "I doubt there's much there you'll find very interesting."

He pulled away and sat back on his haunches, which gave her the room she needed to lift out the single gown she owned that was suitable for Sunday service. Once she did, she realized she had no place to put it that was not coated with dust.

"Hopefully, this trunk is empty so I can store this inside. Scoot yourself over to the bed so I can open it," she suggested and waited until he climbed onto the bed before she set the travel bag alongside him.

She lifted the lid to the trunk with her free hand and grinned. "It's empty. See?"

Ethan leaned forward, peered over the lid, and nodded.

After bending down to place the folded gown inside, Ellie stood up and pointed to her bag. "There are two aprons next. Will you hand them to me?"

He did, although she had to discreetly refold them as she added them to the trunk and then closed the lid. "We can put the rest into the chest of drawers."

Ethan acted on her suggestion before she scarcely had the words out, tugging the travel bag. But in the process he lost his balance on the soft mattress and plopped down bottom first, while the travel bag flipped off the bed. It landed upside down, scattering most of the contents across the bare planked floor as it fell.

When Ethan took one look at what he had done, he promptly burst into tears. Not silent, tiny baby tears—huge, noisy, marble-size tears that rolled down his cheeks, accompanied by heaving, heart-wrenching cries that rumbled from deep within from his narrow chest.

Driven by a maternal instinct that seemed to surface quite naturally, Ellie swooped the child up into her arms and sat down on the bed. She rocked him from side to side, cherishing the opportunity to hold him close and comfort him, just as her mother had always done for her. "Hush, now. Don't cry, baby boy. All is well. There's no harm done. All is well," she crooned and blinked back tears of her own when he snuggled closer, just as he might have done with his own mother.

When Ethan's little body trembled against her, his tears dampening her bodice, she sighed and laid her head against his. She rocked him and rocked him, not only to comfort him but also herself, until his tears were exhausted and his body lay limp and very still, save for an occasional hiccough.

Holding this little one close to her felt good and it felt right. She could not imagine feeling closer to a child of her own, and she tucked the memory away to cherish over and over again whenever doubts about her place in his life, as well as his father's, nibbled at her faith.

Despite the fact that she had much to do before Jackson and Daniel returned home, she continued holding and rocking little Ethan.When he finally began to stir, she patted his back and smiled. "Would you like to help me gather up everything that spilled on the floor now?"

As if hearing her voice reminded him that the comfort he had received had come not from his mother, he wrenched free and clambered off her lap.

His rejection cut deep as she studied his little face and form, and Ellie could not recall seeing a more forlorn little waif. His deep-set blue eyes and plump little cheeks were swollen and red from crying, his nose was running, and his oversized clothes were more disheveled than ever. Using a handkerchief from her pocket, she wiped his nose and dried his face. "There. That's better, isn't it?"

His bottom lip quivered.

Determined to distract him before he got even more distressed, which was bound to make Jackson question her ability to keep a three-year-old happy, she slipped to the floor and dropped down on all fours, despite the fact she was kneeling on a thick layer of dust. In an exaggerated move, she looked around the floor, saw most of her things had survived intact, lifted up the side of the quilt, and peered under the bed. "Oh, dear! However did my hairbrush end up all the way there under the middle of the bed, right next to one of those blocks you and your brother like to play with?"

When he continued staring at her warily, she lay flat on the floor. She tried to slide forward, but stopped, even though the bed was high enough off the floor that she would have fit beneath it. "Mercy! I'm too big! I don't fit. And I so wanted to use my hairbrush," she whined.

He sniffed but continued to stare at her.

She worked her way into a sitting position and sighed. "I suppose I'll just have to wait for Daniel to come home and ask him to crawl under this bed to get my hairbrush for me, as well as that wooden block."

Finally!

Ethan crawled under the bed, snatched her hairbrush, and carried it back to her before the echo of her words had died, along with the tiny block and a good bit of dust.

She clapped her hands and grinned. "Ethan! What a dear boy you are. Thank you!" she exclaimed and put the brush into her pocket. After he stuck the block into his own pocket, he stood still while she brushed off the dust on his clothes and in his hair, tugged his shirt back into place, and tucked it back into his overalls. "Let's see who can pick up the most of my other things," she suggested.

When he did not seem interested, she decided to make a game out of it and crawled around the floor on all fours—no easy task considering her skirts kept getting tangled between her legs. She had to stop more than once to sneeze and decided the first order of business tomorrow was to give this room a thorough cleaning.

As she had hoped, he dropped down onto all fours, charged ahead of her, and snatched her change purse. He shook it and frowned when he heard the barest jingle of coins, then quickly reached for the pair of handkerchiefs lying within his grasp.

She grabbed for her comb before he noticed it, but froze when she saw him pick up the square of faded canvas she had tied shut with a bit of green ribbon. Trying not to panic, she kept her movements slow and her voice soft as she approached him. "I think you were able to pick up much more than I did," she noted gently and sat down beside him.

Ethan ignored her, intent on untying the ribbon.

"Would you like me to help you?" she asked, fearful he might inadvertently damage the one possession she treasured more than any of the others.

To her surprise, he handed the canvas packet to her, albeit reluctantly. After she untied the ribbon, she carefully unfolded the canvas to reveal a miniature pair of silhouettes of her parents, which had been cut from black cloth on their wedding day and laid atop a light paper background.

"This is a silhouette of my mother," she whispered. As she traced the outline of her mother's image with the tip of her finger, memories of the years she had spent caring for her invalid mother unfolded, along with many loving memories of the man whose silhouette image lay next to her mother's.

Ethan's gaze locked on the image of her mother, and she did not stop him when he traced the outline of the silhouette, exactly as she had done. Satisfied he was being gentle with her treasure, she left him for a moment and laid her comb and brush on top of the chest of drawers next to her father's silhouette and the canvas wrapper.

She had to tug hard to get the top drawer open. After she stored her coin purse and handkerchiefs inside, he walked over and reluctantly handed her the silhouette of her mother without being asked. "Thank you," she murmured and rewrapped both silhouettes back in the canvas wrapper. She placed it into the drawer under her handkerchiefs and closed it before taking Ethan's hand again. "I'm really hungry. Are you?"

He nodded so hard his cowlick danced.

Laughing, she crossed the room with him and shut the door behind them. She had just sat him down at the worktable while she made a snack for them when she thought she heard footsteps on the porch.

Startled, Ellie looked up to see Jackson and his oldest son coming into the kitchen. "Did you forget something?" she asked as Ethan charged across the room and ran straight to his father.

Jackson hoisted up his youngest son as soon as he was within reach and frowned. "I was hoping to find supper ready when we returned."

"Supper?" she said as she scrambled to her feet. "Already? But you just left with Daniel not—"

"Two hours ago," he said. "And we've both worked up an appetite, haven't we, Daniel?"

The five-year-old nodded and rubbed his tummy. "I think Ethan's hungry, too."

Embarrassed, Ellie apologized. "I-I'm sorry. Ethan was helping me unpack, and I suppose I just lost all sense of time," she explained. No wonder she and Ethan were so hungry. "It won't take me long to reheat the soup I made yesterday and set the table. I . . . I apologize for not having supper ready. I won't let it happen again." She hurried over to get a fire started in the cookstove.

Daniel followed right behind her. "Supper was never late when my mother was here, and she never forgot to keep a fire in the stove, neither."

Ellie forced herself to give the boy a smile. Apparently he

had not forgotten any of her mistakes, and she wondered if she would ever do anything right where this child was concerned. She looked over at Jackson, hoping he might defend her.

He merely shrugged without bothering to ease the frown he still wore, but she could not tell if he was frowning because she expected him to defend her or because it was the *second* time in nearly as many days that his supper was going to be late.

Ellie squared her shoulders. She had gotten herself into this situation in the first place.

Nine

By Sunday morning, the gentle rain that had arrived late Friday night had strengthened into a torrential downpour.

Lying abed, Jackson could hear the rain hammering at the roof, and he could see the blades of rain slashing at his bedroom window, but the thunder and lightning during the night had finally quieted. He knew without even getting out of bed that it was too dangerous to cross the river to attend Sunday services today. He did not have to worry that Ellie would argue the matter with him, either, because he had made it very clear to her before they had gotten married that he would not take the family to church in bad weather.

Relieved he would not have to attend services, he shivered in the damp cold that permeated the room, rolled over in bed, and yanked the quilt tighter around his body. Adding wood to the stove was pointless now because he had to get up soon and go downstairs anyway. He burrowed deeper under the quilt for a bit more sleep, since he had spent half the night comforting his two sons when the storm woke them up. Waves of resentment still hounded him since Rebecca had died, leaving him to raise their sons alone. Alone to face the scandal she had left behind.

Jackson lay still, silently studying the ceiling beams overhead until his bitter memories receded. When a gust of wind forced a branch to bang against the window for several long seconds, he groaned. He had learned to leave to fate what any storm might do to his orchards, but he had no desire to start his day by repairing a broken window in the midst of a storm.

When his stomach growled, he groaned again. He doubted his new wife would likely ever prepare an entire day's meals worth eating. He closed his eyes, but tempting visions of a good hot breakfast that was neither burned nor undercooked made his stomach growl even louder. If he got up and went downstairs now, he could get a good fire started in the great room and the cookstove, too, which would chase the chill from the rooms before anyone else rose for the day. Grumbling under his breath, he climbed out of bed. Shivering with cold, he wrapped the quilt around him and managed to shave before dressing, all the while trying to be as quiet as he could for fear of waking Ellie, who was sleeping in the room directly below his, and the boys, who were sleeping in their room just across the hall.

He crossed the room on tiptoe, eased his door open, and shut it again. When he turned and cautiously opened the door to the room Daniel and Ethan shared, he frowned. Even in the dim light he could see the blankets on both beds were a tangled mess. The quilts were on the floor, but the beds themselves were empty.

"Rascals," he muttered, checking under the beds where he had found them hiding more than once before. He sneezed twice. Other than a heavy blanket of dust, there was nothing under the beds.

Half afraid the boys had slipped downstairs to get into some sort of mischief, he made a mental note to start locking the door at the bottom of the staircase when he went to bed at night. He also checked the last bedroom, where Rebecca used to keep all her "pretties," a term she used to describe all her frilly, frothy clothing and accessories that were now stored away in attic trunks.

Satisfied the boys were not there, either, he went directly down the stairs to the great room and shut the staircase door. He was relieved to see the door to Ellie's room was still closed, which meant the boys had not disturbed her. When he turned, without catching as much as a glimpse of the kitchen, luscious smells made his stomach growl loud enough to startle him.

He was surprised to see a good fire already blazing in the fireplace, but it was the table directly across the room from him that gave him pause to stare. He recognized the blue-striped tablecloth resting beneath the serving dishes, plates, and utensils that had been set out for a meal, but he had not seen picture-perfect biscuits piled high on a platter near the center of the table since he had fired Widow Hill some weeks back.

Lured to the table, his mouth started to water and his stomach began to growl, despite his best efforts to stop it. Bowls filled with corn relish and pickled beets he recognized as ones Alice Grant had sent over last week sat on either side of the large plate of buttered biscuits. As unusual as this meal would be for breakfast, he was not going to utter a word of complaint.

Not a single one.

Squeals coming from the kitchen, however, reminded him of his real mission, and he set off to investigate, but not before he snatched one of those heavenly buttered biscuits and devoured it in a single bite. He reached the kitchen in a matter of steps and rocked back on his heels. The heat in the room was almost stifling, and his brain was a bit slow catching up with what he saw.

To his relief, Daniel and Ethan were straight ahead. To his amazement, they were sitting together in the brass tub, so busy splashing and playing with each other they didn't even notice he had entered the room.

"Don't get too close, unless you're prepared to duck."

His gaze followed the sound of Ellie's warning. She was standing at the cookstove fiddling with a knob with one hand and stirring a pot of something that smelled like lamb stew with the other.

"Pappy! Look!" Daniel cried, pulling Jackson's attention away from her and back to his sons.

Grinning from ear to ear, Daniel scooped up a cup of water and poured it over Ethan's head.

Sputtering and batting his eyes, the three-year-old squealed and wiped his face with the back of his hands. With a grin, he returned the favor and drenched his older brother, spilling half his cup of water on the floor.

Jackson's heart raced with emotion. He had not seen his boys this happy for months, especially at bath time, and he had not heard much of a sound from Ethan for a while, either. "I must be dreaming," he managed and walked over to the tub.

The soapy water Daniel splashed onto Jackson's sleeve convinced him this was definitely not a dream, and he stepped back. He narrowly averted the water Ethan sent in his direction, but almost lost his footing on the slippery floor. "Keep the water inside the tub," he cautioned and kept his expression stern until the boys let their cups sink.

He thought he heard Ellie giggle. When he looked at her out of the corner of his eye, he caught just a glimpse of her blush before she turned away. For a moment the image of Dorothea flashed in his mind's eye, and his heart slammed against the wall of his chest. Whenever she blushed, which was often, she became more than beautiful, but she never looked more beautiful than when she blushed after he stole a kiss from her. Amazed that a glimpse of Ellie's mottled blush and plain looks had inspired a memory of his lost love, he turned his attention back to his sons. "I'm surprised to find you two rascals taking a bath before breakfast," he teased.

Daniel grinned again. "Me and Ethan had breakfast, and then we helped Miss Ellie, and then we had a snack, and then we took our bath."

Confused, Jackson narrowed his gaze. "You had breakfast and a snack? Already?"

"Yup."

Ethan nodded in agreement.

"It's almost noon," Ellie offered.

Jackson swung around so fast, he slipped and had to grab on to the nearby table when he started to lose his footing again. "Noon? It can't be noon. I've never slept that late in my entire life. Never, ever," he insisted, even though the evidence set out on the table in the other room added credence to her words, as well as Daniel's.

He cast a long, hard look at the windows, but they were

so steamed up from the heat in the room he could not see anything other than a dark gloom outside.

Ellie left the stove, grabbed a couple of towels, and carried them with her as she joined him. "There's no harm done. You wouldn't have stayed abed for so long if you didn't need the sleep, but I was hoping you'd be up soon. I could really use help getting the boys dried and dressed. The stew is nearly ready for dinner, and I'm afraid to leave the stove for too long, although I think I've got the heat well under control now," she said, setting the towels down on the table.

Closer to her now, he noted the dark circles under her red-streaked eyes. "You didn't sleep well?" he asked.

She shook her head, lifted Ethan out of the tub, wrapped him in a towel, and handed him over to his father. "I don't care for storms," she murmured.

He saw her hands tremble before she buried them in her skirts, and he felt guilty for being relieved that it was the storm that had upset her and not second thoughts about marrying him so hastily.

He started to towel Ethan dry while she reached out for Daniel, but the boy braced both hands on the side of the tub and shook his head. "Pappy's here now," he insisted, his mood shifting like quicksilver.

He watched her swallow hard before she managed a smile. "While you're waiting for your turn, would you hand me the cups you and Ethan were playing with? I need to rinse them and store them back on the shelf again for next time."

Daniel shoved one hand under the water, brought up both cups at the same time, and handed them to her.

"Thank you," she said and set the cups onto the table near the water pump.

"I'm sorry I slept so late. I'm afraid I stole one of your

biscuits, too," Jackson admitted as he dried Ethan's hair. "It was delicious. As a matter of fact, that stew smells awfully good," he said, catching a whiff of something familiar and sweet. He looked around the room but could not find the source. "Is that apple pie I smell?"

She laughed nervously and pointed to the highest shelf above the tableware. "Yes, it is, along with a few other goodies."

When he raised his gaze and saw the shelf was filled from end to end with a cake, two pies, and half a dozen loaves of perfectly baked bread, he nearly choked. "What did you do? Spend the entire night in the kitchen?"

She shrugged. "Almost. Like I said, I don't like storms. I tried to occupy myself so I wouldn't spend all my time worrying. Since I wasn't trying to cook and bake at the same time on the cookstove, I managed not to burn too much of anything," she said proudly and moved closer with Ethan's clothes.

Jackson urged his youngest son to let Ellie help him get dressed before he lifted Daniel out of the tub and started to towel him dry.

The five-year-old tugged at the towel to get his father's attention. "Miss Ellie burned her hands, but she didn't cry like Ethan did that time when he burned hisself. I told her that Mama didn't burn her fingers when she cooked."

Jackson frowned. "You burned your hands?"

She shrugged. "There are bound to be casualties in battle, but this war I have with that cookstove of yours is one I intend to win. Hopefully soon," she added.

"May I see?"

She paused and held her right hand out for a moment before quickly pulling it back. "It's nothing serious," she insisted and tugged Ethan's shirt over his head. When she started to ease him into his overalls, she winced and caught her lower lip with her teeth.

"What about your other hand?"

"Just a few blisters. They'll heal soon enough." She buttoned the straps a bit awkwardly and gently patted Ethan's shoulder. "There," she said proudly. "Show your father how nice you look."

Ethan hooked his thumbs behind the straps on his overalls, tugged on them, and smiled.

Jackson shrugged. Ethan appeared to be wearing the same shirt and overalls he usually wore, which were exactly like the clothes Daniel was struggling to get into.

"I found a sewing basket on one of the kitchen shelves and took in Ethan's clothes a bit so they fit him better now," she whispered when Jackson looked to her for help.

"And I look nice, too," Daniel announced and took his brother's hand.

"You're right. You both look nice, and you both look very clean, thanks to Miss Ellie. Try to stay that way," he cautioned.

Before either one of the boys could respond, Ellie charged past the three of them and headed directly for the cookstove. He followed her with his gaze, caught the now-familiar scent of a burnt meal, and let out a sigh.

"Mercy!" she cried, grabbing the end of her apron with each hand and lifting the pot off the burners on the middle step of the stove. Almost immediately, she let go of the pot, which dropped to the floor, splattering stew in every direction.

With her cheeks flaming and bits of stew clinging to her apron and the hem of her skirts, her eyes filled with tears. She paused for less than a heartbeat before she charged past him to get to the sink and frantically pumped water over one of her hands.

Concerned, he stood up and walked over to her, with both boys right on his heels. “Are you all right?”

She blinked back more tears and waved them all away. “I’ll be fine, which is more than I can say for your dinner. I’m afraid I burned it, again, which really doesn’t matter now that it’s nothing more than a mess all over the kitchen floor.”

A sudden, heavy pounding at the back door made it pointless to offer her a single reassuring word, but he murmured it anyway before he turned and walked over to the door to see who might be calling.

Ten

The last thing Ellie needed or wanted right now was a house full of visitors, expected or otherwise.

The moment Jackson opened the door and not one, but four, people barged inside, bringing a burst of cold, wet air in with them, whatever pride or self-respect she had left completely disintegrated. Unfortunately, with the mess of dinner and soapy water on the floor and the brass tub taking up a lot of room, they had to stand shoulder to shoulder.

The gaiety that erupted spontaneously in front of her did little to soften the disappointment of her most recent disaster in the kitchen. She was too sleep-deprived and too bothered by the blisters on her left hand to join in or to even care that her apron was badly stained or that some of the stew was stuck to the hem of her skirts.

As each of the visitors handed their wet outer garments to Jackson, he introduced them to her. "You know Michael Grant, of course. This is his wife, Alice," he said, taking a rain slicker from a very round, cherry-cheeked woman, who appeared to be nearing sixty.

"Just call me Alice. I hope you don't mind our invasion, but I didn't want to wait another day to meet Jackson's new wife," she offered after removing her bonnet.

Ellie mustered a small smile. "I don't mind at all, though I'm surprised anyone would venture out in a storm like this."

When Alice laughed, her belly shook. "We've had worse storms. Besides, that new covered wagon your husband bought to keep his precious apples out of the weather when they're headed to market kept all of us fairly dry, except for Michael," she teased, leaning forward to wipe away the water dripping from her husband's brow.

"I had a feeling you'd find good use for the wagon, too," Jackson quipped, then turned his attention to the young woman struggling to hold Ethan on her hip while Daniel clutched at her skirts.

The girl appeared to be young, not yet twenty. The spectacles she wore, however, were very thick and magnified her deep-set hazel eyes, making her appear older.

Jackson smiled at her. "This is Grizel, their daughter, who might just have to convince the boys to let her remove her cape before they—"

"I'm fine, and my cape is nearly dry," she argued and offered Ellie a smile. "It's good to meet you, Mrs. Smith. If you wouldn't mind, I'll just hang up my things in the other room and keep the boys occupied there with something or other," she said, then disappeared with them into the great room.

"Grizel's spent a lot of time helping with the boys for the past few years," her mother explained.

Envious of the close relationship Grizel seemed to have with both Daniel and Ethan, Ellie had little time to wonder about the other smaller girl who still had her back to her.

Jackson handed Michael the outer garments he had been holding and helped their final visitor remove her bonnet and cape. "And this is a very, very special neighbor I'd like you to meet, Ellie," he murmured before he pressed a kiss to the girl's forehead.

Moving slowly, the girl turned around to face Ellie.

Much to Ellie's surprise, she was not a girl at all. She was a very small, but very, very old woman. Pale, parchment-thin skin dotted with dark brown spots fell in heavy creases over her cheeks. Wisps of short white hair, like bleached strands of corn silk, hung limply to the tips of her ears, but her clouded eyes still carried a bit of a twinkle.

"This is Michael's grandmother, Widow Polly Palmer," Jackson offered with affection. "Gram, this is my wife, Ellie."

The aged woman shuffled over to Ellie and looked up at her. "You can call me Gram like everyone else. I'm a hundred and two. Now that Nellie Burke has passed, I'm the oldest woman in Dauphin County, but I still make the best apple butter on either side of the Susquehanna and I have the blue ribbons to prove it. How old are you?"

"Th-thirty-one," Ellie stammered.

"I've outlived three husbands, four children, and a fair number of grandchildren. You ever married before?"

"N-no, but—"

"No children, then."

Ellie gasped. "No!" she blurted, as shocked by the woman's blunt questions as she was to learn the woman was over a century old. Gram might be the oldest woman Ellie had ever met, but there was nothing frail about her spirit or her authority, which permeated the entire room.

Widow Palmer edged very close to stare at Ellie.

Instinctively, Ellie pulled back, but she held the woman's gaze for many heart-pounding moments. Finally, the older woman smiled and snatched hold of Ellie's hands. "I think you'll do," she pronounced and squeezed hard.

The pressure on Ellie's burned hands unleashed a jolt of pain that bolted up each of her arms, and she winced. Battling tears, she tried to ease her hands free, but the aged woman held them firmly and turned them over, giving them both a full view of the damage Ellie had done to them over the course of the night, as well as this morning.

Gram's eyes opened wide, but instead of making a comment, she waved the others away. "Go on. Go about your business. Michael, you and Jackson ought to unload the foodstuffs in that wagon. Alice, you can clean up that soapy water on the floor next to that tub and that spill over there by the cookstove later. You probably should go with Michael and Jackson to make sure they put things where they belong in the root cellar instead of just dumping it all inside the door. Me and Ellie here have some gettin' acquainted to do."

Ellie was not surprised when everyone did the woman's bidding and slipped away without a single word of argument. Once they were finally alone, Gram pulled out one of the two chairs at the worktable, which was quite removed from the tub as well as the cookstove, and pointed. "Sit yourself down right here."

When Ellie sat down and laid her hands palm up on her lap, she was nearly eye level with her companion.

"Looks to me like you've been havin' more than a fair bit

of trouble with that newfangled cookstove Rebecca just had to have."

Ellie nodded. "I'm afraid so."

"I'll fix somethin' up for those poor red hands of yours."

Ellie stared at her hands and shook her head. "The burns aren't all that bad. I was just pumping water over them when you arrived. They actually feel much better now," she insisted, making a mental note to get to work on that overgrown herb garden, if only to keep some healing herbs handy.

"You've got some good blisters and more comin'," Gram quipped and edged past Ellie to sort through a basket Ellie had not noticed before that was stored close to the window on the lowest shelf. "I'm afraid I didn't help matters much by squeezin' those hands of yours like I did, which means I should make amends."

"There's no need. Truly," Ellie argued.

"Every wrong should be made right, and no right should be forgotten. And no woman should have to cook on a pile of iron plates, which is why I won't let Michael put one of those contraptions in that kitchen of his for Alice," Gram countered with a crooked grin.

After she moistened several diamond-shaped pigweed leaves she had selected from the basket, she placed them, one at a time, on the tender, reddened flesh on Ellie's palms with hands gnarled by more than ten decades of use. Cool sensations took the sting away almost immediately. "Leave them sit a spell. You'll still blister some more, but not as bad. You'll heal quicker, too."

"That feels much better. Thank you." Ellie was curious as to how Gram knew where Rebecca had stored her healing herbs. "Did you visit here often?"

"Often enough to know Jackson as well as I know my

own grandson," Gram replied before she frowned. "Where's your ring?"

"My ring?"

"Your wedding ring."

Ellie lowered her gaze. "Oh, I . . . I don't wear it when I'm doing housework."

Gram put a finger under Ellie's chin and tipped up her face. "Don't tell me Jackson didn't take the time to buy you a proper ring and gave you one of those rings Charles Burke whittles for somethin' to do."

Ellie swallowed hard. "We didn't exactly . . . that is, we decided to get married fairly suddenly. He didn't really have time to buy a ring."

Gram plopped herself into the chair next to Ellie. "Good girl."

Ellie cocked a brow.

"Defending your husband, regardless of which busybody tries to malign him, is a good and proper thing to do. I always defended all three of my husbands, bless their souls, at least until we got back home behind closed doors again. Still, I wouldn't let that man of yours off too easily. He can afford a proper ring. Make sure he gets one for you, one you can wear no matter what you're doing. It's important for other folks to see."

"I try not to put much stock in what other people think," Ellie replied. Recalling the images of women who had looked at her with pity for years, she shook her head. "That's not entirely true. What other people think matters to me . . . sometimes."

"Good girl." Gram patted her arm. "Honesty seems to come naturally to you, although there are times when I believe the good Lord forgives a lie, 'specially when it's done to keep from hurtin' someone who doesn't need hurtin'. Just don't tell Reverend Shore I said so. He gets a bit touchy sometimes, especially if you interrupt his dinner. Acts like he's the only one who knows the real meaning of the Word sometimes, too, but he's young yet. He's only sixty-seven."

Giggling, Ellie shook her head. "He had to leave his dinner to marry us a few days ago, and he did seem to rush through the ceremony."

Gram laughed, revealing the few yellowed teeth left in her mouth. "Let's take a look at those hands of yours again."

Ellie lifted up the leaves. "Most of the redness is gone." She wriggled her fingers. "The skin isn't as taut as it was before, and the blisters don't appear to be anything that will last more than a day or two," she said. "I don't know how to thank you for helping me."

Gram smacked her lips together. "You could try cutting me a big wedge of one of those apple pies I spied up on that top shelf before the others get back and start digging into them."

Ellie chuckled. "I'll do more than try, and I'll even top it off with a thick slice of cheese."

"Good girl. I do think we might get to be friends, Ellie."

"I hope so," Ellie replied. She figured if she had any hope of making a success of this very unconventional marriage of hers, she was going to need a friend. A very wise, very kind, very caring friend . . . just like Gram.

Eleven

Market Day in the city had always been hectic, though nearly always profitable for Jackson. But rarely had it ended without an argument between him and Rebecca.

In mid-September he finally brought his family to the weekly Wednesday event, simply because he could think of no rational reason why the boys could not accompany him as they usually did, which meant Ellie needed to come along to help him keep a close eye on Daniel and Ethan.

When they arrived several hours after first light, Jackson started unloading his apples, fully aware that their presence here today for the first time as a married couple would likely invite a good deal of gossip. But whether the curious folks who showed up at his stall would actually make a purchase remained to be seen.

He unloaded a bushel of Maiden Blush apples, the last of the season, from the wagon at the rear of their stall while Daniel and Ethan helped fill up small bowls of apples for their customers to sample from the rickety wooden table in the front. The pale yellow apples, tinged with a blush of pink, offered a good contrast to the greenish bronze Roxbury Russets, which had reached harvest a couple of weeks earlier than usual this year.

Ellie worked alongside the boys setting out an assortment of miniature apple turnovers and applesauce cakes she had made using that old brick-back oven behind the house instead of the cookstove. He could hear her humming as he hoisted the basket to one shoulder and carried it back with him. For half a heartbeat, he pictured Dorothea standing at the front of the stall waiting for him, but he dismissed the idea as absurd. Dorothea was far too delicate to spend the entire day catering to his customers. Even Rebecca had never been happy at market until he had finally relented and sent her off shopping for more pretties while the boys stayed behind with him.

Ellie, on the other hand, had seemed content, if not relieved, when he had told her he expected her to work alongside him in the stall the entire day.

He nodded as she passed him on her way back to the wagon to get another basket of baked goods. Although she was smiling and humming as she walked, her smile was a tad too tight and her humming too deliberate to be natural. He suspected she, too, was a bit nervous about facing the inevitably curious customers who would appear at his stall once word of her presence at market had spread through the crowd.

After having negotiated the terms of their marriage contract with her, however, Jackson had no doubt she would not back down from those gossipmongers, either.

He set the bushel of apples down behind the front table, took one whiff of the sweets she had made, and urged his boys to silence by holding a finger to his lips. He swiped one of the bite-size apple turnovers and quickly polished it off with another before breaking one in half for Daniel and Ethan to share. Unfortunately, he did not have time to wipe the sugary crumbs from either of their little faces or hands before he heard Ellie approaching.

Turning, he saw her struggling to carry not one, but two baskets of her goodies and hurried over to her. "Here, let me do that," he insisted, easily lifting both baskets out of her arms and setting them down on top of the table for her.

Apparently a bit chagrined by his greater strength, she glanced at the array of sweet treats she had already set out, put her hands to her hips, and narrowed her gaze. "If I didn't know better, I might think a few certain people I know were stealing something I made for our customers, which might be why a particular someone wanted to be so helpful."

The half grin she wore now was a lot more appealing to him than the tight smile she had been wearing, and her eyes were sparkling for the first time that day.

"We didn't steal nothin'. Pappy took two turnovers first, then he gave one to us," Daniel blurted.

"Guilty, but you better make that three," Jackson admitted, grinned, and popped another one into his mouth.

"Me and Ethan had to share one. We want more."

Ethan pumped his head up and down, setting his cowlick into motion.

Ellie folded her arms and waited.

Daniel sighed. "Please? Can we . . . may we have more, please?"

"Yes you may, but only because you remembered to ask

politely." Grinning more fully now, she broke another turnover in half and handed it to the boys, whose manners had improved dramatically under her care. Jackson could not say the same for their behavior toward her, but he continued to wait and watch as she struggled with their rejection.

"Not too fast," she cautioned as they gobbled down their treat. "There's no more for either of you. Or for you," she said to Jackson. "If you three don't stop eating what it took me an entire day to bake, there won't be any for the customers."

"You give the turnovers away. No one pays for them," he argued.

"No, they don't, but once they taste how delicious they are, they'll be certain to buy more of your apples than usual, don't you think?"

With the sweet taste still in his mouth, he could not argue that point and held up his hands in surrender. Fortunately, she did not remind him that he had not been very supportive when she suggested the idea of making baked treats for his customers. To his credit, however, he had moved a stack of firewood closer to the outdoor bake oven so she would not have to carry it so far. And as she had promised, she had made an amazing array of sweet treats to give away and had not burned a single loaf of bread in that oven for their own table, either.

Before he went back to the wagon for more apples, he glanced up and down the wide aisle of the open-air market that had been located here on Market Square for as long as most people could remember—except for Gram, of course. Protected by the wooden roof overhead where fire ladders hung from heavy beams, most vendors were busy setting out their wares. Sam Brooks and Earl Chastings, his market neighbors on either side of him, had yet to arrive. Very few customers were here yet, either, but within the next hour, they would crowd the market so he would scarcely be able to see past his own stall.

With so few people walking about now, he could see Widow Jane Spence was already sitting on an old bench at the far end, waiting to tempt young and old alike with her mint sticks and sour drops. At the other end, her older sister, Mrs. Paula Harrington, had trays of gingerbread and molded cakes ready for sale. Two constables standing near them were idle, waiting for the crowds to develop so they would have to start patrolling for the band of boys who had been turning Market Day into Mischief Day.

Between the sweet confections at either end, the variety of goods for sale ranged from barrels of *schmier käse*, a soft cheese he did not favor, butter, and eggs to sausages and meats. Salted fish was also available, but he had no fear it would show up on his dinner table because Ellie apparently disliked salted fish even more than he did. The usual summer bounty of produce being set out had thinned, as far as he could see, but the fall harvest of apples and root vegetables appeared to be well under way.

"I could use an extra pair of hands, neighbor."

Startled, Jackson turned toward the voice he had heard.

Standing back by the wagons, Sam Brooks tapped the arm tucked into the sling he wore over his left shoulder. At sixty, he was a robust man, and he took as much pride in the sausages he made as he did in his multicolored beard. Stripes of red, gold, brown, and gray hair stretched from his face to the top of his belly, although the sling now obscured some of it.

"I'll help," Jackson offered and hurried back to the wagons with both boys on his heels.

Sam greeted their arrival with a sheepish grin. "Thanks, Jackson. I knew I'd be able to count on you, which is what I told my missus. She's feeling too poorly again to come with me today. I see you finally brought that new wife of yours with you and your boys, too. I don't suppose there's any hope nobody will ask how I broke my arm, is there?"

"Did you get kicked by that old mule of yours?" Daniel blurted.

"Daniel!" Jackson snapped, a bit harsher than he intended.

The boy bowed his head, and Ethan clutched at his father's trouser leg.

Sam chuckled. "There's no harm done, Jackson. The boy's just curious, and I shouldn't be so set on holdin' on to my pride," he insisted, ruffling Daniel's hair. "Old Jonas isn't the most agreeable mule I've owned, but no, son. He didn't kick me, mostly because I've learned not to give him the chance. I'll tell you what, though. You guess how I really did break my arm, and I'll let you have a whole parcel of those sausages."

When Daniel kicked at the ground instead of replying, Jackson let out a sigh. "Go ahead. You can guess."

Daniel looked up and scrunched up his face. "Did you fall out of a tree?"

"I'm too old to climb trees. Mostly I sit on a stump to rest now and again when I have the chance, but you're close."

"Did you trip over one?"

"Even closer. Do you remember that storm a few weeks back?"

Daniel nodded.

"Well, it seems a bolt of lightning hit one of my trees and snapped off a limb. And that old limb smashed right to the ground. Seems I had the misfortune of standing right by that limb when it happened, and that's how my arm got broken. 'Course, I shouldn't have been caught out in that storm, but that's what happens when you don't keep a keen eye on the sky," he said. He grabbed a small parcel from the wagon and handed it to Daniel. "You come pretty close, so here. Since your new mama is here today, give this to her so she can cook up some sausages for your supper tonight."

"Go ahead," Jackson urged when Daniel hesitated.

Daniel took the parcel. "She's not my mama. She's just Miss Ellie, and she can't cook sausages as good as my mama did." He took Ethan's hand and led him away.

"Boys haven't taken to her yet?" Sam questioned.

"Not yet, but they'll come around. Let's see if I can get this wagon unloaded for you," he replied.

By the time Jackson set down the first of the sausages on top of Sam's table, Daniel was already busy retelling Sam's tale to Ellie. " . . . then that big old limb fell right down and broked his arm," he explained, swooshing his arm in the air to reenact the event.

"B-broke his arm," she correctly gently, even though her hands began to tremble.

"And then—"

"That's enough said for now," Jackson interjected when he noticed that Ellie's face had paled. This was not the first time she had reacted poorly to the mere mention of a storm, recalling that she had even lost an entire night's sleep to that same storm.

"Come along, Daniel. You can help me," he suggested. By the time he and Daniel had Sam's wagon unloaded, the market had come to life with customers who started to appear in waves, leaving brief moments to refill the supply of apples behind the table and the sweet treats on top of it before another wave appeared.

As he had expected, some of the folks clearly came to his

stall out of curiosity about the newcomer who was now Mrs. Jackson Smith, because they left without buying as much as a single apple. Others arrived when word had spread about the sweet treats they were giving away, but no one had said anything untoward to Ellie, although he was certain that his constant presence by her side had discouraged them.

By midday, he had but two bushels of Maiden Blush apples left behind the table, and most of Ellie's wares were gone, as well. He was hot, tired, hungry, and a bit crotchety, although he was relieved none of those mischievous troublemakers had shown up at market again this week.

Taking advantage of a lull of customers, he left Ellie and the boys by the table to go to the rear of the stall and started to brush out the empty wagon bed. He was sorely tempted to pack up early today and head for home, like Earl Chastings had done after complaining of a sour stomach, but he did not want to leave until all his apples had been sold.

When he heard a brief scuffle and Ellie's tense voice, he looked up just in time to see her holding both boys by the hand as she marched them back to him.

She let go of their hands and pointed to the wagon seat. "Up with you both. I want each of you to sit there quietly, one on each end of the seat, until you're ready to apologize," she said firmly.

Daniel glanced up at his father, folded his arms over his chest, and planted his feet. "I don't hafta. You're not my mama."

Ethan mimicked his brother's stance and remained silent for several long moments before he did as he had been told, although Ellie had to give him a little help to get up on the seat.

When Ellie looked to Jackson for support, if not his help

in making Daniel obey her, he didn't step in. If she expected him to intervene every time Daniel refused to do as he was told or every time he compared her unfavorably to his mama, Jackson would have little time left for his own work.

Scowling, she scrunched down until she was eye level with the obstinate five-year-old. "Daniel Benjamin Smith, I don't care whether you think of me as your mama or not. You may not like me very much, either, but you've certainly lived with me long enough now to know that I keep every one of my promises. And I can promise you this: When you misbehave for me, you're going to be punished. Now you have precisely five seconds to scoot yourself up onto that wagon seat like I told you to do, or I can also promise you that you will not taste a single one of my desserts for a solid month," she said firmly before straightening up again.

Daniel glanced up to his father again for help. When Jackson did little more than glance back at him, the boy's bottom lip began to quiver and Jackson's resolve weakened. "It would help if I knew what the problem was that apparently got you into trouble, son," he ventured.

Ellie looked at Jackson and frowned. "The nature of the problem shouldn't matter at all," she said, then walked back to the table, apparently more disappointed in Jackson at the moment than she had been with Daniel for not obeying her in the first place.

Annoyed with himself for falling into Daniel's trap and undermining Ellie's authority, he pointed to the wagon seat. "Miss Ellie's right, Daniel. Like it or not, you have to obey her and accept your punishment when you don't. Climb aboard and sit quietly at the other end of the seat. But keep an eye on your brother."

Daniel frowned but quickly did as he was told.

Although Jackson was tempted to leave the boys for a moment to speak to Ellie and apologize, he decided to finish brushing out the wagon bed first, if only to decide exactly what to say to her.

"Jackson? Would you mind helping us?" Ellie cried.

Annoyed that he had not even noticed a customer arrive, he set down his broom and cautioned his boys to stay put. As he walked back to join Ellie, he got a good view of the woman standing in front of the table and tightened his jaw. He should have known better than to think they might actually escape back home today without having the queen of gossip show up at his stall.

"Good morning," he greeted the stout woman, who had a mouth full of one of Ellie's treats and an applesauce cake in each of her hands.

"Mrs. Fielding wants a full basket of Russets, but she hasn't any way to get it home," Ellie explained.

"You don't live very far. I'll be happy to carry it for you. You can pay me then," he offered, hoping he might get the woman away while her mouth was too full for her to speak to Ellie.

To his complete dismay, the woman literally gulped down her food. "That's the best applesauce cake I've ever had," she managed, unaware or unconcerned that crumbs were still caught on her lips as well as the tip of her chin.

"It's the apples," Ellie explained. "The Russets are wonderful dessert apples. They're almost as good as the Pippins, but they won't be ready for harvest until October."

"It's not just the apples. Not at all, my dear," Mrs. Fielding insisted before polishing off both of the applesauce cakes she had been holding. "You're a far sight better at baking than I am, and I daresay Jackson and those precious boys of his are fortunate to have you in the kitchen."

She paused to lick her lips, studied Ellie, and shook her head. "I see what I've heard today is true. You are indeed a far sight plainer than Rebecca, may she rest in peace, but I'm not one to judge others by their appearances, am I, Jackson? Did you tell your new wife that we're practically neighbors?"

He took a step closer to Ellie. Although he had been surprised by how easily his new wife had shared her limited knowledge about the apples he grew, he was not surprised by his customer's audacity. "Actually, I haven't had time. I've been pretty busy with the harvest," he said, convinced the woman would not leave until he told Ellie that they were indeed city neighbors. "Mrs. Fielding's home is—"

"Just down the square from his Sunday house, although I saw Rebecca there much more than anyone else, since Jackson rarely brought his family to the city to stay there so they could attend Sunday services," she said, her mouth twittering as if she could not get her prattle out fast enough. "Rebecca never did like living out there on that island, but . . . well, I suppose it's understandable that your husband hasn't mentioned anything about that Sunday house." She leaned closer to Jackson before lowering her voice to a whisper. "Under the circumstances, I must say I'm relieved that I don't have to tolerate such goings-on as when Rebecca stayed there, leaving you and those poor boys alone while she—"

"These apples dry well, too," Jackson blurted, determined to intercept the woman before she added any more tidbits of gossip, particularly when he noted how pale Ellie's face had become. "If you like, perhaps Ellie can write down the recipe for those applesauce cakes, since you seem to enjoy them so much."

Easily distracted, the woman clapped her hands. "Oh, would you?"

Ellie nodded. "Of course. I'll bring it with me next week."

"That would be so lovely! As I said, I'm not much of a baker, but my sweet sister Donna is, which means I'll need to take both baskets of apples you have left, since I can't very well ask her to bake any cakes for me unless I give her some apples to use for herself," she suggested and handed her coins to Jackson.

He placed the coins in his moneybag, stored it in the box sitting in front of Ellie, and smiled, even though his hopes to leave early today fell flat to the ground. The woman's sister lived a good mile away from here, and the heavy street traffic in the city on Market Day eliminated any hope of delivering the apples by wagon. He was left with no choice but to deliver them on foot.

While he had some qualms about leaving Ellie and the boys for the ten or fifteen minutes it would take him to carry the apples to Mrs. Fielding's house, he had no desire to leave them for the hour or so it would take to walk the apples to her sister's and return.

"We can come along with you," Ellie murmured, as if sensing his reluctance to leave her alone.

"No, the boys are tired as it is, and you've been on your feet all day, too. Stay right here with them. Don't leave the stall for any reason, and keep an eye out for that band of mischief-makers. They're bound to show up today at some point, and I don't want you or the boys caught up in their shenanigans," he cautioned sternly. "I should be back in fifteen minutes or so for the last basket, but it'll take a good hour more for me to deliver the last one."

"We'll stay here," she promised and handed Mrs. Fielding yet another applesauce cake to eat on the way.

As he had hoped, he made quick work of delivering the first bushel of apples. When he got back to his stall at the market, he found the boys sleeping in the back of the wagon bed, and Ellie was at the stall next door helping Sam with his customers. He hoisted up the second bushel and waved to Sam. "Keep a good eye on my family while I'm gone," he said, hoping any other gossipmongers who might arrive while he was gone would soon move on when they realized there were no apples left for sale. Ellie would simply have to wait for him, just as she promised.

When Jackson returned an hour later, after stopping on his way back to buy Ellie something very special to show her how much he appreciated her efforts at market today, he took one look at his stall and realized he had been a fool.

A total fool.

Daniel and Ethan were gone, and so was the woman he had left in charge of them. In fact, his stall was empty, and so was Sam's. His wagon was empty, too, save for the broom Jackson had been using earlier in the wagon bed and the small wooden box where he had stored his moneybag.

With his heart pounding, he looked inside the box and scowled. No moneybag.

"I'm not just a total fool. I'm a stupid fool," he grumbled, certain Ellie had gone off shopping, just as Rebecca had always done. Breathing hard, he charged back to the front of the stall and scanned the crowd of shoppers, hoping to get a glimpse of Ellie or the boys.

Battling memories of Rebecca's waywardness, if not her

outright defiance of his wishes, his anger flared. That Ellie had gone off to spend his hard-earned cash was irrelevant. His frustration was that he would not be there to protect his sons, who knew nothing about their mother's scandalous behavior or even how she died, if gossipmongers dared to babble their tales about Rebecca's behavior in front of them.

Breathing hard, he charged through the crowd. Finally, he got a brief glimpse of his boys before catching sight of that drab brown gown of Ellie's, and his heart pounded with relief. When he finally reached them and saw that she was carrying a parcel from Mrs. French's Ladies' Shoppe, visions of Rebecca carrying similar pink-ribboned parcels flashed through his mind. His anger swelled and washed over him, drowning every good thought he'd had about the woman he had married. She was proving to be no better than Rebecca.

Barely mindful of the people around them, he snatched each of his boys by the hand and glared at her. Leaning close, he found the wherewithal to keep his voice low, so only she could hear what he had to say. "You broke your promise. You disobeyed me and left. For what?" he gritted. "For that parcel of pretties you no doubt purchased with funds you pilfered from my moneybag? I hope they were worth it, because that's the last thing you'll ever do. Hand over my moneybag. I'm marching you straight to the lawyer's office."

Twelve

Ellie's heart hammered so hard it punched the air out of her lungs before pounding disbelief throughout her body with each unsteady beat. Her hands tightened hard on the parcel she was carrying, but she was unable to blink back tears of humiliation that blurred her vision.

She battled the instinct to flee as far as she could from this man, locked her knees to keep them from buckling, and struggled to maintain what little dignity she had left. Once her vision cleared, she stared back at him, only to be wounded again by the profound disgust glaring back at her. And disapproval. And disappointment, as deep as the hurt she had wrapped around her own heart. And fear, she noted with some surprise.

Without saying a word, she slapped the moneybag against his chest.

He promptly stored the bag in his pocket. "Well? Have you nothing to say?"

His curt whisper sliced through the last bit of anger she refused to let take control of her emotions. "No. No, I haven't, for the plain and simple truth of the matter is that you aren't really prepared to listen to anything I might say. So it shall remain unsaid until you are."

He narrowed his gaze, but Daniel tugged his attention away from her. "Pappy! Miss Ellie, look!" he cried, jumping up and down and pointing behind Ellie.

Jackson turned his head to glare down at the five-year-old. "Not now, Daniel. It's rude to interrupt adults when they're talking."

Distracted by a growing commotion behind her, Ellie glanced over her shoulder, saw the crowd parting, got a glimpse of the danger Daniel had recognized, and reacted instinctively. "Get Daniel! Move!" she cried and tossed her parcel away. She picked up Ethan because he was closest to her, wrapped her arms around him, and pulled him with her as she lunged out of the way.

Ellie watched in horror as Jackson heeded her warning just a second too late. He scarcely had time to push Daniel out of the way in the opposite direction before she saw disaster strike for the second time that very afternoon.

The two rambunctious boys she had seen earlier, just after Jackson had left, were racing their wheelbarrows through the crowd again. One swerved away and kept going. The other boy, however, rammed his wheelbarrow straight into Jackson. As he fell backward, the wheelbarrow tipped forward, spilling an entire load of manure on top of him as he landed on his back.

A very large, very fresh, very pungent load of manure.

Grinning, the boy snatched his wheelbarrow and charged away, just as she had seen him do earlier. One of the constables who was chasing after the pair of rascals offered little more than a wave of reassurance he would catch them, but the laughter was loud, if not raucous, from the rush of onlookers.

Wailing, Ethan burrowed deeper within the protection of her arms. She crooned to comfort him and watched Jackson move his limbs to shake off whatever manure he could. Apparently unhurt, he eventually sat up, glanced around, and frowned, as if unsure he could get up and out of the spilled manure without slipping and sliding right back down again. One of the few men who could stop laughing long enough to help reached out to offer Jackson a hand and pull him to his feet.

The crowd clapped and cheered.

Two very high, exaggerated steps later, he was finally standing free of the mess on the ground.

Now that the show was over, the crowd quickly dispersed, no doubt anxious to escape the pungent odor that was spreading through the air. Daniel appeared unhurt as he scrunched up his face and pinched his nose. "Pappy stinks!"

After tugging free, Ethan joined his brother and mimicked his actions, much to Ellie's dismay. "You shouldn't take pleasure in another person's misfortune," she cautioned, though she could not have chosen a more well-deserved rebuke for the man after the way he had misjudged her and spoken to her.

"I'm sorry, Pappy," Daniel murmured.

Ethan nodded his apology.

Jackson sniffed the air and let out a sigh. "I'm sorry, too. It's a long ride home, and you're both going to have to put up with this smell until we get there."

Ellie walked around, carefully skirting the pile of manure, searching for the parcel she had tossed aside, but to no avail.

Jackson scowled and pointed a few feet ahead of him. "Is that what you're looking for?"

She saw a bit of pink ribbon poking out from beneath the pile of manure and sighed with disappointment. "Yes, I'm afraid it is."

"I wouldn't want you to lose your pretties, considering the price you must have paid for them," he snapped, giving the ribbon a few tugs. The parcel eventually emerged, but the brown wrapping paper was covered with manure. Before she could get to the parcel, he knelt down, slipped off the ribbon, and peeled back the wrapper.

He studied the contents, which appeared to have survived without any damage at all. When he finally looked at her, his gaze was smoldering with guilt he justly deserved. "There doesn't seem to be enough fabric here for a gown," he said hoarsely.

"No, but there's enough to make a pair of overalls for two growing boys."

He swallowed a lump in his throat that was large enough for her to see. "And the flannel?"

"The boys need new shirts, too."

Daniel clapped his hands. "Me and Ethan are gonna get new clothes and Miss Ellie's gonna make them. That's 'cause Mrs. French said Miss Ellie was real nice to help her after those boys with the wheelbarrow almost knocked her down. We helped Mrs. French walk back to her shop with Miss Ellie, too. Mrs. French said Miss Ellie could pick out anything she wanted as a present, and that's what she picked," he said, pointing to the fabrics. "Right, Ethan?"

The three-year-old shrugged.

"He's still mad 'cause he wanted to eat the gumdrops Mrs. French gave us for helping her, but Miss Ellie said we had to wait till after supper tonight. Miss Ellie let me keep 'em in my pocket 'cause I'm the biggest. Wanna see?" Daniel asked, pulling out a small parcel tied shut with a pink ribbon.

Jackson nodded. "That was very nice of Mrs. French to give them to you," he said before turning his gaze back to Ellie. "It was very nice of Miss Ellie to pick out something to make new clothes for you, too," he murmured, but Daniel was too busy showing Ethan the parcel and describing the gumdrops inside to pay any attention.

Jackson's remorse was so sincere and so palpable, she could almost touch it, but the echo of his harsh accusations and his threat to take her straight to the lawyer's to end their marriage still rang too loud and clear in her mind to ease her annoyance with him.

"I'm so very sorry," he whispered, handing the parcel to her.

She swallowed hard but held her gaze steady, even though her heart was still trembling. "No one has ever spoken to me the way you did. Not one. Not ever."

He flinched. "I'm sorry."

"And well you should be," she countered. "Don't ever, ever speak to me like that again."

"I won't. And I . . . I had no right to threaten to take you to the lawyer."

She tilted up her chin. "No. You didn't. And thanks to Mrs. Fielding, now that I know you were less than honest with me before we were married, you'll be quite fortunate if I don't consult a lawyer myself."

He actually paled, but she felt no pity for him. "You brought this on yourself because you've misjudged me, perhaps from the very start."

"I was cruel. And hurtful. And . . . and I was wrong."

"Yes, you were," she said, satisfied that he now understood how very much he had wounded her today and how tentative the state of their marriage was at the moment.

He looked down at his manure-stained clothes and smiled sheepishly. "I don't suppose you'd find fault with the notion that having a pile of manure dumped on top of me was nothing more than what I deserved, would you?"

"Not at all, but I do have one other point I might take issue with." She crinkled her nose. "I don't think the boys or I should be punished by riding all the way home with you, since we did nothing wrong."

"Pappy needs a bath," Daniel interjected, apparently interested in the adult conversation again.

"A change of clothes might suffice, at least until we get home," his father countered reluctantly. "I suppose it's the least I can do to make amends."

"At the very least," Ellie retorted, quite certain he would have to do much more.

"I wonder if I might ask your cousin for a change of clothes, although he and his wife weren't exactly overjoyed about our getting married."

"No, they weren't," she replied. "Since you smell like a barnyard filled with waste, I'm afraid Cousin Mark or Olivia wouldn't want you anywhere near their shop, and most especially, not their customers."

"Let's go to the Sunday house. You can change there. Please, Pappy? Please?" Daniel cried.

Jackson arched his back. "Daniel's right. I have clothes I can change into at the Sunday house."

"Is it far?" she asked.

"No," he gritted.

After hearing what Mrs. Fielding had to say about Rebecca and the goings-on there before Jackson managed to silence her prattle, Ellie could not blame his reluctance to return to the Sunday house.

But as hesitant as he might be, Ellie suspected he would be even more reluctant to sit down with her tonight. For she expected him to share with her every detail of the scandal surrounding their marriage and Rebecca's untimely death.

The Sunday house was just as small as Ellie had imagined it to be, and she followed the boys, who quickly scampered ahead of her once Jackson had unlocked the door.

Like other homes kept by folks who lived a good distance away, the single-room house was only meant to be temporary shelter for one or two nights at a time to provide accommodations when the family came to the city for Sunday services or special occasions. The very thought that Rebecca had used this house to betray her husband seemed almost sacrilegious, and Ellie distracted herself from that thought by looking around the room.

A bank of bunks sat against one wall, while a table with benches was positioned in front of the fireplace on the opposite wall. A corner cupboard held tableware and cookware, and a pair of open trunks, overflowing with women's apparel, sat next to a single closed one.

Jackson entered the house right behind her but left the door open, which helped to ease the smell he carried inside with him. He seemed unusually tense, even agitated. Although she suspected he was anxious to get out of those awful-smelling clothes, she also sensed he found returning here, to the very place his wife had betrayed him, extremely difficult.

She walked around the room, finding the whole décor distinctly feminine. Panels of frilly curtains covered the front window. A delicate lace cloth covered the table. Colorful gowns, as pretty as a field of summer wild flowers, matching bonnets, and white, ruffled petticoats hung on pegs above the beds.

Ellie shook her head. No work gowns. No aprons. No clothes for the boys or for Jackson, as far as she could see, unless they were stored in that closed trunk. "Just Rebecca's pretties," she whispered, recalling the room upstairs at home where Jackson said Rebecca had also stored them.

Getting this glimpse of the woman who had been the first Mrs. Jackson Smith also gave her a bit of insight into why he had assumed Ellie had gone off to purchase similar pretties for herself.

"Mama? Mama?"

Daniel's cries distracted her from her thoughts, and she saw him wandering around the room touching his mother's things. Little Ethan, however, had climbed up onto one of the bunks, where he was tugging at the ribbons on one of Rebecca's petticoats. When he finally pulled them free, he clutched some in each fist and scrambled down from the bunk. Daniel walked over to the same bunk, claimed the pillow, and hugged it to his body.

Jackson stepped around her and walked over to the bunk to stand next to Ethan. "We haven't been here since long before Rebecca died," he said quietly before looking down at his sons and shaking his head. "I'm sorry, boys. Your mother's not here. She's in heaven now. Go with Miss Ellie and wait for me outside. I should be able to find some of my clothes and change quick enough."

Ellie reached out to take Daniel's hand, but he turned his back to her, protecting the pillow he was clutching. "I want my mama."

She dropped her hand. "I know you do, and I know she'd want to be with you if she were here. But she's not here anymore. She's with God in heaven now."

"Then I wanna go to heaven."

"We all want to go to heaven someday, but only God decides when we get to go there," Jackson said firmly.

"But one day, we'll all be together again in heaven with people we love," she added and scrunched down low to be at eye level if Daniel turned around. Out of the corner of her eye, she saw Jackson and Ethan watching her, but she kept her focus on Daniel for the moment. "Was that your mama's pillow?"

Daniel's head bobbed up and down.

"Would you like to keep it and take it home with you?"

Daniel looked back at her over his shoulder. "Could I keep it on my bed? When she comes back, she's gonna want it, and I can give it back to her."

"Of course you can," she replied and turned to Ethan. "You can take something of your mama's home, too. Maybe those ribbons you seem to like so much."

Jackson frowned. "No ribbons. Ribbons aren't for boys. Take something else."

Silent as always, the three-year-old simply shook his head, tightened both fists, and looked straight to Daniel for help.

Daniel stated the obvious. "Ethan wants the ribbons."

"He's not asking to wear the ribbons," Ellie offered. "He just wants to hold them."

Jackson sighed. "Fine. But put them into your pocket for now," he said reluctantly.

Daniel climbed over the bunk to help Ethan stuff the ribbons into his pocket.

"Let's wait for your father outside," she suggested. "While he changes, you two can see if those gumdrops from Mrs. French taste as good as they look."

Daniel accepted her invitation by turning and racing straight for the door, right ahead of Ethan.

"Thank you," Jackson said as she passed by him.

But she did not reply.

She simply walked out the door.

Thirteen

Surrounded by silence, save for the creak of her rocking chair or an occasional crackle of wood, Ellie sat in front of a low fire burning in the hearth in the great room later that night and continued to pray.

For patience.

For understanding.

And for the grace to know that this was truly where God wanted her to be.

When Jackson finally came back downstairs and closed the door at the bottom of the staircase, she kept her gaze on the glowing embers that cast only slivers of light into the room as she twirled the wooden ring on her finger. "We need to talk."

The floorboards moaned a bit as he approached her. "I

wasn't certain you'd still be here when I got back downstairs." He sat down in a straight-back chair next to her.

She looked at him and shook her head. "Where would I go at this hour? It's nearly eight o'clock at night, and it's so dark outside, I'm not certain a firefly could find its way back to the city."

He shrugged, but the strain of the day's troubles simmered in the depths of his dark blue eyes. "I don't know. I figure you'd like to be anywhere but here with me after what I did to you today."

She caught her breath and held it for a moment. "Do you want me to leave?"

His eyes widened. "Of course not, but—"

"That's good, because I don't really want to leave," she said, glancing back to the fire.

"You don't?"

"No."

"Why?"

She braced her feet on the floor to keep the rocking chair still. If she expected him to be honest with her tonight, then she had to be honest with him, too. Besides, she had spent several miserable months keeping Cousin Philip's secret and refused to make a mistake like that ever again. After drawing in a long breath, she met his gaze and held it. "If I leave here, I really have nowhere else to go," she admitted, although it pained her to let him know how desperate she would be if he ever decided to have their marriage annulled.

He furrowed his brow. "What about your cousin Mark? I know he wasn't pleased with your decision to marry me, but I can't believe he'd actually refuse to take you in if you wanted to leave here."

"Believe it," she argued. "Cousin Mark made it very clear I

couldn't return to his household if I decided to stay married to you. He doesn't want me any more than Cousin Philip did."

He cocked a brow. "You have another cousin?"

"Philip. He's Cousin Mark's brother. I lived with him and his wife in Philadelphia up until a few weeks ago, when he refused to let me stay within his household any longer," she admitted. She nudged the floor with her feet to get her chair rocking again in hopes the creak of the rocker would chase away the echo of her Cousin Philip's parting words.

When Jackson did not offer a comment or a question, she glanced over at him. "Wouldn't you like to know why I had to leave?"

He moistened his lips. "Only if you want to tell me. To be perfectly frank, I don't see why what happened in Philadelphia has anything to do with our misunderstanding today."

"Then you'd be wrong," she stated.

"It wouldn't be the first time today."

"That's true, but there wouldn't have been any misunderstanding today if you and I had been completely honest with each other before we decided to get married."

"Fine," he snapped. "What happened in Philadelphia?"

She gripped the arms on the rocking chair to keep from twisting her hands together. "I moved in with Cousin Philip and his family after my mother died. Mostly, I helped around the house and such, but some months ago, Philip asked me to help out at the store he operated with his partner so he could spend more time calling on new customers."

"What kind of store?"

She cast him a glance of frustration. If he kept interrupting her, she would never have the courage to finish her story, let alone get him to open up about his past.

He grimaced and raised one hand in surrender. "Fine. I

suppose it doesn't matter. Go on. You were working in his store . . ."

"Yes, but I left early one day to deliver a package his partner's wife had forgotten at the store earlier that morning. When I got to her home, I discovered she wasn't there alone. My Cousin Philip was there, and they were . . . that is, he was . . . Well, he wasn't calling on new customers like he was supposed to be doing while I was working at the store. That was just an excuse he'd used to see his partner's wife more often."

Nearly overwhelmed by reliving the memory of that awful day, she blinked back tears and rocked a bit faster. "Apparently he'd been having an affair with her for some time, but once I found out, I refused to be a party to it. I told him that if he didn't end the affair, I'd have no choice but to tell his wife as well as his partner."

When she looked at Jackson again, he was sitting forward in his chair, staring at her. "Did he end it?"

"He promised he would, and I believed him, so I didn't tell anyone. I only discovered later that he had continued the liaison and secretly contacted his brother here in Harrisburg, my Cousin Mark, to arrange for me to live with him. I had no idea I'd be leaving until half an hour before the stage was set to depart, but by then it was too late to tell anyone."

"Then your cousin Mark knows why you had to leave Philadelphia."

"Oh, he knows, which is precisely why he contacted Reverend Shore and offered to have me volunteer to be your housekeeper for a few weeks. Walking back and forth from the city to your home and working all day for no payment at all was supposed to be my penance, although Reverend Shore had no idea of my cousin's intentions."

Jackson snorted. “Your penance? For what? For standing up for what is right and decent?”

“For interfering with family matters that didn’t concern me.” She locked her gaze with his. “I didn’t volunteer to come here, as you assumed, but I didn’t come here unwillingly, either. I was hoping to do well enough that you’d give me a reference so I might find a decent position in a household somewhere so I could support myself. As it turned out, I didn’t think I’d get much of a reference after failing so miserably with that cookstove of yours. But then I married you instead.”

“Because you had no other real option,” he murmured.

“Other than returning to the city and begging Cousin Mark to allow me back into his home? None, but you suspected as much and practically told me so, remember?”

He straightened his back. “I remember, although I had no idea that your situation was quite so desperate. Why didn’t you tell me when you first arrived that it wasn’t your idea to volunteer here in the first place? I wouldn’t have expected you to continue or to—”

“I’m afraid I rather liked your admiration. I still do,” she admitted, “which only makes your behavior today all the more horrid. I didn’t do anything to deserve how you treated me today, but unless you tell me why you overreacted and why you were so angry when you discovered that I’d left your stall, I’m afraid you’ll do it again.”

“I promised I wouldn’t,” he insisted and sank back into his chair. “But you’re right. You deserve more than just an empty promise.” He stared at the fire as if it held all the secrets he had kept from her. “I’ve told you that my marriage to Rebecca was difficult,” he began. “She went to market with me each Wednesday, but she didn’t stay to work with me or to keep an eye on the boys. Market Day for Rebecca meant a full day of shopping for more pretties, and when I saw the package you were carrying, I recognized it as one of Mrs. French's, and all I could see after that was Rebecca, laughing at me for complaining about how much she had spent or for ignoring the boys all day. I'm sorry. I'm truly sorry. I wasn't really angry with you today. I was angry with Rebecca."

"But you're angry with her for doing more than just overspending or avoiding her responsibilities to the boys," she prompted. "She betrayed you. Mrs. Fielding said as much today, but, Jackson, it wasn't the first time I'd heard that gossip. Cousin Mark's wife told me the same thing when we stopped to collect my things."

When he looked up at her, his expression was hard and his gaze was cold. "Rebecca's betrayal is not something I care to discuss."

Ellie turned in her chair to face him more directly. "I have no intention of judging you or Rebecca, for that matter, but now that we're married, I have a right to know how she died or why there was any scandal surrounding her death. And I'd rather hear about it from you right now so neither one of us has to be constantly on guard, waiting for someone to tell me what you should have told me yourself."

He narrowed his gaze but continued to stare into the fire. "Last February, Rebecca was crossing the river to come back home from the city on a rickety raft late one night when a sudden storm hit. The raft apparently tipped and tossed her into the river, and she drowned. We didn't find her body for nearly a week," he said, his voice hoarse with emotion.

Ellie caught her breath. "How awful! B-but I still don't understand why there'd be any scandal attached to her death. It was a tragic accident."

His gaze grew even darker, and she could see he was

struggling to keep his anger under control. "Rebecca wasn't alone. Some workmen found her body lying on the shoreline just south of town, along with the body of the man who had been her lover."

Horrified, Ellie clapped her fingers to her lips.

"I'll never know whether he was simply escorting her home or if she was returning with him for the boys so she could take them with her when she ran off with that scoundrel. The gossipmongers, however, prefer to think the latter, which means the man you married wasn't even man enough to keep . . . to keep his own wife from abandoning him."

Ellie clasped the handles of the rocker as she tried to come to grips with the depth of Jackson's humiliation. As scandalous as the circumstances of Rebecca's death had been, it was nothing like the scandal that would have ensued if Rebecca had chosen to leave him and take his children with her.

Her heart trembled. Cousin Mark's wife was right after all. Jackson had asked her to marry him precisely because of who and what she was: a plain, very ordinary spinster woman few other men would want as a wife and no man would ever consider as his mistress.

"Now that you know the whole ugly truth, are you still so certain you'd like to stay?"

Ellie blinked hard, so lost in her own thoughts she barely realized he had spoken to her. "I'm sorry. What did you say?"

When Jackson reached out to still her rocking chair, she lurched forward and realized she must have been rocking very, very fast. "I asked if you'd still like to stay married to a man like me, especially now that you know the real nature of the scandal attached to me and to anyone who carries my name."

She moistened her lips, met his gaze, and held it. "I'd like to stay, but not unless you can promise to be totally honest with me in the future. There can't be any more secrets between us. Ever."

"Or burnt desserts," he replied, clearly relieved enough by her answer to tease her.

"One might hope," she grumbled, but it was only later, when she laid her head on her pillow, that she realized he had never actually agreed to be honest with her in the future.

Foolish man.

Or was she the foolish one for believing this marriage of theirs had any chance at all to succeed?

Fourteen

Several days later, anxious to prove he was grateful to Ellie that she had decided to stay in their marriage, Jackson snatched one last piece of bread from the platter before she carried it back to the kitchen after dinner. "The bread's really good," he praised.

She laughed. "You mean it's not burnt, like the pudding I wanted to serve for dessert."

"That, too, although I must admit I have a weakness for honeyed bread," he countered and slathered the bread with a generous dollop of honey and reached for another while the boys played on the far side of the room with blocks their grandfather had cut out of different kinds of apple wood for them.

"You have a weakness for anything sweet," she teased, waiting for the jug of honey.

He shrugged. "You know, winter's not all that far off. We had three feet of snow dropped on us last winter, more than once," he said before taking a bite of the honeyed bread.

"I don't mind snowstorms," she murmured, picking up the jug of honey and starting for the kitchen again.

"Only thunderstorms," he ventured, regretting his words when he saw her flinch. "Even so," he continued, hoping to ease the frown forming on her lips, "I should think you'd be of a mind to figure out how to use the oven in the cookstove so you don't have to tunnel through a dozen yards of snow to get to that old bake oven outside."

She paused and turned around. "I'm trying," she managed as a blush stole across her freckled cheeks.

"I know you are, but I was wondering if maybe it's not your fault that you've been burning things. Maybe there's something wrong with the cookstove."

Her eyes widened with hope. "Really? Do you think that's possible?"

He shrugged. "I honestly don't know, but Caden James would. He sold me that cookstove and the rest of the stoves in the house we use to keep warm. We usually see him on Sunday at services, and I thought maybe I would ask him to stop by and look it over. Maybe all he needs to do is give the inside as good a cleaning as you gave the outside."

"What if it's not the cookstove? What if he travels all the way out here and the stove is fine and the only thing wrong is that it's . . . it's just me?"

He shrugged again. "I'm sure he can show you how to use it. He showed Rebecca. He even has women come to his shop to practice, or so I've been told."

"Well, I can hardly do that," she murmured and started chewing on her lower lip, as if anxious to avoid having the man travel all the way here and take back tales of her ineptness in the kitchen.

Jackson picked up his plate and stacked it on top of his sons'. "If I'm not mistaken, James also left some written instructions for her, but I haven't seen them."

"Neither have I," she admitted.

Grinning, he walked toward her. "Then it's settled. I'll talk to him the day after tomorrow at services."

"Assuming it doesn't rain again and we can ferry across the river safely."

He chuckled. "I've never seen it rain four straight Sundays in a row, but we'll have to wait and see."

"If I didn't know better, I might suspect you were praying for rain just to avoid going to services. It really is important to go to church, and I'm not just thinking of the boys."

"I know," he said, but he brushed her comment aside. "Daniel and I only have a few hours of work to finish in the orchards this afternoon."

She nodded, took the plate and jug of honey into the kitchen, and returned seconds later.

"Do you want me to take Ethan with us?" he asked, hoping to give her a bit of time to herself.

When she hesitated and looked over to the boys, he followed her gaze. He saw that the ends of the ribbons Ethan insisted on keeping were hanging out of his pockets as he sat fiddling with a few blocks, and frowned.

Daniel, however, walked over to them, apparently anxious his father would leave without him.

"Ethan really needs a good nap," Ellie replied. "Maybe I can convince him to take one in the kitchen with me again so he won't put up as much of a fuss. He likes to sit on the window ledge in the kitchen to watch you leave and then wait for you to come home again, you know."

"Ethan's not looking for Pappy when he sits at the window," Daniel interjected. "He's looking for Mama and waiting for her to come home again."

"You don't know that," Jackson murmured, concerned at how often Daniel reminded Ellie that her place here was temporary and how often he used his brother to reflect his own feelings.

"Yes I do," Daniel insisted.

"You couldn't," Jackson countered.

"But I do."

Jackson let out a deep breath and tried to be patient, as much for his sake as for Ellie, who was watching and listening to the entire conversation. "No you don't, Daniel, because Ethan hasn't spoken to anyone. Not for months, and it isn't fair of you to—"

"He talks to me. He does. He talks to me," Daniel blurted, stomping one foot.

Jackson froze and had to remind himself to breathe. "Ethan talks to you?"

Daniel nodded.

Swallowing hard, Jackson looked at Ellie and saw his own shock mirrored in her eyes. "Why didn't you tell me?" he asked his son firmly. "You know how worried I've been. Or why didn't you tell Dr. Willows?"

When Daniel merely shrugged, Jackson suspected the boy had no answers to his questions because there were none. Ethan couldn't have been talking to Daniel without Jackson having some inkling it was happening—the only time the boys were all alone for any length of time was at night. Since their bedroom was just across the hall from his, he would have heard them talking together at least once in the past six months.

Troubled that Daniel would lie to him, he did not want to put his son in a situation where he had to defend his lie, which would make it harder to admit to the truth. "Can you tell me why he won't talk to anyone other than you?" he asked, deliberately making his voice as gentle as he could.

" 'Cause he's not mad at me," Daniel said with conviction.

"But he's mad at me?"

"Y-yes."

"Why?"

"He thinks you sent Mama away," Daniel whispered.

Jackson gulped hard. The anguish he saw in Daniel's gaze and the pain he heard in his son's voice was too real to be denied. The only way to lead Ethan to the truth was to get him to understand the very concept of death, as well as the loss of his mother. Repeating words he had used with his sons for months now, words he had heard Ellie say to them, as well, seemed pointless, yet he still was not prepared to tell them the true circumstances around their mother's death because they were far too young to understand them.

"Why is he angry with *me*?" Ellie ventured. Her voice was soft and gentle, and Jackson saw no hint in her expression that she did not believe the tale Daniel had been spinning.

"You know," Daniel replied and dropped his gaze.

"I think I know, but I can't be sure I'm right unless Ethan tells me or you tell me."

He held silent and studied the floor as if it were the most interesting thing he had ever seen.

"If you know why Ethan is mad at Miss Ellie, please tell her," Jackson prompted, wondering if his son would be more comfortable explaining himself to someone he did not know well, which would give Jackson an opening to get the boy to admit to his lie.

" 'Cause when Mama does come back and sees you here, she'll think we don't want her anymore, and she'll leave for good. That's why."

Ellie paled.

Jackson drew in a long breath. His patience gone, he sent Daniel back to play with his brother.

"You don't believe him," Ellie whispered, her voice laced with disappointment.

"I believe he's hurt and confused enough to fabricate a lie because he has no other way to face his grief. Ethan is too young to keep up a ruse for this long, and I would know if he had spoken to anyone in the past six months. They would have told me, or I would have heard him," he replied in self-defense, keeping his voice low, too, so the boys would not hear their conversation.

"Just because you or anyone else, for that matter, hasn't overheard him doesn't mean Ethan hasn't been talking to his brother," she argued. "Think about what Daniel said. If he's right, if Ethan has been talking to him and has told him he's afraid their mother won't come back to stay if I'm here, wouldn't that also explain why he hasn't spoken to any of the other women who've come to help out, either?"

"What about the Grants, especially Grizel? Why wouldn't Ethan talk to any of them? And why hasn't anyone who's been around the boys heard Ethan talking to his brother?" Jackson charged, unwilling to accept Daniel's words as truth or her arguments as valid.

"I don't know," she admitted and glanced over to the boys for a moment. "Ethan's only three, like you just said. He's still trying to make sense of a world that's been terribly cruel to him, and so is Daniel, really. I don't presume to understand why God allowed Rebecca to die, but He did and . . . and while you and I might have our faith to help guide us to trust in His wisdom, Daniel and Ethan are still trying to understand who and what God might be to them."

"I understand that," Jackson insisted, reluctant to admit to her or anyone else that he had yet to accept God's plan for him and his sons. "But if Daniel is telling the truth, that Ethan is so upset with me that he won't talk to me, why isn't Ethan angry with me all the time?"

Her gaze softened. "I'm not sure, but nobody, especially a little child, can be angry every minute of every day," she argued. "If Ethan truly needs and wants to talk to someone, maybe he turns to his brother because he's the only one who doesn't pose a threat to him. Daniel's his lifeline, at least for right now, and he's fortunate to have him."

Jackson heard the pain in her voice and suspected she had not had someone close to her when she had needed a lifeline of her own. Then again, he hadn't, either, until he had come to this island and met James Gladson.

She sighed, as if arguing the matter was pointless. "The longer Ethan remains angry and confused, the more likely it is that he'll never speak again to anyone other than Daniel. And the less likely it is that we'll be able to help both Daniel and Ethan become the happy children I suspect they once were. My mother used to say that we're the angriest when we're afraid. If she was right, and I believe she was, it means that unless we discover what has scared Ethan so much that he won't talk, we'll never be able to help him."

Jackson blinked hard. The idea that this woman could presume to know his sons better than he did, even if she had been well-intentioned, was so preposterous he stiffened. "I know a lie from a truth, and I know what Daniel and Ethan need right now. They're my sons," he argued, not bothering to hide his annoyance with her.

She dropped her gaze. "I'm not denying that, but—"

"Maybe it will be better all around if Ethan spends more time with me and less time at the house. From now on, I want him to come with me and Daniel in the afternoons to work in the orchard, like he used to do when I didn't have anyone helping out after Rebecca died," he said, reluctant to remind her that one of her duties was to obey his wishes, not question them.

"But what about his afternoon nap?" she argued.

"Ethan's slept under a tree before. It won't be anything new to him," he countered. Anxious to reassert his authority over her, as well as his sons, he turned his attention to the other end of the room. "Daniel? Ethan? I want you to start picking up those blocks and storing them away. Ethan, come over here."

When Ethan complied, Jackson pointed to the boy's pocket. "I thought you were going to keep those ribbons in your room."

Ethan looked down and poked the ribbons deeper into his pocket.

"Hand them over, son."

Ethan's eyes filled with tears, but he tugged the ribbons out and gave them to him.

Jackson held the soiled ribbons by the ends, wondering how they could have gotten so dirty in a matter of days. He was about to tell Ellie the ribbons were bound for the trash pit when he saw the tears trickling down his son's cheeks.

Moved, he bent down to wipe the tears away. "I want you to let Miss Ellie wash these ribbons for you. Once they're clean again, we'll have to think of a special place for you to keep them," he said and handed them to Ellie. "Now hurry back and help Daniel with the blocks so you can come with us to work together in the orchards this afternoon."

Ethan managed a smile, but Daniel whooped and hollered and ran over to his brother. "Come on, Ethan! Pappy just said you could come today. You can help me pick up all the apples that dropped on the ground, just like you did before," he gushed and tugged his brother back to the pile of blocks.

"I'd appreciate it if you'd launder those ribbons as best you can. Maybe by the time they dry, Ethan will forget all about them."

"I doubt he will," she noted.

"You may be right, so when you're making those new overalls for him, don't bother to add any pockets."

After she disappeared back into the kitchen without argument this time, he watched his sons fill the canvas bag with blocks. His heart swelled with love for his boys, even as his mind wrapped around the remote possibility that Ellie was right and Daniel had been telling the truth about Ethan.

What that meant for Jackson as a father was just as telling as what that meant for him as a husband. Then again, he reminded himself as he walked over to help his sons, he was not a real husband. He was just a man. He loved his sons. He loved his work. He loved this island. And in his own fumbling way, he supposed, he loved his God.

There was no room in his life and no need for him to love anything or anyone more.

Fifteen

Ellie walked around the kitchen to make sure she had not left anything undone. She paused and fingered the white ribbons she had laundered for Ethan and hung from one of the shelves to dry, convinced she could find a way for the boy to keep them.

She turned and walked over to the cookstove. Now that the burners on the cookstove were barely warm, she gave them one last swipe with a damp cloth, put her hands to her hips, and stared at her nemesis.

The three-tiered stove, constructed of heavy iron plates, did not look that complicated to use. The highest tier was a bake oven. Four round iron plates of various sizes, used as burners for pots and pans, made up the middle tier. The lowest tier was the narrowest and offered scant room to rest utensils or cookware that needed to cool.

Hinged doors on the top two tiers opened easily to insert the hickory wood used for fuel, porcelain knobs for each of them allowed for the fires to be controlled separately, and smoke escaped by way of a large pipe that came up from the stove and out through the back wall. But the only advantage of using this contraption she could discover was that she did not have to wait more than ten or fifteen minutes for the fire to be hot enough for her to prepare a meal, saving her hours of time each day.

"If I had my way, I'd drag you outside myself and leave you to rust and have a nice hearth built right here in your place. You're lucky I don't, you finicky old thing," she grumbled.

In the end it was a matter of pride, and she was reluctant to spend what little pride she had left by having Caden James teach her how to use it after he checked it out, assuming the day was clear on Sunday.

She glared at the cookstove and tapped her foot. "Maybe Jackson's right. Maybe it's not me at all. Maybe it's you. And maybe all you need is a good cleaning on the inside to make you work," she said.

She had the time and opportunity. She had the motivation. And she certainly had the wherewithal. After her father had died suddenly, leaving her alone to care for her invalid mother, she had been forced to learn how to handle tasks normally left to men, and she was not daunted by the prospect of cleaning the inside of the cookstove, even if that meant she had to take it apart, plate by plate.

She eyed the stovepipe and decided she would somehow find the strength to take that apart to remove the soot that must have accumulated there, too. After removing her wooden wedding ring and storing it safely on a high shelf, she set straight to the task.

"Go . . . back . . . in . . . to . . . place. Go. Go. Go!"

Several hours later, Ellie used all of the strength she had left to give that detestable stovepipe another shove to get it back into place. Meanwhile she attempted to ignore the pain from the new blisters she had gotten on her hands after discovering the inside of the stove was still a lot hotter than the outside.

That stovepipe did not budge. Not a hairsbreadth.

Before the muscles in her arms twitched themselves into knots that would take a week of Sundays to unravel, she eased down from the seat of the chair she had been standing on. She set the end of the stovepipe down on the floor next to a host of kitchen gadgets she had tried to use as wedges to force it back together and sighed.

Once she was on solid ground again, she blew a lock of hair out of her eyes. She did not need to look into a mirror to know she had as much soot on her face again as she did on her gown, which she had used twice already as a wiping cloth after her very last apron got too soiled.

She used the back of her hands to wipe the sweat from her brow before she wiped off most of the soot on her poor hands. She glanced around the room and looked for something else to use to knock that pipe into place. "Nothing," she grumbled, but a burst of an idea sent her charging out to the side porch and back inside again wielding a piece of firewood that had not been split into smaller pieces to fit inside the cookstove.

She stumbled twice when she tried to get back onto the chair without dropping the wood or the end of the stovepipe she was trying to balance on one of her shoulders. Finally, when she had both feet planted firmly on the seat of the chair, she took a deep breath, lifted the stovepipe to the right height, and banged at it with the firewood.

For her efforts, she was rewarded with a palm of splinters before the end of the stovepipe slipped and went clunking to the floor, landing right on top of that piece of firewood. "Miserable hunk of iron. I hope you . . . you rust," she hissed and climbed back down again.

"Having a problem?"

She swirled about, saw Jackson standing in the open doorway that led to the side porch, and wished that stovepipe was large enough that she might crawl inside.

"Define problem," she managed and hid her hands in the folds of her skirts. Why that man had even a hint of a smile on his face was a mystery, and she was in little mood for unraveling anything that complicated when she clearly could not even put a simple stovepipe back into place.

He glanced at the mess of utensils on the floor, as well as the half-hidden piece of wood and the errant stovepipe, and shrugged. "I thought we decided to ask Caden James tomorrow to tackle that cookstove."

She gulped hard. "You did, but since I had some free time, I . . . I thought I might be able to do it myself. Unfortunately, I think the stovepipe must have warped or something when I scrubbed it clean. It won't go back into place."

He shrugged again, walked over, and picked up the end of the stovepipe. "Iron doesn't warp," he quipped and snapped it back into place with one hand.

She gasped. He did not even have the courtesy to pretend it took any effort to do it at all.

"Michael agreed to keep an eye on the boys because I needed to come back home. I forgot to tell you that we're having supper with the Grants tonight at six-thirty," he said casually. He picked up the hunk of firewood and carried it back with him to the doorway.

"You forgot?" she managed, unable to fathom how she could possibly get herself cleaned up, let alone her gown, in time to go to supper at the Grants'.

He winced. "I'm afraid I did."

"W-when did they invite us? This morning?" she asked as her mind raced for a reason to politely decline.

"No. Actually, it's not an invitation at all. It's more of a tradition during harvest season my father-in-law started, but I forgot you haven't been here to celebrate it until Michael mentioned it to me today."

"Tradition? What tradition?"

"There's a full moon tonight," he answered, as if she knew what that meant. "I stopped working so I could come back to tell you now instead of waiting until we finish working this afternoon so you would have time to get ready. Obviously, that was a good idea," he teased.

She looked down at her filthy gown and rolled her eyes. "Obviously."

"I thought I'd meet you at the Grants', since it's closer than coming back here. You can't miss their cabin. Just follow the road to the landing and bear left."

"I'll find it," she gritted. "Did you say six-thirty?"

"I did. Why? Is it a problem?" he asked innocently.

"Define problem," she whispered in return, but he only grinned and waved before hurrying back to the orchards.

She stared at the open doorway for several long moments before she sighed. "The problem, dear man, is that you have no idea of how inept you just made me feel," she said.

She was not prepared, however, to pose the question of why she also found his grin so irresistible or his dark blue eyes so intriguing or his opinion of her so important, for fear the answer might make this marriage of hers far more complicated than she dared to think.

She had more pressing concerns.

She had no idea if she could actually remove all the dirt and soot from her face and hands, or under her fingernails, for that matter, in the space of an hour or two, but she was quite certain there was nothing at all she could do to salvage her gown to make it presentable.

Especially with a full moon outside.

"Of course there's a full moon tonight. Why shouldn't there be a full moon?" she griped. "That way, everyone will be sure to see what a mess I made of my gown and then they'll all have a good laugh when Jackson tells them how easily he put that stovepipe back into place."

She turned and glared at the cookstove. "Mark my words. One day I will drag you out of this house, and I won't need his help to do it," she promised, tilted up her chin, and marched straight to her room.

Sixteen

With one large great room, three doors leading to bedrooms, and supper bubbling on an open hearth, the Grant cabin looked and smelled just like her childhood home.

The moment Ellie stepped inside, she forgot all about the two new blisters on her one hand and the one stubborn splinter on the other that was lodged too deep to remove quickly. The unease she felt at wearing her Sunday gown slipped off as easily as the cape she gingerly handed to Mr. Grant.

But it was seeing what was left of the intricate design winding three feet wide around the perimeter of the packed dirt floor that made her heart beat a little bit faster.

Mesmerized, she studied the design at her feet and embraced the memories it inspired. Growing up as an only child, Ellie had spent years watching her mother, before she was old enough to help her, etch designs on their dirt floor with sticks her father had sharpened for that very purpose. Every holiday or special occasion demanded a design of its own. No design lasted intact more than an hour or so once guests arrived, either, and this design was no exception.

Still, she could see enough to know that Alice and her daughter had created a design quite unlike any she had ever seen before, and she wished she had not been the last to arrive.

"We're glad you're finally here," Michael offered as he hung up her cape on a peg next to the others.

Standing at the long planked table, Alice smiled and waved her knife over the platters of food she had already set out while her daughter tended to the large kettle in the hearth. "You're just in time. Supper won't be but a few more minutes. Michael, why don't you try to convince your companions over there it's time to end that game of yours?"

He grinned and left to join Jackson and the boys at the opposite end of the room. To her surprise, they were sprawled on the floor playing jackstraw. They were so engrossed in the game they had not noticed she had arrived, but she did not feel slighted. She once had lost all sense of time playing the game with her father. One time they played, Ellie had been concentrating so hard, trying to remove a stick from the bottom of the pile without disturbing the others, she had not even realized her father had teasingly slipped a barrette out of her hair.

"Don't bother tiptoeing around," Alice suggested. "As you can see, the design's already gotten plenty of footsteps traipsed all over it."

Ellie sidestepped as best she could through the design, if only to get a better sense of it. "I haven't seen a decorated floor for many years, and I must admit I've never seen one quite like this," she murmured. She approached the opposite side of the table from Alice, who was slicing bread—beautifully browned, perfectly shaped bread, just like Ellie used to make every day, almost without fail, before she met that cookstove.

Alice nodded over her shoulder. "Take a peek over there. Grizel, show Mrs. Smith that one section nobody's trampled yet."

Grizel stopped stirring the pot of chicken bubbling on the hearth, paused to wipe the steam from her eyeglasses, and motioned for Ellie to join her.

When she did, she took one glimpse of the perfect design and caught her breath. Set between two thick lines, a single scene stretched for four or five feet in a straight line before it repeated itself over and over again. A full moon, surrounded by a halo of stars, shined above a majestic apple tree, its limbs bent beneath the weight of the fruit. Etched in the trunk of the tree, a simple cross. "It's incredibly lovely, and very time-consuming to create," she murmured.

"We enjoy making it, but it was Mr. Gladson's idea," the girl replied.

Ellie furrowed her brow for a moment, then remembered the name belonged to Jackson's father-in-law. "He asked you to do this?"

"Every year for the full moon at harvesttime, which is July through October. There really is a tree that looks exactly like that. You'll see it after supper when we go outside for our little celebration, but I'm sure your husband explained all that," Alice offered without leaving her task.

Reluctant to tell the woman otherwise, Ellie kept her questions to herself and walked back to the table. "May I help you with something?"

Alice set the last piece of bread onto the plate and started slicing another loaf. "And risk getting something on that pretty gown of yours? Just sit and keep me company. Next time, don't bother changing from everyday, especially when you visit us. We're just regular folks."

Ellie pressed her lips together. By the standards of the day, the gown with just a bit of lace at the collar saved it from being overly plain. The gown's narrow skirts made it old-fashioned, but Alice was right. The thin fabric and light color made the garment hardly suitable for ordinary wear.

Grizel giggled. "Mother, don't be silly. Mrs. Smith didn't dress pretty just for us."

Ellie's cheeks burned as she wondered what either of them would say if they knew the real nature of her marriage.

"I apologize for my daughter. She can be as outspoken as her great-grandmother," Alice said before casting her daughter a frown.

"There's no harm done."

"You're kind to say so," Alice countered. "If you'd really like to help, maybe you could let Gram know that supper will be ready soon, which will give me a few moments alone with my daughter to remind her of her manners. Gram's room is the last one to your right," she said, then shook her head. "No, it's the last one to my right. It's to your left. Just be sure to knock hard. She still hears as good as most, but she tends to nod off about this time of day."

Ellie nodded, but looked over to where the men and children were playing and caught Jackson looking at her. Before she could say anything, he simply nodded and turned his attention back to the game again without as much as a smile to let her know he was glad she was there. Disappointed, she went to Gram's door and knocked. Then knocked again, harder this time.

"Come on in."

She opened the door and winced at the creaking sound it made. To her surprise, the light that filtered into the small bedroom now that the door was open was no match for the light within. The aged woman must have had half a dozen candles burning on the chest of drawers next to her bed, and there were another two burning on either side of the chair near the open window where she was sitting, an open Bible on her lap.

"Ellie! You came after all," she said, closing her Bible. "Close the door and sit with me a spell before I have to share you with all the others."

She hesitated. "Alice just wanted me to tell you that supper will be ready in a few minutes."

"Nonsense. My nose is telling me supper won't be ready for a good half an hour yet. Sit right down there on the bed so I can see you best."

Ellie closed the door behind her. "I'm sorry I'm a bit late."

"You got here tonight for the celebration, which is more than I can say for Jackson's first wife, may she rest in His peace."

Ellie eased onto the foot of the bed, directly across from Gram. "Rebecca didn't come for the celebration?"

The aged woman shook her head. "Not once she got married. She told Jackson she'd done it enough as a child, and he couldn't change her mind any more than her father could," she explained. "Did Jackson bother to tell you tonight's tradition?"

"No, he didn't," Ellie said, at ease returning the woman's frankness with her own after the single visit they'd had several weeks ago.

"I suspected as much."

Ellie laughed. "You know him that well?"

"I've known that boy since the day he first set foot on this island looking for a place to plant his own roots, but that's a tale for another day." Pausing, she leaned toward Ellie, stared into her eyes for a few moments, and shook her head. "Having a bit of trouble with him, are you?"

Ellie averted her eyes for a moment, wondering if the elderly woman could actually see the truth about the odd marriage she and Jackson were sharing. "Trouble? No, I just—"

"Every new bride has a bit of adjusting to do," Gram said gently. "I suspect you've already discovered that being Jackson's bride is a lot more difficult than you thought it would be."

Ellie swallowed hard. As much as she wanted to seek Gram's advice, she was mindful of her own insistence that no one, other than Ellie and Jackson, would ever know that their marriage was in name only.

Before she could think of anything to say that would not invite more questions, however, Gram raised her hand. "I suppose you think I'm more nosey than most, and you'd probably be right. That said, there's something I want to share with you, if you'd care to hear it."

Ellie nodded, but when she went to twist the wooden ring on her finger, she realized she had forgotten to put it back on again.

"In a way, Jackson's no different from the rest of us. He's not perfect, even though he likes to think he is, and his faith isn't all it should be. But the truth of the matter is that we've all got cracks in our spirits, and we have to remember they're only there because we need them."

Ellie furrowed her brow. "We do?"

"Of course we do. Otherwise, how could God's grace filter in deep enough to give us the joy and peace we're all searching for in this world? It couldn't, plain and simple."

"I never thought of it quite that way before," Ellie murmured, hopeful Gram was not able to see how very cracked Ellie's own spirit had become.

Gram chuckled. "When you get to be as old as I am, all you have time to do is think. And pray. I know Jackson doesn't seem much interested in keeping his faith strong right now, but if you pray for him, like I do, he'll find his faith again. And I suspect you will, too."

Surprised by the aged woman's insight, Ellie dropped her gaze. "I . . . I don't know what to say."

"You don't have to say anything right now, but if you ever want to chat about anything, I'll be sitting right here, ready to listen," Gram offered and patted Ellie's arm. "That's sure a pretty dress you wore today."

Grateful to change the topic of their conversation, Ellie shook her head. "Alice said I shouldn't have worn it."

"Don't pay her any mind. She's a ninny. A good woman, but a ninny at times. You dress to please that husband of yours and don't worry about her."

Ellie let out a sigh. "In all truth, I didn't have another gown to wear," she began and told the sorry tale of her battle with the cookstove. "I won't know if my work gown is completely ruined until I try to launder out the stains. Until then, since this is the only other gown I have, it will have to suit just about anything I do. Unfortunately, I also singed every apron I own and the two I could find in the kitchen, so I'll have to be very careful not to soil this gown."

"You can't make do with two gowns," Gram argued and pointed to the several gowns she had hanging on the wall next to her door.

"It hasn't been a problem before," Ellie countered.

"Well, it obviously is now. If you have the good sense I think you have, you'll let Jackson know what you need, whatever that might be. Speak up for yourself. He'll respect you for it, but more important, you'll respect yourself," she said.

Leaning forward, she lowered her voice. "I just happen to know he had an account with a number of shops for Rebecca, including Mrs. French's. I doubt he's given any thought to closing them, but if he did, then tell him to open them again for you. Get some fabric for yourself on Market Day and make yourself a new gown or two."

Ellie thought of the incident from two days ago. "I will. Soon," she promised as she mulled over Gram's advice. On the day he proposed, Jackson had mentioned something about having accounts in town, although she was reluctant to approach him about using them so soon after their misunderstanding at market.

"Don't wait too long," Gram suggested. "Now, in the meantime, I can help you with a few more aprons. Take a peek into that second drawer over there and take whatever you like. I don't need as many as I have."

"I couldn't possibly—"

"Yes you could, unless you want to disappoint a very old lady who doesn't get the chance to do much for anyone else these days," she prompted and sniffed the air. "Supper's just about ready, so hurry yourself."

Ellie did not have the heart or the energy to argue. She found the aprons stored in the drawer easily enough, but frowned as she sorted through them. All of them had been skillfully embroidered, and there was not a stain on a single one of the aprons. "I really shouldn't take any of your aprons."

"Why not?"

"B-because I'm afraid I'll ruin them doing housework, just like I ruined the others."

"Fine. Then they can continue to sit in that drawer and rot from lack of use rather than serving a good purpose," she teased. "Go on, take three or four, or else I'll have to get these old bones out of this chair and do it for you."

"Fine, but I'm only taking two. If I need more, I'll let you know," Ellie said and took the two aprons lying on top. When she held them up for Gram to see, she realized the aprons were made for a much smaller woman. Reluctant to hurt Gram's feelings by declining her generosity now, she refolded them and laid them on her lap when she sat back down on the bed. "Thank you."

"You're very welcome. You might want to wear one later when we go outside for the celebration, but since this is your only gown at the moment, you probably shouldn't plan on doing much climbing tonight. Don't worry," she said, patting Ellie's lap. "You won't be the only one. I quit that part of the tradition when I turned ninety-four. You can keep me company watching while the others do."

Ellie gasped. "Y-you climbed trees until you were ninety-four?"

"No, not trees. I haven't climbed a tree since I was a girl. I meant ladders, but you'll see that for yourself soon enough. Tell me about little Ethan. Is he talking at all yet?"

"No," Ellie admitted and shared the details of the conversation she and Jackson had had with Daniel. "Do you think it's possible that Ethan is talking to his brother? Or do you think Daniel's just using Ethan as a way of explaining Daniel's own confusion over losing his mother?"

"Anything's possible," the woman replied and tapped the Bible on her lap. "I really can't see well enough to be able to read the words anymore—"

"But weren't you reading when I knocked at your door?" Ellie asked.

"Not with my eyes, Ellie. I've read the Good Book so many times, I can see the words in my head and I can feel them in my heart when I run my fingers over the pages," she explained. "God's never abandoned anything or anyone He's ever created, and I don't believe He's done so with those two boys. Daniel and Ethan are just learning that faith lesson a little younger than most people do," she said, with as much authority as Reverend Shore had when he stood in his pulpit to preach.

Ellie sighed. "I keep praying He hasn't, but how can you be so sure?"

Gram tapped her Bible again. "Because I truly believe He brought you here to those boys and to Jackson, too. He needs you as much as his sons do. He just doesn't realize it yet, and neither do you."

Seventeen

A full moon illuminated the landscape. As always, ever since his father-in-law's death, Jackson led the group to the ancient tree, and as always, memories of celebrations from times past walked alongside him. The first time he had celebrated a harvest at full moon on Dillon's Island, he was eighteen years old. Except for the man who had become his mentor, James Gladson, he had been alone in the world, without family or friends to care about him.

Now, eight years later, Dorothea, the first and only love of his life, was married to another man. His father-in-law and mentor, as well as his first wife, were dead. His second wife was merely his partner in a marriage based on duty and need, not affection. The Grants had become his friends, and he now had all the family he needed: his two sons.

The path that led from the Grant cabin, Gladson's original homestead, was narrow, and he held Daniel's hand as he led the others. He glanced over his shoulder and saw that Ethan had already given up walking. He was settled contentedly on Ellie's hip, which undermined Daniel's assertions about Ethan's feelings toward her, at least for the moment.

But Jackson could not blame Ethan for being confused about his feelings for Ellie. For he, too, felt at odds within himself regarding this woman he had married.

"It's not much farther," he said, noting that the Grants had fallen back to accommodate Gram. At her age, the fact that she was able to walk as well as she did was a marvel, but he could not imagine this celebration without her and slowed his pace.

Daniel yanked on his hand. "Can't we go faster, Pappy?"

"Gram can't walk as fast as we can. She needs some help walking this far, so the Grants—"

"I'll help her," he cried, charging back to his brother. "Come on, Ethan. You can help Gram, too."

Ethan clambered down from Ellie's hip, but she held his hand fast and looked to Jackson for permission to let go.

"Stay on the path," Jackson warned, watching the boys to make sure they listened.

Alice gave him a wave. "We'll watch them for you. Why don't you tell your wife more about what to expect once we get to the tree?"

Ellie smiled and took the arm he offered to her. "I must admit that I'm more than just a little curious," she said as they resumed walking.

"I thought I'd have time to tell you about it over supper, but Gram tends to monopolize the conversation. I definitely didn't want to interrupt her."

She laughed. "Neither did I."

"We're actually keeping two traditions tonight. The first directly involves you and only you. Whether or not you choose to participate in the second, however, will be entirely your choice," he explained and guided her away from an old stump in the path.

"Which one involves climbing a ladder?"

He met her gaze and held it. "I thought you didn't know anything about—"

"Gram mentioned it, but our conversation got sidetracked," she said quickly. "Gram also said she didn't stop climbing the ladder until she turned ninety-four. Is that true?"

"Sure enough," he said, chuckling. "I saw her last climb myself, but that's part of the second tradition. You don't need to worry about climbing a ladder tonight. Besides, no one could expect you to risk spoiling your Sunday gown," he teased.

Her gaze flickered. "I should thank you for not telling anyone about what a disaster I made of myself and my work gown today."

"Like I said, Gram monopolized the conversation," he replied. Unfortunately, it was easier to shrug off her compliment than it was to shutter memories of Rebecca's refusal to participate in either tradition once they were married, not even for the benefit of their sons.

With the ancient tree now in sight, he looked over his shoulder. The others were a good ways back, which would give him time to explain how important it was for her to continue this first tradition. He led her through the small clearing at the northernmost tip of the island where the wild apple tree stood.

Thick, unpruned branches rose high, as if trying to reach the moonbeams that fell on what little ripened fruit remained.

A mild wind moistened by the river rustled the leaves and thinner branches and filled the air with the scent of the island's bounty. Shadows nearly obscured the heavy veins of gnarled roots that covered the ground at the base of the tree, but the thick roots below had held this tree steady against summer storms, floods, and snowdrifts alike for decades.

When she stumbled and grabbed his arm tighter for support, he caught his breath. "Watch your footing," he cautioned and tucked his arm closer to hold her fast so she would not actually fall as he guided her through the maze of ground roots.

"It's hard not to stare at the tree. It's magnificent, especially by moonlight."

He noted the awe in her words before seeing it in her gaze and smiled. "That's exactly how my father-in-law said he felt the first time he saw it," he said, pointing off into the darkness beyond the river. "As he told the tale, he'd been traveling for months, looking for a place to settle down. He'd about given up hope of finding anything in this area and decided to take advantage of the full moon to leave and continue his search elsewhere. That's when he saw the tree from right over there, on the old road that led north from Harrisburg, over forty years ago."

"The tree's that old?"

"It's that old."

"But it couldn't have been so massive."

"No, but he said he was so intrigued, he turned around and rode straight back to the city. Just after dawn, he found someone to ferry him over to the island. By noon, he'd walked the island from end to end and side to side four times. By dusk, he had the deed in hand, and by moonlight that very night, he carved a cross into the trunk of that tree, carved his initials below it, and dropped to his knees to thank God for leading him here. To this very tree," he said as they stepped below the bottom branches into the shadows.

"He did? Where? Where are his initials? Show me," she asked.

Once his eyes adjusted to the dimmer light, he moved them closer, saw the cross at shoulder level, and pointed just below it. "His initials are here. JG."

"For James Gladson," she murmured, letting go of his arm and tracing the letters with her fingertips. "And the other initials?"

"By tradition, which he started, they belong to anyone who has called the island home, including the Grants."

"Where are yours?"

He stepped closer to the trunk. "Here," he said, pointing to the initials he had carved into the tree exactly one year to the day after he had arrived.

"And the boys'?"

"Next to Rebecca's."

"It must be difficult for you to see them there," she murmured.

"Life is always difficult. That's why faith and family are all that truly matter. James Gladson taught me that when he took me in and treated me like I was his own son," he replied. "Now I have the responsibility to teach that to my sons, his grandsons. By following the traditions he started and by giving them roots in faith and family as strong as the ones that have held this tree fast for over forty years," he said.

Reminded by his own words of how weak his faith had become since Rebecca's death, he drew in a long breath. "Now that you're part of the family and you call the island home, you'll need to carve your initials here, too," he said, just firmly enough to make it clear she had no choice in the matter.

For the briefest of moments, he saw concern flash through her eyes. She may have forgiven him for his mistreatment of her on Market Day and accepted the truth about the scandal surrounding Rebecca's death, but she apparently did not trust him completely yet.

Hopefully this tradition tonight would ease her concerns, as well as his own. He pulled the old folding knife from his pocket and handed it to her. "This is the same knife my father-in-law used to carve his initials and every set of initials since. I keep the blade good and sharp, so if you want me to help you carve your initials, I will."

"No. I can do it," she insisted.

"Then be careful not to—"

"Jackson Smith, if you have your wife carve a single mark before we get to you, you'll never taste my apple butter again!"

Jackson laughed, turning around just in time to catch Daniel and Ethan from charging straight past him to start climbing the tree. He gave Gram a peck on her cheek when she finally reached him. "I wouldn't start without you. I was just telling Ellie a little bit about the tradition and warning her to be careful with the knife."

"She's a capable woman. She knows how to handle a knife." Gram held on to her grandson with one arm and his wife with the other. "Prayer first, though," she reminded him.

"You're the oldest, Gram. You get to say the prayers," Daniel prompted.

"Daniel!"

"Don't fuss at the boy, Jackson. He's right. I am the oldest, and I should get to lead the prayer."

Jackson switched his hands from the boys' shoulders to their hands. Ellie took little Ethan's other hand. The rest joined hands with them to form a circle under the tree branches and bowed their heads.

"Heavenly Father, we gather tonight under the light of the magnificent moon you created to welcome Jackson's wife, Ellie, to our island home. Bless her, as you continue to bless us all. Love her, as you love us all. And reward her faith in you with good health and a long life to serve you. Amen."

The chorus of "amens" had barely faded before Daniel was tugging on Jackson's hand. "Now can we climb the tree and watch? Can we? Please?"

Jackson laughed and let go of Daniel's hand. "You go ahead. I'll help Ethan," he urged and lifted his youngest son up to a low branch that would be strong enough to hold both the boys. "Hold on tight," he cautioned, but he did not let go of him until Daniel had claimed a place next to him and held his brother tight.

"I'll watch them," Grizel offered as she pushed away a lock of hair that had fallen in front of her spectacles.

He stepped closer to Ellie and handed her the knife.

"Where should I carve my initials?"

"Next to Jackson's initials," Gram prompted. "Rebecca's aren't there because her father had already carved them into the tree next to his on the day she was born. And there's more room beside Jackson's for more initials, should God bless you both with children."

"Press the tip of the knife hard. The trunk is tough," Jackson cautioned.

Although her hand trembled a bit at first, she soon had her first initial carved into the tree. She paused and looked over at him. "Do I put a K for my maiden name or an S?"

"S," he murmured, wishing he were helping Dorothea carve her initials next to his. "Are you certain you wouldn't like some help?"

"No, I can manage," she insisted with confidence. She had the top curve of the letter done and had started scrolling down to form the next when she yelped and dropped the knife. With her lips pursed, she pressed her thumb against her forefinger and picked up the knife with her other hand to inspect it. "The blade's fine. The tip didn't break off."

"What about your finger?" he asked.

"There's lots of blood," Daniel offered nonchalantly as he leaned down for a better look.

"It's just a nick. Truly," she insisted. "I must have hit a knot or something that I didn't see because of the shadows."

He moved closer. "Let me see."

When she stepped back and touched the trunk to indicate where she had stopped carving, he could see blood dripping from her finger. "Not the tree. Your finger. Let me see your finger."

Her eyes widened, but she let him inspect her hand. "You'll need a stitch or two," he said and wrapped the end of her finger with a handkerchief from his pocket.

"Can I watch?" Daniel asked.

"All I need is a good tight bandage," she insisted and held up her finger. "See? The blood's stopped flowing already."

"I can stitch it up for you," Alice Grant offered.

"No, thank you. I'm sure it'll be fine with just a bandage. Just let me finish up here so we can go on to the second tradition tonight before it gets too late. The handkerchief will be all I need until then. Where's the knife?"

He held up her left hand. "You're holding it," he said and narrowed his gaze. "Where's your ring?"

"Oh, I . . . I took it off to clean the cookstove. I'm sorry. I just forgot to put it back on," she explained.

Disappointed, he made a mental note to replace the wooden ring, which he should have done by now, and put his hand over hers. "Let me help you finish up."

When she nodded, he used his greater strength to help her carve through the knot she had hit and finish the rest of the letter.

"Finished! Now I'm officially a member of the island family." Ellie handed him the knife, then traced her initials with her uninjured hand. She even stood more erect, as if more confident now of her place with him on the island. The joy on her face was so sincere and the wonder in her eyes was so real, however, it almost transcended her very plain features.

Surprised by the mere possibility he might ever find her appealing in any way, he folded up the knife, stored it back in his pocket again, and looked up through the branches to the moon overhead. With the exception of his two sons, his life had been filled with nothing more than bitter disappointment and he had no desire to invite more. He dropped his gaze and stared at Ellie's initials in the tree. Despite those newly carved marks, he had absolutely no intention of thinking their marriage could be any more than it was: a business proposition.

Nothing less.

And certainly nothing more.

Eighteen

"I still want a turn."

Before Jackson could argue with her again, Ellie shifted Ethan, who had fallen asleep in her arms, and laid him down on the ground in a patch of clover next to his sleeping brother. Pleased that the boy had not woken up, she hitched up her skirts with her unbandaged hand. She started for the ladder, which was still leaning up against the apple tree, leaving Jackson standing near his sons.

She passed by the canvas bag bulging with apples and snatched up the other bag that was still empty. After she had looped the canvas strap over her head to her shoulder like the others, the pouch rested against the front of her bodice. Satisfied, she looked up through the branches to decide how high she would have to climb to reach enough apples to pick and pursed her lips.

Harvesting apples by moonlight at near midnight instead of the full light of day would not have been how she would have chosen to pick apples for the first time since she had been a child. Wearing the gown she usually reserved for Sunday services to perform that task would not have been her first choice, either.

But climbing the ladder and keeping her balance while she filled the picking bag when she had a bandage on her finger that was stiff with dried blood, as well as a few blisters and that stubborn splinter on her other hand, made for the greatest challenge of all.

Except for convincing her new husband that she was serious about picking some apples by herself.

"I told you before, you don't have to keep this tradition tonight. There's still one more full moon in October when we harvest the Russets. Wait until then; otherwise, you're going to fall and break your neck tonight, and you won't ever be able to pick up anything heavier than your stubbornness," Jackson warned.

"I don't plan on falling," she countered, grateful that the Grants had already finished picking their apples and had gone home so they would not be witness to the test of wills she and Jackson were having. Cotton gloves would have protected her hands, but apparently they were only worn when picking apples that were going to be shipped to markets well beyond the city.

"Maybe not, but if you back that argument up a bit, you'd have to admit you planned on cutting your finger—which I rather doubt you did, since you'd already damaged your hands enough for one day."

"How gallant of you to mention how inept I am," she retorted. Jackson had been up on a ladder just like this one when she had spoken to him about accepting his proposal, but she had not noticed, at the time, that the ladder was so oddly designed.

Instead of side rails set an equal distance from one another from the top to the bottom of the ladder, the rails narrowed from the bottom up, nearly forming a triangle, which would make it easier to fit the ladder into the branches of the tree. The rungs of the ladder, by necessity, narrowed as well, so that the top rung was barely wide enough for a man's foot.

"We have enough apples for you to make the apple fritters tomorrow, and you were here during the picking. The tradition's been kept," he suggested as he started to close the gap between them.

"Unless I burn the first batch of fritters and need more apples than usual, in which case I need to pick a few more."

He walked around her and stood in front of the ladder. "You're not going to burn anything tomorrow."

She cocked a brow. "Really? Why would you say that?"

He shrugged. "You cleaned out the inside of the cookstove today. End of problem. Even the stovepipe looked as clean as it did the day Caden James delivered it."

"Which you know firsthand, because you simply waltzed in this afternoon and put it back in place like it was nothing at all, when it should have been very clear to you that I'd been struggling with that stovepipe for a good while," she blurted as she faced him through the rungs of the ladder.

He shrugged. "I thought I was helping."

"You were, but . . . never mind. You wouldn't understand."

He folded his hands across his chest. "I won't understand what you mean unless you tell me."

She chewed on her bottom lip. She had no right to complain

unless she was willing to explain why. "I appreciate the fact that you helped put the end of the stovepipe back into place, but I would have appreciated it more if you had said something to acknowledge that it was hard for me, because I'm not as tall or as strong as you are."

"You're nearly as tall as I am."

She rolled her eyes. "See? I knew you wouldn't—"

"I was teasing." His voice was soft. "I'm sorry. I really thought I was just helping you. I didn't mean to flaunt the fact that I'm stronger than you are or hurt your feelings."

"Again. You hurt my feelings again."

Jackson's chin rose a fraction. "I thought you'd accepted my apology for what happened in the city."

She shook her head. "I did. I wasn't referring to that. I meant earlier today."

"Today? When and how did I do that?" he asked, arching his back.

"You didn't treat me very nicely. No, that's not quite right. You didn't treat me with respect when you disagreed with me about whether or not Ethan was talking to Daniel."

"That wasn't disrespect," he countered. "I simply asked you to remember that these are my sons. I know them better than you do, because I've been a part of their lives since the day they were born."

"No, you didn't ask me to remember. You warned me to remember. There's a difference, isn't there?"

He let out a long sigh and lowered his arms. "Yes, there is, but—"

"But unless we respect each other enough to listen and learn from each other, like I thought we did the other night, the next eighteen years, which is how long it will be before Ethan reaches his majority, are going to be more than difficult. They'll be impossible. And unless we can continue to be completely honest with each other and stop constantly suspecting one another of doing something wrong, the lessons we inadvertently teach Daniel and Ethan along the way are not lessons you or I should want to teach them."

She paused and moistened her lips. "Daniel and Ethan are your sons. Yours and Rebecca's. I'm not likely to forget that, but they're my sons now, too, and Daniel and Ethan are the only children I'll ever have the privilege to raise as . . . as my own." Ellie waited, heartbeat after heartbeat, for him to reply and prayed he would not misinterpret her words or her motivation.

"You're quite a bit bolder tonight than you even were the other night, which was a distinct change from how you've been for the past several weeks since we got married," he finally offered, arching his back.

"That's because I didn't have my initials carved into that tree before tonight," she said confidently, now that she truly had tangible proof she belonged here. In all truth, it was the cross carved into the tree that had given her the greater comfort that this is where the Lord wanted her to be. For the first time in many years, she tried to embrace His will and her faith fully. She prayed Jackson might one day do the same.

"And that's what makes the difference," he suggested.

"Yes it does."

"Because . . ."

"Because now I know you won't set me aside unless I do something so terribly wrong and hurtful that you'd be willing to sacrifice the magnificent tree that lured James Gladson to this island."

He cocked a brow. "Sacrifice it? How?"

"By gouging the trunk of that tree so deeply that it would

kill it or by cutting it down, which are the only ways you'd be able to remove my initials. And I know you won't do either of those things, because James Gladson also taught you the importance of traditions like the ones you shared with me tonight.

"Family traditions," she added before he stopped her from finishing her thoughts. "I've waited a very long time to share my faith and my life with a family of my own and with traditions that will help to keep the family strong. I would never do anything to jeopardize that, and they mean a great deal more to me than those legal documents we signed might indicate."

He did not reply. He just stood there, staring at her, as if she had said things he could not or would not believe. Finally, he let out a long, slow breath.

"I still think you're wrong about Daniel and Ethan."

She cocked a brow.

"But . . . but I'm willing to consider your opinion, as long as you remember that my place is at the head of this family. I reserve the right to make decisions I feel are best for Daniel and Ethan, even if that doesn't coincide with what you want."

"Agreed," she said without reservation and held out her hand. "Can we declare a truce now? A real truce?"

He took her hand, gently, and shook it. "Truce," he murmured before his lips curled into a smile. "Now that that's settled, I'd like to ask you to do something for me."

She caught her breath and held it, ready to prove she had meant every word she had said.

"Don't bother trying to salvage that brown gown you've worn since the first day you arrived. It's drab and ugly. Burn it. Cut it up into rags. Do whatever you like, but please don't wear it again; otherwise, people will think I can't provide for you properly."

She gasped. "Ugly?"

He grinned. "You wanted honesty. Or did you intend to reserve the privilege of being honest just for yourself?"

"No, but a bit of tact might be nice, as well," she said. "Is there anything else that's been bothering you?"

"I can't think of anything."

She narrowed her gaze. "No complaints about burnt food?"

He shrugged. "Not really. I've gotten accustomed to the flavor."

"Fine," she said sweetly and lifted her skirts again. "I'd like to pick a few apples now, and I'd appreciate it if you'd hold the ladder to make sure it doesn't slip while I'm on it."

He sighed. "Are you sure I can't change your mind?"

"No. I mean yes, I'm sure," she said.

"It's that important to you?"

"Yes it is."

"Go ahead, then," he grumbled before taking hold of the rails to keep the ladder steady. "If you fall and break your neck, I'll make sure you have good care while you lie in bed, paralyzed for the rest of your life," he cautioned as she started up the ladder. "Of course, I'd have to start looking for another wife, since I'd need someone to help me take care of the boys."

She paused halfway up and stopped to pick a few apples within easy reach. "You can't be married to two women at the same time," she warned, ignoring the pain from the splinter in her hand as she slipped the apples into her pouch.

"True, but I could have the marriage annulled."

She glanced down and glared at him.

"Sorry. Don't get all huffy. This is just conjecture."

She huffed anyway and climbed up another rung. Stretching as hard as she could, she managed to reach a pair of apples but slipped when she tried to transfer both of them to the pouch at the same time. She managed to stay on the ladder, but the apples dropped right onto his head. "Oops. Sorry," she said and climbed higher still.

"Oops?" he gritted, shaking his head. "Of course, if you were higher up on that ladder and fell, you'd hit the ground so hard you might not survive at all. Then I'd have to bury you right here on the island, which means I wouldn't have to bother having our marriage annulled. I'd be a widower again and legally free to marry for the third time."

"That's odd. James Gladson was married three times," she noted as she leaned to the side to reach half a dozen more apples she put into the pouch. "I suppose it might be just another tradition for you to follow if you had to marry again," she said.

As she turned to right herself again before climbing back down, an apple popped out of her pouch.

To her horror, once again it landed right on top of his head.

Fortunately, she stifled her giggle before it escaped.

"No, thank you. I'm not that attached to traditions," Jackson said, rubbing his head. "Having had two wives is more than enough for me, assuming I can survive living with the second one."

Nineteen

The following afternoon, when Ellie remembered she needed to wear her ring tomorrow to services, she went to the shelf in the kitchen where she had stored it.

Ethan's ribbons were still hanging there, but the ring was gone.

"That's impossible! I put it right here, next to the ribbons I laundered and set to dry for Ethan," she mumbled. Hoping the ring had somehow rolled or slid away, she looked behind every plate, every platter, every jug, and every pitcher on that shelf.

No ring.

Even though her finger was throbbing beneath the second bandage of the day, she checked the two shelves below just in case she had accidentally knocked the ring off the high shelf.

No ring.

Ellie dropped to her knees. She crawled back and forth across the kitchen floor, hoping the ring might have rolled free of the shelves.

Still no ring.

But she had leaned on her palm with that stubborn splinter once too often. Between the splinter and the slice on the tip of her finger, her hands smarted enough to bring tears to her eyes.

She blinked them away and sat back on her haunches, more confused than panicked. A wooden ring could slide or roll or fall, but it could not simply evaporate or get up and walk off on its own. Since she did not take the ring, someone else must have. The question was who that someone might be.

If Jackson had spied the ring lying on the shelf, he would likely have cautioned her to be more careful before returning it to her. But he hadn't, and neither Daniel nor Ethan was tall enough to see the ring lying on that shelf. Since no one else had been in the house since yesterday, Ellie had no choice but to set blame for losing the ring squarely on her own shoulders.

She pursed her lips and glanced around the kitchen floor to see if it had fallen there, even though she had swept out the room twice today already and would have noticed the ring if she had swept it up. "Unless it got snagged on the broom!"

Her excitement was short-lived when she found the broom empty of all but a bit of dust. She set the broom down and thought back over the day. "It's got to be here somewhere. I just haven't found it yet."

Impatient with her own carelessness, she tapped her foot. She had two good hours left to herself before she had to start supper for Jackson and the boys. She could use that time to search for the ring, which had to turn up sooner or later. Or she could use the time to do something she knew would be more productive, like hemming the overalls she had made for Daniel and Ethan.

She headed straight for her room and prayed the ring would turn up by the time Jackson returned. If not, given the understanding they had reached with each other last night, she would just be honest with him, explain why she did not have her ring, and pray he would understand.

As Ellie approached the door to her room, she tripped over one of the boys' wooden blocks and frowned. "They must have missed this one."

With a quick glance around the room, she found a canvas bag lying in the corner where the boys had tossed it. Grabbing it by the drawstring, she peeked inside to make sure the boys had not put something other than blocks into the bag.

Intrigued by a bit of ribbon clinging to several of the blocks inside, she took the bag over to the dining table and carefully let the contents slide free.

The seven identical natural wood blocks that emerged were thinner than any of the others she had seen the boys use, and she knew immediately that these blocks were not part of the set the boys' grandfather had made for them. They were a set unto themselves, a set once held together by the bits of tattered ribbon that still remained to make a toy she remembered from her childhood, although the blocks on hers had been painted different colors.

"This is a Jacob's Ladder, or it used to be," she whispered. She did not know if it had belonged to Daniel or Ethan, but it was quite clear that the toy, as well as the biblical story of how Jacob had had a vision of angels ascending and descending a ladder that reached all the way to heaven, had been abandoned.

Convinced the toy's message was one that would help the boys, especially Ethan, she carefully lined up the blocks in a single row and straightened the ribbons that had held them together as best she could. Sadly, they were too old and tattered to repair, and there had been no one here to replace them.

"But I'm here now," she whispered and grabbed hold of an idea that warmed her heart. She hurried back to the kitchen shelf where she had put the ribbons Ethan had pulled from his mother's petticoats and prayed they would be long enough to remake the toy.

She laid the ribbons out on the table next to the blocks and studied them. Individually, the four pieces were each shorter than the row of blocks. But if she measured carefully and sewed well, she just might have enough ribbon to turn the blocks back into a Jacob's Ladder again and start to mend a little boy's broken heart, too.

An hour later, Ellie had to give up.

She was only halfway finished sewing the ribbons to the blocks, which meant she was still a good bit away from helping Ethan, but her hands just hurt too much to continue.

When she heard the back door bang open and heavy footsteps in the kitchen, she caught her breath. Jackson charged into the great room carrying Ethan, who was asleep. "I didn't expect to see you so early."

He glanced at the table where she had the blocks spread out and shook his head. "I didn't expect to find you playing with blocks," he replied and hurried past her.

Frowning, she slid the sewing basket in front of the blocks to hide them.

"More important, I didn't expect Ethan to get stung by a

couple of yellow jackets, which is why I brought him home. He fell asleep on the way, so I'm going to put him on the settee in the parlor so you can hear him if he wakes up."

She leaped to her feet and followed them. "How did it happen?"

"I don't know. I was up on the ladder, so I didn't see it happen, but Daniel said they were putting apples into one of the drop baskets when Ethan got stung on his arm," he said as he entered the parlor.

"Did Daniel get stung, too?"

When he laid Ethan on the settee, she handed him the lap quilt lying across the back. The sleeve on one of Ethan's arms had been rolled up, and there was a wide swath of mud across one of his forearms.

"No, Daniel's fine. This little man will be fine, too," he said as he covered his son. "He's just all worn out from crying, mostly."

"Poor babe. Did you get the stinger out?"

"Both of them. Once I had a good mud pack on the welts, Ethan felt better, but he wouldn't have been stung in the first place if he hadn't been out in the orchard with me," he stated.

"Ethan loves going with you and Daniel in the afternoons," she said, hoping to ease the guilt that shadowed his features as they stood together watching Ethan sleep.

"That may be, but I obviously can't watch him properly when I'm working. He'd be safer here with you."

"But he's happier with you," she countered. "Maybe we can compromise."

He raised a brow in question.

"After dinner each day, Ethan and I can go back to the orchard with you and Daniel so the boys can both be with you for a while. I'll take something along, some sewing perhaps, so the boys won't think I'm watching them every minute."

" 'Sewing,' " he repeated as his lips formed a smile. "No blocks?"

"Definitely no blocks and probably not any mending, either. Not for a few days, anyway," she said reluctantly and held up her hands. "You were right. I do think I need a stitch or two, and I've got a splinter that needs to work its way out, as well."

He placed his hands under hers, studied them, and frowned. "Follow me," he said.

She hurried after him. "I didn't mean for you to . . . W-what are you doing?" she asked when he walked straight to the table where she had been working.

He pointed to the bench closest to his chair at the head of the table. "Sit."

She braced to a halt.

"Please."

Ellie walked over and sat down.

"We'll take care of that splinter for you first," he said and took a needle out of the pincushion where she had left it. He smiled. "Rest your hand on the table."

Having someone remove a splinter for her with a needle was not that odd. Her father had removed splinters from her hands more than once when she was little, so she laid her hand, palm up, on the table in front of her without hesitation. "I tried getting it out myself, but it was too stubborn."

When he grinned, she let out a sigh. "Poor choice of words," she muttered, recalling his description of her last night.

"No, I'd say your choice of words was perfect." Jackson had the splinter out almost before she realized it—but not before she noticed it felt rather nice to have his finger brush against her hand. "Now let's see that cut on your finger," he suggested as he sorted through the sewing basket.

She tried to unwrap the bandage, but the dried blood held it fast. "I'll be right back," she said and went to the kitchen. After pumping water on her finger for a moment or two, she was able to lift off the bandage and clean her finger, but the effort had started her finger bleeding again. She wrapped a clean cloth around it and returned to the great room to find him holding up two spools of thread.

"Gray or brown?"

"Whatever made you pick brown?" she asked nervously as she took her seat again. "I thought you found the color drab and ugly."

"No, I said your brown gown was drab and ugly. Your eyes, on the other hand, are brown, and they're neither drab nor ugly," he said as he leaned very close to stare into her eyes. "They're quite lovely, actually. I never noticed they even have flecks of gold in them, too."

His words made her cheeks burn. The open admiration in his gaze, as if he unexpectedly realized she might not be quite as plain as she knew she was, made her heart race so fast she felt light-headed.

He pulled back and cocked his head to study her face for a moment, then quickly looked away to stare at the two spools of thread.

"U-use the gray," she stammered, aware that this was the very first time anyone, other than her own parents, had found anything attractive about her at all. That Jackson might find her appealing, even momentarily, made her heart skip a beat.

He cleared his throat. "Gray it is." He even managed to guide the thread through the eye of the needle, despite the fact that his hand trembled ever so slightly.

Surprised by how comfortable he was handling notions normally reserved for a woman's skilled hands, she tensed up. Allowing him to stitch up her finger was an entirely different matter than having him remove a splinter, and when he asked her to put her other hand on the table, she tucked it on her lap. "Are you sure you know what you're doing?"

He tightened his jaw and stared at her, holding the needle and thread ready.

She swallowed hard and switched tactics. "Are you sure I need a stitch at all? Maybe we should wait a day or two more to see if the finger heals without one."

He let out a sigh. "It'll heal eventually, but in the meantime, you won't have much use of that hand. Maybe you should have rested it up today instead of using it to slice up all those apples to make fritters."

She shrugged. "I thought it was important to keep up tradition."

"Which one? Making fritters or keeping your hands injured?" He smiled.

Ellie pulled her hand away. "I changed my mind. I think I'd rather let my finger heal on its own."

He shrugged. "Fine, but it seems to me you have enough trouble using that cookstove with two hands, so how you'll manage with one . . ."

She put her hand back on the table. "Have your way, then."

"Try to hold still," he cautioned, then placed his free hand under hers to cushion it. "This is going to sting."

She did not know if the tingles that raced up her arm were from sheer nervousness or the fact that his hand felt so good beneath her own again, but she clenched her jaw and looked away to avoid watching him push the needle through her flesh.

"Tell me about those blocks you were playing with," he said, apparently hoping to divert her thoughts away from what he was going to do to her finger.

Ellie was quite certain he had no idea how much his touch was affecting her ability to think clearly at all. "I wasn't playing with them. I was trying to string them back together with the ribbons I laundered for Ethan," she offered.

She scarcely had a chance to move the sewing basket with her free hand to show him when she felt the first prick of the needle. Swallowing hard, she pressed her lips together and blinked back a few tears before she continued.

"You said you didn't want your son carrying the ribbons around, but I didn't think you'd object to having him play with a toy made with ribbons. Especially a Jacob's Ladder. Ouch! That hurts a lot," she blurted, but Jackson held her fast and would not let her pull her hand away.

Ellie glared at him. "Are you quite certain you've done this before?"

"I've stitched myself up more times than I care to remember, but I've never actually tried stitching up anyone else before right now."

She gasped. "You stitched your own cuts?"

"Orphan kids put out for bid by the town for a family to take them in don't usually warrant much attention, other than to make sure they earn their keep," he murmured and shuttered his gaze.

Too late.

She had already gotten a glimpse of the hurt he had endured as a child, still shining as deep in his spirit as the hurts he had suffered as an adult.

Twenty

For the fourth Sunday in a row, a thunderstorm with torrential rains and howling winds kept Jackson from crossing the river and venturing into town with his family to attend services.

By midafternoon, however, when he opened the front parlor door and stepped out onto the porch, he met bright sunshine, clear skies, and crisp air, heavy with the pungent smell of moist earth. Grinning, Jackson turned around to go back into the house and order everyone outside when his oldest son marched out of the house and looked up at him.

Daniel's cheeks were flushed and damp with fresh tears. "Make Miss Ellie go home, Pappy. Please. Can't you send her back? Today?"

His son's words were spoken so plaintively, Jackson had to fight to keep from scooping him up into his arms to comfort him. "What's wrong?" he asked, noticing that Ellie now stood silently just inside the door, watching them.

Daniel sniffled. "Miss Ellie doesn't like me and Ethan like Mama did."

Taking a handkerchief from his pocket, Jackson bent down and wiped his son's nose, as well as his cheeks. "What makes you say that?" he asked gently, remaining in a crouch to be at eye level with the boy.

"She won't let me and Ethan play."

Jackson waited for Daniel to explain.

"She won't. Mama always let us play in the attic, but Miss Ellie said we can't and made us come down, and then she said we can't have any pie for dessert tonight for punishment and . . . and can't you just send her back? Me and Ethan want you to send her back."

Jackson glanced up at Ellie for a moment, noted the frustrated expression she wore, and sighed. "Miss Ellie is right. You shouldn't be playing up in the attic. It isn't safe up there for you two to play alone, and you know very well that I don't want you playing in the attic, either," he said firmly.

Daniel's eyes filled with fresh tears. "But Mama said we could!"

Frustrated that Rebecca's penchant for letting the boys do whatever they wanted was still causing him trouble, Jackson had to struggle to keep his voice soft and even. "Your mama shouldn't have gone against my wishes and given you permission to do something she knew I didn't want you to do. But she's gone now and Miss Ellie's here, and you and Ethan must obey her, just as you obey me. Understood?"

Ever so reluctantly, Daniel nodded.

Jackson got back to his feet and patted his son's head. "Now, go find that brother of yours and get your boots. We're going for a walk, and maybe, just maybe, if you and your brother can behave, I can talk Miss Ellie into letting you each have a piece of pie for dessert tonight."

"A great big piece?" he asked, his face brightening.

"A great big one. Now scoot!"

Daniel charged from the porch and gave Ellie a wide grin as he passed her.

Ellie's expression, oddly enough, was even dourer than it had been just a few moments ago.

Jackson walked toward her. "What's wrong?"

"What's right?" she asked, without bothering to step aside to let him into the house.

"What's right?" He raked his hand through his hair. "I supported you, didn't I? Isn't that what you've wanted me to do—support your right to tell the boys what they can or can't do and to discipline them if they disobey you?"

"You supported your authority, not mine," she argued. "Did it ever occur to you to ask *me* what happened in front of Daniel? Or to include me in your conversation? I was standing right here, but you and Daniel both acted like I was invisible or that whatever I might want to say would be irrelevant. And then you took it upon yourself to suggest the boys might avoid their punishment by being good now, instead of holding them responsible for what they'd done."

He let out a long breath. "I didn't think there was much point because—"

"Because you assumed Daniel was giving you the full tale of the boys' misadventure."

"I take it he didn't?" Jackson asked hesitantly.

Ellie pursed her lips for a moment, as if trying to sort through the words she wanted to say. "What Daniel neglected to tell you was that I had told the boys twice this morning that they weren't to play in the attic, but they took advantage of the fact that I was busy cleaning up after putting a pie into the oven to slip up to the attic anyway. Daniel's complaint wasn't really about whether or not I had the same rules as their mama, like he claimed it was. It's about whether he and Ethan can deliberately disobey me and not be punished."

He shook his head. "I always made it clear they had to obey you."

"But just now you made it clear that you can undermine my authority over them by suggesting you'll help them to avoid their punishment, which is precisely what Daniel hoped you'd do. Or did you intend to teach the boy that no matter how badly he behaves, he can avoid punishment later by being good?"

"No. I mean, you're right," Jackson admitted, finding it hard to balance his role as both husband and father. "I'll speak to Daniel and Ethan and make it clear to both of them—"

"Don't bother. It's too late for that now, but I'd appreciate it if you'd include me when Daniel comes to you with a complaint in the future so we can all discuss it together." She stepped aside to give him room to enter the parlor.

"I think we all need to get out of the house for a spell. Would you like to come for a walk with us, or would you rather have some time alone?" he asked.

"I'll come, but don't look for any dessert tonight. You're not having any pie, either."

He snorted. "Don't you think I'm a bit too old to be punished by taking away my dessert?"

She shrugged. "You're not being punished at all. The pie burned to a crisp while I was searching for the boys."

Crouching down, Jackson helped Ethan put on his heavy boots. Ellie sat on the other side of the dining table in the great room and struggled to lace up an old pair of his work boots she had insisted on borrowing so she could go along on their outing.

"We're not going out to play, especially in the mud," he cautioned as he secured the second of Ethan's boots. "Once we check the orchards to see if trees are damaged and how many apples fell to the ground during the storm, we may have time to stop to visit the Grants. I don't want you two all muddied up."

Daniel stood next to Ethan watching Jackson work and shifted from one booted foot to the other, apparently as anxious to get outside as his father. "If lots of apples felled down and got hurt, then you can't take them to market, right, Pappy?"

Jackson looked up at his eldest son, hoping all he lost were some apples. "That's right, Daniel. Where will we take them?"

"To Mr. Haines's mill so he can mush them up and make them into cider."

"Very good," he said and patted Ethan's boots. "You're all ready to go."

"I'm ready, too," Ellie announced, although the frown she wore made it appear she would rather not go along with them at all.

"Are you sure those boots aren't too big?" he asked, concerned that she would end up with blisters again, this time on her feet.

She rolled her eyes. "My feet are as big as boats, so the boots are just fine. Is Daniel right? Will all the apples that fell wind up as cider?"

He drew a long breath. "Probably so. People in town

certainly can't store bruised apples, and I can't ship any of them, either. That leaves the cider mill, which is where I take all the drop apples. They don't return as much profit, but it's better than no profit at all. If we've lost as many as I think we might have, I'll need to let Michael know we're starting earlier than usual tomorrow to get them up off the ground," he said, without sharing his fear that he may have lost a fair number of branches, too, if not trees.

"Then we'll just have to hope that most of the apples were able to stay on the trees again this week," she said cheerfully.

Surprised by her upbeat words, he studied her face. Her frown was gone now, but faint circles under her eyes told him she had found little sleep last night during the storm.

Daniel took Ethan's hand and led him into the kitchen toward the back door. "This time you get to show us which path to take to get to the orchard, but don't worry about those yellow jackets. They don't like rain much, so they flew far, far away."

Jackson waited for Ellie before following along behind the boys. Once they were outside, they had to walk around broken tree limbs and branches that littered the yard. Once they passed that huge puddle in the side yard, he let the boys run a fair distance ahead of them. Maybe if Ethan thought they were far enough away, he might say something to Daniel—something that Jackson might overhear, even though he still doubted Daniel's claims that Ethan spoke to him. "Have you heard Ethan talking at all?" he whispered.

"No, not a word. He hasn't even asked for his ribbons, which I thought he might, but Daniel hasn't mentioned them for him, either. Have you?"

He let out a sigh. "No. I've been awake half the night for the past two nights, hoping to hear him talking to Daniel, but

I haven't heard a word from either one of them. I did hear you pacing about your room last night, though," he admitted.

She seemed embarrassed. "I'm sorry. I didn't mean to disturb you."

"You didn't. I told you, I was awake, listening for the boys. How do your hands feel?" he asked.

She held them out in front of her. "Much better, thank you, although I don't think the two stitches will be able to come out for a few days yet."

"I see you still haven't found your wedding ring."

She dropped her hands as well as her gaze. "Not yet."

Jackson stopped, forcing her to stop, as well. He reached into his pocket and took out the narrow gold band that he had bought on his last trip to market. "I've been meaning to give this to you. It's not anything fancy, but it's solid gold, so you won't have to take it off when you're doing housework or anything else," he said and slid it onto her finger.

As he hoped, it fit her perfectly and she closed her hand into a fist. "Thank you. I won't lose this one," she promised. "Well, the wooden ring isn't lost, exactly. It's probably in the kitchen somewhere, since I put it on the shelf before doing some housework. I'm sure I'll find it," she offered weakly, obviously embarrassed that he would think she was irresponsible.

Jackson looked ahead, but when he realized he had lost sight of the boys, he started forward again at a faster pace. Once he spied them walking right along the path as they had been told to do, he slowed his steps again. "Was it the storm that kept you awake? It's not the first time I've noticed your fear of storms. Have you always been afraid of them?" he asked.

She continued to match his pace but gazed straight ahead instead of looking at him. "No. As a child, I don't think storms bothered me too terribly, but I don't think it's fair to say I'm afraid of storms now. It's more like I'm petrified," she whispered and glanced up through the tree canopy, as if searching for any sign of a storm cloud in the sky overhead.

"The storm passed by a good while ago. I wouldn't bring you or the boys outside if I thought it hadn't," he said to reassure her.

She glanced at him and smiled a bit tenuously. "Storms can be very unpredictable. I don't trust them."

"You had a bad experience?"

Ellie was silent for so long he thought she had not heard him. When she finally did reply, her voice was barely above a whisper. "You might say that, although I'd argue that my father had a far worse experience. He was caught out in a storm when lightning struck a nearby tree. In turn, the tree fell and struck him. He lived just long enough to draft and sign a will giving my invalid mother full title to the farm and the little bit he owned before he died. There wasn't enough to support us both for very long, even though I kept the farm going as long as I could."

Jackson ran a hand through his hair. "I thought you looked a bit shaken when Sam Brooks told Daniel how he'd broken his arm during a storm, but I had no idea. . . . I'm sorry," he murmured.

She tilted up her chin. "There's no need to be sorry. You couldn't have known. It took me a very long time to stop being angry with my father for leaving us and with God for taking him home, so I can understand how angry Daniel and Ethan must be about losing their mama," she said, her voice getting stronger. "I'm mostly at peace now with what happened, but I still get frightened every time there's a storm and I hear a clap of thunder or see a bolt of lightning flash across the sky.

I'll have to try harder, though. I wouldn't want Daniel and Ethan to catch my uncommon fear of storms."

"Pappy! Pappy, look!"

Daniel's cries interrupted their conversation, and Jackson looked ahead again, only to see Daniel jumping up and down at the edge of the woods. He was pointing straight ahead to the orchards now in view, but there was no sign of Ethan.

Silently berating himself for not keeping a closer eye on his sons, he rushed forward, Ellie matching him step for step. "What is it? Where's Ethan?" he shouted and closed the distance between them in a matter or strides.

When he looked in the direction where Daniel was pointing, he saw Ethan sitting on a low branch of an apple tree, grinning with pride.

"See? Ethan climbed up all by himself. I didn't even have to help him," Daniel explained.

With his heart pounding, Jackson nodded. "Yes, I do see him," he said, took Daniel's hand, and walked over to the tree. Fearful he might startle Ethan enough to make him fall, he kept a smile on his face and his voice low. "You're up there pretty high, son."

Ethan nodded.

"You climbed up there all by yourself?"

Another nod.

Daniel climbed up right beside him. "I helped Ethan practice climbing when Miss Ellie was busy cleaning," he said as he wrapped his arm around his brother's shoulders.

Frowning a bit, Ellie looked up at the boys. "Did you teach Ethan how to climb back down again, too?"

When Daniel's face fell, Jackson laughed. "I guess I'd better do that right now, but I don't want you slipping outside for any reason unless Miss Ellie gives you permission," Jackson cautioned as he helped Ethan clamber back down. "Now, let's hurry and check on those fallen apples."

"I don't think you have to hurry," Ellie murmured as she scanned the rest of the orchard.

Jackson looked for himself and shook his head. "I don't believe it. There isn't a tree that's lost a limb and there are hardly any more drops than there were yesterday. It's as if the storm veered off after hitting the southern tip of the island."

"Storms are unpredictable," Ellie repeated.

Twenty-One

The following Wednesday, Ellie missed Market Day to stay home with Ethan, who was a bit feverish and gesturing he had a stomachache.

Even though it was barely light enough yet for anyone to see her standing at the kitchen window, she gave a final wave to Jackson and Daniel, who had promised to take good care of the baked treats she had made again this week, despite the fact that she had had to punish him earlier for playing too roughly with his brother. Jackson had also promised to make time to stop at Caden James's shop to ask the man to visit the island soon to teach Ellie how to properly use the cookstove.

She was just as anxious to make the best use of this unexpected day at home, especially now that the stitches in her finger had been removed and her hands had almost fully healed.

Humming softly, she filled a bucket with fresh water and carried it upstairs, where she had already put her broom, cleaning rags, soap, and fresh linens for the beds in the hallway. She glanced down at the apron Gram had given her, frowned, and loosened the ties on one of the aprons so she could tug it down to cover more of her dark brown gown, and sighed. The delicate blue flowers embroidered on the apron, as well as the ties, only made the stains she had not been able to launder out of her gown look worse, and she deeply regretted not being able to buy some fabric today to make herself a new one.

She made a mental note to let the hems down on both the aprons from Gram when she had the sewing basket out later today to finish sewing the boys' new clothes and the ribbons on the Jacob's Ladder.

When she peeked into the boys' room and saw that Ethan was lying on his back, sleeping soundly for the first time since last night, she said a quick prayer of thanksgiving. The winterberry tea she had made for him finally seemed to be working. She tiptoed across the hall and opened the door to Jackson's room very slowly to avoid waking the boy.

After she moved her cleaning supplies into the room, she left the door slightly ajar so she would hear Ethan if he cried out in his sleep or woke up. She did not come to the second floor very often. In fact, this was only the second time she had come upstairs to clean and change the bed linens. It was also the first time she had been upstairs without Daniel at her skirts, watching and criticizing every move she made, especially when she was in the room his mother had shared with his father.

She quickly surveyed the room to see what had to be done, even though she felt as if she were trespassing. Other than the quilt bunched up along one side of the rumpled bed and the shaving stand he used each day, there was little else in the room that appeared to be personal in nature. None of his clothing lay strewn about, and there was nothing lying on top of the chest of drawers.

There was, however, a good bit of dust and dirt on the floor. Feeling too warm already, she opened one of the windows to let out the heat still coming from the warming stove. She bunched the hem of her apron together to protect her hand and opened the stove to see if she needed to empty the ashes once the embers died down.

There were no embers at all, only cold ashes, which meant there was only one reason she was feeling so warm. She shut the door but also closed off the very idea she was flustered from being in his room where Jackson slept in the marriage bed he had shared with his first wife.

Unfortunately, changing the man's bed linens and wiping down his shaving stand only left her feeling more overheated. She opened a second window, swept out the room, and washed the floor. Convinced she was acting like a silly schoolgirl instead of the matron she was, she leaned against the doorframe and brought to mind the documents stored in the parlor and the initials carved into the ancient tree at the far end of the island.

Legally, as long as she kept to the guidelines she had agreed to follow, she had the right to reside here. Ellie twisted the gold ring she now wore on her finger. She could never deny that Jackson was an attractive man, because he was. She also could not deny that he could be a caring, giving man that any woman would treasure as her husband—if he ever truly learned to control his anger.

Unfortunately, the longer she lived here with him, the more often she had to remind herself that their marriage was based on nothing more than mutual need and duty. And the longer she lived here with him, the more difficult it was becoming to deny that her feelings for him had changed and grown into affection—true affection that urged her to want more than just his name or the status of being a married woman.

She wanted his heart.

She let out a long sigh and turned away from the window and the impossible dream that he might come to love her, too. He wanted a housekeeper. He wanted a caregiver for his sons, but he most definitely did not want a wife. Even though their relationship had eased into a comfortable companionship and he was more open and honest with her now, he had made it very, very clear there was no room in his heart or his life for anyone other than his sons.

"Unless he made room," she murmured. Perhaps if she knew more about him, other than the fact that he had been an orphan, she might find a way for him to open his heart to her. There was only one person on this island she knew and trusted who could tell her what she needed to know: Gram.

Feeling hopeful and determined to make another visit to the Grants soon, she crossed the room, stepped into the hallway, and eased the door to his room closed. She tiptoed between the pile of soiled bed linens and her cleaning supplies and returned to the boys' room.

Curled beneath the covers now, with his stubborn little cowlick sticking up from the pillow, Ethan was sleeping with his face to the wall nearest the hallway. She tiptoed to his bedside and gazed down at him. His cheeks were paler now, only slightly flushed. His breathing was even and deep. Ever so lightly, she placed her hand on his forehead and smiled. His fever was gone now.

Relieved, she closed her eyes and prayed over him to thank God for helping him to recover, although she suspected his fever might return again in late afternoon. She had seen that happen often enough with her mother when she cared for her and decided that when he did wake up, another dose of winterberry tea might be in order.

The boys' room did not feel nearly as warm as their father's, and she checked the stove, where she found a good bit of embers that would keep the room comfortable for a few hours yet. She dismissed the obvious difference in how she felt in the room, turned around, and looked about to see how much work it would take to clean it.

Because Jackson insisted on keeping the blocks downstairs, there were none scattered on the floor, but it was as dirty as Jackson's had been. Daniel's bed, set on the other side of the room along the outer wall, was also in total disarray.

She tiptoed closer. Two pillows, including the one he had brought home from the Sunday house, lay in the middle of the bed under the quilt, which had been used to make a tent large enough for both boys to sleep under. She smiled and tried not to feel self-righteous. Maybe this is why Jackson never heard the two boys talking together at night. They were on the side of the room farthest from the hall under a quilted tent that would keep their voices from being heard.

Reluctant to start cleaning and disturb Ethan's much-needed sleep, she returned to the hallway, carried Jackson's bed linens downstairs to the kitchen to be laundered later, and scrubbed the stairs and hallway clean. When she finished, it was nearly midmorning. Ethan was still asleep, so she went back down to the kitchen for her second breakfast of the day but kept the door at the bottom of the staircase open so she would be able to hear him if he woke up.

She returned to the boys' room an hour later. Ethan was in the same position, still sleeping soundly. At this point, she probably should give him another dose of tea, but she did not have the heart to wake him just yet.

Instead, Ellie simply decided to start cleaning the room. If he woke up from the noise, fine. She would stop to care for him. If not, she would wake him up when she finished. By then the rest of the room would be done, and she would only have to change the linens on his bed to have the upstairs finished by the time Jackson and Daniel returned late this afternoon.

She tackled Daniel's bed first. After folding the quilt, which had been the makeshift tent, she set it on the foot of Ethan's bed and returned to Daniel's. The lace-trimmed pillowcase on Rebecca's pillow definitely needed to be laundered, but she did not want to upset Daniel by replacing it with a new one.

Ellie hesitated and glanced out the window. The sun was getting stronger now. If she laundered the pillowcase right away and hung it outside, it might be dry in time for her to put it back on the pillow before bedtime. She picked up the pillow, felt something hard beneath her fingertips, and knew immediately there was something else inside the pillowcase other than a pillow.

Curious to know what treasures Daniel had hidden inside, she sat down on the bed, put the pillow on her lap, pulled the pillow free, and set it alongside of her. She held the remaining pillowcase open with one hand and reached inside to retrieve his treasures so she could put them in a safe place until the pillowcase had dried.

When she finally had the treasures on her lap and set the pillowcase aside, however, she did not know whether she wanted to shout with joy or to cry with disappointment. She only knew that she could not put the treasures back, regardless of how Daniel might feel about losing them.

Swallowing hard, she stared at the wooden wedding ring

she thought she had lost. Apparently, Daniel had either found it or taken it and hidden it here, oddly enough, with his mother's pillow. But it was the silhouette of her mother lying on her lap that forced Ellie to blink back tears. She had not realized the silhouette was even missing, yet here it was. She caressed the outline of her mother's loving face with her fingertips as her tears fell free.

To think that Daniel would take her ring and something as precious as her mother's silhouette made her heart ache. He must be far more troubled by his mother's death and much angrier with Ellie than she suspected. She had done everything she could to befriend the child, and he had repaid her with behavior she could understand but not condone.

Until a sudden thought made her stop and think and wonder.

She did not know how Daniel had come to have her wooden wedding ring, but she was certain he had not been with her when she had unpacked her travel bag and stored away her things, including her parents' silhouettes. Ethan had been with her, but not Daniel. He had been with Jackson in the orchards the entire time, and she and Ethan had been in the kitchen, not her room, when Daniel and Jackson had finally returned.

Ellie thought long and hard about the last few weeks, but she had never once mentioned the silhouettes to anyone. In point of fact, she had not even looked at either of her parents' silhouettes again, or she would have noticed that one of them was missing.

Other than Ellie, Ethan was the only one who knew the silhouettes existed, that this silhouette was of her mother, and where she kept the silhouette stored. Since the drawer where she kept the silhouettes was too hard for Ethan to open, she could draw only one conclusion: Ethan had to have told Daniel about the silhouette, who it was, and how important it was to her; otherwise, Daniel would never have known about it, let alone taken it.

"He had to have told him. Ethan had to speak to Daniel to tell him," she whispered. She had proof that Ethan could talk and did talk to Daniel, exactly as he claimed.

Ellie wondered how Jackson would react when she showed him proof that she had been right to believe Daniel's claims that Ethan talked to him. Was there a way to tell Jackson that wouldn't result in punishment for Daniel—hardening his heart toward her even further?

Unless . . . unless she did not tell Jackson at all. But that made no sense, since she was the one who insisted they should not keep secrets from each other. Besides, even if she did not tell Jackson, Daniel would know she had found the ring and the silhouette when she changed the pillowcase. When his father did not confront him, Daniel would know she had not told his father, which would only condone the idea that married couples keep secrets from one another, a lesson she definitely did not want to teach him.

Troubled and confused about what to do, she slid the pillowcase back over the pillow and tucked the ring and the silhouette into her apron pocket before she did the only thing she was certain she should do: She bowed her head and prayed.

Twenty-Two

When a sobbing, hysterical young woman barged through the back door later that morning, Ellie instinctively leaped up from the worktable to stand in front of Ethan. He was sitting in his usual place on the window seat, apparently fully recovered from his malady. But the woman's shocking appearance had startled him into a full wail.

"Help us. You have to help us," she pleaded, tugging at Ellie's hand. "Please, you have to hurry."

Only now, when she noticed the young woman's spectacles, did she realize the young woman was Grizel. She pulled her hand free, put Ethan on one hip to calm him, and tried to hug Grizel to her. "I'll help. Of course I'll help," she said calmly, even though her heart was pounding in her chest. Her current worries about when to tell Jackson about what she had found upstairs in Daniel's pillowcase quickly evaporated, replaced by concern for Grizel that was much more urgent.

Grizel stiffened and latched on to Ellie's hand again. "Now. You have to come now," she managed between gulping breaths of air. "Please!"

"I said I'd come, but you need to tell me what happened so I know how I can help. What's wrong?"

"It's Gram. She can't breathe right. Mother's tried all sorts of remedies, but nothing's helped. Nothing. Please! Won't you please come? Father won't be back for hours yet, and by the time he gets back . . ." She dissolved into tears, unable to voice the fear that her great-grandmother might not survive.

Ellie patted Ethan's back and rocked him from side to side and held fast to Grizel's hand to try to get them both to stop crying or she would not be able to go anywhere. "Shhh, it's going to be all right," she crooned, over and over again.

Ethan stopped crying first.

When he started patting Grizel on the shoulder, she finally stopped crying, too.

"Tell me what you want me to do," Ellie prompted, prepared to do anything to help Gram, although she could not imagine what she could do that Alice would not be able to do better.

"Can you ride a horse?" Grizel asked as she removed her spectacles to dry off her tears.

"I'm sure I can stay astride, although I haven't ridden for a good many years. Why?"

"Can . . . can you swim?"

Ellie's eyes widened. "Yes, but—"

"Are you certain?"

"I can swim very well. Why?"

The young girl let out a huge sigh as she put her spectacles back on. "Good. Mother said you probably could. I know Mr. Jackson will be very, very upset that we even asked you, but . . . but we need you to ride across the river to fetch Dr. Willows," Grizel gushed. "There's no way to ferry anyone across because my father and Mr. Jackson left everything on the other side. I don't ride or swim, and neither does my mother. We . . . we just never had to learn, so . . . so you're our only hope."

Ellie gasped. "Y-you want me to cross the river on a horse? And ride to Harrisburg?"

Grizel blinked back a fresh flow of tears. "I know it's a lot to ask, but my mother can tell you where the river won't be all that deep and won't reach up much past your knees if you're astride."

Ellie shook her head. "I can't believe the river is that shallow."

"Only in places," Grizel countered. "There's a rift of bedrock here and there that rises up like a roadway under the water at either end of the island. There's even one near the bridge in Harrisburg, where the water is so low sometimes this time of year that people actually drive their wagons or cattle across so they don't have to pay the toll for the bridge."

Ellie narrowed her gaze. "Then why can't I just walk across, instead of riding?"

Grizel paled. "You can't get to the bridge from here. Even though the river isn't very deep in places, the bottom is very rocky and the current is really strong. It's safer to ride, but you'll have to be careful to stay astride. If . . . if something happens and you can't, the current will take you to the other side eventually. As long as you know how to swim, you should be fine. Just please, please say yes. We haven't any time to lose.

I'll keep Ethan at our house with us, just in case Gram . . ." She dissolved into tears again.

Ellie did not have to think it over for longer than a heartbeat before handing Ethan over to Grizel. "I can't ride in this gown. I'll need to change first, but I need your help while I do," she said, then removed her apron and shoved it into the sewing basket, along with the overalls she had been hemming for Ethan.

"A-anything," Grizel promised. "Please. Just hurry!"

"Just in case Mr. Smith arrives home before I do, I need you to write a note for him. Be sure to tell him Ethan is with you at your house," she said and handed her the bit of scrap paper and pencil she had seen in one of the kitchen drawers.

"I know what to write. I've left notes for him before."

"Fine," Ellie replied and patted Ethan on the head. "Be good for Grizel. I'll be right back," she promised and charged upstairs to Jackson's room. Silencing the echo of his warning never to leave the island alone, she found a pair of his overalls and a shirt and quickly changed into them. Once she had rolled up the sleeves on the shirt and the hems of the overalls so she wouldn't trip, she retraced her steps downstairs to find the old boots she had worn just the other day and put them on.

By the time she was ready to leave, Grizel was more composed, although her eyes were swollen and red from crying. "I finished the note for Mr. Jackson. Where do you want me to leave it?"

Ellie stood near the back door and pointed. "Right there. On top of the sewing basket. Hopefully, it'll be the first thing he'll notice when he comes through the door," she said and opened the back door.

Grizel did as she was told and hurried past Ellie and out

the door, with Ethan still on her hip. "Follow me. I know a shortcut."

Ellie shut the door, drew in a long breath, and rushed to keep up with the young girl. If ever she needed God's help it was right now, but the prayers she offered were not for herself. They were for Gram and the family who loved her so very much.

Instead of following any of the three paths that led through the woods to the orchards, Grizel cut into the woods, crossed the clearing with the family cemetery, and led Ellie along a narrow path that hugged the western shore of the island. The distance between the island and the mainland to the west was a good bit greater than the distance Ellie would have to cover on the other side.

Even so, the river was higher than she remembered after the last rain, but the current appeared to be just as swift. She swallowed her fear of crossing the river on horseback and held on to the hope that Gram might have improved by the time they reached her.

She was out of breath and had a stitch in her side by the time they reached the Grant cabin. While Grizel kept Ethan distracted with a bit of taffy, Ellie entered the sickroom. Although the room was dimmer than the last time she had been inside, she could still see the worry in Alice's face and she could hear Gram coughing and wheezing, struggling for each breath. Kneeling at the aged woman's bedside, Ellie took her hand. It was cold and damp, and she could see the sweat beading on Gram's face and the fear in her eyes.

"She's getting worse, and I just don't know what else to do for her. I . . . I hope Jackson won't be angry with me for asking you to help," Alice whispered as she mopped Gram's brow. "After all he's been through, I wouldn't want to remind him—"

"He would expect me to help, and I want to help. I'll get the doctor," Ellie promised, mindful that Rebecca had lost her life on the very river Ellie would have to cross now.

Gram tried to lift her head from the pillow and fought to speak but ended up coughing even harder.

Ellie traced a cross on the aged woman's forehead and gently helped her lay back against the pillow, just as she had often done for her mother when she suffered from one of her spells.

Gram smiled and squeezed Ellie's hand.

"I'll be back soon, but I know the Lord will be with you and help you while I'm gone," she whispered and glanced up at Alice. "Tell me how to find Dr. Willows and where to cross the river," she said and listened to the directions the distraught woman gave her.

By the time she got back outside again, Grizel had an old bay mare, with a distinctive white patch covering her rump, waiting for her. She was holding the reins with one hand and Ethan with the other. "Patience won't give you any bother crossing the river, and she knows the way into the city. Just give her her head. I don't know how to put a saddle on her, though, but there's one in the barn that you could—"

"I don't need a saddle," Ellie said and took the reins from Grizel. After drawing in a long breath, she grabbed hold of the horse's mane. She managed to get astride on her second attempt and wrapped her legs around the horse. "Your mother told me where to cross just below the landing, so you don't have to show me. Just keep a close eye on Ethan for me," she said and smiled down at the three-year-old. "Be a good boy."

He blinked up at her, as if he could not believe she was

sitting on the horse. She saw his lips begin to move, as if he was about to speak, but just as quickly, his lips stilled, and he lowered his gaze. "I'll be as quick as I can," she murmured and urged the horse forward.

Ellie reached the landing easily enough. Patience managed her way over the multitude of river stones there to reach the river's edge. Ellie continued along the edge until she spied the buttonwood tree with the scarred trunk that Alice had described. The noon sun was strong overhead, but she shivered with anticipation as she stared at the distance between the island and the mainland. The half mile seemed much more daunting than when they were ferried across and she had had the wagon to hold on to.

She bent low over the horse and patted her neck. "Take your time and watch your step so we'll both reach the other side together," she urged. After whispering a quick prayer, she gave her mount a gentle nudge with the heels of her boots and loosened the reins to give the mare her head.

Crossing the river was not quite as easy as Grizel had suggested. The horse had to walk very slowly and slipped several times, forcing Ellie to hold on to the mane with every ounce of strength she possessed. The old mare had been steady against the raging current, however, but the water that gradually rose to Ellie's thighs was cold enough to have her shivering by the time they reached the opposite shore.

She shortened the reins a bit when they reached the road that led to Harrisburg and urged the mare into a jog. The sooner they reached Dr. Willows, the sooner he would be on his way to help Gram. Given the noon hour, she expected Jackson was still at the market, but she dismissed any notion of riding there after sending Dr. Willows to see Gram. She was dressed quite inappropriately, especially for the city, and the overalls she had borrowed from him were dripping wet and clinging most immodestly to her legs. She would be far better off riding back to the island with Dr. Willows and changing before Jackson got home.

While she rode, she prayed hard. For Gram. For the Grants. For Jackson and herself, that they might all accept God's will if He called Gram home today, a woman who had been such a precious gift to them all.

Twenty-Three

Four hours later, Ellie finally arrived back on Dillon's Island with Dr. Willows.

Her relief that Gram was still alive quickly gave way to anxiety. Dr. Willows, along with Alice, had been with Gram in her room now for nearly half an hour. Ellie had spent that time with Grizel, waiting and praying that the doctor would be able to help the aged matriarch while Ethan took his afternoon nap in Grizel's room.

Finally, Alice emerged from her mother-in-law's bedroom and eased the door closed. "She's doing better. For now," she whispered, hugging her daughter first and then Ellie.

"For now?" Grizel asked, her troubled gaze magnified by her spectacles.

"Her heart's failing," her mother replied and cupped her

daughter's cheek. "Gram's one hundred and two years old. She can't live forever, but she's more comfortable now, and Dr. Willows seems to think the next few days will tell whether she'll rally or slip away. Even so, we've always known her time with us was waning," she murmured before turning to Ellie. "Bless you for helping us. Bless you."

"I'm so happy we weren't too late. Dr. Willows wasn't at home, so I had to ride several miles out to the homestead where he had been called to treat an entire family struck down by some sort of food poisoning," she explained, hopeful that Gram would recover.

"Yes, he told me. He also told me that you were to get out of those wet overalls and get warmed up, or you were going to wind up being his patient, too."

Ellie nodded. "I've warmed up a bit here with Grizel in front of the fire, but I surely would love to change into something dry and . . . and more appropriate," she added, mindful of her last visit here when Alice commented on the gown Ellie had worn.

"I'd have worn men's overalls myself if I'd been able to ride for Dr. Willows, but we can't have that husband of yours coming home and finding you dressed like this."

Grizel spoke up. "It'd be a pity to wake Ethan up—he just fell asleep. Leave him here with us, go home, change, and come back. By then, my father and Mr. Jackson should be back. I'll have Mr. Jackson wait here so you can all walk home together."

"That's a good idea," Alice said and ushered Ellie to the door. "By the time you get back, Gram might be feeling up to seeing you, too."

"Are you sure you don't want me to take Ethan home with me?"

"I'm not going to wake up that child after he was up half the night with a sore belly. Are you?"

Ellie laughed. "No, but I won't be long. I'll use the shortcut Grizel showed me and be back as soon as I can," she promised and slipped out the door.

Ellie's waterlogged boots were heavy, and after having ridden for hours, every muscle in her body screamed in protest with each step she took. Her overalls were still damp, and she grew cold now that she was outside and away from the fire. But she was more worried about Gram than anything else, even what Jackson would do when he returned home and learned she had left the island today.

Because she had had the presence of mind to tell Grizel to write a note for Jackson before she left, she was not worried about suffering through another misunderstanding like the one that had erupted on Market Day if he returned earlier than usual. Still, she was grateful she would get home before he did so she'd be able to tell him face-to-face why she had left today.

When she finally reached the overgrown cemetery, she was shivering and still suffering with every step she took. She glanced at the overgrowth and made a quick mental note to spend some time here with the boys to clear it out. But that would not be today. All she wanted right now was to get out of these wet overalls and into something dry and to sit down in front of the fireplace in the great room to get warm enough to head back to the Grants'.

When she emerged from the woods and stepped into the side yard, the late afternoon sun was still bright. She stopped for a moment to enjoy the warmth while her eyes adjusted. When they did, she saw Jackson walk out onto the side porch, place something there, and walk back into the house.

"He's home."

Her heart skipped a beat, and question after question swirled through her mind as she started for the house, searching for an explanation of how he had arrived home before she did.

Had she left the Grants' just before he returned there with Michael? If so, they would have told him she was using the shortcut home. Why didn't he follow her? She certainly was not walking very fast. He would have caught up with her. But he hadn't.

Maybe they forgot to tell him she was using the shortcut, and he had used one of the three dirt roadways instead. Had she taken so long walking home that he was able to get home before her? And what was he putting out on the porch?

The closer she got to the side porch to see exactly what it was that he had put outside, however, the faster her heart had begun to beat. The band of disbelief that wrapped around her chest grew so tight, she could scarcely draw a breath.

She did not dare climb the several steps to reach the porch itself. Instead, she simply stared at her travel bag lying there just beyond the top step. Apparently, he had packed the bag with everything she owned so quickly, he had not noticed that the embroidered ties on one of the aprons Gram had given her were hanging out.

She shook her head, as if trying to make the travel bag disappear, and pressed her knees together to keep her legs from shaking. When the door opened again, she looked up at her husband, hoping he could offer a reasonable explanation for what he was doing.

She stared at the overalls he was wearing. They were wet, just like the ones she wore. He must have crossed the river, too, but he must have been on foot since his overalls were damp clear up to his waist. He also must have crossed at this end of the island; otherwise, he would have met up with her at the Grants'.

When she finally met his gaze, she found no answers to the many questions she had. She found only disappointment and anger staring back at her.

He reached down and handed her a note without saying a word. She recognized the note as the one Grizel had written for her to leave for him but read the actual words for the first time:

> *Your missus went to the city. Don't worry.*
> *Ethan is with me. Grizel*

"I believe the note says it all," he murmured and tossed a few coins, which landed at her feet yet stung her very spirit. "You left the island. You left my son. Now take your things and leave again. But this time, don't come back. There's enough money lying in the dirt to get passage on the next stage. Be on it."

"L-leave again?" she managed. Although she was disappointed that Grizel had not mentioned the emergency that had sent Ellie to the city in the note, she could not understand why Jackson had not waited for her to explain herself.

"You apparently know your way back to the city, so forgive me if I don't have the inclination to escort you. I have more important things to do." He turned around and walked back into the house.

When he shut the door, she flinched.

When she heard the bolt slide into place, the blood drained out of her face.

It really did not matter anymore why he had crossed the

river to get home. The only question pounding for an answer was whether she was going to be as stubborn as he claimed she could be and fight to save this odd marriage of hers.

She drew in a long breath and squared her shoulders. There was only one answer that made any sense to her at all. She grabbed her travel bag as well as his coins and charged off before she changed her mind.

Twenty-Four

Jackson braced his back against the door and stared at the floor.

His shock and disappointment in Ellie was still profound, but his blinding anger at her for leaving Ethan when he was not feeling well and going to the mainland had already been spent. All that remained was the utter sense of emptiness he had known most of his life.

Even though he was still wet and cold after crossing the river on foot, he refused to take a single step away from this door until he heard her drag her travel bag off the porch and walk away. His mind and his heart were also closed tight against any pleas or explanations she might offer to excuse what she had done.

Finally, when he heard her charge off as if she could not

leave fast enough, he relaxed against the door. The tension in his frame slowly ebbed, his heartbeat dropped back to normal.

Until he heard footsteps inside the house. "I forgot to bolt the parlor door," he gritted.

"Yes, you did."

Agitated again by the cheerful tone of her voice, he looked up and found her standing in the great room, just beyond the doorway to the kitchen. She was wearing one of his shirts with the sleeves rolled up. A pair of his overalls, still damp from her little adventure, clung to her legs. Her nose and cheeks were pink from the sun, and her hair lay matted against her head.

She waltzed into the kitchen carrying her travel bag as if she were dressed in her Sunday best. She stepped around her mending and sewing notions scattered on the floor—where they had landed after he had shoved them off the table in a fit of anger.

After setting the coins and her travel bag on top of the worktable, she glanced at the floor again and shook her head. "You've tracked in an awful lot of mud. I suppose you're better off if you wait until it dries before you do anything about that mess, but if you're going to act like a brute, please have the courtesy to pick up after yourself and put the sewing notions back into the basket."

He clenched his jaw until he could trust himself to speak without raising his voice. "I thought I told you to leave."

"I heard you," she said, then walked past him to get to the pump and proceeded to wash her hands.

"Then leave," he insisted. Growing more frustrated by the second, he unbolted the door and opened it. "Leave. Wash your hands—as if that really matters, given the rest of your appearance. Don't even bother to change so you can return my clothes. You'll obviously need them, since I have no intention of asking Michael to ferry you across the river. Just leave."

She wiped her hands dry with a clean cloth. "You're right. I might need to wear these clothes again, but not today," she said, glancing down at the damp overalls, and shrugged. "In all truth, I think these fared pretty well, considering I crossed the river twice and rode for miles today, but you obviously don't want to hear about that."

Utterly annoyed that she would have the audacity to be so self-righteous after what she had done, he squared his shoulders. "No, I don't."

"Good, then I won't bother to tell you," she said and put the cloth down next to the pump. Sidestepping the mud and the sewing notions on the floor, she passed by him again and stopped in front of her travel bag sitting on the table. "Although I'm curious about how you fared at market today, I'm afraid I really don't want to engage in any further conversation with you until you're in a better frame of mind."

He bristled, reluctant to admit how many had come to his stall asking for Ellie today. Many of his customers were disappointed she had not come with him today, although they were quite pleased he had brought her baked treats with him.

She picked up her travel bag. "If you'll excuse me, I've had a long, difficult day, and I need to get into some dry clothes and get warmed up before I go for Ethan. Where's Daniel? Upstairs?"

"No, I sent him home with Michael. I came directly home, but you weren't here."

"I'm here now," she said sweetly, as if she had been waiting patiently here for him all day.

He bristled again. "But you should have been here taking care of my son, instead of gallivanting off to the city and leaving him with Grizel. If we hadn't broken a wagon wheel on our way home, I'd have gotten here hours ago, packed up your things, and taken them back to your cousin's so you wouldn't have needed to step back into my house again," he said firmly.

"If you'll recall, I'm not welcome there," she quipped. "And I had no choice but to leave, but you've already said you don't want to hear about that, so I won't bother explaining myself," she said and started out of the room.

"There's no need for an explanation," he argued. "I heard quite enough from Christina Schuler," he said, quite certain Ellie would remember the woman who had been at her cousin's shop the day they had stopped there to tell her cousin and his wife they had gotten married.

Ellie braced to a halt and very slowly turned around to look him in the eye. Her face was pale, but her gaze was steady.

"Christina was returning home earlier today from visiting with a friend who lives just north of the city. She was a good distance away, but she saw you," he said, still shaken by the shock and embarrassment of learning about his wife's adventure today, especially from that woman.

"And even though I've only met the woman once, weeks ago, Christina Schuler was so certain it was me that she made a special point of going to market to tell you," she murmured, her gaze growing troubled.

He shook his head. "No, she recognized Patience. The mare's got that distinctive patch on her rump, remember? Since Grizel is fair-haired, her mother is twice your size, and Gram is far too old to ride, and you weren't wearing a bonnet or a hat again, it wasn't hard to guess who the rider might be. At the time, I didn't have a reasonable explanation to give her for why my wife was out riding, bareback, wearing men's clothing, and I have no need for one now."

"Nonetheless, she'll no doubt enjoy sharing that bit of news with the gossipmongers in the city, along with the rest of her tale." Ellie turned and walked away.

Jackson's jaw dropped, and he stared so hard, he forgot to blink. She . . . she just walked out of the room! By the time he had gathered his wits and followed her into the great room, she was already disappearing into her bedroom. "You can't walk away from me. We haven't finished this conversation," he argued, mindful that this was not the first time she had simply walked away from him when she was upset.

"We weren't having a conversation. You were conducting an inquisition," she said and shut the door only a footstep before he reached it.

"Flippant woman," he muttered and knocked on the door.

When she did not respond, he knocked again. "Open the door."

He heard the bolt click on the other side of the door.

Rankled, he knocked again. He could hear her moving about in the room, but she made no effort to come to the door to open it. He was tempted to take the hinges off the door, just to prove he could get that door open. Instead, he braced both feet on the floor and cocked his head. He could hear clothes rustling. Maybe she was merely changing her clothes before she left, in which case, he did not want to do anything that might delay her.

Shivering hard, he left to build a fire in the fireplace to take the chill off the room instead. Drawing a deep breath, he added one final log and stoked the fire. He did not relish telling the boys that he had made a mistake by marrying that confounded woman, but he did not think the boys would be very unhappy to learn that Miss Ellie was not going to be a part of their lives anymore.

He was still down on his knees stoking the fire when he heard the door to her room creak open. She had indeed changed into a gown, but the smile on his face died the moment she pulled a rocking chair closer to the fire and sat down wearing that drab brown gown of hers.

"Thank you for making the fire for me," she said and held out her hands to warm them. The gold wedding ring he had given her only days ago caught the reflection of the flames, but he was not moved by any emotion other than regret.

He stood up and folded his hands over his chest. "I built the fire for myself and the boys so the room would be warm when they got home, not for you. You're leaving, remember?"

She shrugged. "Remind me again why I'm leaving." Silence. "Oh, dear—you can't remind me at all, because you never told me. You just ordered me to leave, or did I misunderstand you?"

He snorted, her coy words nearly draining the last of his patience. "Is this some sort of game you're playing? Because if it is, you'll have to play it by yourself. Better yet, you can play it with my lawyer when you get to Harrisburg. I need to get to the Grants' and fetch the boys. I'm finished talking," he snapped and walked away.

"At least Ethan has an excuse for not talking to me. He's a child. What's your excuse, Jackson?" she demanded.

He froze, practically in midstride, and caught his breath. He turned and walked back to her, if only to convince himself he must have misheard her. "What did you say?"

She moistened her lips. With her hands folded on her lap, she kept her gaze on the fire. Her words were softly spoken, even calm. "I said I understand why Ethan doesn't talk to me, but I was wondering why you won't."

"Discussing why you left earlier today is pointless."

She nodded. "That's one perspective, although I must say it's an improvement. The last time you leaped to a wrong conclusion where I was concerned, you hurled angry words at me, which you regretted. You did throw coins at my feet, which was rather crass, but I suppose that's better, too, unless—"

"Yes, I did, but there is no 'wrong conclusion' this time," he argued, too annoyed to care that he was talking to her, in spite of himself. "Mrs. Schuler told me she saw you today, and you don't deny it. When I got home, I read the note more than once, even though I've seen notes like that from Rebecca more times than I care to remember. I know you left the island and rode off today. Why you left makes no difference to me. You left and you let Grizel take care of Ethan, even though he was sick."

"That's true, but—"

"But in case you don't remember, let me remind you that there were a few things you agreed to do when we got married. One of them, the most important one, was to honor my wishes never to leave this island alone and leave the boys with someone else. Or do I need to get the papers from the parlor to show you?"

She shook her head and sighed. "No, I don't need to see the papers. I remember everything we agreed to."

"Then I don't understand why you won't leave now, as I've asked you to do. You deliberately broke your word, and I won't tolerate it. I can't. Not again. Not ever again. I've made that mistake once too often before," he said, fighting bitter memories that erupted in his mind.

"With Rebecca."

His chest tightened. "Yes, with Rebecca. As it turns out, you're no better at being a wife or a mother than she was. You're just like her."

"No, I don't think I am, but I can't say I know enough about your first wife to be certain of anything other than she was younger and smaller and far prettier than I am."

"You're right. You don't look anything like her. But inside, where it really matters, you're one and the same. You're selfish and you're never satisfied with anything you have. You must have more. Always more," he insisted, struggling for control.

But he failed, and angry words gushed out of the deep well of his disappointments before he could stop them. "You act like you care about me and about the boys, but you don't. You act like living here on this island is enough, but it isn't. Not when you take the first opportunity you get to leave to pursue whatever it is that truly makes you happy. I've been such a fool, but then again, it seems to be a habit I can't break." Jackson then reached into his pocket and pulled out the wooden ring he'd found when Ellie's sewing basket had fallen to the floor. He held it out so she could see it.

She did not flinch. In fact, Ellie did not seem surprised or concerned at all that he had found it. "The day I put this ring on your finger, you said it was the only ring you ever wanted. But that wasn't true; otherwise, you never would have hidden it away in your sewing basket. I can only presume you planned to pretend you'd lost it so I'd be forced to buy you a better one. But you didn't know I already had, did you?"

"Please. You don't understand—"

"Oh, I think I do. But what you don't know is that I actually bought that ring weeks ago, right before I wound up in that pile of manure. I didn't want you to think I was trying to bribe my way back into your good graces by giving it to you right then," he admitted.

When she remained stoic, as if his words meant nothing to her, he tossed the ring into the fire. "That's where the ring belongs. In the fire, where it will be reduced to ashes," he said. He watched the ring bounce off the log and roll into the corner of the fireplace, knowing the fire would consume it eventually. "This marriage was over before it even began, because in the end, it's all about what you want and what suits you, regardless of who gets hurt in the process, isn't it?"

She paled, tilted up her chin, but held silent. He thought he saw tears welling in her eyes, but she blinked them away before he could be sure. Just when he thought she might never answer him at all, she cleared her throat.

"No," she said. "It's all about doing what's right, regardless of how difficult or inconvenient that might be. It's about caring more for other people than yourself and being there for them when they need you. It's about talking through misunderstandings. And it's about trusting the woman you've chosen to raise your children to use her judgment when need be, instead of insisting she follow rules that are so rigid, there's no room for her to be . . . to be the woman she wants to be instead of the woman you think she is."

Jackson swallowed hard, but before he could find a single word to say in his own defense, Ellie got to her feet and faced him.

"You're a good man at heart, Jackson Smith, but you're still so angry that you've lost the woman you loved and so mired in memories that seem to be as bitter as they are sweet that you can't even recognize that I'm not Rebecca at all. I wish I were, for your sake as well as the boys', but I'm not. I thought that one day you would learn to trust me and to accept me as I am. Obviously, you haven't yet, but if you don't do it soon, the boys never will, and you'll end up getting them more confused than they already are."

Her words were so sincere, he had to steel himself to keep from weakening and telling her that the only woman he truly loved was still very much alive or that he had yet to give up hope they might one day be together.

But it was the deep anguish in Ellie's gaze and her concern for his boys that gave him pause to really consider what she said, as well as the awful possibility that he had indeed jumped to a wrong conclusion today. He cleared the lump in his throat, but she held up her hand to keep him from saying another word.

"I need to get back to the Grants'. If you insist on walking with me, fine. I can't stop you, but I think I've heard enough from you for now. We can talk more tomorrow, after you've had time to think about what it is you really want from me."

"You don't need to go to the Grants' for the boys. I told you I was going to fetch them."

She drew in a long breath. "I wasn't going back just for the boys. I was going back to see Gram. I only pray I'm not too late." She stepped around him and walked out the door to the front porch.

He charged after her. "Late? Late for what?"

She paused at the top of the porch steps and held on to the railing without turning to look at him. "Gram took ill today. She may be dying. Dr. Willows wasn't certain, at least while I was there. All he could tell Alice and Grizel was that her heart was failing."

His own heart thudded hard against the wall of his chest, and he knew the answer to his question before he even asked it. "How did Dr. Willows even know Gram was sick today?"

She bowed her head for a moment and drew in a long, long breath. "Because I rode to the mainland and brought him back to care for her," she whispered, then walked away.

This time, he let her go.

Jackson was too ashamed and too embarrassed by his own behavior to ask for her forgiveness again right now.

But before he followed along behind her to get his boys and to see how Gram was faring, he ran back into the house and straight to the fireplace. He found the wooden wedding ring he had tossed there in anger and pulled it free with the poker. Although charred, the ring had not been reduced to ashes yet.

He used the end of the poker to snag the ring and carry it out to the kitchen. After he pumped water over the ring to cool it, he set the poker down and slid the ring back into his pocket before charging out the kitchen door.

When he saw just a flash of her skirts at the edge of the woods, he hurried his steps so he could follow along behind her just closely enough to make sure she reached the Grants' safely.

Twenty-Five

The fire in the hearth was low at midnight, but hope within the household that Gram would continue to rally still remained high.

While the rest of the Grant family slept, Ellie limped out of Gram's room but left the door ajar so she could hear if Gram made any sounds of distress. Gram was sleeping peacefully and her breathing was much less labored now than it had been when Ellie had gone to fetch Dr. Willows, and she hoped Alice and Grizel were also getting some much-needed rest before they resumed their bedside vigil.

She paused for just a moment to rub the small of her back before she started pacing as quietly as she could to walk out the cramps in her feet and legs. She cringed now and again when her muscles protested, but she pursed her lips and kept walking. If she stopped, the cramps only worsened, a lesson Ellie had learned well while taking care of her mother without anyone to help her.

She glanced at the low-burning fire, but quickly looked away because it only reminded her that her wooden wedding ring was now nothing but ashes in the fireplace at home.

"Ellie? Is everything all right?"

She clasped her hand to her heart and spun around. "Alice! I'm so sorry. I didn't mean to waken you."

"You didn't at all. My husband can take credit for that. You couldn't hear him snoring all the way in Gram's room, could you?" she whispered as she approached, wearing a long robe and a nightcap.

Ellie shook her head. "I just needed to walk off a few leg cramps," she explained.

"I knew it was too much for you to stay with Gram tonight, especially after all that riding you did," Alice replied as she walked along beside her.

"I wanted to stay. Besides, you and Grizel needed some rest, and Jackson's been taking care of the boys on his own for a good while. He knows how to get them both into bed."

"I still think you should have gone home with your family when they left after supper. Jackson was very understanding and forgiving with us for asking you to ride for Dr. Willows, but he did seem a bit reluctant to leave without you. I hope he isn't upset with you for staying."

Ellie swallowed hard. She was not about to tell this woman that he was upset because he wanted her off the island, not back at home with him or even here with the Grants. As far as she knew, he still felt that way; otherwise, he would have caught up with her and apologized instead of following along behind her all the way here. Once they arrived at the Grant homestead, there had not been a moment when they had been alone, even if he had wanted to apologize. "He knows how important it is for Gram to have someone with her," she said finally.

Alice took Ellie's arm and stopped, forcing Ellie to stop, as well. "I'm up and awake now, and I'd like to stay with Gram. I'm sorry I haven't a bed to offer you, but there's a good quilt on that rocking chair by the fire. You could rest fairly well there till morning."

"Are you certain you've had enough rest?"

Alice laughed. "As certain as I am that my husband will be snoring for the rest of the night."

"Then if it's all right with you, I think I'd like to go home so I can be there in the morning to fix breakfast."

"You want to go now? It's the middle of the night!"

"I know, but I could use the walk home to get rid of these leg cramps, and I wouldn't have to worry about waking anyone," she insisted, although she really did not like traveling after dusk, let alone when it was completely dark outside.

"But you hardly know your way around the island yet."

Ellie chuckled and took both of the woman's hands in her own. "I can hardly get lost if I stay on the roadway. Please promise you'll send for me tomorrow if you and Grizel need a rest or if Gram needs anything at all."

Alice squeezed her hands. "I will, but my husband will be here to help us. You be careful now. If anything happens to you on your way home, that husband of yours will not be as forgiving with me as he was today."

"I'll be fine," Ellie insisted. Without bothering to correct the woman's assumption about Jackson, she returned her hug and left for home. The moment she stepped outside, however, she had second and third thoughts about walking alone in the dead of night, even though the air was mild and there was not even the hint of a breeze.

The new moon overhead scarcely cast any light at all, which made it hard to see, and the amazing bed of stars tempted her to look overhead instead of where she was walking. Crickets and other critters filled the air with sounds both familiar and unfamiliar, but Ellie kept reminding herself as she walked that there were no predators on the island that would find her good prey.

When she passed the landing, she knew she was headed in the right direction and her confidence grew, along with her strength, now that her leg cramps had finally eased up. She could hear the river lapping at the shoreline to her right, just beyond the stand of trees, and she could smell the apples in the nearby orchards.

The only unnatural noise she heard at all was the crunching of her shoes on the roadbed as she made her way home, but the sound was not loud enough to drown out the echo of the order Jackson had given her when she had arrived home earlier today or the sound of those coins when they landed at her feet.

" 'Just leave,' " she said quietly, then stopped and looked up at the sky, searching above the dim shadow of the new moon and beyond the twinkling stars to heaven itself. She knew so little about Jackson, other than the fact that he had grown up an orphan and suffered yet more tragedy with the death of his young wife. She did know, however, that there was only one being in the entire universe who might help to heal his wounds and to heal hers, as well.

"Dear heavenly Father," she prayed. "I have come to trust that you brought me here as an answer to my prayers, but this marriage is so very hard for me and for Jackson, too. Please help us, Father. Help Daniel and Ethan, too, so that we might live in peace together now and one day, with your blessing, be a true family, all in accordance with your will," she whispered. The tears she had fought back all day fell freely.

When her well of tears was finally empty and all of her fears and troubles were gentled by the gift of His comfort and peace, she wiped her face and headed for home again with her heart not quite as heavy as it had been all day.

Renewed, she smiled when she finally saw the dark outline of the house, although it was still some distance ahead. A sudden rustling of the brush along the river side of the road behind her, however, sent her feet racing straight down the roadway toward the house to escape whatever animal was lurking about.

When she was too winded to take another step, she hid behind the first sizable tree she found close to the roadway. Panting for air, she tried to remind herself that there were no wild predators on the island that posed any real danger to her—but that did not prevent her imagination from suggesting that a bear or a panther or some other dangerous animal had managed to swim here to sample some of the fruit in the orchards or the animals kept at the Grant homestead.

Once her heart stopped thudding in her ears, she listened hard to hear if the animal had come this way. Eventually, when all was quiet, she ventured back to the roadway, snapping twigs underfoot as she walked through underbrush that snagged her skirts now and again.

She was no sooner back on the roadway than she heard that same rustling sound, only closer and much more ominous. This time, she did not look back. She simply picked up her skirts again and ran as if her life depended on it. She broke through the edge of the woods and dashed to the back porch steps, taking them two at a time.

Once she reached the porch, she lunged for the kitchen door. Trembling with fear and gasping for breath, she was inside the kitchen and had the door closed again before she realized she had not even had time to stop and make sure he had not bolted it against her.

She pressed her back to the door and closed her eyes. With her chest heaving and her heart pounding, she tried to soften her breaths to keep from waking everyone while she said a silent prayer of thanksgiving for arriving home all in one piece.

When she was no longer shaking and her heart was beating normally again, she opened her eyes. The weak light filtering into the kitchen from the great room was too dim to come from any of the oil lamps. Treading on tiptoe, she made her way through the shadowy kitchen to the doorway leading to the great room, where she discovered the light was coming from embers still burning in the fireplace. The great room itself was cast in shadows, with barely enough light to guide her steps.

Since Jackson did not expect her home for hours yet, she knew he had not left the door unbolted for her. She also knew he had not built the fire for her, either, but accepted both gestures as unexpected gifts. Treading on tiptoe, she paused when she found the door to her room closed. She was too unnerved to find sleep anytime soon after her harrowing experience, so instead she carried a chair over from the table, set it close to the fire so she could remove some of the debris caught in her skirts, and sat down.

"I certainly didn't need this," she grumbled as she pulled off a bramble caught in the hem of her skirts. When she realized how many brambles and thorns were caught on her clothing, she let out a sigh of exhaustion and frustration and let them drop.

"Maybe Jackson is right," she whispered. "Maybe this gown is so drab and ugly, I shouldn't bother with it at all. I could simply make do with the gray one until I can get to the city again. Unless he forces me to leave tomorrow, in which case, I'm lost. Totally lost."

"You're not lost, Ellie. I am."

She screamed and leapt to her feet, realizing only too late that the voice she heard belonged to someone she knew—someone who was apparently sitting on the settee right behind her.

Twenty-Six

When his wife bolted out of her chair so fast he thought she might fly up and hit the ceiling, Jackson rushed over to her. "It's only me. Jackson. Don't be afraid."

"You! You . . . you frightened me half to death!" she cried, clasping her hands to her heart.

He raked his fingers through his hair. "I'm sorry. When you first came into the room I thought you'd seen me sitting here."

"How? You were almost completely in the dark, and it's so late, I expected you to be in bed. You're never up at this hour."

He let out a long breath. The last thing he wanted to do was to turn her against him when there was so much he needed to say. "You're right. I'm sorry, but when you sat down and started talking to yourself, I realized you hadn't seen me, but there was no easy way to let you know I was there, either," he explained.

She frowned and cocked her head, as if listening for

something. "I hope I didn't wake the boys by screaming the way I did."

He shook his head. "I have the staircase door closed. Once they're asleep, there isn't much that can wake them up, other than a good storm. It's the middle of the night. Whatever possessed you to come back home, by yourself, no less? Is Gram any better?"

"No, she's doing about the same. Alice woke up and wanted to sit with her, so I decided to come home so I would be here to make breakfast," she murmured and looked down at her skirts, which were liberally covered with brambles and bits of brush. "I'm afraid I might have ruined my gown for good this time."

He grinned and thought he saw the corners of Ellie's mouth turn upward, as well.

"I thought I heard some kind of animal thrashing about on my way home, so I ran off the roadway part of the way home. That's how I got all this nonsense stuck to my skirts."

"Animal? What kind of animal?" Jackson asked, thankful the darkness masked the apprehension on his face.

She shuddered. "I didn't stand around waiting to find out. I'm afraid my imagination got the better of me. All I could envision was a panther or something had crossed over from the mainland, though I know that's not possible."

"Actually, it is possible," he said, concerned that something dreadful could have happened to her along the way if indeed it was a dangerous animal she had heard.

Her eyes widened. "It is? But you told me there weren't any dangerous animals here."

"I know what I said, but there has been a time or two when predators actually swam or walked across the river this time of year, because they're trying to fatten up before winter. I'll check around the island with Michael tomorrow, but just to be safe, you and the boys should stay close to the house until we're sure it wasn't anything more than a raccoon or possum out there tonight."

She wrapped her arms at her waist and nodded. "That's a request I'll gladly promise to keep."

"But you still haven't answered my question," he reminded her, anxious to distract her from her bad experience tonight. After he added a log to the fire, he pulled over another chair beside hers, sat down, and urged her to sit down again, as well.

She did so with a sigh. "Yes, I did answer you. I just told you, I wanted to be home to make breakfast."

"I heard that much, but I guess what I really want to know is why you came home at all," he said, his head downcast.

"You mean, why did I want to come home after how badly you misjudged me again? Or why I'd come back to an extremely unpredictable man who turns into an angry brute at a moment's notice and actually throws coins at his wife's feet? Or a man who doesn't trust his own wife when she's done nothing to deserve his mistrust or his disdain, a man who can't even support her as she tries to establish her own authority in order to raise his sons? Is that what you mean?"

Flinching at the coldness of her words, he swallowed hard. "Yes. That's what I mean."

When she held her silence, he studied her as the reflection of the fire danced across her face. Her dark eyes were glistening, as if they had captured every hurt he had inflicted upon her and shined them back at him. The heavy circles beneath her eyes, however, testified to her weariness, yet she sat here talking to him when she had every right to simply dismiss him.

"I came because I believe this is where I belong," she finally whispered as she twisted the gold wedding ring he had given her only days ago. "I don't know what you truly think of me when you're not blinded by your own anger, but I know how I try to think of you and the boys."

He stiffened, prepared to hear the worst, because he could not imagine her saying much good about them.

"I once thought that you and the boys . . . that you were God's gifts to me, gifts that I could hold on to for a lifetime, but now . . . now I wonder if you were all nothing more than temporary gifts, like the rainbow that lights up the sky after a storm or the rare flower that blooms in the midst of a snowstorm. Gifts that the Lord shares with us for just a moment," she said, her voice hushed. "As strong as I think my faith has become, it's not sturdy enough to withstand your anger and your mistrust. I'm not certain how long I can continue to remain here, but I'm not willing to give up just yet . . . which means I have no choice but to continue to pray for strength to be able to forgive you for what you did today and pray, as well, that you'll be kinder and more respectful of me in the future."

"Gifts," he repeated and looked off into the fire. "I've been called many things in my lifetime—most of which are not suitable to repeat in your presence—but a gift? Never that," he admitted, hoping one day he could silence the harsh, ugly words from his childhood that still echoed in his mind after all these years.

"You mean as a child?" she asked gently.

He nodded.

"Before or after your parents died?"

"Only after," he said quickly. "I don't remember much about them. I was only eight when they died in a freak carriage accident. Since I didn't have any brothers or sisters, knowing that my parents loved me was all I clung to when I shifted from one house to another for the next eight years."

He heard her draw in a long breath. "How many families did you live with?"

"All told? Six."

She gasped. "Six?"

He let the memories surface, one by one, then shoved them to the back of his mind again. "I never knew when I was going to be sent away again until I found my pathetic little bag sitting on the porch steps. It happened once or twice near the end of the year when another family bid lower and I was forced to move so the town could save money. Other times . . ."

He shrugged. "They never really said much, other than I had done something wrong or broken the rules and I had to leave. No further explanation. Just leave," he said, suddenly making the connection between his experiences as a child and his actions today. "I realize now that I was just treating you the same way they treated me. I know that doesn't make it right. But—"

"No, it doesn't," she said. "What happened after you left one of those homes?"

"I'd be sent to live with another family. And then another and then another. I finally ran away for good when I turned sixteen. I wandered around a bit, finding work wherever I could, and landed here two years later. I burned that old travel bag the same night James Gladson invited me to carve my initials into that tree."

"I'm so sorry," she whispered, meeting his gaze when he looked at her. "I had no idea how very, very difficult your childhood had been after your parents died."

"I thought I'd put that all in the past," he offered. "Obviously, I haven't." He was silent a moment before he finally voiced the thoughts rolling over and over in his mind. "I'm sorry, Ellie. I'm truly, truly sorry. I really wouldn't blame you if you wanted to leave after how badly I've acted today. But if you really meant it when you said you wanted to stay, I need you to know that I am going to try much harder not to ever misjudge you again."

He removed the thong of leather he had fashioned into a makeshift chain that was hanging around his neck. After easing it over his head, he held it out so she could see the object hanging from the narrow strip of leather.

Her eyes widened as she stared at the badly scorched wedding ring. "Is that my ring?"

"Yes."

"But I saw you toss it into the fire," she argued, her gaze glistening with tears.

"I did, but—"

"But why? Why would you do something so cruel?"

As he laid the leather thong with the ring onto his lap, he lowered his gaze and swallowed hard. "I've sat here for hours asking myself the same question."

"Did you ever come up with an answer?"

He let out a long, deep breath. Admitting his faults to himself had been hard. Admitting his faults to her now was even harder, but he raised his gaze to meet hers. "I knew how much the ring meant to you. I think I even knew that you wouldn't have hidden it away from me and that you must have found it over the course of the day. But I was so angry when I read the note Grizel left, I deliberately kept it, instead of packing it into your travel bag with that silhouette I found."

She blinked back her tears. "If you were so angry with me, why would you want to keep my wedding ring?"

"In all truth, I'm still not certain," he replied, holding her gaze. "Then later, when you were so stubborn and insisted on staying here, even though I told you over and over that you had to leave, I think I realized the only way to get you to go was to hurt you so badly you wouldn't want to stay. That's when I tossed the ring into the fire. I'm sorry. It was cruel of me."

She moistened her lips but did not look away. "Yes, it was very cruel and very hurtful."

"Fortunately, for both of us, the ring took a good bounce and ended up lying in the corner of the hearth. I managed to get it out of the fireplace before the flames reached it."

Ellie made a fist with her hand, as if protecting the gold ring she now wore. "I don't understand why you'd try to destroy that ring one moment, rescue it the next, and then loop it onto a thong of leather to wear around your neck."

"Because of you."

Her gaze was wary.

"No matter what I said or did, I couldn't make you leave. I couldn't even make you angry enough to lose your temper. But it wasn't until you told me you were going back to the Grants' to check on Gram and to fetch the boys home that I finally realized my grave error. Once I realized the ring hadn't been destroyed, I thought I should keep it as a reminder of a promise I made to myself—a promise I want to make to you now—that I won't ever let my anger blind me again and jump to conclusions before I give you a chance to explain. And . . . and I'll be more supportive with Daniel and Ethan, too."

When she nodded, he could see the hurt he had done to her was still shimmering in her eyes, but he did detect just a glimmer of relief, too. His relief was just as real, and he quickly slipped the leather thong over his head and tucked it beneath his shirt again.

"Would you like to know where I found the ring?" she asked.

"I assume it was somewhere in the kitchen, but that's not important now. What's important is that—"

"I found it in Daniel's pillowcase, along with a silhouette of my mother that had disappeared from my room. Actually, they were both in the pillowcase with Rebecca's pillow, the one he brought home with him several weeks ago from your Sunday house."

Shocked, he listened carefully as she explained how she had discovered the missing treasures, as well as the boys' secret tent they had been using during the night.

"The only way Daniel could have known about the silhouette is through Ethan, which proves he does talk to Daniel. There's no other explanation," she concluded.

He could draw no other conclusion, either, and told her so. "What do I do with Daniel now?"

Her gaze softened. "I don't know. I put the pillowcase back on the pillow again. Once he realizes the treasures he's collected are gone, which he may have already done, he's bound to worry about where they've gone. I suspect Ethan will tell him I was in the room earlier today cleaning, so Daniel will just assume that I found them and reclaimed them."

"Which means he'll expect that you'll tell me and then he'll worry about what I'm going to do to punish him."

"I think that's likely, too."

He swallowed the lump in his throat. "If I punish him, which he deserves, he'll only turn against you more than he already has. But he has to learn that what he did was wrong."

She shifted in her seat. "I think I'd like to talk to him first. Perhaps I can convince him to come to you and confess what he's done," she suggested. "Then we can sit down together, all four of us, since Ethan is involved, too, and decide what to do."

"When?"

"I don't want to wait too long. Later today. Perhaps he could stay home with me this afternoon. Once Ethan takes his nap, Daniel and I would have some time alone to talk."

"Then you're really not leaving," he said, shaking his head.

She sighed, but it was several very long, tense moments before she answered him. "No. I'm not leaving."

"I suppose I still find that hard to believe."

She sat up straighter and squared her shoulders. "Please don't mistake my view of you and the boys as gifts or my commitment to our marriage as some sort of invitation to continue exploding at me whenever you get upset with something I do. I want to stay and I want to make our marriage work for the boys' sake, but there's little hope I'll be able to do that. Not unless and until you do something about the anger you've been carrying around for so long that you don't even know it's there until it erupts and nearly consumes you and everyone around you."

Jackson stared at her. No other woman, or man, for that matter, had ever had the audacity to talk to him like this. No other woman had ever challenged him the way she had over the past month. No other woman had ever been as confident of herself or her faith, either.

He had not anticipated her boldness or her honesty. He had not invited her tenacity, for that matter. But since she apparently had no immediate plans to leave, he needed to prove to her that he could be just as bold or honest or tenacious as she was.

Starting right here and right now.

Twenty-Seven

Ellie caught her breath and held it, but when Jackson stiffened his back, she knew she had spoken to him too brashly.

Unfortunately, she was too exhausted to care much about his feelings, unless he was so offended he would try to put her out of the house again. In that case, she was not so sure she would not end up sleeping on the porch, when all she wanted was the comfort of her own bed.

"You make it sound as if I haven't tried to control my anger. It's not that easy," he argued.

His gaze was so cold Ellie shivered and shifted her gaze from him to the fire. "It's never easy."

"As if you'd know," he quipped. "Did you grow up as an orphan? Do you know what it's like watching other kids grow up with their parents, knowing you'll never have that again?

Do you know how hard it is to fall asleep at night when you're barely ten years old, knowing no one cares, really cares about you? Or that you're all alone in this world?"

His words were so harshly spoken, she nearly cringed. "No, of course I don't, but—"

"Then please don't tell me it's never easy. You'd never know how hard it was for me, because you grew up with parents who loved you."

"That doesn't mean I don't have hurts I have to forgive or resentments that dig deep into my soul," she replied.

"That's not the same thing at all."

"Why? Because you assume that growing up with my parents was idyllic? Or that I may have suffered my hurts or harbored my resentments more as an adult than as a child? They're still as real to me as yours are. The only difference between you and me is that I'm trying to let go of my disappointments and my anger, while you continue to hold on to yours," she charged, unable to stop the flow of her thoughts as they became words.

To her relief, he did not reply right away, but when he did speak, his voice was low and even. "What resentments?"

She sighed and looked at him again, grateful to see his gaze had actually softened a bit, too. "You're a man. You couldn't possibly . . . understand."

He crossed his arms over his chest.

"Fine. Then I'll tell you," she said, although the thought of sharing details of her life with him when she had not shared them with anyone else before made her uncomfortable. "When you were eighteen and found a home here with James Gladson, I was turning twenty-one, still living at home with my parents. My mother had been an invalid for almost as long as I can remember, so I was expected to stay and keep house for my parents, which I did willingly. After my father died, I cared for my mother until she finally died, too. That was three years ago."

"That much I knew, although I didn't realize your mother had been sickly."

"What I haven't shared with you was that by the time I was free to marry, I was twenty-eight. I was too old to be considered a good marriage prospect, which is not something men have to worry about, is it? Men can marry or remarry at any age and still have children. Women can't." She twisted the ring on her finger as her cheeks warmed.

"I loved my parents, and I treasure my memories of them," she added before he misconstrued what she was trying to say. "I'll never regret the years I spent caring for them. I was obviously much older when I became an orphan than you were, but all I was left with after they had both died was a travel bag that held what little I owned, memories of the two ridiculous proposals I'd turned down over the years in order to care for them, and a deep resentment, even anger, that I had to depend on the charity of my cousins just to survive."

He furrowed his brow. "You were angry with your parents?"

"For a time, yes—but I was also angry with God," she admitted and bowed her head for a moment. "I couldn't understand why He'd given this lonely, difficult life to me. Other women my age had already married. They had husbands and homes and children of their own, while I ended up with nothing. All I had to look forward to was spending the rest of my life living with Cousin Philip, which turned out to be much harder than I thought it would be, as I've already told you. Being sent off to live with Cousin Mark didn't improve things, which only made me angrier," she added.

"Then why are you lecturing me about my being angry when you just admitted that you get angry, too?" Jackson asked.

"Because I know in my heart that uncontrolled anger is wrong. It's destructive and . . . and it's pointless . . . so I've tried to forgive others who hurt me, because it's what God expects me to do. It's what we should all do. I'm still struggling to do that, because if I don't, I know I'll never be able to embrace the gifts God has chosen for me, instead of longing for the gifts He's given to others."

He snorted. "Through forgiveness."

"In part, yes," she said, troubled that he did not understand what she was trying to say. After taking a deep breath, as well as a leap of faith, she swallowed hard. "Do you know what Cousin Mark's wife, Olivia, said when I told her we had gotten married?"

He shrugged. "I would hope she offered her sincere congratulations."

"She wanted me to know that the only reason you married me was because I was so uncommonly plain, you'd never have to worry that I'd betray you like Rebecca had done simply because no other man could possibly want me. But that was only after Cousin Mark wanted to know how I could possibly decide to get married without asking him first, especially since I had chosen to marry a man whose name was still tainted by scandal."

"How charitable of them," Jackson quipped.

"I agree, but we're all less than charitable at one time or another. I'm not saying I'm not deeply, deeply hurt and disappointed with them or with you for wanting to toss me out of your life today without giving me a chance to explain why I'd left the island, but I wasn't angry. Just hurt. I still am." To be honest, what hurt even more was that Jackson did not even try to soften her cousin's assessment of why he had married her.

Jackson shook his head. "I still don't understand why you're not angry with me. It's not the first time I've misjudged you."

She stifled a yawn. "I'm not certain I do, either, but I think it's because I'm no longer afraid you'll set me aside, because in all truth, there isn't a thing I can do to stop you if that's what you really want to do."

Before he could offer a word in his own defense, she held up her hand before she lost the courage to finish what she had to say. "My mother gave me some good advice many years ago, but even though I truly believe her advice was good, it's still a struggle for me to follow it," she admitted.

"What advice would that be?"

"She said that fear was the root of all anger, but forgiveness was the balm that could put most fears to rest. And it's through faith that we find forgiveness for ourselves and the courage to forgive others."

He shifted in his seat. "What are you trying to say now? That I'm only angry because I'm afraid? And that I need to forgive all those people who mistreated me as a child?"

She moistened her lips. "I think we have no other choice but to forgive anyone who's hurt us. Eventually."

Her words hung in the air as he turned away and stared into the fire. Jackson had been angry for so long she was not certain he could recognize his fears and let that anger go, especially if that involved forgiving all the people who had ever hurt him. Including, she suspected, his late wife.

Ellie wanted to reach out to touch him, to let him know that he was not alone in his struggle, but she kept her hands folded on her lap. She could see him wrestling with her words by the way he clenched and unclenched his jaw and prayed that he would not reject them in the end.

"I wouldn't know how to begin," he murmured.

She smiled when he looked up at her. "You claim to be a man of faith. If you are, you'll let Him guide you. Going to services faithfully each week might help, too, as long as the weather cooperates."

"What if I fail?"

"Then you'll just have to do what I do. Pray harder and try again."

Jackson shook his head. "I can't imagine you fail at anything you set your mind to do."

She snorted. "Remind me to tell you someday of the time I tried to milk a bull cow."

He laughed out loud. "A bull cow? You didn't!"

"I've got the scars to prove it," she protested as her cheeks started to burn. There was no way this man was ever going to see those scars unless he was her husband in every sense of the word. To add to her embarrassment, her stomach growled so loudly it practically echoed in the room.

Grinning, he patted his stomach. "I wouldn't mind a snack myself. I wasn't in the mood to eat much at supper."

"Neither was I," she admitted. Between worrying about Gram and wondering what Jackson was going to do or say when they were finally alone together, she had barely touched the supper Alice and Grizel had made.

"Alice sent some apple muffins home with me. We could sample a few," he suggested, "although I think Daniel and Ethan are looking forward to having some with breakfast."

"As long as I make griddle cakes for the boys, I think they'll be happy. But if they're disappointed the apple muffins are all gone, I can always make more," she offered.

He cocked his head. "That reminds me. I never did stop to see Caden James today."

She waved off his words. "You needn't bother. I'm getting better at using that iron contraption on my own."

"You've had a long day. Are you sure you aren't too tired to stay up for a snack?"

When her stomach growled again, she sighed and got to her feet. "I'm exceedingly tired, but I'm afraid I've never been too tired to eat."

He stood up, too, and smiled. "Spoken like a woman who could steal any man's heart."

She walked alongside him as they tiptoed to the kitchen together. There was only one man she knew who could steal her heart, and he already had, despite how deeply he had hurt her. He just did not know it, and he never would, because the one fear she had yet to conquer was still too new: She was afraid she might have to spend the rest of her life with a man who would never be able to love her back.

Twenty-Eight

With little more than a few hours' sleep, Ellie rose at first light to a clear sky and the promise of balmy weather. After making a fresh batch of apple muffins to replace the half dozen she and Jackson had polished off, she spent the rest of the morning planning and preparing for her talk with Daniel. Fortunately, Jackson had agreed that Ethan needed to be part of that discussion, too, and had left it up to her to decide exactly how she wanted to approach the boys.

Anxious to introduce her plan now that Jackson had confirmed there was no evidence of any predators on the island, she set a pan of warm apple crisp onto the dinner table. Grinning, she sat down to join the rest of her family for dessert.

"Is something funny?" Jackson asked as she dished out a large serving for him.

"Not really," she said and passed the bowl to him. "There's cream in the pitcher. Daniel, will you pass the cream to your father?"

Daniel nearly knocked the pitcher over but managed to keep it upright. "Can I have a big bowl like Pappy's?"

Her grin widened. "May I?"

He bobbed his head. "May I have one like Pappy's? Ethan wants one, too."

"You both have to eat it all," she cautioned.

When they grinned back at her, she dished out a serving almost as large as the one she had given Jackson and set one in front of each of them. She poured a generous dollop of cream on top and smiled. "Taking a nap for most of the morning has done wonders for your appetites," she teased as they started to devour the dessert.

Having a few hours to herself did wonders for her, too. Everything she needed for their talk was packed up in a large basket she had set outside on the back porch.

Jackson paused between bites. "Who took a nap this morning?"

"I did," Daniel replied. "Ethan did, too."

Ethan bobbed his head, dripping apple crisp down his chin to the front of his shirt.

Ellie dabbed it off with her napkin. "Since the boys couldn't go outside to play until you made sure it was safe, the boys wanted to play upstairs in their room," she explained. "I'm not certain whether they got bored or tired, but they ended up sleeping away most of the morning."

Jackson shrugged. "Napping wouldn't account for a good appetite. It must be something else that's made them eat so well at dinner. Maybe it's because they're celebrating something," he teased as he scooped up the last of his dessert.

Hopeful he had actually noticed what she had managed to do, her heart skipped a beat. "What might that be?"

He held his spoon in midair as if offering a toast. "Congratulations. This is the finest meal you've cooked for us."

She grinned, her heart bursting with pride. "Thank you. And thank you for not saying this was the first meal where I didn't burn a single thing."

"You're welcome," he said before polishing off the last spoonful.

She glanced at Daniel, wondering if he would have his usual comment about how well his mother had always cooked, but he was too busy eating to say anything.

"What are your plans for the afternoon?" Jackson asked, giving her the opening she needed.

"Since the boys have been inside all morning, I thought we could walk back to the orchards with you like we usually do and then leave to collect some river stones."

Daniel's head popped up. So did Ethan's.

Their eyes were wide with interest, but Jackson's gaze narrowed. "River stones?"

She savored a bite of dessert and swallowed it. "Yes. They make a good border. I saw lots of them at the landing, which is probably the safest place to collect them. The boys wouldn't even have to get close to the river's edge to get what we need."

"Can we, Pappy? We wouldn't get our shoes wet," Daniel promised.

"I'll watch them very, very carefully, although I can't promise their shoes won't end up drying on the porch by the end of the day. The Grants are nearby, so I thought we might stop to see how Gram is doing, too," Ellie added. If Jackson did not allow them to go, then her entire plan for how and where she wanted to talk to Daniel and Ethan would fall apart.

Daniel looked at his father. "Please, Pappy? You let Mama take us to the landing for river stones. We'll be good, good, good for Miss Ellie, too."

When Jackson hesitated, she thought for certain he was going to refuse her request, especially when he gave both his sons a hard look. "You must listen to Miss Ellie and do everything she tells you to do. Everything. Is that clear?" he said sternly.

"Yes, Pappy."

Ethan grinned.

So did Ellie. If the afternoon continued to be as fruitful, it would be a very fine day, but she had no illusions. A great deal depended on what would happen this afternoon.

"Aren't you going to finish your dessert?" Jackson asked.

"You can have it if you like. I need to change my gown before I take the boys to the landing."

He glanced at the gray gown she was wearing and groaned. "You only have one other gown. I thought you said it was ruined."

"The brown gown will do just fine for collecting river stones," she replied and hurried to her room.

If Ellie had not been so driven to succeed with the boys, she would have given in to sheer exhaustion by the time they reached their final destination of the day.

Instead, she pulled out the last of the weeds from the family cemetery and let Daniel and Ethan add them to the pile sitting just beyond the border of old river stones that were as easy to see now as the headstones. After visiting for a brief spell with

Gram today, however, Ellie was concerned it would not be very long before the aged woman was called home.

She was also surprised that neither boy seemed to be overly troubled being here at the cemetery and wondered whether or not they had been here when their mother was buried or if they had blocked out all memory of that day. She still was not certain they even realized the significance of the headstones or the cemetery itself, even though she had explained it as best she could when they had first arrived.

At least here, protected by the canopy of trees, they all had some relief from the sun, and she did not have to worry about either of them wandering too close to the river. If she had known how much work it was to collect the stones and then carry them all the way back here, however, she would have packed a snack for all of them, too.

When the boys returned, she opened the bags of river stones they had collected earlier. "Just add these to the line of stones on the ground so it's wider. If there's a special stone you'd like to keep to take home, you can put it in the basket," she suggested.

Daniel pulled a dark stone out of his pocket and put it into the basket. "My mama liked the dark ones."

"I like the lighter ones, I think," she offered as she helped Ethan get a handful of stones. "Which ones do you like best?"

Ethan shrugged, but she noticed he had picked out several more dark stones for himself.

Taking a handful of stones, she added them to the original border and followed the boys as they worked the perimeter of the final resting places for their grandfather and mother. By the time they were finished widening the border of river stones, they had also filled half the basket with stones to take home.

All of them were dark in color.

After saying a silent prayer that God would help her to find the right words to say, she stood at the edge of the border facing the headstones, which lay stark and bare against the earth now, and took each boy by the hand. "Thank you both. You did a fine, fine job," she said and looked down at Daniel. "Would you like me to read the names on the headstones for you before we leave?"

He scrunched up his face. "Which one is for Grandpa?"

She led the two boys to the headstone and knelt down so she would be at their level. "This is his stone. His name was James Gladson, and it's etched right here," she said. Pointing to the letters, she realized that it was probably time to start teaching Daniel how to read and write and made a mental note to ask Jackson about doing so.

"Do you remember your grandfather?"

Daniel shook his head. "No, but Pappy said Grandpa made my blocks."

"That's right," she said and saw Ethan smile. "He lived here on the island first," she continued and pointed to the first of the three headstones on the other side of his grandfather's. "His wife, Emily, is buried next to him. She was your grandmother, but your grandfather had been married twice before they were married. His first two wives are buried here with him, too," she said, hoping the boy would realize that his father was not the only one who had had more than one wife.

"Grandpa's not here. He's in heaven," Daniel countered, letting go of her hand. He walked around to take hold of Ethan's other hand. "Mama said so."

"Your mama was right. His soul is in heaven, but we have a stone here with his name on it, just like we have one with your mother's name on it, to remind us how very much they loved you. That's why it's so important to keep the cemetery looking pretty, like we did today," she said, hoping this simple explanation would not be too much for either boy to accept.

Daniel hesitated for a moment, let go of Ethan's hand, and walked over to the small headstone next to his grandfather's. "Is this my mama's?"

When she nodded, Daniel knelt down and traced the etching of her name with his fingers while Ethan watched. "Does it say Mama?"

She swallowed the lump in her throat. "Yes. It has her name and then it says 'beloved wife and mother.' Some people say that when someone they love has died and gone to heaven, they like to visit the cemetery and sit by their loved one's headstone so they can remember them better," she ventured.

"Pappy brought us here once, but it didn't look pretty like it does now," Daniel replied.

"It's too late to plant flowers here to replace the ones the weeds strangled, but maybe you and Ethan would like to help me plant some in the spring," Ellie suggested.

"We don't need flowers. My mama liked river stones. Come on, Ethan." With his brother following right on his heels, they ran back to the basket and returned with handfuls of dark river stones. They laid them around the base of Rebecca's headstone.

"The stones look beautiful there," she said. She reached into her apron pocket and fingered the silhouette of her mother. "I'm sure your mama would like that much better than flowers. Maybe another day we can collect more stones, and you could put them around all the other headstones, too."

Standing with his brother near the top of the headstone, Daniel looked up at her, his eyes wide with expectation. "Can me and Ethan really come here again?"

She smiled. "Yes, you may, but you can't come out here alone. Your father or I need to come with you and Ethan until you're both a little older."

When Daniel frowned at her response, she frowned, as well. "I wish I could visit my mother's headstone," she said.

"Your mama's in heaven, too?" Daniel asked.

Her heart started to race in anticipation of confronting Daniel with what he had done, although his question confused her. If she was right to assume Ethan had told Daniel the silhouette existed, then he should have told Daniel that her mother was dead, too, unless Ethan had not told him everything.

"My mother died three years ago. I can't visit her headstone because it's a long, long way from here, but I have something else that's very precious to me, something that reminds me of her and how much she loved me." She kept her voice as soft and gentle as she could.

Trusting in God to continue to guide her, she took the silhouette out of her pocket and held it up for both boys to see. "This is a silhouette of my mother's image. I hadn't even realized someone had taken it until I found it yesterday, hidden inside the pillowcase with your mama's pillow."

When Ethan's little face crumpled and giant tears tumbled down Daniel's cheeks, she caught her breath. She was not surprised that both boys were crying, now that they both knew they had been caught stealing. She was determined to use their transgression to help them learn from this mistake, but she would need the Lord's help to lead them to accept her place in their lives, as well as their hearts.

And so she waited, patiently and prayerfully, for the boys to exhaust their tears, with all of their futures hanging in the balance.

Twenty-Nine

"I didn't take it. I didn't," Daniel cried, his cheeks glistening with the last of his tears. "Ethan did it. He took it, not me."

Still resisting the urge to take each of the boys into her arms to console them, Ellie held firm against Daniel's lie. "Ethan can't open the chest drawer by himself, can he?"

Daniel sniffled back a few tears, but his face was berry red. "No."

"Then you must have opened the drawer for him."

"Yes."

"After he told you about the silhouette?"

He nodded, albeit reluctantly.

"Did Ethan take the silhouette out of the drawer?" she asked, knowing how literal a child could be when it was necessary or convenient.

Another nod, but this time, Daniel reached over to put his arm around his younger brother, as if protecting him. "He loses stuff, so I kept it for him."

"But why? Why would you help him keep something that belongs to me? And, Ethan, why would you take something that you knew was so important to me?" she asked gently.

She hoped Ethan would be tempted to respond, but as always, he let his brother speak for him. "He said the lady in the picture looked like our mama," Daniel whispered and arched his back the same way his father tended to do when he was being defensive. "She does. Ask Pappy if you don't believe me. She really does. Ethan just wanted to be able to look at the picture when he was feeling sad."

Her heart trembled, unleashing the memory of watching Ethan trace the image over and over again the day he had found the silhouette when he was helping her to unpack. Knowing that she was right to believe Daniel when he claimed Ethan talked to him mattered very little now when so much more was at stake. "Is that why you took my wooden wedding ring, too, and hid it from me? Because it reminded you of your mother's?" she asked. She slipped the silhouette back into her pocket, doubtful that Rebecca would have worn a ring as simple as the one Jackson now wore on the leather thong around his neck.

Daniel dropped his gaze, as silent now as his brother.

She waited, giving the boy time to answer. Her patience, if not her confidence that she was doing the right thing, was stretched nearly to the breaking point when he finally spoke again.

"I didn't take the ring. I found it on the floor in the kitchen under the cookstove."

She sighed. She had looked under the cookstove twice, but

Daniel had apparently taken the ring already. "What were you doing looking under the cookstove?"

"Ethan lost one of our blocks again. I was trying to find it," he explained. "I thought you didn't want the ring anymore, so I kept it."

"Your father gave it to me. Why wouldn't I want it?"

Daniel shrugged his narrow shoulders. " 'Cause it wasn't pretty. My mama only liked to wear things that were pretty."

Ellie swallowed hard, recalling all the pretties Rebecca had kept at the Sunday house. "You kept my ring without asking me first if I wanted it back?"

"Pappy bought you a new one. It's lots prettier," he countered.

"Yes, he did, but that's not the issue," she insisted. "You and Ethan were both wrong to take something that didn't belong to you. You upset me. And you upset your father."

The moment she mentioned their father, each boy unleashed a fresh round of tears. Still, she held her ground, knowing it was important for each boy to feel remorse, even if it was simply because they had gotten caught or feared the punishment their father would mete out. Recognizing what they had done as a sin that their heavenly Father would forgive them for was something she and Jackson needed to continue to help them to learn.

"Pappy's terrible mad, isn't he?" Daniel managed between hiccoughs.

Ellie shook her head. "He's not angry with you now. He's disappointed in you. Simply apologizing won't be quite enough this time, will it?" she asked, reminding them of the apologies she had accepted after they had disobeyed her and ended up in the mud puddle, then tracked in mud on her newly scrubbed floor.

Daniel's eyes widened. "But we're really, really sorry, aren't we, Ethan?" he asked, receiving a nod in reply.

"Being sorry for what you've done is important, but it's your father's place and my place to make sure you learn never to steal something again. If that means a punishment of some sort, I'm sure we'll be fair to both of you, especially if you remember that stealing is a sin and you need to ask for God's forgiveness, too, when you say your prayers tonight."

"When do we have to tell Pappy?"

She smiled. "I'm hoping we can all sit down and talk this through later today. In the meantime, I have something I want to give back to you to remind you that God's angels are always here to help you when you're tempted to do something wrong."

The boys looked at her as if she was a bit touched by the sun for offering them a present, but they eagerly followed her back to the basket. "Before I give this to you, I want you to understand that you have to share it."

"We will," Daniel promised for both of them, although his gaze remained skeptical.

She lifted out the canvas pouch she had stored inside the basket and removed the Jacob's Ladder she had repaired. When Ethan reached for it, she let him hold it. "You both remember this, don't you?"

Daniel nodded. "But ours broked."

"Broke," she corrected gently. "But it's not broken anymore. I fixed it for you, with your mother's ribbons. The ones Ethan brought home the day you took your mother's pillow, remember?"

When Ethan had trouble getting the blocks to fall, end over end, Daniel helped him, but all Ethan wanted to do was finger each of the ribbons. "I remember this toy. Mama gave it to us."

"Did she tell you the story of Jacob?"

"She said he dreamed about angels on a ladder that reached all the way up to heaven. They climbed up the ladder and down again and up and down and up and down," Daniel replied as he used the blocks to demonstrate. Annoyed, Ethan grabbed at the blocks and held them still, and Daniel surrendered the toy to his brother.

As the boys took turns playing with the Jacob's Ladder, Ellie had visions of many repairs to the toy that lay waiting for her in the days ahead. But she also had hope that one day soon, these two precious boys would discover there was still room in their little hearts to love her as well as their mother. Inspired by how nicely they were sharing the toy, just as they always shared their blocks, she took the silhouette of her mother out of her pocket again.

She caught both boys' attention. "I have an idea," she said, encouraged by the way Ethan's eyes lit up the moment he saw the silhouette again. "Instead of keeping this in my drawer, I think I should ask your father to make a frame for it, and one for my father's silhouette, too. That way, I could hang them up where we can all see them anytime we want," she suggested and handed the image of her mother to Ethan. "I can't let you keep the silhouette, but I'd like to share it with you. Would you like to carry it back home for me?"

His eyes fairly danced with joy and he bobbed his head so fast his little cowlick danced, too.

Not to be outdone, Daniel puffed out his chest. "We share our blocks from Grandpa, too."

"And you share your bedroom, too," she added. Instead of mentioning the makeshift tent they also shared, she tried to expand the concept of sharing to the adults in their lives. "Does anyone else you know share their things?"

Daniel shook his head. "Pappy doesn't like to share his dessert 'cause he wants to eat all of it."

She chuckled. "That's true, but he shares everything he works for and his house with you. He doesn't keep them to himself. Can you think of anything else he shares with someone?"

Ethan appeared to be ignoring her. He was too engrossed rubbing the silhouette image with his thumb, and she tried not to worry that he was smearing dirt on it.

Daniel, on the other hand, was fully engaged in their conversation. "After that big, big storm, with all the wind and rain and stuff, Pappy shared his old boots with you 'cause you didn't have none."

She brightened, too pleased with his example to correct his grammar. "Yes, he did. He shared his old boots with me several times since then, but I couldn't keep them. They belong to your father," she offered and smiled at each of them. "Your father is a very kind and generous man, and he loves you both very much. He knows how much you miss your mama, but he needs someone to help him to take care of both of you. That's why he married me," she said.

She paused to glance down at Rebecca's headstone for a moment before looking back at both of the boys. "Do you think your mama would mind very much if your father shared me with both of you?"

Daniel studied his mother's headstone for a very, very long time. Even Ethan turned his attention away from the silhouette he was holding to do the same. When Daniel finally looked up at Ellie again, his gaze was troubled. "We wouldn't have to keep you, would we?"

She blinked back tears, hopeful that one day they would not only want to keep her, but love her. "No," she murmured. "You wouldn't have to keep me, but I'd be there for both of you whenever you needed something, like the new clothes I made for you or the toy I repaired for you."

"Or griddle cakes. Me and Ethan need them for breakfast every day," Daniel suggested.

"Or griddle cakes," she said, chuckling.

Daniel shrugged. "I don't think Mama would be mad at us, as long as we just shared you with Pappy and didn't keep you for good. If she comes back, she'll just be mad with Pappy," he reasoned, still shifting from understanding his mother was in heaven to believing she might come back someday.

"I don't think she'd be mad at you at all, Daniel," Ellie ventured and stooped down in front of Ethan. "What do you think, Ethan? Do you think it would be all right if Pappy shared me with you, too?" she asked, hoping he might be tempted to speak to her for the first time.

But that precious boy did not speak, leaving Ellie to wonder if he would ever accept her at all.

Thirty

Three days later, Sunday morning arrived without any sign of rain at all for the first time in over a month!

The sun was bright and the air was fall crisp, promising cooler weather now that September was waning away. After attending services for the first time since they had gotten married and speaking briefly with Reverend Shore about his sermon today, Ellie held on to Jackson's arm as they left the redbrick church that overlooked the Susquehanna River.

There were a lot of families in the treelined yard in front of the church who milled about in groups, but instead of worrying about whether or not Cousin Mark and his wife were there, waiting to greet either her or Jackson with a snide comment, Ellie kept a good eye on the boys, who had gotten permission to race ahead to enjoy a rare opportunity to play with the other children.

She spied the boys playing tag and smiled. The long faces they had worn at breakfast again today were gone, but she knew they would return tomorrow morning. Being denied a single bite of griddle cakes for a month might not seem to be much, but the punishment she and Jackson had devised for the boys suited them perfectly.

Glancing down at her cape, however, her smile faded into a frown. She was not nearly as well dressed as the other women who had been at services today, and she felt more than a little self-conscious about her appearance. If it had not been Sunday, when all of the shops were closed, she might have been tempted to take the boys with her to Madeline French's shop instead of taking them for a walk while Jackson cleaned out the rest of Rebecca's things at the Sunday house.

Disappointed to have to wait until Market Day, she glanced over at her husband as they made their way down the brick steps and moistened her lips. Although he was unusually tense, if not distant, he looked positively dashing in his navy frock coat, which was nearly the exact color of his eyes. To her, he was the most handsome man there, and judging by the way a number of other women had looked their way during the service, she knew they found him equally attractive. She also suspected there would be a fair number of women, as well as men, who might agree that the new Mrs. Jackson Smith looked even plainer than usual when she stood by his side.

Jackson caught her gaze, smiled briefly, and leaned toward her. "I'm not certain, but I think except for the Grants, every member of the congregation actually came to services today," he offered.

"Including us," she teased. "The fact that it's rained every

Sunday for the past month might have something to do with it."

"Perhaps," he replied, "though curiosity is probably the most likely reason many of them came." He scanned the churchyard.

When they reached the bottom of the steps, she pointed to the right. "The boys are over there, next to the oak tree."

Avoiding the different groups of people chatting in the churchyard, he guided her off the walkway and across the lawn toward the front of the parsonage to stand next to a row of fading lilac bushes, where they had a bit of privacy, yet still had a good view of the boys.

"Curiosity about what?" she asked when he finally stopped them.

He glanced at her again, his gaze troubled. "They're bound to be curious about both of us, but I'm fairly certain they're far more interested in talking to me than they are you," he admitted and eyed the churchyard again, as if trying to decide if he wanted to stay to talk to the other members of the congregation or simply collect the boys and head for home.

"Why are you so worried about talking to anyone here? We're at church," she questioned.

"That may be, but if the last place you'd expect to find a few people willing to engage in vicious gossip is at church, you'd be sadly mistaken—since there are any number here who are hiding their evil intentions beneath a cloak of self-righteousness," he countered.

"But they should be happy for you now that you've remarried, because they must know how hard it's been for you raising the boys on your own," she argued more forcefully.

His gaze darkened. "They all knew Rebecca, too." He cleared his throat, caught her gaze, and held it. "I wanted to talk to you about something last night, but by the time I got the boys in bed after visiting Gram, you weren't up."

"I was tired," she replied, which was only partly true. In point of fact, now that he had started to spend time each night sitting in front of the fire reading the Bible, she had started retiring to her room earlier to give him a bit of privacy, particularly since he had never invited her to join him. "If I'd known you wanted to talk to me—"

"No, it's my fault. I shouldn't have waited until the last minute, which sounds ridiculous now, since we've already been to services and it'll be difficult, if not impossible, to leave without stopping to speak to anyone."

She smiled. "Then just tell me quickly now."

He cleared his throat again. "I've already told you why there was a good bit of scandal surrounding Rebecca's death."

"I remember."

When he narrowed his gaze, she felt the muscles in his arm tense. He clenched and unclenched his jaw, but she held his gaze and refused to look away. When he finally spoke, his voice was just above a whisper. "I don't want to stay and introduce you around to the entire congregation today and receive their good wishes, only to reappear next week or the following week having to explain that you left me because . . . because you didn't want to stay married to a man like me any more than Rebecca did."

Ellie tightened her hold on his arm and looked at the man who was gazing at her now, silently asking for her support and understanding as he struggled with his fears and his anger, if not his very faith. "I'm not Rebecca. I'm Ellie, and I'm trying very hard to trust you when you tell me you want to change and that you want to make this marriage work, especially for the boys' sake. What matters to me is that we're both trying our best and we're both relying on God to help us. Now, can we please join the others? I think once we—"

"Yoo-hoo! Mr. Smith, don't slip off with that new wife of yours quite yet. There's someone I want her to meet."

Ellie looked up and saw Mrs. Fielding waddling toward them with an elderly woman. "I don't think we have anything to fear from Mrs. Fielding today, do we?"

He shrugged and reluctantly led her toward the two women. "Not unless the woman wants a basket of apples delivered to her sister again this week, in which case I'll have to make sure I have a spare set of clothing, just in case I happen to run into another young rascal with a wheelbarrow filled with manure."

Chuckling, Ellie caught a glimpse of several other members of the congregation following the two women before Mrs. Fielding blocked her view. Half an hour later, Cousin Mark and his wife passed by with little more than a curt nod, but Christina Schuler, the woman Ellie had met at Olivia's shop on her wedding day, quickly approached, accompanied by two other elegantly dressed women.

She took a small step closer to her husband and noted his smile had slipped into a frown.

Wearing a stunning russet cape trimmed with fur, which Ellie assumed her cousin's wife had made, Christina dismissed Ellie with a sweep of her gaze and smiled at Jackson. "I see you finally managed to escape that awful island and join us for services."

Jackson ignored the woman's comment and quickly introduced Ellie to Sarah Callahan and Olympia Wagner, who had apparently known Jackson for as long as Christina had.

"I wrote to Dorothea again just yesterday, but if I'd known

for certain you'd be at church today, I would have waited so I could have told her that, too," Christina offered.

"Dorothea has such a fine life for herself now," Sarah said as she leaned closer to Ellie. "I haven't been to market to Jackson's stall since his late wife met her sad demise, but I hear you bake such heavenly treats that I'm determined to try one this week. I do hope you haven't been bothered overmuch by all the scandal she caused."

Olympia sniffed, which set the ridiculous host of feathers on her bonnet into a wiggle. "People do go on so—you'd think the scandal would die out now that you're remarried, Jackson, but no one should argue with your choice of a new wife. What a woman lacks in looks, she makes up for in other ways, I always say, and a man would be foolish indeed to prefer looks over a woman's talents in the kitchen."

Sarah nodded. "Rebecca certainly had her faults, but she was clearly blessed with such extraordinary looks they led her straight into trouble, and it shouldn't have come as a surprise to anyone that Jackson would want a wife who—"

"Ellie is a fine wife and mother for my sons," Jackson said curtly. "Now if you'll excuse us, we really do need to collect the boys—"

"Mr. Smith? Mrs. Smith?"

Caught between the sting of the women's audacious and meanspirited remarks and pleasure at her husband's defense of her, Ellie noted the arrival of Madeline French with relief.

The woman smiled as she stepped in between Ellie and the three women. "I'm so sorry to interrupt, but Reverend Shore didn't want you to worry about the boys. He and Mrs. Shore are taking them back to the parsonage for a snack," she explained and glanced at Jackson. "Reverend Shore also wanted me to tell you that he forgot to ask if you'd have a moment to discuss something with him before you leave for home."

Jackson nodded. "Of course."

"Then I'm sure you wouldn't mind if I took your wife back home with me for a bit to take care of those matters we discussed last market day," she said and turned to the three women behind her. "Ladies, would you excuse us, please?" she said, hooked her arm with Ellie's, and led her away before Ellie or Jackson or any of the women had a chance to argue with her.

Thirty-One

With her head still spinning from her unpleasant encounter with Christina Schuler and her friends, yet grateful for Jackson's support, Ellie accompanied Madeline French to her shop.

Unlike her first visit there, after she had helped the poor woman recover from a nasty spill on Market Day, she had a feeling this visit today would touch off a round of gossip about the new Mrs. Jackson Smith, especially if Christina Schuler or her two friends had anything to say about it.

At forty, Madeline French was nearly ten years older than Ellie, but with her flawless porcelain skin, vibrant red hair, and eyes that sparkled with vitality, she looked far younger. She wore the very latest fashions, which included the rather remarkable purple cape she wore today that Ellie suspected

Olivia had made. For her part, Ellie felt totally frumpish as they walked side by side down Second Street together.

Although Ellie was grateful that Madeline had interrupted an awkward situation, she was more than a little reluctant to accept the woman's invitation to come to her shop today when it was actually closed, along with all the others in the city. Someone other than Christina or Sarah or Olympia was bound to notice her entering the shop on a Sunday, which was supposed to be a day of worship and rest.

Since Madeline French was no stranger to gossip herself, however, Ellie could not have chosen anyone better to be her companion, as well as her champion. From what she had learned at market from some of Jackson's customers, this stunning woman, who had also insisted that Ellic call her by her first name, had kept gossipmongers guessing the truth about her for the past ten years while maintaining her dignity and her grace, as well a reputation as a fine businesswoman.

Some gossipmongers argued that Madeline French had moved here from New York and was not married at all. Her husband, they argued, was a figment of her imagination, because she wanted to escape the pitiful title of spinster. Others claimed her husband had abandoned her many years ago in Massachusetts. While he had gone west, either alone or with another woman, depending on who was telling the tale, she had moved here to avoid scandal. Yet others claimed the couple had lived in Boston where they had divorced, for as many reasons as there were types of fabrics for a woman to choose from for her gowns.

Indeed, the only thing gossipmongers could agree upon was that no one, other than Madeline French herself, had ever seen or met the woman's husband, Oliver Caldwell French.

Still, Ellie was relieved when they arrived at the shop and proceeded to walk around the building to the back door.

"You may not know this, but your husband told me last week you were to choose at least three fabrics that you'd like for your new gowns," Madeline stated as she led the way inside and down a dark hallway to the front of the shop.

Ellie frowned. "I still don't see why this couldn't wait until Wednesday when we'll be coming in for Market Day. I'm sorry, but I'm afraid I'm not comfortable shopping on Sunday."

"You weren't comfortable listening to some of the bolder members of the congregation who wanted to share a bit of scandal with you just before I arrived, either, but you survived," Madeline said as she drew up the canvas drape covering the single window in the shop to let in more light. "In fact, from all I've seen and heard, you're one of the few women in the city who can face down gossip almost as well as I do. But don't fool yourself. Gossipmongers like Christina Schuler and her friends don't give up easily. They'll be waiting to test you again next Sunday."

Ellie felt her cheeks warm. "I'm not certain why some of them seem so determined to be so mean."

"Because they have pitiful lives and even more pitiful faith, although they'd be the first to spout platitudes at any silly fool willing to listen to them," Madeline argued as she led Ellie over to the bolts of fabric on the counter along the far wall. "All of which means you need to be prepared, and I'd like to be the one to help you, since I have much more experience doing that than you do."

"How are you able to do that?"

"You need to select some fabrics," Madeline suggested, without answering Ellie's question. "Or if you're still feeling uncomfortable, just tell me which ones you don't favor. I'll choose several for you tomorrow morning and get them to Dr. Willows so he can bring them with him when he comes to check up on Widow Palmer in the afternoon. That way you'll have much more time to make a new gown by next Sunday," she said before studying Ellie's cape and frowning. "You really should pick out some fabric to make a new cape, too."

Ellie cringed but narrowed her gaze. "How did you know Dr. Willows was coming to the island tomorrow?"

Madeline patted her arm. "Dr. Willows told me. He also told me poor Widow Palmer had taken a turn for the worse. Now, what about those fabrics?"

Ellie shook her head. "If it wouldn't be too much trouble, I think I'd rather have you choose for me. I'm not very good at selecting fabrics for myself, anyway," she admitted, although she did not hesitate to point out several fabrics in dark brown as ones she did not favor, since Jackson did not like the color. She also excluded anything with a hint of gray or black, simply because she had worn those colors for years. "I think that's all. Except for this one," she added when she spied a deep maroon print that reminded her of the color of the gown she had worn when David Shepherd had withdrawn his request to court her after she had insisted that her mother must be included in any household she established with him.

Madeline chuckled. "Whether it's fabric or sweets or gossip, there's always room for more, isn't there?"

Ellie's spine began to tingle. She had the distinct impression that Madeline had chosen her words deliberately and had invited her here as much to spread more gossip about Jackson and Rebecca as to accommodate him. "If there's more gossip about my husband or his first wife, let me assure you—"

"If there is, then you should hear it," Madeline argued and crossed her arms over her chest. "The only way to best anyone who wants to hurt you is to know exactly how they intend to do it. From what I could gather today, after listening to bits of gossip here and there before overhearing Christina and her friends, I'm not certain you know enough about Jackson or Rebecca to be able to do that."

"Jackson told me all I need to know," Ellie countered, stiffening her back. "I know Rebecca betrayed him with another man, and I know she died with her lover," she blurted.

"But did you also know that Rebecca and her lover had their little trysts in the Sunday house? Or that she made certain she was seen around town with that man?"

Ellie grew still. Although Mrs. Fielding had suggested Rebecca had used the Sunday house for sinful purposes, Ellie never would have guessed that Rebecca had actually flaunted her affair by appearing in public with her lover.

"I didn't think so," Madeline murmured and walked over to stand beside her. "Jackson is a good man. Regardless of the circumstances of his marriage to Rebecca, he didn't deserve what happened to him, and you don't deserve to have your happiness with him destroyed by it any more than he does."

Ellie turned around to face the woman. "Then why are you spreading such gossip about him with me?"

"Because others will. They tried today, and they'll try again and again, until you prove to them that you know absolutely everything about the man you married and you still love him," she said with such absolute sincerity Ellie was tempted to believe her.

"Why should I trust you? Why should I believe that you're any different from them?"

Madeline sighed. "You probably won't. Not unless I trust you with something I've never told anyone here—something I'd rather you not tell anyone, including your husband," she said and drew in yet another long breath. "Did Jackson tell you the name of the man who was Rebecca's lover?"

"No," Ellie replied. "But I don't see how knowing the man's name makes any difference in whether or not I should trust you."

"His name was Arthur Rutledge, which is common knowledge. What no one knows, however, is that he . . . he was my brother." Her eyes glistened with tears.

Ellie's eyes widened. "Y-your brother?"

"Yes, he was, although why neither one of us ever acknowledged our relationship to each other is not something I'm prepared to share with you today," she said. "I'm not proud of the fact that he involved himself with Rebecca the way he did, but he was my brother and I loved him. He may not be here to right the wrong he did, but I'm trying to do that for him by helping Jackson and helping you."

"I don't know what to say," Ellie managed.

"You don't have to say anything, but if you have any questions at all about Rebecca or Jackson, questions you might not feel comfortable asking him, please come to me. I'll answer them as honestly as I can."

"I don't like keeping secrets from my husband or sneaking behind his back to talk to you when I should talk to him."

"I understand," Madeline said sadly. "Tell him about Arthur and me, if you must. Get him to talk to you about Rebecca, but don't stop there. Ask him about Dorothea, too, because the gossipmongers are bound to bring up her name sooner or later."

Ellie furrowed her brow. "Dorothea?"

"Christina Schuler's sister."

"Yes, I know. Christina mentions her every time I see her,

but I haven't asked Jackson why the woman seems so obsessed with mentioning her."

Madeline let out a sigh. "Because my brother told me that according to Rebecca, Dorothea was the only woman Jackson ever truly loved."

During the walk back to the parsonage, Ellie set aside thoughts of Rebecca, but she had a hard time setting aside what Madeline had told her about Dorothea.

She remembered Christina Schuler referring to letters from her sister, Dorothea, every time they met and how defensive Jackson had been when Dorothea's name was mentioned. But the notion that Jackson was still in love with a woman he had not seen for many years—he had, in fact, married another woman instead—was so farfetched she dismissed the very idea as simply an excuse Rebecca had used to justify betraying her husband.

After all, she reasoned, Jackson had promised not to keep any secrets from her, and Ellie had to trust that he was true to his word; otherwise, he would have told her about Dorothea long before now.

Fortunately, she was hard pressed to give either Rebecca or the mysterious Dorothea any of her thoughts once she arrived at the parsonage. Mrs. Shore had introduced the boys to a stray dog she had befriended in a fairly obvious attempt to get Jackson to let the boys take it home as their pet.

Ellie found the dog rather adorable, much to Jackson's dismay, especially its dark brown wavy hair. Its lower jaw was oddly prominent and revealed its bottom teeth, which made it appear that the dog was actually smiling all the time.

While Daniel and Ethan crawled around the parlor floor

with the friendly little mutt, squealing with abandon, Ellie sat next to Mrs. Shore on the settee in the parlor and listened to the minister's wife trying to defend her idea against each of Jackson's protests.

Across from them, Reverend Shore sat in a chair next to Jackson's. Judging by the expression on his face, he was hoping his wife would prevail.

"He can't be much of a stray. Look at how fat he is," Jackson argued.

Growing impatient, Mrs. Shore snorted. "It's not a he, and she's only put on a little bit of weight, because I took pity on her after I found those foundry workers pelting the poor thing with stones."

"Is that her name? Poor Thing?" Daniel managed, struggling to talk while the dog licked at his face.

Reverend Shore chuckled. "It may as well be, since that's all I've ever heard for the past two weeks. Poor thing, she can't sleep outside, because those urchins might spot her again. Or poor thing, she hasn't had a decent thing to eat, so she gets more at dinner than I do."

"Poor Thing! Over here," Daniel cried, trying to lure the dog away from Ethan, who was laughing as the dog tried to chew off his cowlick.

Jackson held up his hands. "I'm sure you'll be able to find the poor thing a proper home right here in the city."

"She can't stay here indefinitely," the minister said firmly. "Neither one of us has time during the day to spend with the poor thing."

Mrs. Shore nudged Ellie's arm. "You're at home all day with the boys. Don't you think they'd just love having a dog?"

"Ethan and me want the dog!" Daniel cried.

As always, Ethan expressed his opinion by smiling.

Ellie had the good sense to know that if she even hinted that her answer to the woman's question was yes, Jackson wouldn't care if everyone in the entire state of Pennsylvania had stayed after services to offer their good wishes to the newly married couple without a single whisper of ill-will. He would still send Ellie packing and worry about explaining her absence from his life later.

"If Jackson doesn't think so, then I'd have to agree with him," she said, although she very much wanted to take the dog home with them.

"Phooey! You like the dog, too. You know you do. She's almost the same color as that old gown of yours."

"Exactly," Jackson chimed in, looking smug.

"That's true, but the dog's wavy brown coat is neither as drab nor as ugly as my gown appeared to some people," she said.

Jackson's dark blue eyes softened when he looked at her. "We don't need a dog. Especially a female dog who could have a litter of pups every season," he insisted.

"How many dogs do you have on that island of yours now?" Mrs. Shore asked.

Jackson shrugged. "None. Old Jake died some years back before Daniel was born, and my father-in-law never thought we needed another one."

The older woman laughed. "If you don't have any other dogs there, how could this poor thing ever have a litter of pups? She couldn't."

Ellie smirked, and though Jackson remained silent, a hint of bemusement lit in his eyes.

Mrs. Shore clapped her hands. "Next argument, please, or accept defeat and agree to take the dog home with you."

Before Jackson could respond to the woman's challenge,

little Ethan settled the matter in a way that made it impossible for anyone, especially his father, to say no.

He walked over to his father, mimicked the dog by jutting out his chin, and put his little hand on his father's arm as he looked up at him. "Poor Thing," he said, so clearly and so distinctly, no one would ever believe that this child had not spoken out loud to his father or anyone other than Daniel for over six months.

Ellie's heart swelled.

Poor Thing had found a name and a home with them on the island after all.

Thirty-Two

When the full moon rose to shine its light down on Dillon's Island in late October, sadness also cast long shadows on the lives of everyone who lived there.

Widow Polly Palmer, their feisty, plainspoken, and beloved Gram, had died peacefully during her nap earlier that afternoon. She had, in death, relinquished her title as the oldest woman in Dauphin County to ninety-nine-year-old Spinster Abigail Holtzben, but Gram would forever be remembered as the best-loved woman who had ever called this island home.

At Jackson's suggestion, which he had made several days ago when Gram suspected the end was finally near, her final resting place was here in his family's cemetery on the island. At her request, made only that same morning while Jackson and his family had been in the city attending Sunday services, they buried her beneath the spotlight of the full moon that shone through the thinning fall canopy overhead.

After each of the family had shared their favorite memories of Gram and prayed together, Michael Grant left the cemetery to take his wife and daughter home to begin life without the matriarch who had anchored their lives with wisdom and faith.

Jackson, however, remained at the gravesite a bit longer with his family. Awash with his own memories of the aged woman who had befriended him for so many years, he looked at his wife with awe. Ellie appeared every bit as tired as Jackson felt. But her devotion to him and his sons, as well as her stamina, continued to amaze him.

Day by day, she also challenged him and inspired him to strengthen his own relationship with a loving and forgiving God, but he was far from being the faithful follower of the Word he wanted to be, in spite of the fact he and Ellie had begun reading the Bible together each night after the boys had gone to bed.

To distance himself from the absurd thoughts that there could ever be anything more than friendship between the two of them, he glanced at his boys and smiled. They had definitely gotten their second wind, and their disappointment that Poor Thing had not been allowed to come to the cemetery was long gone. Under Ellie's direction, they were busy adding more river stones to the pile they had started where Gram's headstone would one day be placed. He hoped that their newfound energy would last just long enough to pick a few of the Russet apples tonight so Ellie could make fritters with them in the morning, since this was the last full moon for this year's harvest.

He studied the boys as they raced back and forth between the stones along the perimeter, where Ellie was standing, and the pile of stones at the head of Gram's grave. They obviously did not understand the somber significance of burial or the finality of Gram's death, any more than they understood their mother's.

They had apparently made some connection, because it had been their idea, not his or Ellie's, to decorate Gram's grave with river stones. Actually, it had been Daniel's idea. Ethan merely nodded his agreement, remaining as mute as he had been before saying the dog's name, but Jackson still had hope that the boy would start speaking again soon.

Ellie caught Jackson's gaze and lifted her brows, a new habit of hers that acknowledged his place as the head of their family.

When he nodded in response to her unspoken question, she smiled. "Each of you boys can pick out one more stone for Gram. Then we have to leave, or it'll be too late to pick any apples."

"Can we take Poor Thing with us?" Daniel asked as he walked along the perimeter looking for his last stone.

"No. No dog," Jackson said sternly.

Neither Daniel nor Ethan bothered to argue with him, although he suspected it was less out of respect for him as their father and more because they were too close to the end of their punishment to want another.

When Ellie stepped alongside Jackson, he shook his head. "If I had my way, I'd have taken that dog to the city and left it back at the parsonage house before attending services this morning," he whispered.

She cocked her head. "Even though that dog's sweet natured and gentle with everyone, especially the boys? Poor Thing's even lured Ethan away from his seat at the window in the kitchen to play, and it's kept Daniel so preoccupied, he hasn't followed every step I take to criticize me."

"Granted," he said. "I daresay I'm surprised you'd defend the animal. If it hasn't been snatching some of your aprons or clothes you've hung out to dry, it's scratching at the floor you've just scrubbed clean. And wasn't it Poor Thing that stole supper off the table last night?"

She chuckled. "You know it was."

"Which is why the dog's been banned from the great room at mealtimes, although I'm still not convinced I was right to give the creature one last reprieve," he quipped.

"You know you'll have two very unhappy boys if they have to bid farewell to that dog."

"Maybe Poor Thing will learn how to behave better," he suggested.

She chuckled again. "You might have to pray very hard for that to happen," she teased as Ethan laid his last river stone on the pile.

Daniel added his own, looked down at the mound of fresh earth atop Gram's grave, and put his arm around his little brother. "Gram's in heaven with Mama. What's heaven like, Pappy?"

Jackson walked over to stand alongside them, and Ellie joined them by standing opposite from them at the foot of the grave. "What do you think it's like?" he asked, hoping to get a glimpse of what his son thought instead of simply telling him, which was what Ellie often encouraged him to do.

"I think there are lots and lots of griddle cakes in heaven," Daniel said.

His little face was so serious Jackson had to stifle a laugh. "In six more days, you'll have griddle cakes, too," he reminded him gently. "What else do you think is in heaven with your mama and Gram?"

Daniel opened his arms wide. "A big, big, big ladder. Right, Ethan?"

"For picking apples?" Jackson asked as Ethan grinned.

"Not for that. For the angels," Daniel replied.

Nodding, Ethan pulled the Jacob's Ladder out of his pocket and nimbly let the blocks tumble over on one another.

Jackson rubbed the top of Ethan's head. "Very good! You've got the knack of it now," he said, grateful that Ellie had talked him into letting the boy take Rebecca's ribbons home in the first place, but moved more that she had found a use for them by repairing the toy.

"Do you still love Gram, even though she's in heaven now and you can't see her?" he prompted, hoping to draw some parallel between Gram and their mother that might help them to accept her death.

When both boys nodded, Jackson continued by asking yet another question, something Ellie had done often with him these past few weeks after he had invited her to sit with him to read and study the Bible after the boys were in bed for the night. "What about Gram? Do you think she still loves you back?"

"My mama loves me back and she loves Ethan back, even though she's in heaven," Daniel replied as Ethan struggled to fold up the blocks so he could shove the toy back into his pocket.

"Then Gram will, too," Jackson assured him as he reached down to help Ethan.

Daniel looked at him, his expression still serious. "How old will me and Ethan be when you die and go to heaven to be with Mama?"

Jackson straightened up and swallowed hard. "I don't know, but I think it will be a long, long time before I get to go to heaven. You and Ethan will be grown men by then, with families of your own to love you."

Daniel mulled over Jackson's response for a moment before he pulled Ethan closer. "We'll still love you, so you can love us back from heaven, won't we, Ethan?" he said.

Jackson caught his breath, hoping this would be the time when Ethan would speak again. When he simply bobbed his head up and down again, Jackson tried not to be too disappointed.

Daniel dropped his gaze and looked over at Ellie before he turned back to his father. "Will you still share Miss Ellie with us when you're in heaven?"

Jackson saw Ellie's expression light with joy and smiled down at his sons. "Yes, I will. Why?"

" 'Cause I think we might need her sometimes, like we do now. Me and Ethan still have lots to learn. Do you think Mama gets mad at us when we let Miss Ellie help us learn our letters?" he asked, jumping back from the future to the present in a single breath.

"What do you think?" he asked. Although the boys were paying scant attention to Ellie's presence, he hoped Daniel's answer would not be too painful for her to hear. If it was, he hoped she would find some consolation that Daniel actually enjoyed the lessons she had begun with them after breakfast each day.

"Me and Ethan think Mama is happy. She isn't mad anymore."

"She isn't?" Jackson replied. Surprised by his sons' apparent change of heart and Daniel's willingness to discuss it, he encouraged him to share more. "Why is that?"

" 'Cause she loves us and she wants us to be happy."

Jackson blinked hard to keep the tears welling in his eyes from dropping free. "Yes, she does."

"And we really love Poor Thing. Miss Ellie loves Poor Thing, too," Daniel added, as if trying to let his father know he was the only one in the household who wanted to get rid of the dog. "If me and Ethan went to heaven, we'd want somebody to take care of her for us so nothin' bad happens to her. Do you think Miss Ellie would take care of Poor Thing?"

Jackson swallowed hard. "I think she would."

"We do, too," Daniel whispered.

That's when Jackson knew that regardless of how many times that dog snatched something or how many times he would have to repair the scratches it made on the floor or how many meals it managed to steal off the table, Poor Thing was going to spend every single day of its life right here on this island with his boys.

When he glanced over at Ellie and back at his boys again, his heart began to pound. The dog might be staying for good, but he wondered if Ellie would agree to do the same once she discovered the final secret he had kept from her.

He had to tell her about Dorothea.

Thirty-Three

Several hours later, Jackson sat with Ellie in front of the fireplace in the great room, just as they had done each night for the past several weeks after the boys had been put to bed.

Fortunately, the boys had been too exhausted after leaving the cemetery and picking half a dozen Russets to complain that Poor Thing had stubbornly refused to follow them upstairs to sleep by their bedroom door tonight. Instead, the dog had chosen to lie by the cookstove in the kitchen, on top of two of Ellie's aprons she had snatched while they had been at the cemetery.

As dread pulsed through his veins, Jackson opened his Bible to the verse he had selected to provide the context for their talk tonight. By the light of the fire burning low, he silently prayed for courage before reading Psalm 118, verse 8: " 'It is better to trust in the Lord than to put confidence in man,' " he said and then gently closed the Bible and laid it on his lap.

As always, Ellie kept her head bowed to let his words simmer within her spirit. Flames reflected on the pale gold gown she wore tonight and set her countenance aglow. And as always, she waited for him to express his thoughts about the verse to begin their discussion.

This time, however, he deliberately opened their time together with a question. "What do you think the verse means?"

She lifted her head.

"I decided that you should go first tonight."

"You decided," she repeated, clearly remembering they had mutually agreed to let him begin their discussion each night.

"I did."

She pursed her lips. "Is that supposed to be a clue to understanding the verse?"

"In what way?" he asked, feigning ignorance.

She chuckled softly. "In every way. For a man who used to find our conversations awkward or difficult, you're becoming quite clever."

He urged her, "Tell me why you should go first, within the context of the verse, of course."

"It's rather simple to explain, now that I think about it. You changed the routine we'd established to show that while I can't completely put confidence in you, I can always trust in God to keep His promises," she said, a bit proudly.

"Do you?" he asked, anxious to know if she would be able to forgive him for deliberately misleading her.

"I try, although I'm not always successful at it," she countered, her cheeks turning pink. "But I do know that when others I depend upon disappoint me, just as I'm bound to disappoint them, I must ask Him to help me to forgive them, just as I would expect them to forgive me."

Jackson clasped his hands together. Over the past few weeks he had prayed hard, but he had yet to fully accept his Father's forgiveness for all the mistakes he had made in his life or forgive those who had disappointed him or hurt him.

Ellie's wooden wedding ring pressed against his chest. She had forgiven him not once, but twice, for misjudging her, but he was not certain she could forgive him again for not being absolutely honest with her. "You don't ever disappoint me. Not anymore," he added. "I know I haven't always acted very kindly toward you since we've been married—"

"But you do now," she murmured, her gaze misty. "I know I'm bound to disappoint you now and again, or that we'll disagree about something, but I also know that you've learned to be honest with me, and you're more likely to talk things over with me now than you are to erupt in anger."

He dropped his gaze and stared at the Bible lying on his lap. Recognizing his own failures, instead of others', as he had been forced to do ever since this woman had come into his life, was still hard. But nothing he had ever told her before was as difficult as what he needed to share with her now.

In part, because she had helped him to face the real truth about the difficulties in his marriage to Rebecca by encouraging him to start reading his Bible again. And in part, because he had never wanted anyone's respect as much as he now wanted hers.

He looked up at her. "I haven't been honest with you. Not completely."

"You haven't?" she prompted as she turned in her seat to face him.

"No, I haven't," he said, shaking his head. "It wasn't

entirely Rebecca's fault that our marriage was a miserable failure. It was mine."

Ellie narrowed her gaze. "Yours? How were you to blame?"

"Because I didn't love her. I never loved her and I never could, because . . . because I was already in love with someone else when I married her."

Ellie stiffened. "If you were in love with someone else, why didn't you just marry her instead of Rebecca?"

"Because she rejected me and married someone else—someone who could give her the kind of life she wanted, one I could never hope to give her," he admitted.

"So you married Rebecca instead," she said. "Why?"

He drew in a long breath. "To please her father more than any other reason, I think. When he asked me to marry his daughter so he would have grandchildren who would want to make this island their home, I agreed, because I wanted the future that the marriage would give me and the children I hoped to raise here."

"Did Rebecca know this when she accepted your proposal?"

He took a deep breath. "No. I think she may have actually loved me, in her own way, but she eventually realized I wasn't free to love her, because I was still in love with a woman who was nothing but a memory."

"Was this woman Dorothea?"

"How did you know her name?" he blurted as his surprise gave way to disbelief.

"From Mrs. French," she replied, recounting her visit to the woman's shop.

He listened carefully and resisted the urge to interrupt her more than once. When she finished her tale, which answered all the questions he might have posed, she turned and stared into the fire. Although he was shocked by what she had told him about Madeline French's relationship to Rebecca's lover and chagrined that the woman had told Ellie about Dorothea, at least the woman had given him the opportunity to tell Ellie the rest of the truth himself.

He studied Ellie's profile carefully. With her shoulders slumped and her hands trembling ever so slightly, he knew he had clearly disappointed her yet again. "Dorothea's full name when I knew her was Dorothea Blake, but her name is Cunningham now. Mrs. Stanford Cunningham," he said. "Christina never really approved of us."

"Are you still in love with Dorothea?"

He raked his fingers through his hair. "I don't know. One minute I think I've forgotten about her. The next, I think of her and need to remind myself that she's another man's wife. But there are times when I still wonder if someday she might be free and come back to me."

"I see."

"But I doubt Dorothea has given me a single thought in the past nine years—although I can't say the same for her sister. Christina seems to take great pleasure in reminding me that Dorothea is extremely happy with her new life," he said, anxious to ease the distress he noted in his wife's dark brown eyes.

Ellie dropped her gaze for a moment before looking at him again and shaking her head. "And all this time I thought Mrs. French was mistaken and that you were grieving for Rebecca or trying to forget that she had rejected the love you offered her. But it wasn't that at all, was it? You were really grieving for Dorothea."

Her gaze was misty. "You betrayed Rebecca, just as surely

as she betrayed you, by marrying her knowing full well that you could never love her because you still loved Dorothea. You've betrayed me, as well, by not being honest with me. And you've betrayed your boys, too."

He stiffened. "That's ridiculous. I've never betrayed my sons—"

"Daniel and Ethan both deserve more from you than you've given them," she insisted. "Regardless of how it might affect them, you've made it very clear that you'd marry Dorothea, if that were possible, which means you'd set me aside and put me out of their lives in order to do that. Perhaps someday you'll get that chance, and if you do, you could have our marriage annulled quite easily, couldn't you? That's really why you insisted on those legal papers you've got so safely stored away—because you haven't given up hope that you'll be with Dorothea someday, a hope you kept hidden from me because you knew . . . you knew how hard it would be for me to stay once I knew that no matter how well I followed every one of the rules you set forth in those papers, it really wouldn't matter in the end, would it?"

She had spoken insistently, yet so softly, he barely heard her, but he did not miss the sound of disappointment in her voice—disappointment that he was not the man of good character she had thought he was.

"I'm sorry, but it's pointless to argue about something that will probably never happen. Granted, I should have told you about Dorothea before now, but she's happily married and quite content with her life in Philadelphia, which makes my feelings for her irrelevant. I didn't tell you about her tonight to make your life with me uncertain," he added defensively.

She huffed. "Really? Pray, why *did* you tell me?"

"Because I don't want any secrets between us. And

because . . . because I trust you and depend on you to help me raise the boys. And because I want you to be able to trust and depend on me, too. You're a good wife. I don't want to lose you."

"At least not until Dorothea shows up on our doorstep and you decide you don't want me or need me anymore." Ellie rose from her seat.

"That's not true," he countered as he got to his feet.

But instead of answering him, she went directly to her room without once looking back at him and closed the door, a habit he was too distraught over to complain about.

Thirty-Four

Another note?

Sighing, Ellie unfolded the scrap of paper she had found tucked under her bedroom door again this morning. Anticipating yet another Bible verse that lauded the value of a good wife, she read Jackson's neatly inscribed message:

> *Proverbs 31:25*
> *Strength and honour are her clothing;*
> *and she shall rejoice in time to come. J*

Her heart skipped a beat. This verse, above the others he had left for her to find under her door over the course of the past week or so when she rose to start her day, reached out to her the most. This verse, like the others from Proverbs, did not just recognize her good qualities or her value to his household. This particular verse offered hope that her future here as his wife would be joyful.

"Which is highly doubtful," she whispered, unable to forget that her future depended on whether or not Dorothea ever waltzed back into Jackson's life. She refolded the scrap of paper and put it alongside the others he had written in the trunk at the foot of her bed. She caught a glimpse of the stack of wood he had started carrying into her room each day to make sure she had enough to keep warm now that the nights were growing chillier and sighed again.

He was making every effort to convince her that he valued her as his partner in this odd marriage of theirs, but she still could not let go of the fear that he could easily set her aside one day, in spite of her constant prayers.

Slipping out of her room, she hurried past the silhouettes now hanging on the wall in frames Jackson had made for them, yet another effort on his part to please her. She closed the door at the foot of the staircase, then went directly to the porch to get more hickory wood for the cookstove. Shivering from the morning chill that promised a cold rain by the end of the day, she carried the firewood back inside and thought about asking Jackson to do that chore for her, too.

She headed for the cookstove but took one look at Poor Thing lying in a bed of her aprons and drying cloths and rocked back on her heels. Trembling, she laid the wood down on the floor by the worktable and approached the dog on tiptoe. She stopped when she was an arm's length away and knelt down to get a better view.

"What's all this?" she crooned as she gazed at the two tiny creatures lying together and suckling at their mother. With their eyes closed and their smooth brown-and-white-spotted bodies, they looked more like baby rats than puppies. They were, however, utterly adorable, if not totally helpless little things.

She sat back on her haunches and shook her head. Now it all made sense. The aprons and cloths the dog had been taking. The scratches at the floor. The need to stay by the cookstove where it was warm.

"You were making a nice bed for your babies, weren't you?" she said and chuckled. Jackson had agreed to take a female dog because there was no other dog, especially a male dog, on the island. Poor Thing, however, had fooled everyone. She was already carrying her pups when she came here.

Ellie could guess what Jackson might say when he saw the puppies, but she had no doubt that the boys would be absolutely thrilled.

Until she spied the lifeless little body tucked in the corner of the bed.

Poor Thing growled low as Ellie reached in for the dead pup. "Shhh, I won't bother your babies," she whispered, quickly took the cold pup, and laid it on her lap. She was not certain whether to simply hide the pup and bury it later or to let the boys see it so they would know that death was part of all life, even for animals.

She had just decided to let Jackson decide that matter when she heard the thunder of footsteps coming down the staircase. The door at the bottom opened so fast it banged against the wall, and she cringed, hoping the door had not hit the silhouettes.

"Today's the day! We can have griddle cakes today!" Daniel cried as he tore into the kitchen with Ethan right behind him and Jackson following them both.

Ellie instantly covered the dead pup with her apron. If

Jackson wanted the boys to see it, there would be time for that later. "You have more than griddle cakes to be excited about," she said as they raced over to her.

Jackson chuckled. "I doubt there's anything these boys of ours could want more."

"What about puppies?" she offered, knowing there was not anything their father could want less, and her heart leaped when she realized he had referred to the boys as "ours."

Amazed by the sheer number of griddle cakes both boys were managing to eat for breakfast, Ellie enjoyed the last bit of her warm cider while they battled with their father over naming the two new puppies.

"You don't need to name them," Jackson argued again, although much more halfheartedly than before. "The people who get the puppies will name them, just like you named Poor Thing."

Daniel pouted and pushed his food around his plate.

So did Ethan.

"Poor Thing doesn't want her puppies to go away," Daniel said dejectedly.

Ellie glanced at Daniel's and Ethan's faces, and her heart trembled. Separating Poor Thing from her puppies would only remind the boys how their mother had been taken from them. But even she had to admit that the prospect of having three dogs in the house for the boys' sake would be a bit unnerving.

Jackson took another bite of the apple fritters Ellie had made for him and gave both boys a stern look that closed that much-discussed topic again. "They can't stay here. Period."

"Poor Thing has a name. The puppies need one, too,"

Daniel argued, turning the conversation back to a topic he must have thought he could win.

When Jackson looked to Ellie for support, she shrugged. "I don't suppose naming the puppies would do any harm. The new owners can change their names. I'm certain Poor Thing had a name before we named her," she offered, hoping to talk to Jackson about keeping the puppies later when they were alone.

Daniel grinned at her before looking at his father. "Can we name them, Pappy? Please?"

Ethan grinned, too.

"Fine. Name them, but mind my words: Those puppies are going to leave and get new homes, where they'll get new names, just as soon as they don't need Poor Thing's milk anymore," Jackson cautioned.

"Just because you name them doesn't mean you can play with the puppies yet," Ellie added. "Poor Thing has enough to do without worrying about having the two of you handling her new puppies."

Daniel dipped a last forkful of griddle cake into the syrup on his plate and devoured the food in a single bite. "We know. We can't play with the puppies until they open their eyes, but me and Ethan got names for them already. Wanna hear them?"

Ellie laughed.

Jackson did, too. "Why not?"

"Griddle cakes," Daniel said as he pushed his plate away.

"You say please when you want more to eat, and you can't have a third serving of griddle cakes. You'll get a tummy ache," Ellie cautioned.

"I don't want more griddle cakes. That's what me and Ethan call the puppies. Griddle and Cakes. Can we name the dead puppy, too?" he asked, his expression as innocent as his question as he looked from his father to Ellie.

She nodded toward his father for an answer, more than happy to defer to him, since he had decided the boys had needed to learn about the third, stillborn puppy.

"Do you have a name already picked out for him?" Jackson asked gently.

Daniel shrugged. "We think we should just call him Puppy. Can Miss Ellie help us bury it in the cemetery? Do you wanna come, too?"

Ethan stared at his father, as if anxious to know the answer to his brother's question.

Ellie stared at the boys' father, too, wondering most if he would pose an objection to having the puppy buried in the family cemetery rather than a place in the side yard or the woods.

Jackson set down his fork. "I'll come if you want me to, or Miss Ellie does, but there's rain coming today. I have a lot to do to get ready for tomorrow. It's our last day at market until next year, remember?"

Daniel shrugged. "You don't have to come. We like it when Miss Ellie helps us."

"I don't mind helping the boys alone. Other than the threat of rain, it's certainly safe enough," Ellie offered. "If we go to the cemetery right after breakfast instead of starting our lessons, I think we'll be back long before the rain starts. If the boys move the stones along one side of the perimeter, I think we can make a special place for the puppy there," she added, just to let him know that the puppy would not be buried directly alongside any of his relatives.

"That's fine. I don't think we'll see much rain before dinner, but it's probably wise to get the puppy buried this morning.

I'll get a few small tools ready for you before I head out to the orchards. Perhaps after supper tonight, we can all make a few plans for tomorrow," he suggested.

Ellie narrowed her gaze. "But tomorrow's Market Day."

Jackson shrugged. "I know, but I expect we'll sell out the last of the Russets well before noon, which means we'll have the afternoon to spend as we like."

"We wouldn't come straight home?" she asked.

"Actually, since I had someone get the Sunday house fixed up a bit for us, I thought it might be nice if we took the time to stay the night so you could do some shopping. We should probably stop by and let Reverend and Mrs. Shore know about the puppies, too."

She caught her breath, surprised by his offer for them to spend time in the city. "What about Poor Thing? We can't leave her here alone for two days, especially with the puppies."

"I don't think Grizel would mind coming over to take care of her. Besides, I need the boys to help me with something in town."

Daniel clapped his hands. "We'll help, Pappy, won't we, Ethan? What are we gonna do?" he asked.

"First and foremost, we need to see if we can find anyone in town who'd like to have one of Poor Thing's pups. While we're looking, I was wondering if the two of you would help me decide if Mrs. French's gumdrops really do taste better than Widow Franklin's."

The skies were darkening. The air was growing raw. The smell of rain was thickening.

More than anxious to get back to the house before the storm broke, Ellie shoveled the last bit of dirt on top of the little pup's grave and stepped back. "You can smooth the dirt down now."

Ethan knelt down and started patting the earth with his hands while Daniel raced back from rearranging the stones around his mother's headstone.

"I think Mama's really happy now," Daniel said as he plopped down next to his brother.

"Why is that?" Ellie asked.

Daniel answered without looking up at her. " 'Cause now she has a puppy to play with in heaven."

"They have puppies in heaven?" she questioned, reminded she did not always know what he was thinking.

Ethan looked up at her before Daniel challenged her answer. "Don't they?"

"Of course they do. I was only teasing you," she said quickly to ease their worried expressions. "I think it's time we get back. We have lessons to do."

Daniel stood up and brushed off his overalls, which inspired his younger brother to follow suit. "We can't go back yet. We have to put stones on the puppy's grave."

Ellie looked overhead at the dark clouds gathering there, shivered, and shook her head. "Not today. There's a storm brewing. We don't have time to walk to the landing to find them and bring them back before the rain starts. We'll go tomorrow after the weather clears."

"But tomorrow's Market Day and Pappy said we weren't even coming home. We're staying at our other house," he argued, puffing out his little chest.

Ethan grabbed his brother's hand, silently taking his side.

"Oh, I forgot. Then we'll have to wait a few days to get the stones. In the meantime, why don't you borrow some from over there?" she asked, pointing to the perimeter.

"No," Daniel said, stomping his foot. "The puppy wants new stones, just like we gave our mama."

"No, *you* want them, but you'll have to get them another day. I don't want any of us to be caught outside when the storm hits. Besides, we need to get back to the house for your lessons," she said, far more sternly than she intended.

Daniel grabbed Ethan's hand. "Come on, Ethan. We'll get the stones later," he said and marched away with him.

Holding the larger shovel, Ellie grabbed the two smaller ones the boys had used that were lying on the ground with her other hand and hurried to catch up with them. She rarely had to refuse the boys when they asked to do anything, but she chided herself for letting her fear of the brewing storm make her so tense she had spoken to them more harshly than they deserved.

She was only a few feet behind them, hoping to soften her words with a promise to ask their father to take them to the landing for stones later if the storm did not last long when she heard Daniel whispering to his brother.

"Don't be sad. If Miss Ellie is mean to us again, we don't have to keep her. We can give her back to Pappy whenever we want."

She hurried her steps, more anxious than ever to make amends. She tried to shove aside her fear of storms, but it landed right next to her fear that their pappy would give her back to her old life, too, if he ever got the chance to reunite with Dorothea.

Jackson reached home an hour before dinnertime.

He charged into the house just steps ahead of the storm, which threatened to hit the island much sooner than he had expected. But it was not the storm that had him rushing back here. The gusting wind almost blew the porch door out of his hand, but he managed to grab it and close it behind him.

Confident that Ellie's fear of storms had kept his sons inside with her, where it was safe, he called out for them.

"Ellie! Daniel! Ethan!"

He paused to catch his breath, but when no one answered his cries, his confidence failed.

"Ellie! Daniel! Ethan!" he cried, even louder.

When he still got no response, he glanced around the kitchen, which was unusually chilly. In fact, Ellie did not have anything simmering on the cookstove for dinner. Poor Thing, who was still lying in her bed with her puppies, looked at him as he passed by with those big brown eyes of hers, as if pleading with him to start a fire to warm them.

It was then he spied the note Ellie had left for him on the worktable.

When he read the note, he grew more than alarmed. His body turned cold, and his heart pounded so hard in his chest he found it hard to breathe:

> *We went to the landing for river stones*
> *for the puppy's grave. Ellie*

Fear for his family's safety, heightened by an ominous clap of thunder that shook the house, sent him charging back toward the door again. With visions of the animal tracks he had recently spotted mocking his assurances to Ellie that no wild predators were likely to be on the island, he stopped just long enough to get his rifle and load it.

He ran across the porch and took the steps two at a time.

Startled by a flash of lightning that magnified his fear, he raced for the cemetery, hoping to find them on their way home.

For the first time, however, his fear did not unleash anger at anyone other than himself. Had he taken Ellie's alleged near-encounter with an animal of some kind more seriously and made more than a cursory search of the island for animal tracks, they would not be in danger now. If he had taken the time to go with her and his sons to bury the puppy this morning, instead of worrying about getting his work done to make sure nothing interfered with his plans for their visit to the city, they would not be in danger now, either. They would be here, safe at home.

With a prayer on his lips only God would hear above the wind that whipped at the treetops, he pleaded for help in finding his family and keeping them safe until he did. He knew Ellie would protect their sons at all costs, but he also knew there was only one thing that might prevent her from doing just that: her uncommon fear of storms.

Thirty-Five

"Don't move. Don't even try, or we'll all fall."

Ellie held tight to the boys' hands as they straddled a thick branch some ten feet off the ground. Unfortunately, the tree they had climbed had already lost most of its leaves, and there was no chance of hiding. They also had no protection at all from the elements, and with the wind increasing in strength, she feared nothing short of divine intervention would save them.

To keep her from dissolving into sheer panic, now that the storm was growing ever closer, she kept her gaze focused on the gray-and-white animal that was pacing on the ground directly below them, just as it had done for the past twenty minutes.

She tightened her hold on both boys and glanced down at the bag of river stones she had abandoned below. If she could only get her hands on that bag of stones, she could try throwing them at the animal to force it to leave, but there was no way she was going to risk climbing back down to get it. Not with that animal so close and not without putting both boys at risk by leaving them, even for a moment.

"I wanna get down," Daniel whined as he tried to tug his hand free.

She held him firmly. "Not yet."

"But I wanna play with the dog."

"It's not a dog. It's a wolf, and it's not safe to play with it," Ellie repeated for the third time, trying to keep their climbing up the tree more of an adventure than what it was: a desperate attempt to avoid being dinner for a rogue wolf.

The wolf stopped pacing for a moment, looked up at them, growled, and bared its teeth.

Ellie caught her breath and froze. When Daniel yelped, and Ethan edged even closer to her, she did not think either boy would ask to play with the animal again.

"I'm very glad you're such a good tree climber, Daniel, and I'm especially pleased you taught Ethan how to climb trees, too. Your pappy will be very proud of both of you," she offered to distract them. She prayed that by now Jackson might have realized they were not at home and would come looking for them.

When the first clap of thunder broke overhead, sounding like a giant drumbeat, the tree literally shook, along with Ellie. She might be terrified during a thunderstorm when she was inside the house, but being outside was far, far worse.

Almost paralyzed with fear, she glanced at the boys. Daniel's eyes were dark with terror, and Ethan's hold on her hand was like a vise that was making her fingers tingle.

Her heart constricted. Poor babes. They were just as petrified as she was.

As dark storm clouds swirled closer and the tree branches swayed in the gusting wind, the wolf stopped pacing and howled its objection. Almost in response, a bolt of lightning cracked the sky, and absolute terror shot straight from the top of her head to the tips of her toes.

Both boys promptly burst into tears and tugged at her hands as yet another flash of lightning lit the sky. They tried to edge closer to her, and she had to struggle hard not to lose her grip on them, all while keeping them balanced on the branch. "Shhh. It's all right. Don't cry," she crooned.

"I wanna go home," Daniel wailed.

Ethan's cries overwhelmed his brother's.

"We can't leave. Not with the wolf right there waiting for us," she insisted. She let go of their hands and slipped an arm around each of their shoulders, hoping to keep their little bodies from shaking so hard they all lost their balance and fell straight to the ground.

To her horror, just when she felt more confident about holding them all in place, a gust of wind tore a branch off a tree just yards away and sent it flying through the air like an oddly shaped arrow. It landed too far away to scare off the wolf, but it inspired new fears about the danger of remaining in the tree during the storm.

Daniel tried to tug free. "I don't wanna broked arm like Mr. Brooks," he insisted, apparently remembering the accident that their stall mate at market had told him about some weeks ago. "I wanna go. I want my pappy."

Ellie held him tighter. "Don't be afraid. I'm here," she promised, although she had to admit that the boy's fears were well-founded. "Your father must be home by now, which means he's already found the note I left for him. I'm sure he's already looking for us. We just need to be patient and wait for him," she suggested, then quickly offered a silent prayer that God would protect them all until Jackson could rescue them.

"He won't look for us up in a tree," Daniel cried. "Pappy! Pappy! Come find us. We're up here!"

Ellie was about to join her voice to his when another clap of thunder erupted. Within the same heartbeat, she caught a brief glimpse of the wolf turning and disappearing into the brush, apparently more afraid of the thunder than it was hungry.

"Look! The wolf is going home," she exclaimed, grateful the animal had run off in the opposite direction of the farmhouse.

"I wanna go home, too. Can we go home now? Can we?"

"I think that it's safe enough to try. Here," she said, taking his hands, as well as Ethan's, and pressing them against the branch. "Hold tight while I climb down first so I can help you."

Daniel was sitting on the branch closest to the trunk. "I'm going first," he said and promptly edged his way to the trunk before lowering himself to the branch below before she had a thought to stop him.

Apparently Ethan was also too eager to wait for her. Unfortunately, he was just as agile as his brother, if not a bit more daring. Before she knew it, he had simply lowered himself from the branch they were sitting on to the one below.

"When you get to the ground, don't move another step before I get there," she warned. She reached the ground just as the rain started, and neither boy argued when she grabbed them. The wind kicked up and whipped at her skirts and the thunder boomed even louder. With the storm about to unleash even greater fury, they were too far from home to get there quickly, but they were even farther from the Grants'.

"We need to find shelter until the storm passes," Ellie cried as the rain that pelted them changed from a soft drizzle to hard drops. Praying that Jackson was on his way, she braced herself and led them toward home, directly into the wind.

With her heart pounding louder than the thunderous skies overhead, she forged onward. Little Ethan was so petrified he could barely keep up, so she picked him up to carry him. Daniel, meanwhile, clung to her arm as well as her hand, forcing her to drag him along, step by step, using her own strength.

"Help us, Father. Help us," she murmured against the stinging rain that nearly blinded her.

Seconds later the sky rumbled, followed by a loud boom and an explosion of light and heat that forced her to fall back a few steps. The sound of wood splitting and cracking was so loud and the burning smell so intense, she screamed and yanked Daniel farther back only moments before a giant evergreen started a slow, gentle fall to earth just half a dozen yards ahead of them.

Too terrified to move, she watched in horror as the thick, heavy branches on the tree snapped smaller nearby trees that had already given up their foliage, cutting a wide swath of destruction. Finally, the trunk of the massive tree landed with a thud, shaking the very ground beneath her feet.

Ethan buried his face against her neck and his fingers dug at her flesh. Wailing, Daniel wrapped his arms around her waist, preventing her from taking a single step.

Frantic, she was nearly overcome by the memory of her father's death, when he had been struck in a similar incident. She could scarcely imagine that having a tree struck by lightning right in front of her was God's answer to her prayers, until she realized that the tree posed no danger now to her or the boys.

In fact, the tree would provide the very shelter they needed, a blessing indeed.

"Hurry," she said as she pried Daniel from her waist and the rain soaked clear through her gown to her skin. "We can hide beneath the tree."

"Where's Pappy? I wanna go home," he cried.

"I'm sure Pappy's coming, but we can't wait for him here," she insisted as she tried to convince him to walk a bit faster.

Another boom of thunder added emphasis to her words and he did not resist, even when she urged him to crawl beneath the branches, close to the trunk, as she followed along with his brother. With Ethan's hands wrapped around her neck now and her skirts constantly getting caught between her legs, she made slow but steady progress.

Finally, when they reached a thick canopy of pine needles on tree branches that overlapped one another to form a fairly decent roof of sorts that blocked the wind and rain, she told Daniel to stop. "If you sit up, you can lean against the trunk. I'll be right next to you," she promised as she peeled Ethan's hands from around her neck.

He did as he was told, but the moment she sat down, Ethan scrambled right onto her lap, grabbed her legs, and held on tight. Daniel sat so close to her, she doubted she could slide a pine needle between them. They were all wet and shivering with cold, and she had so much dirt ground into her hands from crawling to get here, she did not know if she would ever be able to soak it all away.

Otherwise, they were all fine. Frightened to their bones, naturally, but physically unhurt. They were also out of the wind and rain. And most important, they were safe, assuming she could trust the notion that lightning never struck the same object twice.

She wrapped one arm around Ethan's waist and the other around Daniel's shoulders. "We'll be safe here," she said reassuringly as she inhaled the scent of scorched pine that enveloped them.

Daniel snuggled closer. "I'm real glad Pappy shared you with us today, but I hope he doesn't take too long to get here. Do you think he'll find us soon?"

"I hope so."

"But he won't see us 'cause we're hiding under the tree."

"But we'll see your father and we'll let him know right where we are."

He leaned even closer. "That was a big, big wolf. Do you think it'll find us here, too?"

"No. That wolf's too scared to be bothered with us now, thanks to the storm."

"I'm not scared anymore," Daniel boasted, even though he found her hand and held on so tight she wondered where he found the strength. "You're not scared, are you, Ethan?"

His younger brother shook his head, but he did not ease his hold on her legs, either, and his bottom lip was quivering.

Daniel sniffled when a round of thunder erupted, although she thought it sounded a bit farther away than earlier. "Are you scared, Miss Ellie?"

"A little," she murmured, reluctant to admit that her heart was still beating so fast, she was afraid it might beat her straight into the next world. "Maybe you and Ethan could do something to keep me from thinking about being afraid."

"Like what?" he asked timidly.

"Well, how about singing a song? I'll even sing with you," she added.

When Daniel looked up at her, his bottom lip was quivering. "I don't think me and Ethan can sing right now. Can you . . . can you just tell us a story?"

And so she did.

Starting with Daniel in the lions' den and Jacob of ladder fame, she told every Bible story she could think of that would give all of them courage. She was not certain how much her stories helped, since her words were often eclipsed by the sound of branches cracking and falling to earth or thunderclaps that had the boys covering their ears with their hands. She only faltered when the torrential rain started to flood their hiding place, although by then, the thunder and lightning had moved on.

When she ran out of ideas, she simply started over. She was halfway through describing the ladder Jacob had seen in his dream when she thought she heard something that made the hair on the back of her neck stand on end.

Thirty-Six

"Daniel! Ethan! Ellie!"

Jackson searched from left to right as he traipsed through the woodlands, desperate for some sign of his family. Near frantic with the greatest fear he had ever known, he dropped to his knees and raised his face to the angry heavens. "Please, Father, help me. Please. I need you," he cried, finally opening his very spirit to reclaim the faith he had once embraced with his whole heart and his whole soul.

As the wind whipped at his body and the rain pelted his face, he remained steadfast and prayed harder than he had ever prayed in his life. For forgiveness. For the strength to forgive others. And for the opportunity to find his boys and raise them to be God-fearing men who loved God and followed

His Word as faithfully as Jackson vowed he would do every day for the rest of his life.

Drenched to the bone, he ignored the chills that left him shivering so hard his bones ached until finally, despite the cold and the wind and the rain, he felt the redeeming warmth of God's all-powerful grace.

After bowing low to the earth to acknowledge his Creator, he stood up, held his rifle high, and plodded forward, confident that God would somehow guide him to his family. Nearly half an hour later, he approached a giant evergreen lying on the ground just ahead and raised his rifle when he detected a sudden movement within its branches.

The instant he saw Daniel and Ethan scramble out from under the protection of the fallen tree, with Ellie climbing out just behind them, he lowered his gun and praised God for His faithfulness and His mercy.

His heart flip-flopped in his chest and relief charged through every pore of his skin. Choking back tears of joy and gratitude, he set his rifle down on the ground and opened his arms as his sons raced toward him.

"Pappy! You found us!" Daniel cried as he charged against him. "You really found us!"

Jackson pulled his oldest son close with one arm and tugged Ethan to him with the other and held them tight against his chest. Ethan, however, struggled free and looked up at him.

"Pappy! Pappy! You saved us, Pappy! There was a bad, bad wolf that wanted to eat us, but Mama Ellie saved us. I climbed a big tree all by myself and Daniel climbed the tree and then Mama Ellie climbed a big tree, too, and we waited and waited, but the bad, bad wolf just wouldn't go away. And then the storm came and the wolf got scared and ran away and Mama Ellie said . . . ."

Overwhelmed by the sound of his youngest son's voice, Jackson lifted him up into his arms and stared at him, just to make sure it was true. Ethan was talking again. He was talking!

With his gaze blurred by his tears of joy, Jackson kissed his son and looked at Ellie, who was making her way to all of them. Her dark hair was plastered against her head, and that awful brown gown she wore was torn in several places and sagged under the weight of the rain and mud it carried. Her hands and feet were covered with mud and pine needles. Tears were streaming down her face, and he knew she had heard at least two precious words Ethan had spoken, too: Mama Ellie. Ethan had called her Mama Ellie.

When he saw the look of pure joy on her face, his heart pounded in his chest. As impossible as it might be, this utterly plain woman had been transformed, for the briefest of moments, into a woman of great beauty and worth, not because she was fair of face or form, but because her very spirit, her kindness, and her goodness reached out to him in a way that he had never quite experienced before.

Not with Rebecca.

Not even with Dorothea.

Not ever.

He cleared the lump in his throat. "Are you all right, too?" he whispered.

She nodded, but as she swayed on her feet, he pulled her into his arms, too. When she collapsed against him, the wedding ring he still wore on the leather thong around his neck pressed against his chest, and he could feel her heart pounding against his own.

As Ethan continued to rattle on and on with his tale, Daniel squirmed his way between Ellie and Ethan, and Jackson hugged his family close.

His heart swelled. His family. They truly were his family. Daniel. Ethan. And Ellie. They were his family, and they were all that mattered, truly mattered to him in this world—a realization that was as great a miracle to him at this moment as rediscovering the faith he had abandoned for far too long.

As overjoyed as he was, however, he was still fearful that the rogue wolf might still be close by. He shifted Ethan in his arms and lifted Daniel up with his other arm. Ellie reached down and picked up his rifle, which was still loaded and ready to fire, if necessary.

With his boys' faces snuggled against him for protection from the rain, he headed for home. His heart and soul were so overjoyed at finding his boys safe and at hearing Ethan talk to him again, he almost felt as if he were walking through the woods on a warm summer day instead of in a cold, drenching rain.

Concerned about Ellie, he glanced over at her, but she was keeping up with him as if she were dressed in finery and heading into church for services instead of marching through the woods in a downpour.

Her devotion to his sons today and her courage was remarkable, if not extraordinary. She had saved both Daniel and Ethan from being attacked by the wolf by having the presence of mind to get them up into a tree. More impressively, she had also conquered her desperate fear of storms to protect them, and he would never, ever forget what she had done for them or for him.

When he finally sighted the house, he nudged his sons with his shoulders as he increased his pace. "Daniel? Ethan? There's our house. We're almost home."

"H-hot c-cider f-for everyone," Ellie stammered.

Both boys, however, continued to shield themselves against him. When he looked at her face again, he could see her teeth were chattering, and she was uncommonly pale. Yet even with the weight of the rifle she was carrying for him, added to the drag of her sodden gown, she still managed to match his faster pace. "The cider's a good idea, but not until we all get into some warm, dry clothes," he suggested as they finally neared the porch. "I'll take care of the boys and get the fire started in the cookstove. You need to get out of that wet gown before it drags you down to the ground."

With rain rushing down her face, she grinned. "If th-that happens, I w-won't have the strength to g-get up, b-but if y-you expect an argument from m-me about h-heating up the c-cider, y-you won't g-get one. I'll m-meet you all in the k-kitchen," she said and hurried up the porch steps when he urged her to go ahead of them.

Later that afternoon, after filling the boys with hot cider and some hot soup for dinner and tucking them in for a much-needed nap, Jackson paused at the bottom of the staircase. Ellie was sitting in front of the fireplace in the great room not ten feet away while the rain continued to lash at the windows. She was so thoroughly engrossed in her task, he was reluctant to interrupt her.

Seated close to the fire, she had unpinned her hair and with long, deliberate strokes of her brush, she was attempting to dry it. The fire cast a gentle glow to her face and form, yet her spirit and faith gave her an inner glow that made his heart lurch in his chest for the second time that day.

He would not be taking a very big leap at all if he let himself fall in love with this woman, and he was surprised at how hard it was at this moment to recall even one of Dorothea's features. The memory of the love they had once shared was actually beginning to fade now, and only a foolish man would want to keep it alive when Ellie was right here.

She paused abruptly, as if sensing his presence, and looked up. "Oh! I . . . I didn't expect you'd be down so quickly," she said. After hurriedly setting aside her brush, she pulled her hair back behind her neck and tied it with a ribbon that was as pink as her cheeks had gotten. "Please. Come sit. The fire feels wonderful. I can do this later."

"No, I can come back, after you've finished," he offered, albeit weakly.

"This is your fireplace," she said as she got to her feet. "I know I have a stove in my room, but my hair will dry much faster by the fireplace. I was hoping I'd be finished by the time you'd tucked in the boys."

"Please don't stop on my account," he suggested as he walked toward her.

Her blush deepened. "I can wait a bit. How are they?"

He chuckled and pulled a chair closer to sit down beside her. "Warm and dry, with their bellies full, and fast asleep, which is what I might say about Poor Thing and her puppies, as well."

She smiled, looked at the rain-splattered windows, and frowned. "The rain hasn't ended yet. I'm afraid the boys and I would still be out huddling under that tree if you hadn't come for us."

His eyes widened. "Did you really think I'd leave you and the boys out in a storm? And with a wolf about?"

"No, but I wasn't certain when you got home or if you knew about the wolf or how long it would take you to find us."

"I came home as soon as I spotted the wolf's tracks. I was hoping the threat of the storm might have kept you all inside, but when I saw your note, I realized you were all in far greater danger, which is why I brought my rifle. I'm sorry. If I had taken you more seriously before when you had that encounter with an animal on the roadway—"

"That's not important now. We're safe and unharmed," she argued. "What are you going to do about the wolf?"

"We're leaving in the morning for the city, but I'll stop and make sure the Grants know about it. Michael may even spot the wolf and get rid of it before we get back."

She shivered and wrapped her hands at her waist. "I hope so, although I suspect we owe the wolf, as well as the storm, a bit of gratitude."

He cocked his head. "Gratitude?"

"Ethan's talking again, isn't he?"

He chuckled. "Nonstop, I'm afraid, although I don't see how that miracle is connected to either the wolf or the storm."

She moistened her lips and smiled but held silent.

He waved his hand to urge her to speak. "If you see a connection, please tell me. I'm more than curious to know what you're thinking."

She nodded. "I don't know that I had much opportunity to think of it until just now, when I was brushing my hair and let my thoughts wander. Do you remember when Daniel told us that Ethan spoke to him?"

"Of course."

"Do you remember that Daniel said Ethan talked to him but wouldn't talk to you because he was angry with you?"

"Yes, but—"

"If fear was at the root of his anger, then he must have been terribly afraid of something that made him so angry he wouldn't talk to you. What's the first thing Ethan said to you today? Do you remember?"

He furrowed his brow. "He called me Pappy, several times I think, but I was so excited to hear his voice, I'm afraid most of the rest is a bit blurred."

"He said, 'You saved us.' He was overjoyed that you saved us, which made me wonder if he was afraid you wouldn't or couldn't save us because he thought you hadn't saved his mama from dying or from leaving," she whispered.

His heart pounded against the wall of his chest. "You think that's what he was afraid of for all these months? That I wouldn't be there for him because I hadn't been there for his mother?"

"I don't know. Ethan's so young, I'm not even certain Ethan realizes it himself, but—"

"But it makes sense." Jackson leaned back in his chair. "I've obviously never told the boys about the difficulties between myself and their mother, although I'm certain they knew all wasn't right. But I never told them exactly that Rebecca died by drowning, either. I thought they were too young, and I didn't want them to develop a fear of the river."

As his mind traveled back over the past few months, he realized he had been so self-absorbed with his own grief and disappointments, he had not really been aware of how deeply his sons were suffering, too. "Do you remember when Daniel told us that Ethan sat by the kitchen window every day because he was waiting for his mother to come back, when we both thought he was waiting for me to return from working in the orchards?"

"I do. Why?"

He tried to sort through his thoughts by saying them out loud. "I was just thinking . . . maybe Ethan was sitting by the window waiting for me, after all, because he was afraid I wouldn't come if he needed me. He just didn't know it or didn't want Daniel to know how frightened he was that I wouldn't be there for them." He gazed at Ellie. "I don't know that I would have made that connection—or any at all—without you."

The color in her cheeks grew more pronounced. "You probably would have, eventually. I'm just glad I could help. You might want to think about something else, too."

At this point, he was so grateful to her he would be tempted to do anything to please her. "Such as . . . ?"

"Such as thinking about keeping Griddle and Cakes, at least for a little while. Separating those puppies from their mother might remind the boys about how they were separated from Rebecca."

He straightened his back and leaned forward. "Keep the puppies? Both of them? And Poor Thing, too?"

She chuckled. "It was just a thought."

He scowled. "Maybe it was, but I'd rather think about what you're making for supper tonight."

"Supper? Or dessert?" she teased.

"Can we have griddle cakes for dessert?"

He turned, saw Ethan racing toward him, and held out his arms. "Right here, little one. Your pappy needs a hug," he said, though a little privacy now and then, so he could have time alone with Ellie, would not be a bad idea, either.

Thirty-Seven

Having any expectation of total privacy when there were two adults and two rambunctious boys sharing a one-room house was a bit like expecting a moth that was drawn too close to a burning flame to survive.

Ellie folded the wood-framed partition that separated her bunk from Jackson and the boys in the renovated Sunday house and slid it underneath the narrow bed. Now that all of Rebecca's things had been removed, the walls were bare but wore a fresh coat of whitewash. A pair of new rocking chairs sat side by side in front of the fireplace, facing the mantel, where a Bible rested, waiting to be read and shared, just like at home.

The embers of her attraction to Jackson had been fanned into flames by the events surrounding that fateful storm, but the flames had grown even hotter these past two days. With the two boys literally underfoot, however, there was no way she could tell if Jackson was developing feelings for her, too, or if she was completely misreading him.

To distract her from the disturbing thought that her feelings for him could never be returned, especially with his heart still in Dorothea's hands, she glanced over at the boys. They were sitting on Ethan's bunk on the other side of the room, talking and playing with their Jacob's Ladder, and she had to smile to herself.

Once Ethan had started talking again, he'd been a veritable chatterbox. In all truth, the only time the child was quiet now was when he was asleep! Still, she did not think she would ever tire of hearing him, or his brother, call her by her new title: Mama Ellie.

To preoccupy herself while they waited for Jackson to return from a private visit with Madeline French, she checked the ashes in the fireplace again and spread them around with a poker to make sure there were no burning embers left. Satisfied, she cleaned them out one last time. She was more than satisfied, if not unduly proud of Jackson for reaching out to the woman who had also been deeply hurt by the scandal, even though her pain was hidden from the rest of the world, while his was very public.

She set the bucket of cold ashes by the front door and looked around the room to see if there was anything else she could do to speed their departure. After deciding to take one last look inside the trunk they were taking home with them, she opened the lid.

In a flash, Daniel and Ethan were right there beside her.

"Can we have some more gumdrops?" Ethan asked.

"*May* we have some?" Daniel asked, correcting his brother's grammar rather proudly.

"You may not," Ellie replied with a grin. "Your pappy put them away for later. There aren't any stores on the island, remember? If you eat all the gumdrops now, you won't have any to look forward to when we get home."

Ethan pouted for a moment before his eyes lit up. "Can we play with Griddle and Cakes when we get home?"

She cocked a brow.

Daniel puffed out his chest. "May we? Please?"

Ellie shook her head. "The puppies are only three days old. They need to stay with Poor Thing for a few weeks yet." After spending the past month with the boys as they waited for their punishment to end, she knew how hard it was for them to understand the concept of time, especially when they were waiting for something like griddle cakes for breakfast or a puppy to play with. She also knew they would ask to play with those puppies every day, all day, unless she could think of something to help them.

"I have an idea, though," she said and rifled through the trunk. When she found two of the half dozen slates Jackson had bought for the boys to use during their lessons, she handed one to each of them.

She found the chalk quickly enough, too, and gave each boy a piece. "Let's sit," she suggested and helped them get settled. "Listen first," she cautioned when Ethan bent down to scribble on his slate. "There are seven days in a week. You'll probably be able to play with the puppies in two weeks. That's another fourteen days."

Daniel scrunched up his face. "That's a lot of days."

"Lots and lots of days," Ethan added for emphasis.

She smiled. "Yes, it is, but if you make fourteen marks on your slate and erase one each day when you have your griddle cakes for breakfast, you'll be able to see how many more days it will be before you get to play with Griddle and Cakes."

"I can count to fourteen," Daniel said and started making his marks right away.

Ethan, however, held back, studying what his brother was doing instead of making his own marks.

"What's the matter?" she asked. "Don't you want to do it, too?"

"I can't count to fourteen. I can only count to ten."

"Here, I'll help you," she said, but before she could take the chalk from him, there was a loud knock at the door.

"I'll be right back. Daniel, help your brother," she instructed and went to answer the door, curious to know who might be calling, since Jackson would not have bothered to knock.

When she opened the door, she took one look at Jackson and burst into laughter. Between the stack of boxes in his arms and the parcels hanging from his hands, she could scarcely see his face. Still laughing, she stepped back to let him inside. "How did you ever manage to knock?"

"I didn't. I had to kick at the door with my foot."

The boys met him midway as he carried his purchases over to the table. "Presents!" they cried in unison as they clapped and skipped, rather awkwardly, along with him. "Presents! Presents!"

"What makes you so certain any of them are for you?" Jackson asked teasingly as he deposited his bounty right on top of the slates the boys had been using.

Ellie managed to slide the slates free, which smeared a few of the chalk marks the boys had made, while the boys climbed up onto the benches to see what their father had brought home.

Jackson cringed. "Sorry. I didn't realize there was anything on the table."

She laughed. "You couldn't see the top of the table. But there's no harm done. The boys can finish their lesson when we get home."

"Which one is mine, Pappy?" Ethan asked.

Jackson looked down at his youngest son with such unconditional love that he nearly stole Ellie's heart. Again. "This one," he murmured. He handed a small brown parcel to Ethan and an identical one to Daniel. "I know you're too young in your lessons right now," he cautioned as they ripped their presents open, "but I wanted each of you to have your own Bible, one you can read each night before you say your prayers at bedtime."

"Mama Ellie's gonna teach me to read first, 'cause I'm the oldest," Daniel said as he paged through the Bible.

Ethan, however, showed little interest in the book, set it down, and started fingering the rest of the packages. "Did you bring us more gumdrops?"

Jackson laughed. "No! Mrs. French gave you both more than enough gumdrops after you told her that you thought hers were better than Widow Franklin's."

"How is Mrs. French?" Ellie asked.

Jackson met her gaze and held it. "She's well. Very well. I'll tell you more a little later," he promised. "In the meantime, perhaps you could make some room in that trunk so the boys and I can put what I purchased for myself inside and we can head home."

Pleased that he had finally bought some things for himself after showering her and the boys with gifts, she shook her head. "I hope they fit."

"Can't we open the rest of the presents first?" Daniel asked.

"They're not presents. They're your father's things," Ellie replied.

"Pappy, did you find any homes for the puppies while you were gone?" Daniel asked as Ellie made her way to the trunk.

He laughed. "No, but I'm not worried. I decided that if all else fails, I'll just take them both to the parsonage, since it's Mrs. Shore's fault we wound up with Poor Thing in the first place."

Before Ellie could remark that Reverend Shore would definitely have other ideas about taking in two puppies, there was another knock at the door that made her turn to face Jackson again and offer him a grin. "Please don't tell me you bought more and had it delivered. There's barely enough room for what you managed to carry home."

"No. This is it."

Curious once again about who would be calling on them, she answered the door, only to find Christina Schuler standing there.

Wearing a black cape and matching bonnet, the woman appeared to be in mourning, although she had not dropped down the veil on the bonnet to shroud her face, and the beaded reticule she carried was far too elegant for a woman in mourning. "I only just heard you were in the city, and I was hoping you hadn't left yet. When I saw your wagon outside, I was relieved I wouldn't have to make that awful trip out to the island to see Jackson. May I come in?"

"Y-yes, of course," Ellie murmured, stepped aside to let the woman enter, and closed the door.

Jackson froze for a moment and acknowledged Christina with a curt nod.

In return, their visitor glanced at the boys, who were standing on the benches looking back at her with curiosity before directing her attention at their father. "What I have to say won't take long, but I'd prefer that I do it with you privately."

With her heart anxious to know exactly what the woman

had to say, Ellie rifled through the trunk, found one of the parcels she thought might be helpful to keep the boys occupied, and walked past the woman to Jackson. "I'll take the boys outside and keep them busy. We'll wait for you there," she whispered.

Jackson took the parcel from her and handed it to Daniel. "Take your brother outside and wait for us in the wagon. Just don't eat every single one of these gumdrops. And if you aren't sitting in that wagon when I get there, you won't see another gumdrop for a month," he cautioned.

Without posing a single argument, Daniel ushered his brother outside.

Once the door closed again, Jackson stood next to Ellie and faced Christina. "What is it?"

Christina reached into her reticule, pulled out a letter, and handed it to him. "I'm not happy doing my sister's bidding where you're concerned, but she is my sister. I could hardly refuse to deliver the letter she took the time to write to you when she's in mourning."

"Did you say *mourning*?" Jackson asked as he put the letter into his pocket.

"Her husband died very suddenly and most unexpectedly just last week. Obviously she's in a state of shock, as we all are. Even so, she's determined to move back to Harrisburg, and I expect she'll be here in a matter of weeks, if not sooner. Quite frankly, I'd expect you to consider her needs and her reputation very carefully, as well as your own, before you do something rash once you read her letter," she cautioned before letting herself out the door, unaware she had taken all of Ellie's hopes and dreams with her.

Thirty-Eight

After losing yet another night to fitful sleep, Jackson woke just after dawn. He blinked hard, surprised by the bright sunshine that filtered into his room. It held all the promise of a wondrously warm day to come, a rare gift with winter drawing so near.

Unfortunately, he had forgotten, yet again, to add wood to the warming stove before retiring the night before, and the sunshine was still too weak to chase off the raw night air that surrounded him as he got out of his bed.

Shivering, he dressed for the day. But the gooseflesh that covered his body and the piercing chill that penetrated his bones was not as numbing as the dreadful confusion that troubled his very soul, despite the hours he had spent on his knees each night for the past week, begging God to have mercy on him and bless him with the grace of wisdom to know what to do now that Dorothea actually wanted to be part of his life again. He still felt as if he were hanging from a precipice by his very fingertips, with overwhelming joy and hope for the future beneath his hands, and dismay and disappointment waiting for him if he made the wrong decision.

Should he forgive Dorothea and reclaim the love they once shared? More important, could he? Or should he accept the fact that his responsibility to his sons was greater than his own needs and stay with Ellie?

Desperate to end the confusion and turmoil that continued to torture him, he sat down on the bed to reread the first letter he had received from Dorothea yet again.

My dearest Jackson,

I mourn for my husband, whom God has seen fit to take away from me, yet I grieve ever more deeply for the loss of the love you and I once shared, a love I so foolishly tossed away. I pray you will find a way to welcome me back into your life upon my return to Harrisburg.

Your Dorothea

Overwhelmed that the only woman he had ever loved still loved him, too, and not only wanted to come back to him but was free to do so, he refolded the letter. Carefully, he set it aside and stared at the letter that Christina Schuler had given to him yesterday when he had gone into the city, alone, to deliver the last of the apples to William Haines at his cider mill. He unfolded the letter for the second time.

More bittersweet memories assaulted him and grew even stronger as he skimmed through the three-page missive.

Disregarding her account of the large inheritance she would receive, he also dismissed her childlessness, which she described as "joyful," and her plans to stay, temporarily, with her sister. Instead, he focused on the final provocative paragraph that made his heart pound even harder than the last time he had read it:

It is with a faithful, trusting heart that
I pray your love for me is still returned,
twofold and forever, as you vowed it would be
so many years ago. I am leaving Philadelphia
soon and will come to you as soon as I arrive.
Your Dorothea

Gently, he refolded the letter, added it to the other one, and stored them away again beneath his mattress. *Twofold and forever.* How often had his heart pounded in his chest when she whispered those very words back to him? How often had he ached to make her his wife, with just a glimpse of her beautiful face or the velvety touch of her hand, and pressed her for an answer to his proposal? "Apparently not often enough, or she would never have left me in the first place," he whispered and got to his feet.

As he started pacing back and forth, walking from his bed to the window and back again, the scorched wooden ring he still wore pressed against his chest, reminding him that his sons were not the only ones who would be affected if he took Dorothea as his wife and welcomed her return as a once-in-a-lifetime dream come true.

His heart pounded hard and fast as doubt and fear and confusion coursed through his veins. Doubt that he could truly trust Dorothea. Fear that she did not love him as fully as he loved her and that she would leave him again one day.

And confusion. A deep, soul-wrenching, heart-perplexing confusion that left him wondering if he even knew the meaning of true love between a man and a woman. Was love the passionate fire in his belly that grew hotter each time he was near Dorothea because she was so physically beautiful, or was that only carnal desire, nothing more than unadulterated lust?

He stopped in place for just a moment and juxtaposed his feelings for Dorothea with what he felt for Ellie. Was love something else, perhaps more like the way his heart warmed when he heard her laughing with his sons or watched her struggle to win her battle with the cookstove? Or was it the way she inspired him and made him feel like he was a man of honor and character and worth because that's how she saw him? Or was he confusing love with nothing more than gratitude for her patience and her goodness and the way she had brought order back into his life, asking very little in return?

Had she been nothing more than a temporary gift, something God had given to him for just a short while, or was she something far more precious: a woman of faith who would be his lifelong helpmate?

Jackson shook his head. He did not know the answers to those questions any more than he knew if he was capable of loving anyone other than his own sons.

Dropping to his knees, he bowed his head and turned to the One who knew his heart and his faults better than he knew them himself. "Father, please help me to know what to do. I don't understand why Dorothea has come back into my life now, just when I was beginning to think I could actually build a good life with Ellie by my side. Forgive me for being so uncertain, but I trust you and I love you. Please help me to make the right decision for all of us, especially for my sons, but most especially, a decision in accordance with your will. Amen," he whispered and got back to his feet.

All too aware that he needed to tell Ellie about Dorothea's second letter and the likelihood that she would arrive very soon, he left his room and crossed the hall. He made sure the boys were still asleep before he headed downstairs and closed the door at the bottom of the staircase before going into the kitchen. Although he welcomed the warmth in the room, he was disappointed that Ellie was not there. Poor Thing was not there, either, but the two puppies were lying there on the floor asleep, no doubt exhausted after spending the previous day playing with his sons.

He noticcd there were three large kettles of water set to boil on the cookstove, which meant she was planning to do some laundry today. He tested the water with the tip of one of his fingers. It was barely warm, so the kettles had not been on the cookstove for very long.

When he saw a note from Ellie lying on top of her worktable next to a full plate of warm apple fritters, he crossed the room, snatched one of the fritters, and ate it while he read her note:

I took Poor Thing for a walk. Ellie

Disappointed, but not deterred, he grabbed his coat and another fritter before heading outside. Since he was planning to spend the entire day working at the north end of the island renovating an old section of orchard, he needed to find Ellie now and ask her if she would sit and talk to him later tonight.

With time to herself while she waited for the kettles to come to a boil, Ellie followed Poor Thing along the southern shore of the island and pulled her new cape tighter against the cold of early morning, although the day promised to turn exceptionally warm later.

She did not venture through the woods in front of the house to come here often, but it was the one place that offered her the solitude she needed. She passed by a copse of walnut trees, the only area on the island where this type of tree still remained, and made a mental note to return here with the boys to harvest the last of the precious walnuts before winter set in.

Unless she was gone before then.

She paused to look up at the sky to offer yet another prayer for patience as well as trust, but hope that her prayers would be answered and Jackson would ask her to stay nipped at her faith. Overhead, a fluff of a cloud was framed with pure golden light from the sun that was hidden from her view. Awed by the sight, she studied the dark nooks and crannies in the body of the cloud within the frame and smiled.

Like the cloud, her life was filled with troubles and doubt, as well as joy. At times like this, she needed to remember that God was always behind her, surrounding her with the light of His love, even though she could not see He was there. She also needed to remember Gram's words and prayed that the light of God's love would reach deep into Jackson's spirit, too.

She resumed her steps, even as her thoughts grew troubled again. She knew Jackson was struggling to decide if he wanted Dorothea back in his life, but she was struggling, too. She still wanted to believe that this is where God wanted her to be, but as the days passed, she had begun to wonder if she was wrong and had misunderstood His will after all. Perhaps, in the end, Jackson and Daniel and Ethan were not gifts He had meant for her to keep, but rather just to share for a brief time, even though she had fallen in love with the man whose name she had carried and loved those boys as if they were her own.

She also knew that unless Jackson loved her, too—truly, truly loved her—staying here with him would only lead to heartache, regardless of how much joy she found in raising Daniel and Ethan.

When Poor Thing stopped suddenly, alert to something Ellie could not see, she paused in her steps again and heard a rustle in the woods that made her heart skip a beat. Although Michael Grant had eventually found and destroyed the rogue wolf while she and Jackson had been in the city, she grew worried that another wild predator had decided to venture here.

Until she saw Jackson emerging from the woods.

He waved and hurried to join her. "I was hoping I'd find you here," he said as Poor Thing ran over to him and received a gentle pat on the head.

She chuckled nervously. "Me or the dog?"

"You," he said, at which point Poor Thing ventured off to investigate more scents.

"I left you a note, but I didn't expect you'd come looking for me," she said as she started following the dog.

He walked alongside her. "Since I'm working at the north end of the island all day, I wanted to talk to you before I left."

She caught her breath and held it, but she offered no reply. If Jackson had something so important to discuss with her that he needed to follow her out here to do it, she was not going to say anything that could discourage him, no matter how difficult it might be to hear what he had to say.

"It's about tonight," he said. "I was wondering if you'd

join me in front of the fire after the boys go to bed, like you used to do."

Relieved, she glanced at him. "I thought you might prefer to have some time alone."

"I miss our talks."

She cocked a brow. "We're talking now."

"That's not what I meant, and you know it."

She paused in her steps, forcing him to stop, as well. "I know you have a decision to make. I can't help you to do that," she murmured. "I also know that while I pray each day that you won't set me aside for Dorothea, which you're legally free to do, I can't control how you feel about either one of us. You once married a woman when you were in love with another. Please don't repeat that mistake and stay married to me if you truly are still in love with Dorothea."

He arched his back defensively. "You know all about my life and the mistakes I've made, yet I know very little about yours."

"I've told you all there is to know."

"You've told me about your family. That's true enough, but you've never once told me about any of your suitors, except that you had two, I think."

"Yes, I had two," she admitted begrudgingly.

"Yet you married neither one of them. Why not?" he asked as he bent down, picked up a small stone, and skipped it across the surface of the river.

"Lots of reasons, but I don't see how—"

"I'd like to hear them," he insisted.

She drew in a long breath and counted out her reasons on her fingers, quickly covering the scar on her forefinger with her thumb. "I didn't want to marry Frederick McKenzie, who was my first suitor, because he was seventy-two years old, while

I was barely eighteen. By the time David Shepherd asked to court me, my father had died and I was living alone with my mother. He withdrew his interest in me because he objected to including my mother in our household once we were married," she said and dropped her hand to her side.

"Did you . . . did you love him?" Jackson whispered.

"I thought I did. Eventually I realized that I was only in love with the idea that I wouldn't spend the rest of my life as a spinster," she admitted. After taking a huge gulp of air, she turned to face him and told him the truth she had kept hidden from him for the past few months. "You're the only one man I've ever loved, Jackson Smith, and I love you with all my heart," she whispered, blinking back tears that threatened to spill before she finished what she had to say. "I've told you many times that I don't want to leave you or our boys, but if you truly love Dorothea and want to be with her, then all you have to do is say so and I'll leave here quietly, with nothing more than what I brought to this island, so you can be with her. All I ask is that you give me a letter of reference, that I might find a position far away from here, because it would be too confusing for the boys to see me from time to time if I stayed in the city."

She dropped her gaze, turned, and walked away, even though she knew she had not told him the whole truth. If he set her aside, she would leave, but with far less than she had when she arrived here that fateful day in August.

Because she would leave behind the one thing she had never given to any other man: her heart.

Thirty-Nine

Since Jackson would be having dinner with the Grants to take advantage of the dwindling daylight now that winter was drawing near, Ellie did not expect him back until suppertime, which still might not give her enough time to forget the disastrous mistake of telling him that she loved him.

Fortunately, she had two rambunctious boys—not to mention two very boisterous puppies and a mama dog—to handle on her own, as well as her housework to keep her hands busy and her mind occupied.

After scrubbing the parlor floor, she stopped for the boys' lessons. As she concluded, however, she glanced at the sunshine pouring through the windows into the kitchen and rebelled. If her days here on this island were going to end soon, she was not going to waste this glorious day in the house when she could be outside spending time with the boys. "Put your slates and chalk on the shelves. We're going for a walk," she announced, then suddenly recalled the walnut trees she had seen earlier.

"Can Griddle and Cakes come with us?" Daniel asked as he scrambled down from his chair.

"We'll watch them good," Ethan promised as he raced ahead of his brother to be the first to put away his things.

Ellie laughed, but also noted that Poor Thing was getting little attention now. "No puppies. We have a special task to do, and I don't want to have to worry about the puppies. I'll have my hands full just keeping the two of you out of the river."

"Are we going to get more river stones?" Daniel asked.

"No, we're collecting walnuts in the woods down by the river, which means you two have to change into some old overalls, the ones you wear when you go outside to play, and put on your boots." She started to untie her apron strings. "Daniel, you help your brother get started. I'll meet you both back here to finish up once I change my gown."

Both boys raced ahead of her to run upstairs, and she hurried to her room. Collecting walnuts could be a dirty business, and the pale blue gown she wore would no doubt end up stained beyond saving. She took the dark brown gown she had mended yet again out of the trunk and quickly changed.

When she returned to the kitchen, she found Ethan sitting and Daniel kneeling on the floor, struggling to help Ethan with his boots. "I'll do that," she suggested. "See if you can reach one of those nice-size baskets sitting up there on the shelf."

Daniel dragged a chair over to the shelf, climbed up, and pulled down two baskets. "One for me and one for Ethan." He carried the baskets over to her.

She laughed as she tried to slide Ethan's boot into place. "That's fine."

"Can we visit Mama and Gram today, too?" Ethan asked.

"Can we get more river stones for the puppy?" Daniel added.

"Well, why don't we collect the walnuts first? If you're not too tuckered out, then we'll see if we can't find a few river stones. We can't go all the way to the landing to get them, because I really do need to get some scrubbing done today, but I think we can find enough stones along the shore near the walnut trees. Ready?" she asked as she patted the bottom of Ethan's boots.

"Ready!" they cried in unison, and raced across the room and out the porch door before she said another word.

Chuckling, she hurried after them, hoping to tuck one more precious memory of these boys into her heart.

At midday, Ellie trudged back home with the boys.

She was hot, thirsty, hungry, and nearly as dirty as the boys, who dragged their feet as they walked alongside of her. She carried their baskets for them and wondered if the dark stains that covered her hands had been worth the precious few walnuts that filled only a quarter of one basket. It was a bit foolish to chide herself, again, for forgetting her gloves, but Ellie knew it would be weeks before she got those stains on her hands out.

As they neared the edge of the woods, she caught a glimpse of the house. Unbidden, a ray of hope shined through her doubt. Jackson had tried very hard to build a life here for his family, but would he really set her aside to marry Dorothea, knowing the scandal that would be unleashed? Would he subject his sons to more upheaval by introducing yet another woman into their lives and expect them to accept her as their mother? What about Ethan? Would he revert to muteness again? And what about Daniel? The poor boy had carried his own grief and confusion, as well as Ethan's, for many months. How fair would it be to expect him to do that again?

She shook her head to erase those thoughts. She glanced

down at the gold wedding ring she wore and thought of the scorched wooden ring that hung from Jackson's neck. She did not want Jackson to keep her as his wife to avoid scandal or for the sake of his sons. She wanted him to keep her because he loved her or because he truly believed he could grow to love her one day as much as she loved him.

She stepped out of the shaded woods into full sunshine and pointed ahead, toward the house that was now in full view. "We're almost home now. The first thing I'm going to do is make us something to eat and drink while you—"

Apparently energized by the promise of food, the boys did not wait for her to finish. They charged straight ahead, but instead of running around the side of the house to enter through the kitchen, they headed straight for the front door.

"Use the back door!" she cried and raced after them. "I just scrubbed that parlor floor!"

Whether they did not hear her or they heard her and decided not to obey was irrelevant. In the next moment they were inside, tracking mud onto the parlor floor.

Determined to keep them from tracking mud through the entire house, Ellie hitched up her skirts and ran after them. She raced across the front lawn and up the steps, bouncing half the walnuts they had gathered out of the basket in the process. She rushed into the house, only to stop dead in her tracks, just a few feet inside the door.

Panting for air, with her heart pounding, she stared hard, but there was not a single doubt in her mind that the incredibly beautiful young woman dressed in elegant mourning clothes, who was sitting next to Jackson on the settee, was the woman Jackson had loved for so long.

Forty

To say that Ellie felt like Cinderella at this very moment would be an understatement. At the moment she was probably dirtier than the hearths the fairy-tale heroine had been forced to clean. She set down her basket and tucked her hands into the folds of her dark brown skirts and managed a weak smile.

Dorothea, however, looked impeccable. Her black gown, made of a fabric Ellie had never seen, fairly shimmered. The veil on her bonnet had been pulled back, revealing tiny raven curls that framed her oval face. Her pale porcelain skin was flawless, and her eyes were sparkling, although they hardened into blue ice when she looked at Ellie.

Jackson rose to his feet looking like a little boy who had been caught stealing candy and nervously cleared his throat and introduced them to each other.

After exchanging a nod, as well as a long, assessing look, Dorothea smiled. "I must apologize for arriving unexpectedly, but it's as difficult to send word out here to the island as it is to get here," she murmured in a soft, cultured voice. "Under the circumstances and in the interest of time, I thought it best to come directly here. It's a blessing to have old friends to rely upon in times of trouble, and it was my good fortune that Jackson came home at midday."

Ellie was tempted to ask her what circumstances she might be referring to, if only to force the audacious woman to admit what she really meant: She had come here to steal another woman's husband!

In the eyes of the law, however, she was not here to steal another woman's husband at all, since Ellie and Jackson were husband and wife in name only. She managed to maintain a smile as she caught Jackson's gaze. "Where are the boys?"

Dorothea shuddered. "He sent them upstairs to change. I had no idea little boys could be so unkempt or get so dirty."

"I told them they could play with the puppies in the kitchen when they were done," Jackson offered, clearly uncomfortable with having Ellie here and anxious to keep his boys away, as well.

She picked up her basket of walnuts, or what was left of them, and addressed his guest with courtesy, although it galled her to do so. "Since Jackson was supposed to be having dinner with the Grants, I was only going to heat up some of yesterday's soup for myself and the boys. You're welcome to stay."

Dorothea looked at Jackson and smiled. "Actually, we were just discussing having dinner together later in the city, weren't we, Jackson?"

"We were, but—"

"Then I'll leave you both to make your plans," Ellie murmured.

She did not know how she found the strength, but she managed to walk away without having her legs crumple beneath her. Fighting back her tears, however, was more than she could do, and she only managed to swipe a few away when she heard the boys' footsteps as they started down the staircase.

She hurried into the kitchen, pumped some water onto a clean cloth, and wiped away her tears before the boys came into the room.

"Pappy said we could play with the puppies," Daniel announced as he headed for the pen with his brother.

"Remember to be gentle," she cautioned. Anxious to escape for just a moment to get control of her emotions before the boys saw she was upset, she headed for the kitchen door. "Stay right there with the puppies. I'll be right back. I want to get some fresh cream to top off our pudding for dessert," she told them and slipped outside.

When she heard the front door to the house open, she hurried off to avoid seeing either Jackson or Dorothea. They certainly had not wasted any time making plans to meet later today, but she had no intention of facing either one of them until she had better control of herself. She slipped into the root cellar, which had been built into a man-made hill, closed the door, latched it tight, and leaned back against it.

Drawing in huge gulps of air, she pressed her arm against her forehead and sobbed as she felt her heart breaking.

Moments later, an unexpected, heavy bang at the root cellar door shook her back and shocked her into silence.

"Ellie! Open the door."

More than a little provoked that Jackson must have seen her and followed her here, she swiped furiously at her wet face before opening the door. She remained standing, however, within the shadows of the root cellar to face the man she loved.

Bathed in sunshine, he stood only inches away from her, gazing at her with his dark blue eyes. "What are you doing?"

She cleared her throat. "G-getting some cream," she managed and looked around. "Where's Dorothea?"

"On her way to the landing," he said, motioning with his hand toward the other end of the island. "We need to talk."

Ellie took one look at the papers he had in his other hand, decided she did not need any cream after all, and walked out from the root cellar without bothering to close the door behind her.

He took a step back to allow her to pass and walked alongside her as she hurried back to the house. "Please don't go off in a huff. I know you're upset. I didn't expect Dorothea to show up here today any more than you did. I mean, I knew she was coming home any day, but I had no idea she'd actually turn up—"

"You knew she was coming home any day? How?" Ellie snapped, without stopping or looking over at him. "You let me read the letter she sent you. She never specifically mentioned when she was coming back to Harrisburg."

"She sent me another letter. I only picked it up yesterday when I went to the city. I was going to tell you tonight, when we sat down to talk, but then later, after I decided—"

"Why did you bring those letters out here?" she snapped and stopped to look down at the papers folded up tightly in his hand. The fact he was carrying around Dorothea's letters while trying to talk to her was almost unthinkable. "To show me in writing how deeply she feels for you? Or are you feeling guilty that you didn't show them to me before now?"

"These aren't her letters," he argued.

She huffed. "Then if they're letters of reference for me, you wrote too many. I only need one. And don't you dare toss any coins at me like you did once before. I'm perfectly capable of walking as far as necessary to find a new position for myself, thank you."

"Look closer," Jackson insisted. "You should recognize these papers. They're the legal papers we signed before we got married, but unless you stop and listen to me instead of leaping to conclusions and charging off again, you won't give me a chance to explain—"

"Since you came out to talk to me with our legal agreement in your hand and you're meeting Dorothea for dinner later, you don't need to explain anything. Your intentions are perfectly clear," she argued. "I also think we've said all we need to say to each other. I have dinner to make. My boys are hungry, but I'm not going to pack my bag until they've had something to eat," she added and started back to the house.

This time, he did not walk with her. If he wanted Dorothea, so be it, but she was not going to listen to any platitudes about how difficult his choice had been or how he was going to get annulment proceedings started or what a wonderful wife Ellie would make for another man someday.

"They're not your boys."

She stopped dead. Heart pounding, she spun around. Defiantly, she glared at him. "Wh-what did you say?" she managed, almost daring him to repeat his despicable words.

"I said, they're not your boys."

Her eyes welled with traitorous tears that threatened to undermine her determination to remain indifferent to him, but she kept them in check. If she had to leave, she would leave with dignity.

He walked toward her, taking one slow step at a time.

When he was only inches away from her, he smiled. "They're not my boys, either."

Narrowing her gaze, she took a step back, but decided to hold her ground to listen to what he had to say.

He captured her gaze with his own and held it. "They're *our* boys," he whispered. "They need you, but most important, I need you and I want you to stay here and be my wife. My true wife."

"M-me? You want me?" she said, so stunned by his words she almost forgot to breathe.

"You," he said, stepping so close she could feel his breath on her face. "I want you to be the first thing that I see every morning, lying beside me when I wake up. I want to listen to you, humming softly, as you make griddle cakes for our sons. I want to hear you smile and laugh during the day, and I want you to climb the stairs with me every night when it's time for bed because I want you to truly be my wife . . . because I love you. Only you," he whispered.

"I thought you loved Dorothea."

He smiled. "I thought I did, too."

"Thought?" she managed, searching the depths of his gaze and finding only love shining back at her.

He smiled again. "I've spent the past week thinking and praying and thinking some more, but it wasn't until I was high up on a ladder just a few hours ago and got a glimpse of that magnificent tree where you carved your initials that I knew I didn't want to spend a single day without seeing or holding or loving one woman. Only one. And that woman is one of His most precious gifts to me, a gift I intend to treasure for the rest of my life, Elvira Kilmer Smith. Because that woman is you."

She blinked hard, struggling for understanding. "B-but

what about Dorothea?" she asked, finding his declaration of love for her, instead of Dorothea, to be confusing.

He smoothed a lock of hair off her face and smiled at her so lovingly that she thought she must be dreaming. "What about her?"

"Aren't you meeting her later for dinner?"

"No," he said firmly.

"But she said—"

"I was sitting right there. I heard what she said, too, but—"

"But if you aren't meeting her later, why are you carrying around those legal papers of ours and why—"

"Are you going to stop interrupting me and listen, or do I have to kiss you to keep you quiet?" he teased, then simply wrapped his strong arms around her and kissed her, long and sweetly, anyway.

Nearly breathless when he finally set her free, she swayed, and he held her close to keep her steady. "Now that I have your attention, I need to tell you that I truly had no idea Dorothea would show up here today, let alone be waiting at the house when I returned to tell you that I wanted to stay married to you," he murmured as he pressed his cheek to hers.

"I only agreed to meet with her later because I wanted to get her out of the house before you and the boys came back and found us there. Unfortunately, you all came home right after I did, and I needed to wait until you and the boys had left the room because I knew she was not going to be happy hearing what I had to say, and I didn't want her rantings to upset the boys."

Ellie held him close, the scorched wedding band pressed tight between them. "What was it you were going to say to her?"

"That I had made the mistake of marrying Rebecca when I was still in love with another woman, and if I married her, I'd only be making the same mistake twice. Sound familiar?" he asked, reminding her of the very words she had spoken to him just hours ago.

He set her back and held out the legal papers he had been carrying. "Now, unless you have any objections, I'd like to take these inside and burn them so we can begin our lives together again, truly as one."

She laughed and cried at the same time. "No, I don't," she managed as her very soul began to sing with joy and gratitude. "It sounds wonderful and miraculous and—"

But before she could continue, Jackson silenced her litany with a kiss that held all the wonder of the married love they would share together.

Author's Note

There are a fair number of islands in the Susquehanna River as it courses through the Commonwealth of Pennsylvania, eventually emptying into the Atlantic Ocean. Some islands are as small as three acres, while others contain nearly one thousand.

Historically, Native Americans used many of these islands during milder months as meeting places to trade or to enjoy the area's natural bounty. Later, settlers moving west claimed these islands. On at least one, there are records of a homestead; on others, there are accounts of settlers living there only for brief periods of time.

During the twentieth century, government and government-sponsored organizations, as well as other philanthropic groups, began to acquire these islands to preserve them as ecological treasures or to create recreational centers. Some islands remain uninhabited by humans or are now protected sites for wildlife to use for nesting. City Island in Harrisburg, on the other hand, is now home to a sixty-three-acre recreational park. The Susquehanna River Trail Association also oversees a fifty-one-mile river trail that runs from Sunbury to Harrisburg and provides day access to twenty islands.

Dillon's Island, however, is purely fictional. There are also no historical records to indicate that anyone ever established commercial orchards on any of the islands, either, although there were orchards on some of the islands, as well as the nearby mainland in the nineteenth century.

Today, the area around Biglerville, Pennsylvania, is an apple lover's dream-come-true. Home to the National Apple Museum, the area is also home to growers who tend thousands of acres of apple orchards. Several major producers of apple juice and applesauce have built their plants nearby, as well.

Technology has changed a great deal since the nineteenth century, too. For women who lived in the nineteenth century, the change from cooking on an open hearth to cookstoves was not always an easy one. Priscilla J. Brewer has documented the change in cooking technology in her scholarly book, *From Fireplace to Cookstove: Technology and the Domestic Ideal in America,* and I relied on her work a great deal. Ellie's trouble with cleaning the stovepipe, for example, is based on a diary entry made by a Connecticut woman in the 1830s.

A quick search of Internet sites can provide interested readers with all sorts of information about Pennsylvania's Susquehanna River islands as well as the apple industry and antique cooking stoves. I invite you all to explore them, as your interests lead you.

I also ask you all for your indulgence as I created my fictional island home for the story I have shared with you. *Hearts Awakening* is, above all, a story of faith and hope and love and His precious gifts to all of us.

Delia Parr